The Way We COLLIDE

USA TODAY BESTSELLING AUTHOR
TIA LOUISE

This book is a work of fiction. Names, characters, places, and incidents are products of the author's imagination or are used fictitiously. Any resemblance to actual events or locales or persons, living or dead, is entirely coincidental.

The Way We Collide
Copyright © TLM Productions LLC, 2025

Cover illustration by Laura Moore, @LCM_designss.
Design by Kari March Designs

Printed in the United States of America.

All rights reserved. No part of this publication can be reproduced, stored in a retrieval system, or transmitted in any form or by any means—electronic, photocopying, mechanical, or otherwise—without prior permission of the publisher and author.

Playlist

"Another Day of Sun" - La La Land Cast
"Hurricane" - Luke Combs
"The Craving" - Twenty One Pilots
"All Too Well" (Taylor's Version) - Taylor Swift
"Cool Again" - Kane Brown
"Stars Like Confetti" - Dustin Lynch
"Sugar" - Maroon 5
"Good Morning Baltimore" - Cast of Hairspray
"Talk You Out of It" - Florida Georgia Line
"This Tornado Loves You" - Neko Case
"End of the Road" - Boyz II Men
"Closer" - The Chainsmokers, Halsey
"Let's Stay Together" - Al Green
"Pony" - Ginuwine
"Queen of My Double Wide Trailer" - Sammy Kershaw
"It Never Rains in Southern California" - Albert Hammond

Listen on Spotify Here.

Dedication

For everyone waiting to see love knock Hendrix on his ass, here we go...

"The cure for anything is salt water. Sweat, tears, or the sea."
—Isak Dinesen

Prologue

Raven

"Where did you get that, Raven Lorrain?" My mother's voice is sharp, and she snatches the chocolate cupcake with the bright blue frosting from my fingertips.

"Zoë's mom had—"

"Zoë's mom…" She cuts her eyes in the direction of a little girl I befriended while we were sitting in our crinkle curlers. "She did this on purpose… Just look at your face!"

I can't look at my face. I don't have a mirror, but I can deduce by the way my mother roughly scrubs my cheek with the damp towelette, something's wrong with it.

"It's not coming off!" The panic in her voice pitches my stomach. "All your contouring is ruined. How are you ever going to be Little Miss Georgia Peach with blue Pillsbury Doughboy cheeks? It's bad enough you're five pounds heavier than you were last year."

She gives my face a little shove as she flicks it away with her wrist, and shame prickles the back of my neck. I look down at my fluffy peach and white chiffon dress, and I notice my fingertips are stained blue from the cupcake frosting, as I'm sure my face is.

"Joining us next, all the way from Peachtree City…" The announcer's polished voice rings out, and a soft growl comes from my mother's throat. "Miss Raven Lorrain Gale."

"Go on," my mother hisses, her brown eyes burning with anger.

Lifting my chin the way I was trained, I walk out onto the stage. Bright light heats my skin, and I can't see anyone in the audience. Still, we've been drilling for this moment for the last six months, so I know what to do.

I walk to the center and hold, looking left, right, then I continue down the runway.

The Little Miss Peach pageant is the next step on the rung leading to Miss Middle Peach. From there, I'd compete to become Miss Teen Peach, leading ultimately to Miss Georgia Peach, which is the very top before Miss Georgia World.

I'm not sure where the peaches go after that.

"Raven is eight years old. She's the daughter of Jeffrey and Roxanne Gale, herself a former Miss Georgia World 1996." The man continues listing my status, and I remember last spring when we visited Mama's family in Perry.

They took us to the state fair, and I saw my very first pig show. As we stood in the audience, owners marched out their prized pigs. A line of judges frowned and studied the animals' sizes and colors, and eventually they pinned a blue ribbon on the biggest one.

I declared it a pig pageant! And everyone laughed except my mom. She looked at me a lot like she's looking at me right now. I wonder if she's thinking about that pig pageant and me.

If she's to be believed, all I do is eat and lie around watching YouTube videos. My face is round, and my cheeks are fat—genetics from my father's side of the family, she muses, doing her best to contour my features with bronzer. *What must everyone think of her having a daughter like this?*

When I reach the end of the runway, I pause, smiling as I look left, right, then I turn and slowly walk back to the top for a final stop in front of the judges.

The lights change, and polite applause fills the hotel ballroom. I wait for a count of five, then I walk off the stage under the penetrating scowl of my mother.

She doesn't speak. She only turns, and I follow her to the dressing area to wait for the results.

Twenty-two eight-year-olds, all dressed in a rainbow of colors with their hair all teased and sprayed and their faces made up to look like grown women proceed to do the final walk before we're called out to line up in front of the judges.

My mother doesn't even bother to reapply the bronzer, and when the time comes for us all to walk out and the winners to be selected, my new friend Zoë is crowned Little Miss Peach.

I walk away with fourth runner-up, and my mother doesn't even look at me. She collects our things, and she sits in the front seat of my father's silver Mercedes sedan facing forward as my father takes my hand and helps me into the back.

He gives me a sympathetic smile before closing the door. I buckle my seatbelt, and no one says a word as we drive home in the rain.

Chapter 1

Raven

"I DIDN'T PAY FOR YOU TO GO TO ONE OF THE BEST SCHOOLS IN Georgia for you to become a weather girl." My dad is using his booming voice, which I guess he thinks will scare me. Hello? Ever heard of thunder? Skyquakes? My mother?

I don't scare so easily.

"They're not called *weather girls* anymore, Dad. They're meteorologists." I bite a Totino's pizza roll in half, holding for a moment while the savory flavors of salty tomato and melted cheese coat my tongue and quiet my insides.

"So now the weather is controlled by meteors?" He switches to his ridiculing voice for this question.

I pop the other half of the rectangle into my mouth. *And to think this man has millions of dollars…*

"The name actually comes from Aristotle. He titled his book *Meteorologica*, using the Greek word *meteoron*, which means 'things in the air.'"

Dad walks slowly to where I stand, arms crossed and

frowning down at me. "You want to waste a brain like that on the *weather*?"

He says it like I just announced I was going to work under a bridge downtown.

"It's actually one of the most useful branches of journalism." Years of experience have taught me to keep my voice calm if I want him to hear me, no matter how I feel. "Weather affects everyone, every day. Extreme heat introduces the danger of heat stroke and dehydration. Extreme cold can lead to frostbite and death, and I don't have to tell you how destructive tornadoes can be."

"No one can predict a tornado, Raven Gale. They're too fast."

Swiping another pizza roll, I don't even try to argue. "I want to be the next female Jim Cantore." Lifting my chin, I say the name with pride.

"Who's that?"

Sad horn.

"Only the most famous hurricane hunter on The Weather Channel. Trust me, Dad, if Jim Cantore shows up in your town, you do *not* want to be there."

"And that's who you want to be?" His voice drips with disdain.

"Yes!" I practically shout—so much for keeping cool. "I want to be the person who tells people to stop sitting on their butts and evacuate. Do you know how many lives I could save?"

"I only care about one life." Dad's arms lower, and he closes the distance between us. "I don't like this career path, Biscuit. I want you to get your MBA and join Amelia and me in the family business."

"Don't call me Biscuit." It's a low grumble.

"Just trying to get through calculus over here." My sister Amelia holds up her pencil from where she sits at the ornate mahogany desk in our father's office on the second floor of his mansion just south of Atlanta.

Being the daughter of a luxury jewelry importer and a former Miss Georgia World, even a late one, is a total double-edged sword.

Money and status make people feel like they have control over you, and the last thing I've ever wanted is to be controlled. I'm way too stubborn for that.

Exhaling heavily, I do my best not to resent my Dad's opinion. Amelia's degree is considered useful, because she'll join the family business. I'm considered a troublemaker, because he doesn't understand my dreams.

"No one ever died selling a watch." Dad's condescending tone annoys me.

"As far as you know." I strain away from his hug. "I don't want to sell Rolex watches, Dad."

"Rolex watches are the backbone of the luxury timekeeping industry."

"Luxury timekeeping." Now it's my turn to be disgusted.

"Yes, timekeeping." Dad's brown eyes lock on mine. "You're talking about the weather. Do you have any idea how critical the business of *time* is? I'd wager it's right up there with tracking a hurricane."

"Only if you're running out of it."

"You're joking, but I'm serious." Dad puts his hands on his hips. "Weather is amusing, but luxury watches are our bread and butter. You are to come back here and take your place at my side like your grandfather before you, and his father, and... all the rest of us."

I'm finished arguing. "Love you, Dad. Don't stay up past your bed*time*."

"Don't patronize me, young lady. You've gone from one harebrained scheme to the next, and now you want me to take seriously an extreme weather venture?"

"It's not like that. I wasn't cut out for those other jobs. Anyway, there's no shame in trying different things. That's the whole point of being young, right?"

"What would your mother say?"

Oh, he did *not* go there.

"Mom would say the camera adds fifteen pounds." I can't keep the irritation out of my tone.

"She'd say you don't know what you want and you need guidance. Your mother was an important woman. She never wanted you to have to rise above the way she did. She wanted you to have stability."

"The root word of which is *stable*, like in a barn," Amelia teases.

"Don't encourage her, Amelia." Dad's tone is clipped.

My little sister doesn't make waves, but I have a feeling there's a rebel lurking beneath her submissive front.

I don't resent my dad. He's actually a pretty decent human being—with occasional spoiled-billionaire-tyrant tendencies. He's nothing like my *very important mother* was.

Miss Georgia World was done with me when I refused to go to fat camp and dropped out of the pageant circuit. To her I was choosing to be a nobody, an overweight failure, which in her mind was the worst kind.

Amelia was lucky she never had to experience that life. Our VIM was gone before my little sister was old enough to *pause, look left, right, smile for the judges…*

The memory sends a shiver down my back, and I snatch the handle of my rolling suitcase. It took me a lot of therapy and a lot of retraining my thoughts to get away from that childhood, but I did it.

Now I hold my head high, and I do whatever the fuck I want.

"I've got to go. I'm due in south Alabama for Dylan's wedding." I kiss his cheek, and turn, bending down to hug my sister's shoulders.

"Who's Dylan?" Dad grumbles. "Is that a boy?"

"Dylan Bradford is a girl, Dad. I met her on the cruise when Amelia graduated high school? I told you this. She was a chaperone for a group of kids from Newhope, Alabama."

"Have a nice time." His tone is stern. "When you get back, you're going to settle down and get serious."

I'm tired of arguing, so I don't even bother to reply.

"I'll follow you out!" My little sister hops out of her chair, catching my hand.

She laces her fingers in mine as we walk out to my car, and I think about how close we've always been. She's nine years younger than me, but it was the perfect time to get a new baby in the house. Her feet never touched the ground, and as the years passed, our bond grew stronger.

"I wish I was going with you." She shoves a clump of dark brown curls behind her ear.

"You have to study for your finals."

Amelia is a student at Emory, and in the fall, she's moving into an on-campus apartment with her friends, which means I'll be home alone with Dad.

It's enough to make me want my own place. If only entry-level meteorologists were paid more. As it is, I'm pretty dependent until I get a promotion, which could take years.

I graduated from The University of Georgia at Athens with a degree in general studies and a desire to do something important, something that would make a difference in people's lives. I just didn't know what.

I tried being a mortician. It sounded interesting, and I thought I could be a kind, loving presence at a difficult time in people's lives. Then I threw up on my first cadaver.

For a whole two weeks, I tried accounting—until my dad busted me sleeping at my desk, and I threw in the towel. It's so freaking boring!

That's when I discovered meteorology. I landed a six-month, unpaid internship at the television station in Athens, and I realized *this* was what I loved. It was fast paced and exciting, and it was news that actually impacted people's daily lives.

I saw first-hand how important weather and hurricane

coverage could be. I saw the destructive power of wind and hail and flooding.

It's possible I was influenced by repeat viewings of the movie *Twister* with Helen Hunt. I look nothing like Helen Hunt. I'm short with thick brown hair that I dress up with gold highlights in the front. I have thick thighs, a big butt, and a narrow waist. I'm more like Helen Hunt-Kardashian, which makes me snort. That's a weird combo.

"Does Larry know about your plans?"

"No." I growl, impatiently shoving my overnight bag into the back of my car. "Why would I tell Larry?"

"I don't know. Aren't y'all supposed to be sort-of getting engaged or something?"

Lawrence Calder O'Halloran is the son of my Dad's business partner Therman. Since we were born, our parents shared the dream of us one day getting married and uniting their jewelry empire.

Larry shared my mother's dream of marrying a Miss Georgia World, and he was on her side when I dropped out of that madness. To them it was the worst mistake of my life. To me, it was freedom.

Don't get me wrong, I don't hate pageant girls. I'm just not one of them.

It was Larry who coined the nickname "Biscuit." Once when we were in high school, I made my signature drop biscuits for him. They're delicious and fluffy, and with cream and honey, they're like little bites of heaven. Larry decided I ate too many of them, and a nickname was born. I wanted to kick him in the biscuit.

Lately, he's been making offhand remarks about how these new compounding pharmacies make off-brand Ozempic at affordable prices.

"I wouldn't marry Lawrence O'Halloran if he were the last man on the planet." Anger heats my throat. "He's a dick."

"But you're going to unite the families." She holds out her

hand, doing a pretty decent imitation of Don Corleone from the classic movie *The Godfather*. "You'll let down your father."

"That ship sailed before I left for college." My throat burns. "I only wish I wasn't so financially dependent."

"Aw, Dad loves you." Amelia blinks up at me with the eyes of a youngest child. "He says a lot of stuff, but in the end, he really just wants you to be happy."

Wrapping my arm around her waist, I pull her in for a hug. Ameila is a little taller than me, and has never had an overweight day in her life. She has no idea what it's like to be the "failure" oldest daughter of someone like our mom.

"I'm sure you're right, Sis."

What makes me *very* happy is knowing that in four short hours, I'll be down at the beach watching one of my dearest friends get married, going to a rocking after party, and having a weekend to be free of condescension and pressure.

"See you later alligator." I give her a little squeeze.

"After while, crocodile!" She calls back, using our standard farewell.

Scooting behind the wheel of my car, I wave out the window as the gates slowly open for me to leave my family's estate.

I can't wait to see Dylan Bradford again. We share a love of cooking and eating and enjoying life, and we're both a little fluffy.

We've kept in touch ever since the cruise, almost four years ago, when we discovered our love of hot peppers and margaritas and Mexico. We text, swap recipes, and she keeps inviting me to come for a visit.

Every Thursday at her family's restaurant, they have a "Dare Night," where she whips up a super-hot pepper recipe for *daring* customers to try. She said it's a fun party, and I've been promising to make time to see it.

I couldn't believe it when she asked me to be one of her bridesmaids. Then she said I'd be walking down the aisle with her brother Hendrix, who I happen to know is the star tight end for the Los Angeles Tigers.

I looked him up, and he ranks two million on the Scoville heat scale. That's hotter than a Carolina Reaper, in case you didn't know.

It's going to be the best weekend, like a mini-spring break, and as my father's mansion grows smaller in the rearview window, my hopes grow bigger.

I'm going to have fun, and who knows? Maybe I'll figure out a way to make a place for myself on the coast and get one step closer to my dream.

"What do you like to do for fun, Raven?" Hendrix Bradford wraps both of my hands in his large ones and smiles down at me.

His sapphire blue eyes sparkle like the deep ocean, and I'm momentarily hypnotized.

We're standing in the large dining room at Cooters & Shooters, and the Thursday Dare Night is winding to a close. I'm sorry I missed all the crazy fun, but my sadness is short-lived when Dylan introduces me to her six-foot-two, muscle-bound groomsman-older brother.

Let me just say for the record, Hendrix Bradford is 300 times hotter in person than he is in the pictures on Google, which makes him 300 times hotter than a Carolina Reaper.

I'm doing my best to be sassy-cool and toss my hair behind my shoulders as I laugh. I'm feisty and fun, and maybe he'll want to give me a kiss after the wedding.

What? That's the whole point of being a bridesmaid, right? Getting to make out with an insanely hot groomsman?

Okay, I know. The point of being a bridesmaid is the possibility of *hooking up* with an insanely hot groomsman... But the thought of Hendrix Bradford wanting a post-wedding hookup makes my stomach jump to my throat and do a roundoff, back handspring, with two backwards flips in a pike position.

Basically, it turns my stomach into Simone Biles.

Amelia once told me that Beyoncé developed a fake persona to help her when she was nervous about going on stage.

Beyoncé's persona is *Sasha Fierce*, so we decided mine would be *Tasha Scarce*, which made me a bit skeptical. Why was Tasha scarce? Was she broke? Had she gone missing? Would she dip out when I needed her most?

Amelia said my *fear* was scarce, and I went with it. All those years of pageant training had to be good for something.

So while I wish I'd made it in time for "Dare Night"-dancing and tasting one of those little cups of vanilla ice cream with the Trinidad Scorpion blueberry sauce, Tasha gives me a fabulous personality to deflect my nerves around this big, rowdy family and their devastatingly handsome men.

"I'm a meteorologist." I blink up at him with a smile. "I chase hurricanes."

His brows quirk, and he steps closer, causing my core to clench. "Are you one of those poor reporters struggling to stand up against 100 mile-per-hour winds while you tell everybody to evacuate?"

"That's me!" I even manage to laugh. "I almost ended up in the ocean once, but as you can tell, I'm not so easy to knock down."

I motion to my sturdy frame, and his sexy eyes slide down my body. It's like a hot caress, and it leaves me feeling completely naked and slippery and I'm pretty sure my ears are pink.

"You look good to me." His low tone lights a fire in my veins, and I won't lie, I like it.

Fighting the blush covering my entire upper torso, I lift my chin in defiance like Tasha would. "I'm going to be the next Jim Cantore."

"Oh, shit." His low laugh tickles my stomach. "If Jim Cantore shows up, you'd better get the hell out of Dodge."

"Exactly!" I tap my finger against his rock-hard bicep. "Imagine how many lives he saves just by his reputation alone."

"I never thought of it that way." Hendrix's smile reveals straight white teeth as he studies me. "That's a pretty cool twist—a life-saving reputation." He nods. "I like it."

"If only my dad agreed with you." I take a sip of the Modelo I'm holding. "He thinks I'm trying to be a weather girl."

Hendrix's forehead crinkles, and even his laugh is sexy. "Does anybody still say *weather girl?*"

"My dad does."

My tone mellows his humor, and he genuinely seems bothered by this new information. "I hate that. You have a dream, and it means a lot to you. Your dad should respect it."

"I think so." My lips twist into a smile, and the gratitude I feel helps with the nerves twisting my stomach. "I appreciate you saying that. It's nice."

He leans closer, and I'm surrounded by his sexy scent—warm vanilla and sandalwood. He smells delicious.

"I know what it's like not to see eye to eye with your family." His chin lifts, and he takes a sip of his own beer. "Or when they try to tell you what you're supposed to want."

I tilt my head, looking up at him. "People actually treat *you* that way?"

"I have three older brothers." He smirks.

"In that case, we should join forces and be rebels this weekend." Tasha is in full control right now. "Leave all those limits behind us."

"I like how your mind works." Mischief is in his eyes, and he lifts my hand into the crook of his arm. "If you're game, we can have a little adventure. Just say the word."

"I never know the right response to that." I lean forward with a laugh. "Is it *word*? If so, then *word*!"

He points at me. "Word up."

Chapter 2

Hendrix

"MOST EMBARRASSING MOMENT—DON'T THINK. JUST ANSWER. GO!"

Raven's brown eyes widen adorably, and her pretty chin juts forward. "What? No way, you first."

The DJ is playing a One Direction song at top volume, and my bow tie is undone. I'm holding an Abita Amber and leaning against a high-top table covered with a white tablecloth.

A small vase is in the center filled with white twinkle lights and an enormous white flower, and Raven is beside me with a clear cup of fireball and cherry liqueur in her hand.

It's some "spicy cherry" brew Dylan asked the bartender to mix up for her bridesmaids. I'm sticking to beer, because the last thing I want tonight is whiskey dick.

We've been going back and forth since we were paired up in the foyer of Miss Gina Rosario's massive, Italian-style mansion overlooking the bay.

I took one look at the gorgeous woman I'd be escorting down the aisle, and all I could think was I had to break the tension somehow. Raven was just too fine to slip away tonight.

My brothers give me shit for being a player, but the truth is, I'm really a nice guy. So while I'm dreaming of seeing this woman naked, I'm doing my best to charm her with my "most embarrassing moment."

"Phew, it was probably when our biggest defensive lineman caught me crying over a Taylor Swift song in the locker room."

Raven's hand flies to her mouth, and her eyes water. "Oh my god…"

Got her. "Did you almost do a spit-take?"

She nods quickly, grabbing the napkin from under my beer to blot her nose.

Dylan's wedding went off without a hitch, and as the older guests have slowly departed the reception, the vibe has gotten a little wilder. Or as wild as we can get at Miss Gina's posh estate.

Miss Gina is a rich old blind lady who kind of became our surrogate grandmother after our parents died. My little sister has been obsessed with her since she was old enough to ride her bike up the scenic highway from our house.

The two of them have been thick as thieves since that first box of Girl Scout cookies, and naturally, Dylan had to have her wedding here.

Legends swirl around the old lady and her family. Some people say she descended from pirates who buried treasure on the grounds of this sprawling property. Some say she's a lost, Italian princess.

We've only ever known her as a kind old lady who dispenses wisdom and kittens, and who played match-maker for Zane and his fiancée Rachel, Miss Gina's young nurse from Birmingham.

Now, in Miss Gina's overplanted garden we're surrounded by fruit trees, tropical plants, and wrought iron trellises all decorated in white twinkle lights.

An arch with magenta flowers growing over it in a vine is situated on a wooden platform with an ornate iron bench. It provides a photo-ready backdrop as the sun disappears into the water.

The flagstone patio is a makeshift dance floor, and my brothers and all of Dylan's bridesmaids are dancing and singing.

"Now *that's* an embarrassing confession." Raven points at me.

My eyes narrow. "Are you making fun of me, Rave?"

"Absolutely." Her laugh is a low, sexy sound with a little rasp that makes my dick twitch.

"Your turn." I take a step closer, and pink flashes from her cheeks to the tips of her ears.

It's really cute, and I've been counting how many times I can make it happen all night. It's like a little signal she's as interested in me as I am in her, and it fans the heat smoldering in my stomach.

I've also been doing my best to keep my eyes from lingering on her perfect breasts pressing against the top of her sheer pink dress like two luscious pillows every time she inhales.

"I need a judge's ruling. Which song?" Her eyes dance as she takes the cherry from her drink and slips it between her teeth.

My breath stills, and for a moment, I'm lost watching her full lips wrap around that bright red fruit. "Ah… the one about the guy who calls to break her like a promise—doesn't everybody cry at that part?"

"Like in that Ryan Gosling movie?"

"Which one?"

"*The Fall Guy.*"

"Never saw it."

She shakes her head disapprovingly. "I can't believe you live in LA, and you don't know movies."

"I know football." I give her a wink, and she reaches for another cherry.

"I'm not even going to ask what you were doing listening to Taylor Swift in the locker room." She's so sassy, it's terrific.

"It's Dylan's fault. She plays her music all the time."

As if on cue, "Love Story" by Taylor Swift begins, and Rachel and Liv and Allie and just about every female at the reception race to clump together in a circle, singing every single word at the top of their lungs.

"See what I mean?" I nod in their direction. "You can join them if you want. I won't judge."

She arches an eyebrow as if it's a dare. "*You* can join them if you want. *I* won't judge."

I bite back my grin, studying the golden flecks in her brown eyes. She's bewitching with that dimpled grin, with her dark hair hanging in smooth waves down her back.

I have to thank my little sister for choosing an off-the-shoulder style with a slit up the leg for their dresses. It's floor-length, but it gives me the most tantalizing view of Raven's gorgeous body. I want to lift, squeeze, and bite every inch of her.

I'm dying to hear what she sounds like when I make her come.

"I'd rather stay here with you." I dip my chin, giving her my best smolder.

"High praise, coming from a true fan."

"I'll show you a true fan." I catch her around the waist, and she laughs, loud and hearty.

She really slays me with that laugh. The dimple in her cheek deepens as she merrily blinks up at me. "Hendrix Bradford, are you trying to get in my pants?"

"Yes. Is it working?"

Her lips twist, and she tries to fight her smile. "Maybe."

Damn, I want to kiss her, which catches me off-guard.

I confess to being a "lust at first sight" type of guy, but this is something different. This kind of lust feels dangerous. I need to bring it down a bit.

I shrug my coat off my shoulders, putting it on the back of a nearby chair. "So you're not a fan of the most popular singer of our generation?"

"Of course, I like Taylor Swift. I'm not sure I believe you like her."

"She's very talented. I even like the songs she writes for other artists."

"Such as…"

"'Better Man' by Little Big Town?"

"That's a good one."

"Sometimes in the middle of the night?"

"I can feel you again."

"Come on, that's just good shit."

"Okay, I believe you." She holds up her empty glass. "And I like a man who can praise a woman so easily. It shows you're very confident."

"You have no idea." Catching her hand in mine, I lead her in the direction of the bar for a refill. "What kind of music do you like?"

The song ends, and a peppy, cheerleader-type dance song begins, causing all the girls to jump up and down again.

"Chappell Roan!" Raven cries, lifting her arms and doing a little twisty move that makes my mouth water.

Dylan's best friend and former ballet partner Craig is on the improvised dance floor with my brother Garrett doing some YMCA-style spelling choreography.

Craig's boyfriend Clint was Dylan's wedding planner and florist, but I'm pretty sure Craig picked out all the music for the reception—with my sister's help, of course.

I'm not much of a dancer, but I don't mind faking it if it means I can wrap my arms around Raven. Watching her move, I think she might be the perfect woman.

If there were such a thing.

The bartender hands me two fresh drinks, and I pass one to her.

"Thank you." She smiles, lifting her chin as she takes a sip.

We return to the tall table where we place our drinks. "So Chappell Roan…"

"Charli xcx, all the Broadway show tunes…" Her full bottom lip goes between her teeth. "Believe it or not, I used to be a pageant girl."

"No shit—"

"I know, I don't look it." She blinks away, and this time the flush on her cheeks isn't like before. It's like she's really embarrassed.

"I wasn't going to say that. I was going to say it explains your poise and how you project confidence."

"I'm a terrific actress." Her voice is quieter.

I slide a lock of brown hair off her creamy shoulder. "I bet the camera loves you."

All of my brothers are on the dance floor now, jumping up and down to some Beastie Boys song. Craig yells for me to join them, but I wave him away. Usually, I'm right there with them having fun, acting crazy, but not tonight.

Tonight, I've found something way better.

She sways closer, the warmth of her body noticeable through the cotton of my shirt, and I can't resist. "Tell me, Raven Gale, do you have a boyfriend back in Atlanta missing you this weekend?"

"Nope." She pops the *P*, and my eyebrow arches.

"Something I should know?"

Her eyes roll, and a cute little growl rumbles in her throat. "The only person back home is Lawrence Calder O'Halloran."

"I already don't like him. What's his story?"

"He's the son of my dad's business partner." She slides another cherry between her teeth. "He's also an entitled asshole who likes to keep me informed of the availability of weight-loss drugs—for my health, of course."

"Hang on." Shaking my head, I process what she just said. "He actually *said* you need to take weight-loss drugs?"

"Oh, no. He would never be so crass. He simply implies I'm a big girl, and don't I think I should be smaller?"

Stepping directly in front of her, I put both hands on each side of the table, effectively caging her in my arms. "Look at me, Raven Gale." She lifts her chin, and her breasts rise and fall as she breathes. "Your body is fucking gorgeous. There are women who would pay good money to have your curves, and I would give my left nut for one night to devour every… single… inch of you."

I lean closer with each word, and her thick lashes flutter. That cute flush creeps up her neck again, and it makes me grin.

"What about you?" It's a breathy question, and her pink tongue wets her bottom lip. "Is there some girl in LA waiting for you?"

"No." My eyes flicker down hungrily. "I don't date."

Stepping back, it's important I lay the ground rules for her as well as for me. Even if she's in Atlanta and I'm in LA, and there's no way this could be anything more than a post-wedding hookup. Raven Gale is a bit too tempting.

Her brow furrows. "But I've seen pictures of you out with women—"

"Don't get me wrong, I have dates for special events or awards banquets, stuff like that, but I never date the same woman more than twice."

"So you're a player."

"Not at all. I actually respect women very much. I had an amazing mom, and I have a cool little sister." Nodding, I put it out there. "I would never want them to be with a guy who loves football as much as I do. I've heard of golf widows and hunting widows—I don't want any kind of widow. It's not right."

"What if you met the love of your life, and you didn't go on a third date with her?"

"I've met the love of my life. It's small and pointy on each end, and I hold it in my arms so tightly. Some people call it a pigskin."

That makes her laugh. "I understand being obsessed with your work, but you're saying you've never met a woman you wanted to date more than twice? Not *ever*?"

"Once."

"Ahh, here we go." She's so smug, but I have nothing to hide.

"Back when I first moved to LA, I dated a woman for a little more than a month, and it was a disaster."

Her brows lift in disbelief. "A disaster how?"

"I told her right from the start, football is the most important

The Way We COLLIDE

thing in my life." I tilt my beer to the side, shaking my head. "She didn't believe me, and from there, it was nonstop drama. I almost never got rid of her."

To my surprise, Raven nods. "She wasn't the one."

"I've never made that mistake again. I love football. I'm not like my brothers. I have goals, and living up to my dad's legacy is the most important thing to me."

"I get that. My career is the most important thing in my life right now—not my dad calling me a weather girl or Lawrence Calder O'Halloran telling me women don't chase storms."

Placing my hand on her waist, I pull her closer. "Want to get out of here and get wild?"

She places her hand on the front of my shirt, curling her fingers in the fabric. "What did you have in mind?"

Leaning closer, my lips brush the shell of her ear, and I inhale the floral scent of her perfume. "I have a suite at the Bayside hotel. We could go there and get to know each other better."

Naked. We could get to know each other naked.

I don't say that part out loud.

I watch her throat as she swallows. She hesitates, thinking, and I'm on the edge of a cliff, hoping she's as curious and as turned on as I am.

Her eyes go to the dance floor, where Dylan is hanging on her new husband, moving side to side to a Justin Bieber song.

"I don't think Dylan will miss me." A hint of excitement is in her tone, and my dick responds.

I have a good feeling about this.

"She's one foot into her honeymoon."

A soft hand slides into mine, and that dimple appears on her cheek. "I'm game—let's do it."

Chapter 3

Raven

HENDRIX DOES NOT HAVE A HOTEL ROOM. HE HAS A PENTHOUSE suite with a view across the bay to the barrier islands. It has a small living room, a cute little kitchen, and around the corner, a full, king-sized bed.

My stomach is jumpy, and I slip into the luxury bathroom as soon as we arrive. It has a separate, glassed-in shower and a large, jetted bathtub, and I'm texting my sister.

> I'm hiding in the bathroom of Hendrix Bradford's hotel suite, and he's out there waiting to seduce me 😬

Chewing the side of my fingernail, I pace back and forth, wondering if she'll even see this message. She's an hour ahead of me in Atlanta.

Relief shoots through me when my phone vibrates with her reply.

> Mimi: Get out there and get seduced!

> I'm nervous, and there's nothing to eat.

Mimi: Eat some dick 🍆

> He's too hot for me—he has a square chin and a scar on his lip that is so. HOT 🔥

Mimi: He's a Category 5 hurricane, and you're The Raven Gale—now face him down!

> He's more like a tornado ready to level my trailer park...

Mimi: Yes, girl... let him level it!

> omg

Mimi: BE TASHA!!! Be fierce and own Hendrix Bradford's dick!

> I might not come out alive...

Mimi: At least you'll go out in a blaze of glory!

> Later gator.

Mimi: After while, dile.

Leaning forward, I cover my face in both hands. My heart beats so hard, I take a few deep breaths to steady my nerves.

Shaking my hair back, I straighten my shoulders, looking at myself in the mirror. "Tasha," I whisper, then I open the door with a flourish.

He's near the balcony with his dress shirt unbuttoned halfway. I can see shadowy lines on the muscles of his chest, and with the sleeves rolled, I notice ink on his muscular forearm. His brown hair is tousled, and his fine ass rests against the back of a leather sofa.

When he turns to look at me, a grin parts his full lips, and my panties go up in smoke. "Everything okay?"

The hot cherry Fireball burns low in my stomach, and I give

him a full smile. "Yeah," I exhale a laugh, shaking my head. "My little sister sent me a text, so I took a minute to reply."

Pushing off the couch, he closes the distance between us, and I swallow air. He moves as gracefully as a dancer. I imagine it's because he's so athletic.

He's a tight end. He has a tight end. The thought almost makes me want to snort, but I hold it back.

"You have a little sister?" His voice is deep and smooth as silk.

My eyes are fixed on his full lips, and I wonder what it will feel like to kiss them. I'm fascinated by that tiny white scar. I want to slide my tongue along it.

"Yeah, Amelia."

His brow quirks. "Another pageant girl?"

"No, thank goodness." I walk over to the granite-topped bar lining the edge of the kitchenette. "She managed to escape that nightmare. She's a business major at Emory."

He's standing beside me, and he's so tall. At five-foot-five, I'm not exactly short, but with my heels off, my face only reaches the top of his chest.

Turning, I look up at him. "I didn't realize you were so tall."

"Six-two." He puts his hands on the bar and steps on foot back so his face is lower. "Better?"

It's what he did at the reception when he said he wanted to devour every inch of me. My chest squeezes, and I'm breathing fast again.

"Yes." I lift my hands to his shoulders, leaning closer. "You smell really good."

He turns his face so his lips brush the top of my ear. "So do you."

Tracing my hands along his unbuttoned shirt, my body trembles when I see his chest and stomach. "It's like you're airbrushed."

He leans back, meeting my gaze. "What?"

"I forgot you don't watch movies. It's a line…"

I want to get back to our banter. I'm more confident when we were joking around—like we did all the way down the aisle and all the way through the reception.

Dropping his lips to my ear, he whispers, "What's wrong?"

My face flames with heat. "I've never done this before." Confusion fills his eyes, and I realize at once what he's thinking. "I mean, I've done *it* before. Of course, I've done *it*. I'm over thirty."

"And by *it*, you mean..."

"I'm not a virgin."

"Glad to hear it." The smile that curls his sexy mouth is pure amusement, and he glances to the side like he's telling me a secret. "I'm not either."

I really do snort that time, and my eyes widen. His dance, and it's better. I'm not sure how he makes me so relaxed, but he does.

"What should we do?" I don't know why I'm whispering.

"May I kiss you?"

My tongue pops out to wet my bottom lip, and I nod.

Long fingers hold my chin, tilting it higher. His eyes hold mine a moment as he lowers his face, then they close as warm velvet seals my mouth. They open, and I don't know how, but he pulls my lips with his.

His tongue slides next to mine, and it's the exact amount of pressure, coaxing and curling. A strong hand is against my lower back, scooping me firmly against his chest, and my pussy clenches when I feel his hard dick against my stomach.

My fingers curl on his shoulders, gripping his shirt and pulling him closer as his mouth continues to ravage mine. I'm doing my best to keep up. He tastes like cinnamon and he smells like warm vanilla and sandalwood.

His body is strong and hard, and my arms straighten then wrap around his neck. I stretch against him like a cat as he wraps his arm around my back, pulling me tighter to him.

I don't want to stop kissing him. He's like the air I breathe.

Moving his lips to my cheek, he speaks in my ear. "You're a good kisser."

"You are too…" I whisper, blinking my eyes open slowly.

Releasing me, he takes a slight step back to remove his shirt, and my jaw drops. I carefully place my hand on the top of his chest, moving it to his rounded shoulder.

Lines of ink trace down his right arm, but I don't have time to study him.

"Now your turn."

"Oh…" Fear tightens my stomach, and I hate it. I hate the voices in my head.

Turning, I go to the bedroom, where two lamps shine from the side tables. A round switch is on the wall, and I reach out to turn it off, plunging us into darkness.

"Whoa," he laughs. "Let me see if I can fix that."

Standing at the foot of the bed, I watch his shadowy form go to the side of the bed and turn one of the lamps on again. It's still too much light, and I look down at my dress.

"I'd rather them off." My voice is quiet.

A confused smile lifts the side of his mouth. "But then I can't see you."

Wrinkling my nose, I shrug. "I'm more comfortable that way. You're less able to see our… differences."

Leaving the light on, he returns to where I stand, and I hate my embarrassment. Reaching for my chin, he forces my eyes to meet his.

"I like our differences." Stepping closer, he leans down to speak in my ear. "I'd even say, I love our differences."

Large hands circle my body, shifting my long hair over my shoulder. He presses warm lips against the top of my bare shoulder, sliding his hands to the zipper of my dress.

The top falls to my waist, leaving me in only my strapless bra. My breasts aren't as big as my butt, but I'm not flat-chested by any means.

"God, you're gorgeous." His voice is husky, and I can't help a laugh.

"No one has ever said that to me."

His eyes snap to mine, and he seems truly annoyed. "Are you serious?"

I shrug. "It's true."

"It's not true. You're a bombshell…" He leans down to kiss my cheek, lifting his hands to cup my breasts over my bra.

His thumbs circle my hardening nipples, and I sigh. "Is that so?"

"A classic beauty." His lips move lower, and he nibbles my top lip. "These sexy lips… Can't you feel what you're doing to me?"

He pulls me close, and I feel his erection against my stomach, and I tease with a line from an old movie. "Is that a wrench in your pocket or are you happy to see me?"

"I'm very happy." He leans down to kiss the side of my neck, and heat flutters my stomach. "Very happy… Now get on that bed and let me taste your pussy."

My back arches off the bed as the orgasm rockets through my body. Hendrix has my thighs over his shoulders, and my legs jerk and shake as another deep moan rises from my throat. "Oh, God… Oh, God…"

"Keep calling me that." Hendrix turns his face, his beard scuffing my sensitive skin right before he bites my inner thigh, making me squeal again. "It's great for my ego."

I start to laugh. The orgasm swirls through my veins, and my insides hum with pleasure. He rises onto his knees again, his lips slick with my come, looking down at me with his erection in his hand.

"I've never come so many times..." I gasp, sliding my hand over the butterflies still fluttering in my pelvis. "In a row."

"We're just getting started, beautiful." Leaning across me to where his pants are on the side of the bed, he fishes his wallet out of the pocket.

He straightens, still on his knees, and I move around to my stomach.

"Your turn," I murmur, pulling his dick between my lips.

"Mmm... Okay."

He's big and thick, and my fingers don't meet when I put my hand around his shaft. Still, I focus on the tip, popping it in and out between my wet lips.

With a hiss, he slides his hands behind my neck, lifting my hair off my shoulders and holding it at the back of my head like a ponytail.

Flicking my tongue all around the edge, I tilt my head to suck the underside while I look up at his heated blue eyes.

His full lips part, exposing clenched white teeth as he groans, and he's so fucking hot. I lick my palm before returning it to his shaft, then I slide my hand, pulling it to meet my lips as I bob my head faster.

"Fuck," he rasps, pulling my hair.

His hips rock, and his cock moves deeper into my throat. Shifting my position, I put my hands to his hips, sucking and pulling, staying with him until his stomach flexes. He shudders with a groan, and he bends forward at the waist.

"Stop." His cock pops from my mouth. "I'm not coming down your throat the first time."

Leaning down, he kisses my swollen lips, parting them and curling his tongue against mine. Holding his cheeks, I kiss him back as he moves to sit beside me on the bed. Our kiss parts, and I wait as he rolls the condom over his erection, then he leans back against the pillows.

"Climb on and ride me, baby."

My brow furrows, and I start to argue. "I don't like that. I'm too... *exposed*."

"That's what makes it so great." He sits forward, wrapping his muscled arms around my waist and pulling me onto his lap in a straddle. "I want you bucking on my cock and calling me God again."

His naughty blue eyes flash, and I can't help a laugh. "Hendrix..."

"Come on, gorgeous. Put those sexy tits in my face."

"Oh, my god." I place my hands on the headboard behind him.

"Now we're getting somewhere." He sits forward, pulling my nipple between his lips.

He gives it a firm suck, and a zip of pleasure shoots to my core. Moving one hand to his broad shoulder, I rise onto my knees, helping to guide his thick cock to my aching pussy.

My breath catches as his tip nudges for entry. It's been a while since I've had sex, and I've never been with a man so endowed.

Our eyes meet as I slowly lower, and they both widen as he goes all the way, balls deep. His brow collapses, and my chin drops forward as we both groan. Just as fast, he sits higher, scooping my mouth with his and invading it with a deep kiss.

Another groan vibrates my lips, and my hips start to rock. Our mouths break apart, and his hands are on my breasts, lifting and pulling them to his mouth as he kisses and sucks my nipples.

I've never been in this position, but I'm already a fan. His cock is deep, hitting a part of me that sends tingles through my pelvis, urging me to move faster. My clit rubs against his stomach and sparks of orgasm flash through my belly.

Reaching forward, I grip the headboard so I can ride him faster. His hands are on my ass, squeezing and pulling me, helping me match his rhythm. My eyes close, and I'm caught up in a whirlwind of sensation.

I hear him chanting and groaning, and my head drops back

as I rock faster, harder. It's rising, growing tighter and hotter. I need more, and the only way to get it is to buck harder, harder. He swears low and loud, and I'm lost, chasing that magnificent release, knowing I'll die if I don't get there.

The bed moves. We're both frantic and grasping. Then all at once, it erupts like one of those fireworks that shoots a blaze of sparks in its wake, scorching me to my toes.

I don't know if I call him God, but I'm definitely soaring through heaven. My body clenches and releases so fast, I moan through shuddering pants. He rolls us so I'm on my back, and with three, four more thrusts, he comes with a shout before collapsing, warm breath panting in my hair.

My arms and legs are wrapped around him, and we're both sweating and shaking. I'm not sure I can move. My eyes are squeezed shut, and I wait, letting the sensations ripple out as I fumble back to reality.

His large palm strokes the hair off my forehead, and I slowly blink my eyes open, meeting his warm gaze, his satisfied grin. "Did I break you, beautiful?"

That makes me laugh, and I shake my head. "Not yet."

"Good, because I want to do it all again."

Chapter 4

Hendrix

I should've closed the blinds before I passed out in Raven's arms.

We spent an epic night fucking. I ate her pussy a few more times. She sucked my cock a few more times. I bent her over the couch. She rode me like a bull. She even let me put my dick in her ass, and holy shit, I came so fast, it was embarrassing.

Now she's lying across my chest. Her thick, chocolaty hair is spread over my skin in silky waves, her full lips are pouty. My eyes glide down her gorgeous body, and she is so damn sexy. I almost wish…

"Ugh… not the sun." She lifts a hand, holding it over her eyes in a way that makes me chuckle.

"You're not secretly a vampire, are you, Rave?"

"I might as well be after last night." She turns her face, burying it between my arm and my side.

Shifting my body, I do my best to shield her from the light while stroking her hair off the side of her cheek. Her eyes are closed, but her lips curl with a smile.

Lifting her chin, she blinks up at me. "We didn't get enough sleep."

"Sleep is overrated."

"I can't believe I'm not hungry. I always wake up ready for breakfast."

"To be fair, you swallowed a lot of cock last night." Her eyes flare, and she pinches my side, making me yelp a laugh. "Ow! I wasn't complaining."

"I could use some coffee." She sits up slowly, and I admire the shape of her body, her narrow waist, the curve of her hips. "I've got to get on the road soon."

A twinge of something like sadness moves through my stomach, but I immediately dismiss it. "I'll make us coffee."

Standing, I walk through the room to the kitchen. Her eyes follow me, but I've never been shy about my body. I fill the carafe with water, and when I turn, she's standing at the bar with my white dress shirt loosely buttoned over her naked body. Her dark hair falls around her shoulders in messy, silky waves, and she looks amazing.

I hit the on button and return to lean across from her. "I can drive you to the house when you're ready."

She nods, looking down. "I wish I had something to wear besides my bridesmaid's dress. Talk about the walk of shame."

"No shame—hold that thought." I walk around the bar, returning to the bedroom where the king-sized bed is several inches away from the wall.

I grin at the sight of it, remembering how wild we got last night.

Scooping up my boxer briefs, I pull them on quickly, stepping over the condoms dropped in a neat stack beside the nightstand. I'll clean all this up later.

For now, I dig in my suitcase, taking out an old cotton practice jersey and a pair of sweats. "These are going to be too big for you."

"I doubt it." She takes the clothes from me. "Do you mind if I take a quick shower?"

"Of course not. Take as long as you need."

I pull out a pair of jeans and a navy tee, and I'm standing in the kitchen with a cup of coffee when she emerges from the bedroom dressed in my clothes.

"I can't believe they fit." She's looking down, with her hair over her shoulder, then when she straightens, my old jersey tightens over her breasts and hips in a way that makes me want to suggest a Round 2… or is it 20?

"That looks better on you than it does on me."

"I think my padding hits differently than yours."

"You look great." Stepping to the coffee pot, I take out the carafe. "Go cup?"

"Nah." She waves a hand. "I'll stop at McDonald's on the way out of town and grab a coffee and some breakfast."

Damn, I hate that she's leaving so soon. I can't help thinking if things were different…

Clearing my throat and my mind, I motion to her dress looped over her arm and her silver heels hanging from her fingertip. "Is that all you brought?"

"And my phone." She gestures to the thin terry-cloth slippers on her feet. "I think it's okay if I keep these?"

"I'm pretty sure they throw them away once they're used." I hold the door, leaving the *Do Not Disturb* hanger out, so housekeeping doesn't try and get in here while I'm gone.

We don't say much on the drive to my family's home, but it's a comfortable silence. My mind filters through everything we talked about over the last twenty-four hours. I think I've told her more about myself than any woman in my life, but I decide not to read too much into it.

Raven's easy to talk to, and we had an instant connection— probably because from the start, we knew it had an end date.

Still it feels like too soon we're pulling up at the house, and when we stop in the driveway, I hustle around to hold the door for her.

"Such a gentleman." She gives me a wink.

"Not always." I give her my naughty grin, and her ears turn pink. *Damn, I'll miss doing that.*

Once we're inside, I wait as she goes to the stairs to collect her overnight bag. "I'll change out of these clothes and leave them in the room for you. It'll only take a minute."

"Keep them. I like to think of you wearing my jersey."

Her nose wrinkles, and she hesitates. "I don't really watch football."

"Maybe it'll inspire you to start."

Taking her bag from her hand, I walk with her out to the car. She changed out of the thin slippers and into a pair of Ugg ankle boots.

I hold the door of her car as she tosses her bag onto the passenger's seat. When she turns and looks up at me with those big brown eyes, my stomach twists. My throat clogs, and I don't say what I'm thinking.

We can't keep in touch. We're too far apart, and it'll only make things awkward.

I remember when I was just starting to notice girls, my dad took me to the side and asked me how much I loved the game.

I said football was the only thing in the world, and he smiled that wise old smile, patting my shoulder. "As long as you feel that way, it's best to keep things easy with the ladies. It'll save you a lot of heartache."

I live by that advice to this day.

"Well…" Raven pushes her hair off her shoulder, blinking up at me. "I had a really great time last night."

"Me too." I smile down at her pretty face. "If you're ever in LA, and you're looking for something to do…"

Her nose wrinkles. "If you're ever in Atlanta and want to risk a second date…"

A wistful smile lifts my cheeks, and I nod. "I'd risk it for you."

"Thanks, Hendrix." She steps forward to give me a brief hug. "You're really sweet."

I huff a laugh. "Pretty sure I've never been accused of that."

Stepping into her car, she grins. "Your secret's safe with me."

"Be careful out there chasing storms."

She pulls the door closed, lowering the window. "Be careful out there getting hit in the head."

That makes me groan. "It's not all like that."

"I think it might be. I just spent the night with you."

Leaning down, I kiss her cheek. "Lucky me."

Our eyes meet, and we hesitate. A fleeting sense of something... a sense of *almost*... passes between us. I'm sure she feels it, too, but it's time to say goodbye.

I've got plans, and they don't include romance—or "widows" of any variety.

She starts the engine, and I step back, crossing my arms over my chest as I watch her drive away.

Chapter 5

Hendrix

Fifteen months later

August is the hottest month in LA, and we're in the final weeks before preseason begins. Before it's time to start another year of football every week, sometimes twice a week.

I can't wait.

Satisfaction unfurls in my chest as I stand on the balcony of my prairie-style mansion. It's concrete with metal beams and a steel roof built into the side of a hill, and as I look out over the city, I'm like an emperor surveying his domain.

I'm alone, but I'm content as I contemplate the year ahead.

Last season my team made it all the way to the playoffs. We fell short of the big game, but this year is shaping up to be different.

Adrenaline beats in my chest as I think about it. I'm so ready to get started. I can feel it—this year is the one. We're going all the way, and I can practically see that championship ring on my finger.

All the sportscasters are talking about it. I'm at the top of my game. It's the pinnacle of my career, and I'm ready to do this.

Then my phone lights up with a text.

> Jack: You got time to come home for a few days?

My brow furrows as I study my oldest brother's question, and I quickly tap back a reply.

> Is something wrong?

> Jack: Nothing's wrong—just family business. We need you here.

My jaw tightens, and I look around the place. I have plans with a few of my teammates tonight, but I can bow out and book a flight to our little hometown on the coast in south Alabama.

I don't know what "family business" means, but Jack never asks me to come home. It must be important.

> I can leave in a few hours.

> Jack: Plan to stay a few days.

> I always do.

It doesn't take long to arrange for the team jet to fly me to the small, private airport ten miles south of Newhope. The pilot needs about an hour to file a flight plan, and in that time I can pack and catch a car to the airport.

As the starting tight end for the LA Tigers, I tend to attract a lot of attention. This small jet has become my go-to means of getting across the country, and the pilot and crew are like old friends.

The attendants welcome me with my usual scotch on the rocks, and I settle into the recliner-sized seat with my headphones in and my phone out. Usually, I watch reruns of past games when I fly across the country, but tonight I'm restless.

My late dad was a legendary quarterback for the Texas Mustangs, and he taught my three older brothers and me everything he knew. He taught us to watch all the games during the season. He taught us to study what the other players in our positions were doing. He even taught us to study past players of his generation to see how they handled situations.

Every weekend, we were in the park running plays and working on our passing game.

As the youngest in a family of star athletes, I loved it. It was my dream to play professionally with all my brothers. Now I'm the only one still at it.

Gazing out into the growing darkness, I think about my dad.

We lost both our parents less than a year apart when I was still in middle school.

Jack had just signed on as the starting quarterback for the Mustangs, and all eyes were on him. As the oldest Bradford Boy, the entire pro-football world was waiting to see if he'd be the next Art Bradford.

He was.

He managed to be the best player in the league and keep us all in line from three states away. Zane, my second oldest brother, helped of course.

He was in college and close enough to keep tabs on us through his last year before signing on as a first-round draft pick with the Baltimore Admirals.

He left and Garrett took over.

It was hard, but all five of us believed in keeping our family together. We didn't get into trouble, mostly because we all had our eyes on our goals. Even my youngest sister Dylan had her sights set on joining the New York Ballet Company—until an accident changed her plans.

We all inherited our dad's laser focus, and when Jack

announced he was retiring from the league to be the head coach at our old high school, I couldn't believe it.

"Retiring?" I stared at him like he sprouted a second head. "Why would you do that? You're a star. Hell, you're on track for the MVP!"

Jack's grin was tight as he messed the front of my hair. "There's more to life than football, little brother."

He tried to play it off like it was no big deal, but his smile didn't reach his eyes.

"What about Dad?" I asked, doing my best to shake him out of it.

"What about Dad?" he said through a chuckle.

"Dad dedicated his life to training us. He taught us everything he knew. He opened the doors, paved the way—"

"Dad taught us the only path he knew to a better life, but there are other ways." Jack's tone was calm, reasonable, and it pissed me off.

"I don't believe that." I pushed back. "Not for you."

My mind tripped back to all the Saturdays we scrimmaged in the park; all the Sundays we sat in front of ESPN.

I'd been sleeping with my head on a football since I was old enough to carry one. I'd been busting my ass to be as good as my three big brothers since the first day Dad told me to get out there and play with them.

At six-foot-two, I'd always been the receiver to Jack's quarterback. Garrett was a born lineman at six-foot-four, two hundred pounds. Dad guided Zane to being a kicker, and for a disinterested loner, had the most natural talent of all of us.

Still, Jack was our constant. He kept us on track like a good team captain, and I always thought we were the same.

Until then.

"You're walking away from your career to coach *high school*?" I couldn't keep the disgust out of my tone. "I don't believe it."

"It's what I want to do, Hen. It's what I've done since Mom

and Dad died. Taking care of all of you changed my priorities. Then Kimmie changed them even more."

His hand slid up and down the back of his sleeping daughter Kimmie Joy. Her head was on his shoulder, and it all made sense. I understood the resignation in his eyes, the smile that wasn't completely genuine.

"This is because of Danielle." I flat-out said it. No point beating around the bush.

Jack's first wife was a two-bit country singer from Fort Worth who caught his eye somehow. I only met her once, but I could tell right away what she wanted.

What I couldn't figure out was why he was with her. Jack never dated girls like that in school. Then she turned up pregnant. Then she ditched him for a singing career in Branson.

"It's not because of Danielle." His voice was low, but I caught the hint of a growl.

"She ruined Texas for you, and you think being here will make it all go away."

Don't get me wrong, I love our hometown on the coast. When Dad decided he couldn't play anymore, he and Mom moved to Newhope and opened our family's restaurant. They raised us in a tight-knit community that rallied around us when we were orphaned.

Still, as sweet as it might be, nobody's getting famous in Newhope, Alabama.

"Sometimes I forget how young you are." He said in that paternal tone that ticked me off even more.

"Don't listen to him." Dylan pushed past me, reaching for the baby, her amber eyes shining.

"Come here, Kimmie! Come see your favorite aunt."

"Her only aunt," I groused.

Dylan is eighteen months younger than me, and she'd love nothing more than for all of us to give up football and move home.

"I'm so happy you're back." Our sister's voice was soft and

high as she talked to the toddler, shaking her head and rubbing their noses. "You're going to love it here. We'll take baby swim classes at the Y, and I'll get you in at the preschool—"

I couldn't take any more, and I *wasn't* finished with our conversation. "You want me to believe that being a high school football coach is better than being the best quarterback in the league? Better than winning the Big Game. Better than getting your championship ring?"

"Being with my daughter, being here with my family, and yeah, coaching the next generation of star players is better than the grind." Jack's tone was firm. "Maybe Danielle did spoil Texas for me, but my goal was always to save enough money to be able to walk away when I was ready. I'm ready."

"I'm so glad you are." Dylan took his hand. "I can't wait for all of you to retire."

"Don't hold your breath waiting on me," I grumble. "I'll never throw away my career for a woman."

"Never say never unless you're hungry," my brother chuckled. "You'll end up eating those words."

"Not me. I know what I want, and it's not quitting."

"I'm not quitting, little brother." He put a strong hand on the top of my shoulder, and gave it a squeeze. "I'm doing what I want to do, and one day, you might find something you love more than football, too."

"Doubtful."

A light touch on my shoulder rouses me, and I realize my memories turned into a doze. The smiling hostess lets me know we've made it to the private airport south of Newhope.

It's dark as I descend the stairs to a waiting black SUV, and by the time I arrive at the hotel, it's after midnight.

I always book a room when I visit home. Dylan and her new husband Logan live in our old family home up the hill from the restaurant, and I like to have my own space in case I meet someone or just want to lie around all day in my boxer briefs and watch football.

Besides, Dylan and Logan are newlyweds. They don't need me lurking around the house, interrupting their marital bliss. They should be able to have sex on the kitchen floor if they want.

I send a brief text to the brother's group chat that I'm here, then I crash for the night.

Eight hours later, I open my eyes to a string of texts telling me to come to breakfast at Cooters & Shooters. The restaurant doesn't open to the public until eleven, but when the family is all home, we have breakfast together.

My little sister's wish has almost come true. She likes to say I'm the lone holdout.

Garrett was the third brother to retire after reuniting with his high school sweetheart at Dylan's wedding and getting her pregnant.

I still can't believe he was so careless.

He keeps saying it's Liv, and I get it. Garrett and Liv were inseparable in high school. None of us could believe it when they broke up in college, and we never got the whole story on why. Garrett only said he blew it.

Then they saw each other again at Dylan's wedding, and it was on like Donkey Kong.

It sounds romantic.

It's not.

Never have unprotected sex, kids.

I park my rented Rover at our family house and walk down the pea-gravel path leading to the long, tin-roofed restaurant. It's a gorgeous place in classic, Creole style. It has cedar plank siding painted white with the oversized French doors and windows.

The hurricane shutters are open wide to allow the bay breeze to stream through the space, assisted by massive ceiling fans down the center of the room. On this steamy August morning, like every other August morning in the south, the breeze makes it tolerable.

Briny sea air touches my tongue, and I do love it here.

One day I'll come back here and retire. I'll be an old, *old* man at that point, and I'll sit around and fish and talk shit with the other old-timers.

I'll be too old to play football, but I'll have a legendary career to look back on with pride. I'll have carried on Dad's legacy like he always dreamed his sons would.

"Hey, bro!" Garrett meets me at the door, pulling me in for a hug. "Good to see you."

He almost seems smug about me being here, which puts me on guard. "Good to see you, too."

Garrett towers over everybody, and today he's in his Deputy Sheriff's uniform. It's made of thick khaki, and at his height and build, with the heavy, black leather gun belt on his waist and all the stripes and badges on his chest, he looks pretty badass.

"Busted any criminals lately?" I tease.

"Just the usual—kids acting up, tourists getting drunk, folks driving too fast." His brow arches. "We've had some excitement, but nothing illegal."

"Oh yeah?" I'm intrigued, but Jack catches me by the arm.

"How was your flight?"

"I slept most of it."

"Come with me to the kitchen."

I'm a little confused as he guides me in the opposite direction of our family and friends, but okay. I go with him.

Zane and his fiancée Rachel sit at a booth watching us. Liv is with them, holding her and Garrett's new baby on her shoulder, patting her back. If it weren't for my brother hustling me to the kitchen, I'd go over and meet my new niece. I can see she has Liv's strawberry blonde hair, and she's a chunky little baby.

Instead, I give them a wave, continuing after Jack.

Dylan is in the kitchen, I assume, and Logan's probably with her—if he's not at that radio station he bought and has been busting his ass to get off the ground.

He wants to make it the premier sports destination on his dad's communications network, and once a month, I drop in for a broadcast Zoom chat to break down the week's games and talk about what's coming. It's pretty cool.

"What's going on?" We're just approaching the kitchen when the doors open on their own, and I stop in my tracks.

My chest tightens, and I'm face to face with a girl I haven't seen since my sister's wedding. I've thought about her... more than once. She's petite and pretty with brown hair and golden highlights around her face.

She has a great smile with a big dimple in her left cheek, and her body is banging. She's soft and curvy, and fuck me, her boobs look even bigger than the last time I saw her.

Heat surges below my belt, and my mind jumps back to the night we shared after Dylan's wedding. We had a lot of fun and *a lot* of sex.

It left an impression.

And I've got to stop thinking about it before I pop an inappropriate boner right here in front of my whole family. Glancing around, they're still watching us, and it's a nice bucket of cold water on that train of thought.

"Raven, hey...." Clearing my throat, I extend a hand. "It's been a minute, but wow. You look great."

Her brown eyes widen, and she seems flustered, which is new. When we were together, she was so confident and bold. She was funny, and our chemistry crackled in the air around us.

"Is he here?" Dylan emerges from the kitchen, with a dark-haired baby on her hip.

I frown, confused. No one told me Dylan was pregnant. Has it even been nine months since I saw her last?

"Yes." Raven's voice is quiet, and her eyes are worried. "Hendrix... I didn't know you'd be here so soon. We didn't exchange contact information, and I... I needed to reach you."

"Why? What's going on?"

"We have a little surprise!" My sister is using her baby-voice as she bounces the infant on her hip, then she smiles up at me brightly. "Hendrix, meet Hayden. She's your daughter!"

My chin jerks back in surprise, and my face cools as all the blood drains from it. "My *what?*"

"That's right!" Dylan leans forward, rubbing her nose against the little girl's and making her smile. "Raven brought us another baby to love. Sweet little Hayden Lucille Bradford. Isn't she *adorable?*"

"I'm sorry…" I'm having trouble speaking around the boulder in my throat. "I don't have a baby."

The room falls quiet. My eyes move quickly over the crowd of familial spectators all watching me.

"Sorry, bro." Garrett steps forward with that smug grin on his face and slaps the top of my shoulder in a forceful way. "Looks like you do."

"Get off me." I shrug him away, stepping closer to Raven and lowering my voice. "But we used condoms every time."

"We did." Raven nods. "I was so impressed by how responsible you were."

"I'm *always* responsible." I'm doing my best not to raise my voice. "I'm responsible so this doesn't happen. How did this happen?"

"I don't know." Raven's voice is equally quiet. "I guess one… failed?"

I swallow air. "Condoms cannot fail. Condoms have one job, and that is *not* to fail."

Raven's eyes drop, and her tone is placating. "I didn't want to tell you this way. It's a shock, and you…"

"Want to hold her?" Dylan extends the baby to me like Rafiki in *The Lion King*.

"Whoa!" Both my hands shoot up, and I take a step back while I try to restart my brain.

The small human blinks at me with wide blue eyes, just like mine.

She's weirdly like looking in a mirror. Her head is covered in shiny dark hair that ends in soft curls around her chubby cheeks, and as I study her, her tiny lips press into an angry scowl.

I don't know shit about babies, but I'm pretty sure this one's about to scream in my face.

Raven steps forward quickly, taking her out of my sister's hands and hugging her little body close to her chest. "It's okay, Haddy."

The baby puts her head on Raven's shoulder and two fingers in her little mouth, sucking furiously.

Then Raven turns to me. "We need to talk." She catches my hand, pulling me with her through the double doors into the kitchen.

We leave my family in the dining room, buzzing with chatter, and if I know my brothers, they're having a field day with this one.

If I know my little sister, she's floating on cloud nine and making all kinds of plans for preschool and baby swim lessons and holy shit.

Raven turns to me when we're alone. "I'm really sorry. This wasn't my plan, but I didn't know how to reach you. I didn't have your number, and I had the worst morning sickness the whole time I was pregnant. I actually *lost* weight. Then after she was born, it took me a minute to get back on my feet, and the longer I waited, the harder it seemed. I knew I had to tell you, but I didn't know what to do."

She pauses to breathe, and I can tell she's stressed. I'm fucking stressed, but when I see other people stressed, I snap into action. It's what I do.

We're adults. We can fix this.

"Hang on. Just slow down a minute." I'm still groggy from the jet lag, but I'm doing my best to strategize. "So you got pregnant after Dylan's wedding…"

Brown eyes meet mine followed by bright blue ones framed in thick dark lashes. "Yes."

Baby Haddy is curious, sucking her fingers and watching me like she's wondering what I'll do next. I have no freaking idea.

"And Haddy is…" The words get stuck, so I clear my throat. "My daughter?"

"Haddy is *our* daughter."

Our daughter.

Adults.

We're adults, but what the ever-loving fuck?

This was *not* supposed to happen.

Chapter 6

Raven

"Haddy is our daughter." Hendrix repeats my words, crossing his strong arms and putting one hand over his mouth like he's trying to pull himself back together.

Haddy is hugged against my chest, and she watches him curiously. She's never been a fussy baby, but she's attuned to my moods. I can tell by the way she's clutching me and sucking her fingers, she's picking up on my nerves, so I try to stay calm.

"I had a ten-year no-vomit streak until this little lady showed up." I laugh, doing my best to ease the tension.

I've outgrown Tasha in the last fifteen months. Now I'm simply Mama Bear, and I hope, if my instincts are correct, I can count on Hendrix Bradford to help me with my problem, even if he's looking at me right now like I just nuked him.

"She's… cute."

"She looks a lot like her daddy."

She really does. Haddy has my dark hair, but the rest of her is all Hendrix, from the bright blue eyes to the full lips to the stubborn streak, although I guess that could come from both of us.

"Do you think she'd let me hold her?" The touch of vulnerability in his tone melts my heart.

"Of course." I step closer, hesitating as I give her a little bounce. "It's okay, Haddy. He's really, secretly sweet."

Her blue eyes are fixed on him, but she lets me pass her over. Only he puts his arm across her stomach, holding her against his ribs like some kind of… *football?*

"Oh, no…" I take a stuttering step, reaching out to lift her. "That's… that's not right…"

I don't want to make him self-conscious on his first attempt, but she's practically upside down.

Dylan's head pops through the door at that moment, and her bright smile turns to a grimace. "Good grief, Hen! You're holding her like a football!"

"So?" He's defensive as she rushes to him, lifting her niece to more of a sitting position on his arm, which actually seems less stable. "I've never dropped a football in my life!"

"Give her to me." Dylan scoops Haddy onto her shoulder. "Hey, pumpkin. Don't worry about your silly daddy. He'll learn."

"I was getting her situated," he protests, and I put my hand over my mouth to hide a smile.

It really was awful—and a bit terrifying.

"Let me have her. You need to talk to her mama." Dylan skips to the door. "Y'all take your time. We'll be right out here."

My eyes are wide when he turns to face me again. It's the first time the D-word has been used on him, and he stands for a moment, seeming winded.

I hate how abrupt all of this feels. I think I know Hendrix pretty well, and I wouldn't have handled it this way if I'd had a choice.

While I didn't want to have this conversation with him with my head in a trash can vomiting the whole time, I certainly didn't want to ambush him.

I know this isn't what he wants, and I would never want him to think I was trying to trap him or change his mind or make him do anything. I would never make him do anything.

It's like the moment I got here with the baby, we got caught up in a hurricane of family love. It's warm and welcoming, but it's still a hurricane.

"I'm really sorry." My voice is quiet. "I didn't expect… all of this." I wave my hand at the door his sister just disappeared through.

"All of this would be my family." His tone is wry. "Now you know why I get a hotel room when I'm in town."

"I think they mean well."

"They do, and I love them. I also love my privacy and being able to decide my business without a committee."

"I get that."

"They're really enjoying this, too." Looking down, he exhales through a grimace. "I've been a shit for so long about babies and poop and… well, you know."

He glances up at me from beneath his brow, and my breath disappears. It's been that way since the first time I saw Hendrix Bradford.

He's too good looking and he smells too damn delicious and his smile is absolutely sinful—and I know how good he is in bed.

Heat crawls up behind my ears, but I clear my throat. *That* is not the direction I'm headed. It's not why I'm here.

"Damn, Rave, this is crazy." He takes a step closer, studying my face. "How have you been otherwise? Are you a storm chaser yet? Is Jim Cantore watching his back?"

"No." I exhale the word. "It's been impossible to work with all the morning sickness, and then when she was a newborn, I had to be with her. I've kind of had to put all my career plans on hold."

"Well, shit. I'm sorry." He briefly pats my arm. "I won't try to fight you on this or anything. I don't have a leg to stand on. She's clearly mine."

The way he says it is teasing, but I squint one eye. "Would you have done that?"

The teasing melts, and he almost seems wounded. "Is that what you think of me?

"No." Dropping my eyes, I know he wouldn't have.

It's the whole reason I'm here preparing to ask him something completely terrifying.

"I guess I'm supposed to *make this right*." He says it in a mock-authoritative voice, and I chew my lip.

"I guess."

"My brother Jack did that, and it was a total disaster."

Nodding, I study my hands feeling my stomach twist as I think about what I'm going to say. I think about the Hendrix Bradford I spent a crazy twenty-four hours with almost two years ago.

The playful one, who fucked my brains out and made me feel confident and sexy. The one who liked to have fun and talk about adventures.

"Are you expecting me to do that?" His voice is quiet, and my eyes cut up to his.

"No—not exactly…" Standing straighter, I square my shoulders.

"I'm glad to help you. Tell me what you need, and I'm sure I can afford it."

A knot is in my throat, and I do my best to swallow it away. "Actually, the thing is… I do have another reason for coming here… besides you needing to know your daughter."

"Okay?"

"It's funny. Growing up, I never really cared about money. You might say it's because I've always had it, and that's a privilege. It's true. My family is wealthy, and I've never had to worry about my next meal. But I also think it's my personality. I'm not afraid to work hard, and I'll do pretty much any job… within reason, of course."

His brow furrows, and I know I'm rambling. "That's good, I guess?"

"Yes, well…" I inhale a shaky breath. "Having Haddy sort-of changed all of that. You'd be surprised by how little money starting meteorologists at local news stations are paid, and well…"

"You need me to give you money?" He brightens.

With a wince, I shake my head. "I don't want a handout. I want to support myself, and you didn't ask for this…"

"You didn't either."

"Still, I could've…" My chest tightens as I consider the alternative. "I could've *handled* it as soon as I found out I was pregnant. Maybe that would've been smart, but I just couldn't. I really wanted her."

"Shit, Rave." His tone gentles, and he takes a step closer. "I wouldn't have asked you to do that. Just because I didn't want a baby doesn't mean I would've told you to end it."

My lips part on my exhale, and I'm glad Dylan has Haddy because I am freaking out right now over what I'm about to say.

"I have a solution. It's completely unorthodox, but I hope you'll hear me out and at least consider it. I think it'll work, because we get along so well…"

"What is it?" His head is tilted, and that look in his eye gives me the one, tiny push I need to say it.

"Hendrix Bradford, will you marry me?"

The room falls silent—except, the hum of the dishwasher, which is suddenly very loud.

He blinks twice, and I realize it might've been nicer to wait a day before hitting him with another life-changing tidal wave.

Oh, well. Too late now.

"Ahh…" He takes a step back. "Sounds like somebody forgot my two-date rule."

He grins doing finger guns, and I have to give him credit. He's pretty good at rolling with the punches.

"When my mother died, she left me a trust fund of six million dollars." I inhale a fortifying breath as I try to explain. "The only problem is I can't touch it until either my father dies or I get married. And while I really want to be financially independent, I'm not planning to knock off my dad."

His brow lowers, and I force a strangled laugh. "That was a joke."

He turns, walking to the large, stainless steel work table in the center of the room. His hand is still on his stomach when he looks back at me. "Fuck, Rave, is that even legal?"

"Knocking off my dad?"

"Putting rules like that on a trust fund. How can she say you can't access it until your dad dies or you get married? Who does that?"

"My mother was an extremely controlling person, and as much as I love my dad, he never defended me." My jaw tightens, and that old bitterness stings in my throat. "Believe me, I would never come here and ask you this if I had any other choice. I never even wanted her 'control-Raven' money... Until now."

The way Haddy looks at me sometimes with so much faith. It hits me hard when I know how little I have to offer her. She's so dependent, and it didn't take long for me to realize I'd do anything to keep her safe and secure, including this.

Frowning, he rubs his stomach as he thinks. "Wouldn't it be easier if I just paid you child support? Then you could hire a nanny or whatever until you got on your feet?"

My body is tense, my neck tight. "That could take years, whereas my trust fund would take care of everything now. You wouldn't have to worry about us ever again."

"I don't want that." He looks in the direction of the doors. "I want to know my daughter. Now that I've met her."

Blinking up at him, I start slowly. "If you'd be willing to give me one year..."

"A year!"

"Six months?" I quickly shave it down. "Three months—and I'll say it's my fault. I don't like football or I don't like LA or I'm too far from home—whatever reason you prefer. Then we'll get a quickie divorce, and it'll all be over."

His eyes hold mine, and he frowns. "I don't like the sound of that either."

"Which part?"

"The quickie divorce. It sounds so… shitty."

"It wouldn't be a real marriage, though. And it would really help me a lot. It would help Haddy, too. I'll sign a prenup, whatever you need—" Taking a beat, I swallow the desperation in my throat. "I can't let her win, Hendrix. She did this to control me, but if there's a chance…" The truth burns my eyes. *If there's a chance I could come out on top for once.* "I don't want to give up my dream. But I love that little girl so much."

It's quiet again, and this time even the dishwasher has stopped, the timer ticking like it's waiting as well.

At last, he speaks. "You'd have to move to LA."

My stomach jumps to my throat at his words. "Does this mean you're considering it?"

"I mean…" He shrugs. "I'd like to get to know my daughter. She's cute, and I could get you a job at one of the local news stations, so… you know, you could work on your dream."

"How in the world could you do that?"

A grin curls his lips. "Not to brag, but I'm kind of a big deal in football."

"Oh, are you?" I attempt to tease, but relief is hitting me so hard, my muscles are weak.

He's going to help me. This might actually work.

"Yeah." His face relaxes, and I think he's catching up to the craziness of what I'm suggesting. "My place is huge, so you could have half the house to yourself."

Now I'm starting to get excited. "And I promise not to intrude in your life or interfere with your plans… It'll go by so fast, and then everything will be back to how it was before."

Except I'll be six million dollars richer.

The dimple appears in his cheek, and he walks closer to

where I'm standing. "One thing—we *cannot* tell my family about this. They'll go nuts, throw a party, insist we move back here."

"Trust me, I've seen enough in two days to know what they're like. It's sweet, but it would seriously complicate my plans."

"We'll be far enough away, so they'll never know."

"But my dad has to know—and his lawyer and the trustee."

We're talking fast, and he seems as eager to help me as I am to accept his help.

"They're in Atlanta, so that's a good buffer zone. We'll let them know, but otherwise…"

"It'll be our secret."

Reaching out, he takes my hand, pulling me to him. "Yes, Raven Gale, I accept your proposal of marriage."

"It'll be so easy. We already have experience walking down the aisle."

"We're old pros." His expression turns sly. "We're even pretty good in bed."

"We made a baby!" I love that he's strategizing with me, making it fun and not terrifying.

"How soon would you like to get started, Miss Gale?"

"The sooner the better."

"We'll do it for Haddy." His muscled arm is around my shoulders.

"For Haddy."

Chapter 7

Hendrix

RAVEN SMILES UP AT ME WITH SO MUCH HOPE IN HER EYES, IT'S LIKE I'm some kind of white knight riding in to save the day.

On the one hand, it's kind of cool to be a hero. On the other hand, I feel like I've been shoved down the scrubby hill outside my LA mansion with no padding.

Or crushed under a pile of 300-pound linebackers.

I'm getting married.

I have a baby, and I'm getting married.

Which undoubtedly means at some point I'll be faced with poop.

Two nights ago, I was standing on the balcony of my mansion in the hills, overlooking the city of LA spread out before me like a king overlooking his domain.

The only thing on my mind was football and having the best year of my career.

I had no freaking idea.

"Ready to run the gauntlet?" A tease is in her voice, and I almost groan.

My family is out there waiting for a verdict, and I just know what the guys are going to say.

"Let me take the lead, and stay close."

We go through the double doors, back to where my entire family is crowded around two tables, introducing my daughter to Garrett's baby Gigi. They're the same age, because apparently we weren't the only ones who got lucky after my sister's wedding.

Of course, I gave him shit for that. The twinkle in his eye tells me he hasn't forgotten about it either.

"We'll call them the Dylan twins!" My little sister announces, bouncing my daughter on her hip. "They're like my very special wedding present from my two big brothers."

"Hey, us ladies had something to do with it," Liv cries, joining us and taking Raven's hand. "I wish you'd texted me. We could've gone through it together."

"I was either in bed nauseated or hanging on the toilet the whole time." Raven follows Liv to where the girls are standing, and Haddy reaches for her.

She pulls the baby onto her hip, and I stop in my tracks, thinking how really beautiful they are. Haddy is a cute little brunette with a button nose like her mom's. Then her head turns, and she hits me with my blue eyes.

"It's kind of uncanny." Zane's voice is quiet at my side. "She's got your face."

"Yeah…" I huff a laugh.

There's no denying whose kid she is.

"You're going to make this right." Garrett still has that grin on his face, walking over in his sheriff's uniform.

"Of course, I am." I hold back an eye-roll. As if I wouldn't. "We talked about it, and Rave and Haddy are going to move out to LA for a little while to live with me."

"Oh, no!" Dylan cries, giving me her sad-puppy face. "We just got her! Don't go to LA, Raven. Make Hendrix come here."

"I've got training camp starting next week." When I get closer to Rave, I put my hand on Haddy's little back. "Then the season starts, and I'll be slammed. It's the only way that makes sense for me to spend time with my daughter."

"Garrett and Liv did long distance," Dylan pouts. "So did Logan and me."

"So you know how much it sucked," Garrett calls, supporting me for once.

"Would you like to hold her again?" Raven's voice is quiet, and I study the baby girl sitting on her hip.

"Will she cry?"

Garrett glances at the large clock behind the bar. "I bet you've got about ten minutes before she starts crying."

"Ten minutes?" I cut him a look like he knows anything.

"He's right, actually." Raven passes our daughter to me, helping me situate her against my chest in a way that puts her little face closer to mine. "For some reason five o'clock is the witching hour. She always gets fussy around that time."

"Haddy?" Raven's voice is gentle. "This is your daddy."

Haddy wobbles on my arm, and I bend my knees, trying to balance her.

"Here." Garrett lifts my hand, putting it on her back. "You have to hold her."

"I know that." *I didn't.*

I don't know shit about babies.

She seems more secure, though. Sitting on my arm, she looks at me several moments before patting her chubby hand against my cheek. It's damp and a little sticky, but I know better than to say *gross*.

Her other finger is still in her mouth, but she emits a squeal-like noise like she's trying to tell me something. It's kind of cute.

I glance at Raven, unsure, and she gives me an encouraging smile. "She likes you."

"Just look at you two." Liv walks over, putting a hand on Haddy's back. "Where's my phone? Dylan, take a picture of them."

"Oh my goodness!" Dylan coos, pulling her phone out and taking several pictures.

I study the little girl on my arm, wondering what she's thinking. I wonder if she's as startled by all of this as I am. She has no idea the gang of family surrounding her, and how they're all ready to steal her away and spoil her rotten.

But I do.

"We've switched to feeding Gina at five," Liv continues. "I figure we can all eat together when she's older."

"That's so smart!" Raven's brown eyes are wide. "I can't believe I didn't think of that."

"It sounds like you've had a lot to think about all by yourself." Liv's smile is sympathetic.

"It wasn't so bad. My little sister Amelia helped me, and my dad was there—disapproving and asking a ton of questions."

"Call me anytime." Liv takes her hand, and they drift over to where Dylan is talking to Rachel. "You have my number."

"Looks like you're getting the hang of it." Jack gives my shoulder a pat.

"You could've warned me." I cut my eyes up at him. "I could've had a whole twelve hours to prepare for this."

"Raven wanted to tell you herself."

"Dylan told me."

Jack's face scrunches with a grimace. "Dylan's always been a wildcard. You know your sister."

"She almost killed me the first time we met." Logan walks up, and I turn, reaching out to shake his hand.

"One of you could've warned me."

"Are you kidding? And miss that look on your face?" Garrett's voice is loud and laughing, and his daughter sits in the crook of his arm. She's pretty much doing the same thing as mine, patting his shoulder and blowing raspberries through her lips. "Let me know if you need me to draw you a diagram. Those poopy diapers are tricky til you get the hang of it."

The last thing I intend to do is let my oversized brother think he's got one on me. "I can handle a poopy diaper."

I can *not* handle a poopy diaper.

"I'll ask Rave to take a video of you handling it." Garrett's on my case. "I can always use a good laugh."

"You got this, Hen." Jack is being team captain as always, keeping me motivated. "If I did it, you can do it. Call me if you need help. Don't call this guy."

"Like I'd ask Sasquatch for help," I growl.

"That's Daddy Bear to you," Garrett replies.

"When are you retiring?" Logan puts his hands in his back pockets. "You'd be a great addition to the show. Our ratings always spike when you drop in for a chat."

My chest tenses, and I guess my grip on Haddy does as well. Her little eyes blink faster.

"Don't get ahead of yourself." I try to keep it light, but my body is tight and a hint of defensiveness enters my tone. "I'm not like you guys. I don't have any plans to retire any time soon."

Jack's voice is a low calm. "There's plenty to do around here if you change your mind."

"I won't change my mind." My voice rises, and Garrett's brow does, too.

He has that look on his face like he's holding a goldfish in his mouth, and by goldfish I mean some kind of dunk on me he's ready to spew. Probably something about making me another pillow with these new words cross-stitched on it.

He never gets the chance to say it, though, because Haddy scrunches up her little face and starts crying. *Loud.*

"Shit…" I hiss under my breath.

Her little face is red, and I'm looking all over the place for Raven.

"It's okay… It's okay…" I'm using the same high-pitched voice I've seen people use when babies start screaming. I even bounce as I walk. "Don't cry…"

"Real smooth, bro." Garrett shakes his head. "You scared her."

I leave my brothers standing around, having a good laugh at my expense, but I've got to find Raven. Haddy lets out another, louder yell, and she even has a little round tear caught on her bottom eyelashes.

My stomach twists. Where the fuck did Raven go? She was just standing over here with Dylan and Liv and Rachel…

I'm about to give up and ask my annoying giant brother for help when Raven bursts through the double doors leading to the kitchen.

"Oh, no!" She has an aqua-colored rubber pacifier in her hand, and the first thing she does is pop it in our daughter's mouth. "Sorry, I lost track of time."

She takes her from me, and I follow her into the kitchen, where Dylan has one of those small, vanilla ice cream cups she uses on her spicy dare nights. It's the kind with the paper top and the small wooden paddle for a spoon.

"Did Daddy pinch you?" Dylan dips a tiny bite of ice cream and slips it into her mouth.

My daughter stops crying right away, and my shoulders drop. "I could've given her ice cream."

"Oh," Liv makes a worried face. "I'm not sure she should have ice cream yet…"

"It's okay," Raven jumps in quickly. "She can eat whatever she wants. I'm not one of those moms."

"No, I just mean… You're supposed to wait until she's a year old for cow's milk." Liv's nose wrinkles like she's sorry for telling us this.

"Right. I didn't think of that…" Raven's eyes widen, and I grab my phone, doing a quick Google search.

"It says here, ice cream is safe for babies at six months, but you should really wait until she's a year…"

"It's Aunt Dylan's fault!" Dylan takes the ice cream cup from Raven. "Sorry, I'm the worst."

"It's okay. She's had a lot of stimulation today." Raven turns to me. "I should take her to the house. Want to walk me back?"

"Of course." I take the purple canvas bag she's holding that has all the baby stuff in it.

Thomas gives me a nod as I pass him. "You remind me a lot of your daddy right now."

"Really?"

"He loved his kids." Our old friend's lips part in a smile as he pats my shoulder. "He just didn't always know what to do with them—but he learned."

"Thanks, T." I grumble as he chuckles, like my ignorance is so hilarious.

I had a really good dad, and if he learned, I can learn. Sometimes life throws you curveballs. Maybe I don't play baseball, but I can do this.

I follow Raven out the back screen door. A flight of three steps leads down to a wide, pea-gravel path lined with small black lights.

My family's home is on the bluffs, up the hill from the restaurant. Haddy has a pacifier in her mouth, and as we walk, she emits little humming noises.

Raven is pretty as ever walking beside me in the growing twilight. Her body hasn't changed, and her eyes, her hair, her full lips, her breasts, all of it has me wondering if our arrangement might include *benefits*.

She's the only woman I've thought about for more than a few weeks. For a while, I wondered what might've happened if we lived closer. Would I have tried dating her? Would it have been a mistake?

I think about that morning when we said goodbye after our wild night. *I'd risk it for you...* Am I about to find out?

When we step inside the back door, she takes the diaper bag, digging through it and taking out a pale blue, crocheted stuffed animal with what looks like purple fans on each side of its head.

The minute Haddy sees it, she leans forward with a little squeal, reaching for it and hugging it tightly to her neck.

"I take it that's someone important."

"That's Axel the Axolotl," Raven explains. "My sister crocheted him for her. We never go anywhere without Axel."

"Got it."

"The good news is Amelia's working on a backup Axel in case something happens to this one."

"Smart," I nod, and she takes our daughter from my arms.

"She just needs her dinner and a bath. Then she'll probably go right to sleep."

"I've got my room at the hotel if you'd like to stay with me." As I'm saying the words, her expression changes.

"I don't think that's a good idea." Her lips tighten, and she doesn't meet my eyes. "I appreciate what you're doing for Haddy and me, but I think we'd better keep things strictly platonic while we're together."

"Really?" I sense all my fantasies from our walk to the house going up in smoke.

"Really." She nods quickly. "I can't do your two-dates thing. It doesn't work for me. I tend to get attached."

"That's okay," I give her a little grin. "But what if we want to blow off a little steam?"

"Nope." Her tone is emphatic. "No dating. No sleepovers. We're just friends, who happen to be parents."

Her eyes flash, and I hold up my hands. "Understood. I respect your boundaries."

"Thank you." Her chin drops, and she almost seems apologetic. "I think it's for the best. Blurring the lines will only make it harder to say goodbye when it's time to go."

The pinch in my chest tells me she's right. Raven might be cool and smart and tempting, but I've never had a problem walking away from a woman.

Our time together will be like training camp. We'll start the clock, and in six months, we'll shake hands and walk away. No misunderstandings. No complications.

Football is my life. I love it, and I like being single. Three months isn't going to change anything.

Chapter 8

Raven

"THIS HOUSE IS INCREDIBLE! AND THIS VIEW…" I'm standing on a concrete balcony with a bronze and glass banister overlooking the city of Los Angeles spread out for miles below. "It's like that house in *Charlie's Angels*. You know, the one where Drew Barrymore falls over the balcony?"

"Never saw it." Hendrix stands at the sliding glass doors with Haddy against his chest.

He's getting better at holding her. In the past few days, all through hiring the movers and coming here, he's gone from stiff and nervous to relaxed and downright sexy holding her.

Not that I'm thinking of him in those terms.

We've laid the ground rules, and I'm sticking to them.

His daughter, by contrast, has no rules and is clearly in love with her daddy. She's gotten to where she'll go to him as quickly as me. He can even get her to stop crying now.

"We've got to do something about your lack of movie

knowledge." I lean my back against the railing, crossing my arms. "Are you not coming out here?"

"I don't want to get too close to the railing while I'm holding her. She might jump out of my arms."

Pressing my lips together, I will not tease him for being overprotective. It's actually kind of cute. "Then I'll come to you."

I walk across the wide balcony, stepping into his posh home. It has heavy, reclaimed wooden floors with rustic columns throughout. All of his furniture is leather and dark mahogany wood. It's designed in a split-level style with the different floors separated by short flights of stairs.

It's very Frank Lloyd Wright, built into the side of the hill and designed to blend with the scenery, concrete and steel.

"Jack said we could hire someone to childproof the house for us." He walks into the living area where a massive flatscreen television hangs over a gas-log fireplace. "We can put pillows around the fireplace mantle, but this coffee table is a hazard."

"We should be okay until she starts walking." I pause at a credenza where several framed photographs are arranged.

One is of Hendrix and Garrett hugging each other on the sidelines. As much shit as they give each other, I can tell from their expressions it's all an act. Pure love is on their faces.

"I adore this photo." I lift it, turning it so he can see.

"Oh, yeah." He stops, walking back to where I'm standing. "I wanted to have one of all four of us together, but Jack retired before I could."

"You have this one of you and Garrett with Logan." It's a shot of the three of them together on the sidelines. Garrett's arms are crossed, but Logan is laughing at something Hendrix has said. "These are so good!"

"That one's from the team photographer." He nods at it. "The other one came from a gossip site. They made a lot of money catching us all together like that."

"Are you saying this is a money shot?" I tease, replacing the photo.

"Definitely."

Following him through the house, I'm in love with the gorgeous, mid-century modern design, then we arrive at another short flight of stairs leading to a whole separate wing.

"This will be your half of the house." He slides his hand over a light switch, and warm yellow light illuminates a spacious sitting area with wood-paneled walls and two doors on either side leading to separate bedrooms.

"Very inviting." I open one of the doors to see a wide-open space with a desk and two chairs in the center. A king-sized bed is near the windows, covered in a pine green duvet with fluffy white pillows. "I take it this is my room?"

"Is that okay?"

"It's beautiful."

My suitcases are stacked beside the closet, and I remember briefly seeing a man at the airport collecting our things and loading them into a black SUV.

Hendrix leads us across the hall, opening the other door to a pretty room painted in a vintage purple color. It has a gleaming wooden crib at the back wall with a pretty mobile attached to the side. Plush, pink and purple fairies hang from it all holding wands with ribbon streamers.

The mattress is made up with a pink and purple crib sheet and a bumper all around the sides. A queen-sized bed is positioned against the opposite wall, and a glider with a footstool is by the floor-to-ceiling windows, which have blackout shades waiting to be lowered.

"I had to tell Coach what was going on, and his wife Christina really wanted to help get the house ready for Haddy." He almost seems apologetic. "I hope that's okay. She was so excited. Their son just left for college."

"That's so sweet. I'll have to send her a thank-you card. The house is all ready for us."

He hesitates, as if he's unsure what to do now. "I hope you'll both like it here."

Hendrix is this big, strong athlete with perfectly messy brown hair and bright blue eyes. He's six-foot-two inches of pure muscle with broad shoulders, a rock-hard chest and abs, and a narrow waist. When he grins, his lips part over straight, white teeth, and that scar… and that dimple. He's a work of art.

He's a total player, and when he reveals these moments of pure vulnerability, it does not help that I remember our one night together so vividly.

I have to be very careful during this time to keep my head straight. I won't lose my heart. It wouldn't be fair to any of us. We have ground rules.

Football is his life. The weather is mine. We share Haddy, and that's where it ends.

"I'm sure we will. Your house is so beautiful, and Haddy's room is so cute. I've always been in the same room with her, so that'll be a switch."

"You can sleep in the bed in here if you want?"

"We'll see how it goes. It's good for her to get used to her own room."

We walk back through the house, in the direction of the kitchen, and when we enter the large living room, I can't resist. "This television is incredible. I can't wait to watch movies on it."

"You talk about movies like I talk about football."

Shrugging, I can't argue. "It's my favorite hobby."

"Is watching movies a hobby?"

"It is how I do it." I gesture to the massive screen. "You can compare camera angles and scenes, contrast the old styles with the new ones to see how they influence each other. You can even compare the way actors walk and their delivery of lines to the way actors did it in the past—especially when they do biopics. It's so fun."

He's ahead of me as we walk, and my eyes drift to his butt. My lips tilt to the side, and I almost sigh over how unfair it is that he's so attractive. It's like a test.

"Are you sure you want to be a meteorologist?" He stops,

turning fast, and I jump, letting out a little yelp which makes his eyes narrow. "Were you just checking out my ass?"

"No!" I say it too loudly, and my ears grow hot, which I know means they're turning pink.

"You were checking out my ass."

"I was not!"

He looks at Haddy. "She was checking out Daddy's ass."

Haddy smiles and pats his cheeks, letting out a little gurgling noise.

"See that?" His blue eyes meet mine. "She said you were."

"Nice try." I step forward, holding back a swoon at how cute they are. "You'll have to watch your language. Her first word can't be a swear."

"Is *ass* a swear?" he teases.

"She can't say it at school."

"Still, we know what you did." He resumes walking, leaning into our daughter. "She was checking out Daddy's butt, Hads."

"I was not checking out your butt!" I cry, even though it's a total lie. I was totally checking out his butt. "I was thinking about what you said, and yes, I want to be a meteorologist."

"You should be a movie critic. You're in the perfect city for it."

"I also want to tour Warner Brothers studios."

He groans. "I'll let you do that on your own."

"It'll be fun! Look, Haddy agrees with me, don't you, baby?" I step forward, but our little daughter's brow furrows.

"See?" he laughs. "She does not agree. She thinks that's a terrible idea."

Her blue eyes lose focus for a minute, and I press my lips together. I know that look. "I don't think that's what she thinks."

The distinctive scent of baby poop permeates the air around us, and Hendrix's eyes snap to mine.

"Haddy!" He cries, lifting her by her midsection and holding her away from his body. "What did you do?"

"She pooped." I hold my nose, trying not to laugh.

"She was just sitting on my arm!" His face wrinkles with a grimace. "How could she sit there and do that on my arm?"

I shrug. "Babies poop, Hendrix."

Her little eyes squint, and her bottom lip wobbles. She holds out her arms to him, starting to cry.

"Ugh—it smells so bad!" He turns his head, dropping his jaw and breathing through his mouth.

"You have to change her."

Panicked blue eyes lock on mine. "I can't do that."

"Sure you can!" I smile encouragingly.

"Raven…"

"She's not on fire, Hendrix, and there's a good chance you'll be alone with her and a poopy diaper at some point." Haddy cries harder, and I take her from him. "Come on, baby."

I snatch up the diaper bag from the kitchen table and carry her into the living room. Haddy puts her little head on my arm.

"You're not going to do it on my rug!" Hendrix's voice is pure horror.

"I'll put a blanket under her. Now get over here and help me." I take a baby blanket from the bag and spread it over the expensive Persian rug, then I take out a fresh diaper and the packet of baby wipes.

He kneels beside me, but when I open the dirty diaper, he falls back on his butt, cupping his face. "Oh, God!"

Then he jumps up and dashes into the kitchen.

"You've got to learn how to do this!" I yell after him.

Haddy's little lip quivers and a tear is on her bottom lashes. "It's okay, sweetie." My voice is soothing. "Daddy is new at this."

I'm smiling, doing my best to calm her down when her blue eyes flash and she lets out an even louder scream that makes my heart jump to my throat.

Hendrix drops to his knees beside me wearing a snorkel mask and yellow rubber gloves.

Haddy cries, trying to twist away, but I hold her. "Take that off—you're scaring her!"

"I can't... that smell!" he argues.

"Hendrix!" I push him with my elbow, and his shoulders drop.

Haddy won't be consoled, and he finally takes off the mask. At once, he jerks forward, holding a gloved hand over his nose and mouth like he's about to vomit.

"You're kidding me," I groan. "Don't you dare throw up on her!"

"Raven..." he cries, gagging again.

Haddy cries more, and I growl. "Go away before she gets too upset."

Pushing off the floor, he sprints out of the living room again. I grab the wipes and quickly clean up our baby.

"He's got a long way to go, Hads." My tone is sweet, and I quickly wrap up her dirty diaper, putting it to the side as I slip on a new one.

She's still making little quivering sobs, and I grab the bag, digging in it for her pacifier. As soon as it's in her mouth, I lift her and she rests her head on my shoulder, curling her fingers back and forth in my shirt sleeve.

I put all the supplies away and wrap the dirty diaper in a plastic bag before putting it in the garbage. Hendrix sits at the bar holding a coffee pod to his nose, and I shake my head at him, doing my best not to growl.

"I can't do this, Rave." His eyes are serious. "I do football. I don't do poop."

"But you're a smart guy." I shake my head. "You'll figure it out."

"I don't know how I'll figure *that* out. I *will* vomit."

"Think of it like you're a doctor. She needs you to help her. She can't do this herself."

"How long before she can do it on the toilet?"

"A couple of years."

His head drops back, and he groans. "Years?"

I walk over and put my hand on his forearm. "I'll give you

a pass this time, but you have to learn to do it. She can't stay in poop if I'm not here. It'll give her a bad rash, and that'll be worse. Imagine if you had to sit in poop for hours."

His lips press, and he puts his hand on our daughter's back. "Hear that, Hads? No pooping when Mom's away."

I shake my head. "Help me with her dinner. Then we can give her a bath and get her ready for bed."

Chapter 9

Hendrix

> Grizz: How's it going, hotshot? Encountered any biohazards yet?

With a growl, I shove my phone into my pocket. If it were anyone else, I'd confess and ask for advice, but there's no way in hell I'm talking to that showoff.

I'll ask Jack later. I've got a lot more respect for him after that poopy diaper incident. He had to do it all by himself after Danielle left. With a shiver, I return to bath time.

Haddy sits securely in a little foam chair in the middle of the garden tub in Raven's bathroom. She's much calmer now that she's had her dinner.

We don't have a high chair or seat for her, so she sat in my lap as Raven spooned mush into her mouth. It was really cute, and surprisingly not too messy.

Raven would hold up a spoonful of bright orange sweet potatoes, and Haddy would open her mouth like a baby bird.

Then she'd do a little shiver like it was the grossest thing in the world, but she kept opening her mouth for more.

I couldn't stop laughing. I might be biased, but I think she's the cutest baby I've ever seen. Garrett can fight me.

Now she's in the warm water, and I lift a sponge shaped like an octopus, sliding it over her teeny shoulder. She's happy, and she seems to have forgiven me for my snorkel misstep.

I guess I did look pretty scary in that mask, but dinner made up for it.

"It's like she has rubber bands around her arms." I use the octopus to wash the three little creases on her chubby limb.

Haddy kicks her feet in the water, splashing bubbles all around us and making happy baby noises. Warmth fizzes in my chest, which is weird. I have *never* been the baby type.

"She's very healthy." Raven sits on the step beside me, lifting a cup of water to wet her hair.

I take the baby shampoo and pour a *pea-sized* amount into my hand before rubbing them together to make a lather. "She's adorable."

A small smile lifts the side of Raven's lips, and she watches me massaging my hands over our daughter's head. When I finish, she uses the cup to rinse the soap out of Haddy's hair, and I hold my hand over her eyes to shield them.

I might suck at poopy diapers, but I've got this bathing routine on lock.

We drain the water, and I make sure she's thoroughly rinsed before lifting her out of the tub. At the last minute, I remember to pull off my T-shirt and place her against my chest.

The hood of her towel is over her little head, and the length is wrapped around her bottom. But her bare stomach and chest are against mine, and I slide my hand up and down her towel-covered back.

Raven sits back on her feet frowning up at me curiously. "What are you doing?"

"I saw a TikTok that said skin-to-skin contact is important for dads to bond with the baby."

As if following instructions, Haddy rests her head in the center of my chest right under my throat and puts her hand on my shoulder. I lift my eyebrows at Raven as if to say, *See?*

"You're watching dad TikToks now?"

"Garrett acts like he's Dad of the Year, but I can do this." I'm even getting better at keeping my voice level. "I'm Dad of the Decade."

"It's not a competition, Hendrix."

"You don't know my brother. It's always a competition."

Her head tilts to the side, and a little smile curls her lips. "Is it because you were the baby boy?"

That makes me huff a laugh. "I was never the baby anything. Dylan was born eighteen months after me. *She* was the baby."

"But you were a baby, too."

"I might've been the youngest son, but Garrett was the baby boy."

Her nose wrinkles, and I know it's hard to understand. Three years passed before I was born with Dylan right on my heels, but Garrett never relinquished his title, regardless of the new additions.

"She probably likes the way you smell."

"Are you saying I smell good?" My brow arches, and her ears turn pink again… third time this evening.

"I mean, yeah." She's so flustered, I'm not letting this go.

"How do I smell?"

"I don't know. Like vanilla and sandalwood." Raven stands quickly, reaching for our daughter. "Let me get a diaper on her before she pees on you, then you can resume your bonding."

Reluctantly, I allow her mom to take her. Haddy makes a little fussy noise, and I nod like I've already started winning.

"TikTok for the win!"

"Okay, champ." Raven shakes her pretty dark head, and I

follow her to Haddy's room, letting my eyes run over her sexy ass. She says no touching, but I can still admire the scenery.

And I'll readily admit I'm checking her out. She was totally lying earlier.

"Hey, don't mention the snorkel thing to the girls." I can just imagine Garrett having a field day with that one.

"Think it'll cost you some 'dad of the decade' points?"

"It'll put me in the hole for sure."

"Don't worry." She puts Haddy on her back on the changing table like a pro. "It was a rookie mistake."

"Just don't mention it to Liv."

"Not ever?" She glances up at me.

I know, I know. Everybody wants a good laugh at my expense. I get it.

"Not until I've gotten a little better at this."

I'm standing beside her at the changing table when my phone goes off. Looking down, I see it's our quarterback Tyler Murray on FaceTime, and I hit the accept button.

"Tyler!" I step away so I don't startle Haddy. "What's up, brother?"

"You're back! What was the emergency in Newhope?"

"Oh, you know. Family shit." I glance over my shoulder, thinking maybe I could start a swear jar or something. Language training.

"We're heading to Jaguar's tonight. Come with!" He's grinning, and my jaw tightens.

Jaguar's is a strip club the guys like to frequent. Occasionally, I'll tag along, and for the first time I feel uncomfortable about *someone* knowing.

"Ahh, I don't know, man." I look over my shoulder again, wondering if Raven is listening.

"What?" Tyler's voice is loud. "Alana's dancing tonight. I know you want to see her, and man, she's got this new move. You're gonna jizz in your pants."

Clearing my throat, I wish I'd have sent this call to voicemail until I was alone. "I'm not really in the mood for that."

"Did I call the wrong number? Who is this? Bodysnatchers?"

Turning away, I duck and lower my voice. "You know that's not my scene."

"Not your scene? You were doing shots off Alana's belly last month."

"That wasn't me." I huff a laugh. *It really wasn't.*

"What's up? You got a girl at the house? You're acting weird, and you keep looking over your shoulder."

"Two girls, actually." I haven't had a chance to tell anybody about Haddy, although I'd love to take her to practice and show her off.

I'm not sure how Raven feels about being shown off. Or why I'm even thinking of showing her off—*what the fuck?*

"Oh dang, I'd better let you go then." A note of admiration is in his tone. "I expect to hear all about this next week."

"It's not like that—"

"Right, and you don't go to strip clubs either. I got you. See you at practice, bro."

The phone goes dark, and I turn to find Raven standing in the doorway of Haddy's room with my baby girl on her hip and a smirk on her lips.

Exhaling a short laugh, I shake my head. "Tyler's our quarterback. We hang out... sometimes."

"No need to explain." She holds up a hand, passing me on the way to the kitchen.

I hustle to catch up with her. "All this has happened so fast, and I wasn't sure what you'd want me to tell the guys."

"It's really none of my business." We're in the kitchen, and I watch as she takes out a bottle and mixes up the formula. Then she pops it into the microwave and hits the button. "We're about to go to bed, so if you'd like to go out with your friends, there's no reason for you to stay home."

She's saying that, but she has that tone in her voice that I know from experience means the exact opposite.

"I really don't like going to strip clubs."

Her head cocks to the side, and her eyes almost roll as she looks at me. Haddy sits on Raven's hip blinking those bright blue eyes at me.

"You're doing me a favor, Hendrix. I don't expect you to change your whole lifestyle for the three months we're here. Go out with your friends."

Slowly, carefully, I cross the space to where she's standing. Holding out my hands, I give Haddy a moment to decide. I'm gratified when she leans forward, allowing me to lift her off her mother's hip and onto my chest.

"I've gone with him a few times." I rub my hand up and down Haddy's back as she lays her little head on my shoulder. "Alana is this old-school, pinup-type of girl everyone was talking about. I was a single dude. I was curious."

The microwave buzzes and she turns away, testing the temperature of the liquid on her wrist. "You don't have to defend yourself. It's not my business."

"I really don't like those clubs," I continue anyway. "Those women are too thin. Their boobs are clearly fake." She's not impressed, so I quickly add, "And they're all someone's daughter or sister."

Her eyes almost roll, but she redirects, holding out her hands for our baby. "Just stop."

"I'm sorry." My voice is quiet, and I don't want to give her Haddy.

I'm not sure why, but I'm invested. I don't want her to think I'm that kind of guy.

"Why are you sorry?" Her voice is equally quiet. "I'm not here to be your ball and chain."

My chest burns. "Still. I care about what you think of me."

"Why?"

"Because you're the mother of my daughter. And we're going to be married."

"It won't be a real marriage."

"It will be for a little while, and I want you to think I'm a good guy. A good dad." I stop short of saying a good *husband*. That feels way too intense. "I don't want you to think I'm an asshole."

"I don't think you're an asshole." She says it like she might think I'm something else, though.

"I don't want you to think I'm a fuck boy either. I want you and Haddy to be proud of me."

"You definitely need a swear jar." She lifts our daughter off my chest. "Bedtime."

Chapter 10

Raven

"AND THEY ALL SAY GOOOOOD NIIIIIGHT…" I sing the last words softly, rubbing my hand slowly over Haddy's back as I back away from her crib.

Her eyes are closed, and a round nightlight in the shape of a moon sits on a nearby table. It projects stars all over the ceiling of her bedroom, and the blackout shades are drawn. The room is cozy and warm. She has a blanket over her and Axel is clutched at her side.

A pacifier is in her mouth, and several more are scattered within arm's-reach around her crib. If she wakes in the night, a fresh paci is always within reach.

Hendrix is beside me, and the two of us tiptoe to the door, quietly slipping into the hall and closing it softly behind us.

We hesitate, waiting. My heart beats quickly, and I look up at his blue eyes, ready to declare bedtime victory when the first of her hiccuped cries begins.

He's ready to charge back through the door, but I grab his arm before his hand lands on the knob.

"Wait!" I whisper, barely above a breath. "See if she'll calm down on her own."

Standing on the threshold, we're still as statues, listening. We're so focused on whether or not she'll cry again, I almost miss how close we're standing to each other.

His luscious scent of warm vanilla woods wraps around me, and much like my baby girl, I want to lean forward and bury my nose in his chest. He really does smell divine.

After a few heartbeats of silence, I take a step away. "Houston, I think we have liftoff."

He grins, allowing his blue eyes to run over my face in a way that makes my skin prickle with heat. "You're really good at all this."

"I've been doing it a while. You'll get the hang of it, too."

"You make it look so easy." The side of his mouth cocks a grin that reminds me of Jacob Elordi.

Or maybe with those blue eyes Austin Butler? He definitely has the young, cocky LA heartthrob down pat, with a touch of southern accent. It's a silly thought I dismiss at once.

"Your voice is so smooth and polished. I didn't know you were such a good singer."

"Remnants of my pageant years." My eyes fall to my hands. "Singing was my talent."

"We'll have to do karaoke! I'd love to hear you sing for real."

"Maybe." I nod, considering it. I've never suffered from stage fright. "I guess that does it. Goodnight, Hendrix."

He's still studying me in that way. "Good night."

I take a few steps in the direction of my bedroom when another round of hiccuped cries begins. Freezing in place, I look over my shoulder, and our worried eyes meet.

Hendrix has been pretty game for learning all this baby stuff, but Haddy's cries really throw him off balance. I can't blame him—it takes getting used to.

He's still right outside her door, but he holds up his hands, whispering. "Should I wait?"

Nodding, I retrace my steps to stand beside him again. Her hiccuped cries are different this time. Now she seems more awake for some reason, and she sounds really pitiful. She sounds like an abandoned child in a dark and scary new room.

Her whimpers grow louder, and our eyes meet briefly before Hendrix and I both burst through her door, hustling to where she's standing inside her crib.

When she sees us, she holds out her arms. Hendrix beats me to her, lifting her straight onto his chest.

"It's okay, baby." His voice is soothing, and he rubs her back as she makes baby humming noises around her pacifier. "We're here. We got you."

My lips press tightly as I watch him, and I have no idea why I'm so sentimental. "She'll probably need a night or two to adjust to the new place."

He nods, pressing his lips to the side of her head. "Everybody needs to adjust to a new place. Why should a baby be any different?"

"I know what will help. Where do you watch movies?"

Shaking his head, he exhales. "We've already established this—"

"Sorry," I interrupt. "*Sports*. Where do you watch sports? Do you have like a home theater or something?"

I'm pretty certain in a house this size and this luxurious (and with as much as he loves football), there has to be a home theater. I've always heard everyone in LA has one.

"Right this way." He takes off ahead of me, carrying Haddy, who's clutching Axel and looking ahead. She seems right at home sitting on his arm.

"Here it is." He opens the door, and I gasp.

"Oh my gosh…" I walk into the dark room with lighted sconces on the walls. "It's exactly like a real movie theater!"

"That's exactly what it is." He reaches out to hit a button.

Black curtains open slowly over a wall-sized screen, and my eyes widen. It really is a small theater. The only difference is instead of rows of seats, there's a large, black leather sofa in the shape of a horseshoe for us to sit on.

Armrests divide it into sections, and I sit beside him as he arranges Haddy and Axel on his lap. She leans back against his chest like she's been doing this all her little life, sucking her pacifier and staring at the white screen.

"What do we do now?" I look from her to the screen as well.

He hands me a small remote. "You tell me. This was your idea."

"Okay, well, back home when we had trouble sleeping we'd watch a movie." I turn the familiar remote in my hand, pressing the home button with my thumb. "What streaming services do you have?"

"All of them."

Of course he does. He only watches football, but he has every streaming service.

"It really is a shame you live in LA and you're completely ignorant of cinema."

"Cinema?" His brow arches. "That sounds ominous."

"Don't worry. We'll get you up to speed... starting... here." I quickly pull up *The Princess Bride*. "Haddy loves this one, and it's just long enough and quiet enough that she should be asleep by the end."

"*The Princess Bride?*" He gives me such a grimace, I almost laugh.

"You've seen it?"

"No, but it sounds like a chick movie."

My brow lowers, and I can't resist. "Would you say it sounds like a *kissing* movie?"

Hendrix watches me suspiciously as I start the show. It opens with the scene of a little boy holding a game controller and sitting in his bed.

"Whoa, look at that video game! What even is that? It's so primitive."

"It doesn't matter." I glance over at him, and Haddy is rooting around, moving into his side so she can rest her little head on his chest.

It's really cute how comfortable she is with him already. He has no problem with her either, even helping her get into a position that's comfortable for them both.

"This movie came out in 1987," I say softly. "It's a Rob Reiner joint."

"Rob Reiner?" He looks at me, and I have to hold back from groaning loudly.

It's so sad. He literally knows *nothing* about film.

"Rob Reiner was a major movie director. He started out as an actor, playing "Meathead" in the TV show *All in the Family*, but he made the transition to film with *This is Spinal Tap*, which led to Christopher Guest making all his mockumentaries."

"I have no idea what you're talking about." Hendrix shakes his head.

"He also made *Stand by Me*? *Misery*?" Nothing. "Where Kathy Bates hobbles James Caan with a sledgehammer?"

"Whoa… That sounds pretty gnarly."

Exhaling heavily, I wave him away. "It doesn't matter. Haddy loves *The Princess Bride*, and she's only been here six months. You'll catch up."

The grandfather bursts onto the scene, and Hendrix exhales a little chuckle when the grandson balks at the ancient fabric-covered hardback book after which the movie is titled.

We watch a few minutes longer, and Hendrix shifts gently in my direction.

"Speaking of brides, I start training camp on Monday, and I'll be pretty much gone every day, all day, for two weeks. Then preseason starts, and it just gets busier." My brow furrows, but he continues. "If you're serious about this marriage thing, we'd better do it a-*sap*."

"Oh!" My stomach tightens, and I sit straighter in my seat. "Right. What do we need to do to get married here? Blood tests?"

"Nope." He shifts back to facing the screen. "I did some half-assed Google research, and we can get a license in thirty minutes. So basically as soon as you're ready, we can head to the county clerk's office. They'll even provide the witnesses."

"What about a prenup?" My voice is quiet.

His lips twist, and he looks at me. "This is about securing your trust fund, right?" I nod, my insides tense. "I trust you."

Blinking a few times, I wish he didn't tug at my heart so. "I trust you, too."

"Okay, then." He exhales a laugh, patting his little girl's back. "Let's do this."

Relief floods my veins. My eyes drop to my hands in my lap, and I blink against the mist clouding my vision.

Maybe it's my friendship with Dylan or what I know of his family. Maybe it's a leftover connection from our night so long ago, but I do trust him.

He's a player, but he's honest. He cares about his daughter and being a good dad. I know he wants to take care of us. He already said as much.

Turning to face the screen again, I swallow the lump in my throat. "How about tomorrow?"

"Sounds good to me."

"We can be there at eleven."

"As you wish."

That makes me grin, and my heart beats faster. *Tomorrow.* I think about standing beside him, holding hands, and reciting vows in front of a judge.

It's not a real marriage. Hendrix is doing me a favor so I can get my trust fund so I can take care of our daughter and follow my dream. The end.

I have no reason to feel anxious or even excited. It's a business arrangement. It's temporary, not life-changing.

It's only life-changing when it's real.

His eyes are on the screen, and I wish I knew what he was thinking. He's so handsome and confident and sure. Am I the only person who makes bold decisions then secretly freaks out about them?

I'm tired and jet-lagged, and I'm sure my self-doubt has something to do with my mother. It always does. She taught me to second-guess everything. I wish I had some popcorn.

Swallowing the growl in my throat, I settle in beside him to watch this movie, hoping it puts our baby girl to sleep.

Hendrix Bradford is acting exactly how I should be acting. *Calm.*

There's no reason for either of us to be nervous. We're simply checking items off a list, and I'm not losing sight of my goals… in this gorgeous mansion with this sexy man who smells like warm, woodsy vanilla and who treats my daughter like a little princess.

I'm a meteorologist. If I plan to face down hurricanes, I'd better be able to marry Hendrix Bradford without being seduced by his charm.

Trust yourself, Raven.

Ninety minutes later, the sun is setting on the screen, our heroes are sitting on white horses, and Wesley leans forward to give Buttercup a kiss.

Hendrix has been quietly asking questions and making comments throughout the movie, but for the last several minutes, he's been silent. I hesitate, watching the kiss occur, before turning to notice his eyes are firmly shut.

A puff of air slips through his lips. It's almost a snore, and I realize he's out cold. Haddy is equally out, her little baby body is spread across his stomach like it's the most comfortable thing in the world.

I happen to know that's not true. His chest is like a slab of granite. Still, it's the most adorable sight. Slipping my phone out of my pocket, I take a quick photo of the two of them happily sleeping hard on each other, thinking one day we'll want to have documentation of their first bedtime together at Dad's house. Their first time falling asleep together in front of a movie.

Only... Glancing at my watch, I wonder if I should wake them. I look around the comfortable home theater, and decide against it. The lights are dim, and the sofa is wide and cushiony. It's perfectly fine for sleeping.

Standing, I walk over to where a square bin is placed beside the wall. I take out a plaid, flannel blanket and carry it to my sleeping people. I spread it gently over the two of them before I straighten, crossing my arms over my chest.

I try to decide what to do with me. I'd rather sleep in the large, king-sized bed in my room on the other side of the house. At the same time, I know the rule—never wake a sleeping baby. But what about a sleeping daddy?

I decide to let them be. Haddy is secure, Axel is in her arms, and the sofa is wide. I lean down to kiss the top of her head, inhaling her sweet baby scent before going to the basket and taking out another blanket.

As much as I want to try out my own luxurious bed, I feel kind of lonely leaving them here. Maybe we're not a real family, but... *is that true?*

The wedding might be temporary, but the bonds between the three of us are lifelong. Hendrix wants to be a good father and a supportive co-parent. We can be a family and still be friends, can't we?

I'm not surprised he wanted to support me. In the one weekend we spent together, I saw the good man hiding behind the cocky player. Otherwise, I'd never have spent the night with him the way I did.

That's my story, and I'm sticking with it.

Chapter 11

Hendrix

> Grizz: Couldn't do it, could you?

Another growl, and again, I shove the phone into my pocket. The brother's chat is filling up with texts I haven't answered.

> Logan: You'll get no shame here. I had to leave the house when Dylan changed Gigi's diaper. I don't know how you do it G.

> Grizz: I can do anything for my baby girl. Whatever she needs, she just asks her daddy.

> Jack: You'll get used to it. After a while, you don't even think about it.

> Zane: Everybody poops.

> Grizz: It's just baby food.

> Logan: Baby food that's been left in the sun and turned into rancid decay.

> Grizz: Damn, you packing a thesaurus over there?

> Logan: Just speaking the truth. Let me know when your schedule lets up so we can record, Hen.

Logan's is the only text I might answer, but not today.

Today, I'm standing in front of a massive desk in the city office building facing an old male judge with white tufts of hair sprouting from inside his ears. He looks like he might be 100 years old, and he definitely could use a visit to the barber.

His bench is positioned on a stage above me, so he's looking down at the scene where we'll exchange our vows. He isn't smiling, and from this angle, it actually looks like he's doing his best to stay awake.

I can't stop hearing the voice of that old priest from *The Princess Bride*. Raven made me watch it, and now we're having our fake wedding ceremony.

Marriage is what brings us together today...

Laughter huffs through my lips. I fell asleep before the movie was over with my baby girl on my chest. A smile lifts the corner of my mouth when I think about her sleeping in my arms like she loves me.

Whatever else happens over the next six months, that little girl resting on me like it's the most natural thing in the world is the best shit ever.

Hayden Lucille Bradford is completely unexpected and very cool.

Raven named her after my mother, which kind of touched my heart. I didn't even know she knew my mother's name was Lucille. Dylan must've told her.

When I woke in the middle of the night and saw Raven sleeping on the couch, I quietly carried Haddy to her crib. She didn't even wake up when I slid her from my chest to her mattress. Her little mouth began to move rapidly, sucking her pacifier, but she hugged Axel over her face and went right back to sleep.

Still, I was nervous to leave her there with me on the other side of the house and Raven in the home theater. So I crawled into the queen-sized bed in her room and went to sleep.

As soon as my eyes opened this morning, I slipped out before Raven could come in and check on her. Call me old-fashioned, but I didn't want bad luck.

This might be a fake wedding, but I know the groom isn't supposed to see the bride before their wedding.

Okay, technically I saw her in the home theater after midnight, but it was dark, and I've chosen not to count it.

I texted her first thing.

> I've got a car service arriving here at ten-thirty. He'll be waiting in the driveway.

> Raven: Are you sure they can take us at eleven?

> I think so. I think it's a first-come, first-served type of thing.

Maybe I should've done a little more than half-assed research on that point. Still, how many people are showing up to get married on a Thursday morning around here? It isn't Vegas.

> Raven: We'll be ready. I got Hads this cute little dress... Where are you?

> Running errands—need to grab a few things. I'll meet you downtown.

> Raven: Wait! Haddy and I are going by ourselves? We can't ride together?

> I can't see you til the wedding... it's tradition—don't be late!

> Raven: Why are you being traditional? Are you dressing up? Are you renting a tux?

> It's not prom… I'm not sixteen. I own a tux.

Raven: Are you wearing it to our fake wedding?

> Our wedding isn't fake. It's temporary, and no, I'm not wearing a tux. I do plan to wear a suit, tho.

Raven: So business casual? I can do that. Now I need to grab a few things 🧳 Do you have a car I can borrow?

> The fob is on a hook in the kitchen.

Raven: Hope I don't get lost.

> Use GPS. See you soon.

Raven: I can't believe you're springing this on me.

> That's a joke, right?

Now I'm standing in this small, wood-paneled, ancient-looking government room waiting for her to appear.

"We'll have the both of you stand here to recite your vows." An older man who looks like he's worked here since the Reagan years is halfway through his instructions when the door opens and Raven steps through it. "The court secretary and I will serve as witnesses, since you don't have your own…"

He continues speaking, but I can't tear my eyes away from the woman who just entered the room. Her eyes hold mine as well, and my lungs tighten as I take in the sight of her.

She's wearing a simple, knee-length cream dress with lace tiers forming the skirt. The top is a round scoop that shows off her mouth-watering cleavage, and it has quarter-length sleeves ending at her elbows with lace flowing onto her forearms.

She's not wearing a veil. Instead, a pretty floral wreath is woven into her soft brown hair, which hangs in waves around her shoulders. Her amber eyes are framed in thick, dark lashes, and her pink lips are full and glossy. My hand instinctively rises to my stomach.

Our baby girl is on her hip, but for several moments, I only see Raven.

Haddy's grumpy fuss breaks my stare, and I see she's wearing a white dress made from that sheer fabric I always saw on Dylan's ballet skirts. Tulle, I think? She also has a wreath of flowers in her hair, too, but they're larger than her mama's.

They're also what's causing her to fuss. A frown twists her small features, and she keeps reaching up to try and lift it off her head.

Raven moves her hands down again, putting a pacifier in her mouth. Axel is tucked under her arm, and when she sees me, everything changes.

She bounces on her mom's hip. Her little hands reach out, and I laugh at how happy she is. Raven's full lips curl with a smile, and I don't know what to make of all these warm and zippy feelings in my stomach.

I've known a lot of people, but none have ever reached in and snatched my heart right out of my chest the way this tiny human has.

Jack's daughter Kimmie always runs and yells when she sees me, but it's different. We're close, but she's a lot more excited to jump on Grizz's back than to hold her arms out to me.

Haddy, by contrast, seems to know I'm her dad, and she likes it.

The muscles in my shoulders tense. What does a baby girl want from a guy like me? I'm still learning, but whatever it is, I'll do my best to give it to her.

Hell, if I have anything to do with it, she'll never have a sad day in her life. Which is pretty much the reason we're here.

The old man is back, touching my arm. "Ready to begin?"

I glance at Raven, who's still waiting at the back door. She gives me a little nod, and I give her an encouraging smile.

"We're ready," I say.

"Let me turn this on!" The court secretary is an equally old lady with white hair styled in a round pouf around her head.

She scurries over to a side table and presses the button on a black, rectangular-shaped cassette player. With a loud click, it begins playing the wedding march.

The speaker is tinny with not enough bass, but the song is instantly recognizable.

Raven walks in time down the center of the room to where I'm standing, and my baby girl reaches for me. I take her, moving her into the crook of my arm, and she rests her head on my shoulder still sucking her pacifier.

I smile down at her pretty mamma. "You okay?"

My voice is quiet, and she blinks rapidly as she nods.

"You look really nice," she whispers. "Very handsome."

"You're very beautiful."

The tips of her ears turn pink, and she blinks away. "I always thought my wedding day would be different."

My smile tightens, and I take her hand in mine. I don't want her to be disappointed.

"It will—when you do it for real. It'll be everything you want it to be."

These words shouldn't be bitter on my tongue. They're the truth. The only reason I'm here is to help her get what she wants. I have to keep my thinking straight.

Her chin drops, and she shakes her pretty head. "I'm sorry. I don't know why I'm being so sentimental. It must be the music."

Thankfully, the old judge cuts in. "Let's begin." Our eyes move to him, and he turns to Raven. "We'll start with the bride. Repeat after me. I, state your full name, take thee, state his name, to be my lawful wedded husband…"

Raven's hand is small in mine, and I look down at her soft, olive skin. We only had one weekend together, but I know who she is. She's independent and strong.

Like me, she has dreams and things she wants to accomplish,

and I'm not going to be the reason she doesn't get to make them come true.

Her voice is soft with a little rasp as she follows his instructions. "I, Raven Lorrain Gale take thee, Hendrix…"

Worried amber eyes fly to mine.

"James," I provide quietly.

"I should know that," she whispers, seeming flustered.

"No you shouldn't." I give her a reassuring smile.

She takes a breath and continues. "Take thee, Hendrix James Bradford, to be my lawfully wedded husband…"

We continue through the rest of the vows. We leave off the part where she promises to obey me, even though I thought we could have some fun with that.

Now it's my turn. The judge tells me what to say, and the room falls quiet.

"I, Hendrix James Bradford take thee, Raven Lorrain Gale to be my lawfully wedded wife…" Our eyes lock, and something moves in my chest.

"To have and to hold, in sickness and in health…"

"…in sickness and in health," I repeat.

I should've expected this to affect me, but *damn*, I had no idea I'd feel this way, like I'm taking ownership.

I'm one of the fastest runners in the league. All of this should make me want to run. I shouldn't have this tightness in my stomach, this feeling that we're doing something important.

Raven's eyes travel over my face like she's studying every reaction I have. I'm pretty sure she's been studying my reactions since the day she arrived in LA to see if I'll let her down.

I won't.

Haddy is a curve ball neither of us saw coming, but Raven can handle it. I can help her. Maybe not with a poopy diaper, but with other things.

We finish the vows, then the judge glances between us. "May I have the rings?"

"Oh!" Raven lets out a soft gasp, but I'm prepared.

"Right here." I place the two inexpensive yellow-gold bands I picked up this morning on his book of vows.

"What…" Her dark lashes flutter, and she looks up at me. "How did you know my ring size?"

"I guessed."

The sales girl told me the average ring sizes, and I picked one from what I remembered, watching her take care of Haddy. She has delicate hands, slim fingers.

"Repeat after me." The old man directs us to put each others' rings on at the same time. "I give you this ring as a daily reminder of my commitment and love for you."

We repeat the words, but this time our eyes don't meet. They're on the gold bands sliding on the third fingers of our left hands.

Raven's tremble. Her voice is quiet. "It fits."

My throat tightens, and we'd better wrap this up before I forget this is all an act. It's the music and the small room, and it's kind of warm in here. I think they're running the heater.

It's been a cyclone of a week. A lot of really big changes have hit me hard and fast, but I can take it. I grew up learning to hang on until the big wave passes.

I'll get back to training next week, and things will go back to normal. Football is my life, and I'm only here to do a favor for a friend.

"I now pronounce you man and wife." The old man holds up both of his hands over us. "You may kiss the bride."

Raven's eyes widen almost like she's afraid of what I'll do. With a wink, I lean down to gently kiss her pink cheek. Her sweet, flowery scent swirls around us, and I want to bury my nose in her hair.

I don't.

"Don't worry, Rave." I move my lips to her ear, speaking so only she can hear. "I know the rules."

Her shoulder lifts, and she blinks away, looking at our little girl as the flush I know so well travels to her ears.

The old lady presses the button on the tape recorder again, and the wedding exit march begins. Haddy perks up, bouncing on my hip to the tune.

She finally gave up on trying to rip her floral headband off her head. Now her attention is back on me, and she lifts her chin, patting my cheeks with her damp little mitts.

"Da!" She announces happily, almost like she's been thinking about it the entire ceremony. "Da-da-da!"

My expression changes, my eyes snapping to Raven's.

She's just as surprised. "Did she just say…?"

I'm not sure.

Haddy bounces on my hip, saying it again. "Da!" Then louder, almost a squeal. "Da-*da*!"

"That's your first word?" Raven laughs in disbelief. "Seriously, Hads? After all I've done for you?"

The little girl's eyes blink, and she laughs that cute baby laugh of hers. "Da-da-da!"

"That's me!" I give her a bounce, pulling her closer to my chest for a hug. "I'm Dada!"

Reaching out, I wrap my arm around Raven's shoulder, drawing her to my side. We're standing in front of this judge who just pronounced us man and wife, and I'll be damned.

My daughter just called me *Dada*.

I don't believe in signs, and I'm not losing sight of what we're doing here, but I won't lie, nothing tops this moment.

Haddy twists against my hug, and I loosen my arm. She continues bouncing on my hip, patting my face and shoulder almost as if she knows she did something impressive.

She also hasn't stopped saying it. "Da… da… da!"

"I'm not sure she knows what it means." A hint of resentment is in Raven's tone, and I chuckle more.

"She knows." I can't resist teasing her. "It only took her four days to figure out who's the man."

Raven exhales a groan. We're walking slowly to the back of the room where we'll sign the paperwork.

"I read somewhere it's easier for babies to say the *D* sound than the *M* sound." Raven is still rationalizing. "It doesn't mean anything."

"It means something," I counter.

"It means you haven't stopped holding her since we got here."

I don't want to argue with her pretty mama on our special day, but this is the cherry on top of a crazy week. I lean down to kiss my daughter's chubby neck as she squeals another *Dada*.

"Let's get some cake."

Chapter 12

Raven

"YOU'RE MARRIED?" MY DAD'S VOICE BOOMS THROUGH MY PHONE.

Before the ink was dry on the marriage certificate, I paid the clerk to have certified copies mailed to my father and the trustee of my mother's estate.

"It's what you kept saying you wanted the whole time I was pregnant." I lower my voice to a pretend grumble, repeating his words to him. "'Where is this young man,' and 'Back in my day, men did the right thing.' Well, we did it."

"A thousand miles away," he grouses.

"Two thousand, to be precise."

"Exactly—and with no family there."

"Haddy was there."

"You know what I mean, Raven Lorrain." He's still scolding. "You ran away and got married like it was something shameful."

"I was under the impression it was." Again, not arguing, simply clarifying the facts.

"I am not ashamed of my family." Now he's indignant.

"Right," I concede.

Being ashamed and trying to control me was my mother's role, all the way to the end—and even after the end.

Imagine my surprise when I discovered being pregnant still didn't unlock my trust fund. Nope, only a husband would do that, which is when I came up with the idea of this marriage.

Hendrix is married to football, but I had a feeling he'd be willing to help me if it didn't interfere with his plans.

He was right. Being in LA, we have a lot more control over the flow of information—at least when it comes to our families.

We quickly learned the paparazzi were stalking him everywhere when we tried to go for cake after our ceremony. Or should I say I learned. He's been warning me since I arrived.

We hadn't even taken the first bite of strawberry confetti cake when he heard the sound of a click. I didn't know what to think when he pulled his blazer over his head and ordered me to grab Haddy and run to the waiting SUV.

After that, we haven't left the house together. We're even keeping the curtains drawn, and he ordered me to wear a black hoodie and shades when I go outside.

He says we're perfectly safe, and it'll blow over as soon as some other celebrity does something crazy, which could be any minute. I've decided just to stay indoors.

All of this is so new and strange to me.

"I'm sorry you weren't here, Dad." My tone gentles. "But it was better this way."

"How was it better?"

Exhaling a sigh, I think of all the reasons, and their last names all start with the letter *B*.

"You just have to trust me. People elope all the time. No one will think anything negative about it. Tell them we're a couple of crazy kids."

"One of whom I know nothing about." We've made it to Pouty Dad, which means he's almost done sulking. "It was very selfish. I'll never have the chance to walk you down the aisle again." My throat tightens at that complaint, but I don't argue. "And what about Amelia? She would've been your maid of honor."

"Mimi will understand." She's one of three people who know about Operation Make Raven a Millionaire. "She's got enough on her plate without having to worry about a big wedding."

"I'd like to see pictures." Now he's coming around. "I'd like to meet this young man, my son-in-law. The father of my only grandchild."

"You will one day, but I told you, he's a professional football player. He started his training camp last week, so he's gone every day. Then the season begins. We'll have to try and do something in December."

In three months…

"What will you do the whole time you're there, alone with a baby while he's playing games?"

He makes it sound so awful, I can't stop an eye-roll.

"We're actually looking into getting me a job at one of the local TV stations here. Hendrix has lots of media connections."

"What about Hayden?"

My lips twist, and I chew the bottom one. It's a good question we haven't discussed yet. I don't know anything about this new city, and I can't imagine Hendrix has been keeping up with childcare options in Los Angeles.

"She'll have a nanny, of course." *When in doubt, make it up!* "The team has a service."

It seems like I read something about football programs providing child care for the players.

"Will you get to interview this person, or will it be whoever those addle-headed people see fit?"

"They're not addle-headed, and of course, I'll get to interview the person."

"Just make sure they place an emphasis on safety. From what

I've observed of that organization, they don't seem to take injuries very seriously."

"Dad!" My voice rises, and I exhale a laugh. "They're not going to let the babies get injured."

In my fantasy, the football-sponsored nanny I made up is a fastidious German woman with very strict rules and a no-nonsense approach. I have no idea why I imagine her wearing one of those navy capes and hats like in *The Sound of Music*.

"I'm sorry, I worry about you. I only want you to have the best." The concern in his voice melts my annoyance.

I smile, tilting my head to the side. "Don't worry, Dad. I'm really fine. Better than fine."

"But are you happy?"

"Yeah," I nod, realizing as I say the words, they're true. "I am."

I'm *hopeful*. For the first time in eighteen months, I'm not terrified it's all over for me. I feel like I have a shot at achieving my dream again, unlike when I was alone with Haddy.

"That's all that matters to me." My father's voice is calm.

Our conversation ends, and I walk through the house, back to the room where I put Haddy down for a nap. Standing outside the door, I listen to her happy squeals and coos before opening it.

She always has been an easy baby, even if my body seemed hell-bent on killing me my entire pregnancy. The nurses would say she was going to have red hair. Then they'd say she'd be covered in hair.

Come to find out, neither of those things was true. Her skin is smooth and nearly hairless like mine. She has brown hair like mine and her daddy's, and his ocean blue eyes.

Dylan sent me a file of baby pictures from when Hendrix was little, and it's pretty amazing how much she looks like him.

As soon as she sees me, she's on her feet, holding onto the side of her crib and bending her knees to bounce.

"Da da da!" she cries happily, smiling and pointing.

"Ma-ma," I say to her, doing my best to demonstrate the *M* by pressing my lips together and humming. "Ma… ma."

"Da da!" Her little voice goes high, her eyes bright like we're playing a game.

Exhaling, I shake my head, lifting her out of the crib and carrying her to the changing table.

"I can't believe you." My voice is playful, and I'm smiling despite my words. "After all that morning sickness, you take his side?"

I shake my face close to hers, and she laughs, switching to blowing raspberries through her lips while I change her diaper.

Dry diaper on, I snap her onesie and lift her off the table. She settles onto my hip as I walk to the kitchen. "This house is so big, I'll get all my steps just walking back and forth to our rooms."

My phone goes off, and I lift it to see my sister calling on FaceTime.

I hit the answer button, and Haddy squeals when she sees her aunt.

"Hadeee!" Amelia coos. "How is my favoritest baby niece today?"

"Da da da!" Haddy bounces on my hip, shaking her hand in reply.

"Whoa. Did she just say *Dada*?" Mimi's brow furrows.

"Yes," I groan, dropping my head back. "In the middle of our wedding ceremony she starts saying *Dada*."

"Haddy, you little traitor!" My sister's voice is a high-pitched tease. "That's right! That's what you are! You're just a squishy-poo little traitor."

Haddy squeals and makes more attempts at speech. I put her on her feet in front of the coffee table between my legs and sit on the couch, holding my phone so Amelia can see both of us.

"How does Hendrix feel about all this *Dada* talk?" My sister's tone is sly. "He's not running for the hills yet, is he?"

"We actually live in the hills, so it would be a short run."

"You know what I mean. How's it going with you three?"

Pressing my lips to the side, I nod. "Really good, actually. Surprisingly good."

"Surprisingly?"

"Yeah..." I think about everything that's happened since we got here. "He's very sweet. He's very invested in Haddy. He helps me bathe her, and he even tries to help feed her. He does *not* change diapers."

"Do any men change diapers?"

"They should!" Now I'm cross. "Where is it written that only women change diapers?"

"I'm just saying they're wimps."

My mind trips back to Hendrix running into the living room wearing a snorkel mask, and I snort a laugh. "It's true."

"What?" A smile is in my sister's voice. "Why are you laughing?"

"It's nothing..."

"Tell me," she cries, and Haddy squeals, reaching for the phone.

I hold it down so she can see her Aunt. Ameila helped me so much with her over the last six months, I imagine Haddy misses her, too.

"Make her tell me, Haddy-boo!"

"Don't say anything because I kind-of promised I wouldn't rat him out." Actually, as I think about it, we never finished that conversation. "Hendrix tried to help me change a poopy diaper, and he almost barfed everywhere."

"Noooo!" she laugh-cries.

"Then he ran out and came back wearing a snorkel mask..." I hiccup, starting to laugh, too. "Haddy almost had a fit. She screamed so loud."

"He probably scared her to death!"

"Oh, my gosh, he totally did." I lean back, placing my hand on my stomach. "It took dinner and a bath to calm her down... And she *still* said *Dada* first. Didn't you?" I bend to the side, kissing the side of her chubby cheek. "Didn't you?"

My baby only pats the couch cushion and coos. She's so close to saying more words.

"Ahh, that's so funny. I can only imagine a big hunky footballer in a snorkel mask." Another soft giggle, and we fall quiet for a beat. "I miss you two. I've almost finished the backup Axel. I'll drop it in the mail with a care package next week."

"Okay!" That makes me smile. "I'll send you pictures from the wedding. The old-lady secretary took a few on a camera that looked like it was from the Stone Age."

"I hate that I missed it." Her eyes narrow. "How was the honeymoon? Is he still as good as the first time?"

She waggles her eyebrows, and my ears heat. I wish I hadn't told her how good he was in bed when I got home after Dylan's wedding. To be fair, I was still reeling—and still feeling every place he'd touched, bitten, kissed, or spanked me. I'd never had so many orgasms.

Shaking my head, I clear my throat. "We're not doing that."

"What do you mean?"

"We're not sleeping together."

"What!" Her shriek is so loud, it makes Haddy fuss.

"It's okay, baby!" I lean forward, rubbing my nose against hers. "Don't mind Aunt Mimi. Way to scare the baby, Mim."

"Why the hell not? You're married now!"

"It's not a real marriage. We're only doing this…" Lowering my voice, I study the room behind her. "Where are you?"

"I'm taking a walk. It's safe."

Still, lowering my voice, I talk through tight lips. "You know why we're doing this."

"What does that matter? You can still have fun."

"No, we can't."

"Ohh…" She's instantly compassionate. "Does he not want to?"

My eyes drift to the ceiling, and I tilt my head to the side. "Um… I think he'd probably be up for anything."

"Then *do itttt*!" She cries again. "Have you seen how hot

your husband is? I googled him when you got home, and let me tell you... I got a little hot around the collar."

"Don't be lusting after your brother-in-law—that's just *ew!*"

"I'm stating the facts, ma'am. The man is a work of art."

Twisting my lips, I nod in resignation. "He is pretty to look at."

"So go crazy, nail his ass! You've got three months to bone til the cows come home."

Haddy laughs, bending her knees and bouncing, and I shake my head, thinking we need two swear jars. One here and one in Atlanta.

"I'm not sleeping with him." She starts to protest, but I press on. "If we start doing that, I'll get attached, and it'll only make it harder to say goodbye when it's time to go."

It already pinches my stomach to think of that day, and we're barely getting started.

Her shoulders lift, and she shakes her head. "Who says you have to go?"

"I say." Now it's my turn to be stern. "Our agreement is for three months, then I'm going back to Atlanta to collect my trust and launch my career."

"Why can't you launch your career in Los Angeles?"

"It's not what we agreed to do."

"So change the agreement!"

"I'm not doing that." My throat burns, and I shake my head. "Hendrix agreed to this to help me, and I won't take advantage of his generosity."

"Who says you would be?"

"He told me very plainly he's not interested in settling down or even having a serious relationship. He's focused on his career. He loves football. He's building a legacy, and I'm not going to get all clingy and make him sorry he helped me." Heat is in my chest. "That's not who I am."

"Okay." My sister's lips pull into a frown, and she exhales heavily. "What a waste."

"Anyway, I'm focused on my career, too," I push back. "I have goals and dreams, and that means sometimes you have to make sacrifices."

"So you're going to sacrifice your libido just so you don't get attached to the father of your child?"

"Yes." My answer is firm.

"I give it two weeks before you're boning til the cows come home."

I'm about to argue when I hear a noise in the kitchen.

"Honey, I'm home!" Hendrix teasingly calls to me, and my neck heats.

"Da da da!" Haddy squeals, bending her knees and dropping to the carpet in an effort to crawl to him.

"Where's my little nugget?" Hendrix breezes into the room, in full view of the phone.

Mimi's eyes widen, and she smiles like she already won. "Make that one week."

"Later, gator." I press the button as she says *crocodile*, and my phone screen goes black.

Hendrix scoops up our baby, and she pats his face, repeating her new word. "That's right, Dada's home."

She continues making noises like she's actually trying to talk to him, and I cross my arms, pretending to pout. It's impossible when he leans forward to kiss her neck, and our daughter lets out a belly laugh.

Hendrix's eyes are shining when they meet mine, and I swallow my swoon. My sister is right. My husband is truly a work of art, all six-foot-two, toned muscles of him.

The ends of his brown hair are damp, like he showered before coming home. His jaw is square with a hint of scruff, and he's wearing a blue T-shirt that stretches across his muscled chest. The short sleeves stretch around his biceps, and his jeans hug his tight ass. Such a nice tight end.

Inhaling warm, woodsy vanilla, I exhale a sigh. It really is unfair how perfect he is, and I've taken a vow of chastity.

"You know on the West Coast, hurricanes are called cyclones?" I find meteorological facts highly effective at killing lust.

Almost as effective as a bucket of cold water.

Full lips part over a straight, white smile. "I think I knew that one." He nods at my phone. "Who was that?"

"My sister called to see Haddy—and to see how things are going." I reach up to rub her little back. "I also talked to my dad."

His dark brows rise. "What'd he say?"

"Oh, you know. He was pouty at first. Then he came around the more we talked. He said he'd liked to have been here, but… you know."

His jaw tightens, and he nods. "I can understand that. It's a big step, and he's your dad."

I can't resist teasing him. "Feeling empathetic?"

"Empathetic?" He's briefly confused, then he quickly relaxes, kissing our daughter's little head. "Oh, no. Haddy's never getting married. She's never even going near a boy. And if I ever see a stinky little boy coming around here…"

He bounces her every time he says it, and she leans forward, cupping his face in both her hands.

Pressing my hand against my chest, I try to deny the swell in my heart. I think about what I said to Amelia. It might already be too late. The sweeter he is to our daughter, the more he falls in love with her, the harder it is for me to stay detached.

"You know, you haven't stopped holding her since we left Newhope. Not even at bedtime."

We've taken to falling asleep every night in the home theater to some bedtime-friendly movie. Every morning I wake up to find Haddy in her crib and Hendrix asleep in the bed in her room or in the kitchen making coffee.

"It's a big transition coming here, especially for a little baby. I'm her dada. It's my job to look out for her."

"You're spoiling her rotten."

"Impossible." He rubs her back, and she rests her head on his shoulder. "Haddy's too sweet to spoil."

My chest squeezes, and it's not just the way he treats our baby. Hendrix projects the image of a player, but he still tried to make our justice-of-the-peace wedding special.

It was so sterile and impersonal, and as kind as the old people helping us were, my sister wasn't there, my dad wasn't there.

I was a little on the brink of tears, which was completely out of character, when Hendrix reached out and took my hand.

He saved the day.

"What happens when you have to be out of town?"

"I expect you to step up, Mamma. Don't let my baby cry."

I laugh, walking into the kitchen. It's dinner time, and I need to mix up her cereal. "She was always a good sleeper. Now, I'm not so sure."

"She's a champion sleeper. I put her in her crib, and she never stirs all night."

Exhaling a nod, I can't argue. "I guess she was sleeping in my room before I came here."

I take out the envelope of organic baby cereal. Hendrix ordered all kinds of organic, non-toxic, biodynamic, who knows what else baby food from a store called Erewhon.

He follows me into the kitchen, putting Haddy in the new baby chair we got for mealtime. "You never told me what you were doing before you came here. Did you get a job at a TV station? Were you at least gaining on Jim Cantore?"

"No." I exhale a laugh. "I got a job at a teeny-tiny station in Pierre Point, Louisiana."

"Where the fuck is that?" I cut my eyes at him, and he quickly edits himself. "Where the *fonk* is that?"

"South of Baton Rouge, north of New Orleans, near French Settlement and Port Vincent. I loved it. Best people in the world."

"What happened?"

"This little girl happened. I found out I was pregnant, and all hell broke loose. My morning sickness was so bad…" I remember not being able to get out of bed except to vomit. "I didn't even know it could be that bad."

"Dang."

"Tell me about it." Taking the warm cereal out of the microwave, I stir it with a plastic baby spoon.

Haddy watches me all ready to eat, and I squint my nose with a smile. "I was sad to leave them, but I wouldn't trade anything for my Haddy."

"My sister Dylan dreamed of dancing with the American Ballet Company in New York. She worked so hard all through high school. Craig was her dance partner, and they were really, really good."

"She told me a little about that." I think about his feisty little sister, my friend. "Then she broke her foot?"

He nods. "My brother Zane fell on her when we were playing a family football game. He never forgave himself for it, but he's like that."

"What's he like?" I think about his second-oldest brother, the tall, dark, and quiet one.

I want to know all about his family. They're Haddy's family now, too, and from what I've observed, they're big and warm and rowdy. I can't deny the knot in my throat wishing I was…

Not going there.

"Let's see," Hendrix sits beside me as I feed the baby. "Zane was our mom's favorite until Dylan came along."

"Your mom did not have favorites."

"She said he was like her dad. He likes to read and take walks by himself. He's probably seen all these movies you make me watch. He'll be a great dad right out the gate."

"You're being pretty great right out the gate." I don't know why I feel protective of him.

"You think?"

"I do." I give him an encouraging smile.

Haddy's a good baby bird. I hold out the spoon, and her little mouth pops open.

"I don't know how great of a girl dad I'll be."

"Girls just want a dad who'll listen to them. They want

someone who loves them and who'll stand beside them against the bullies but still let them be strong, independent women."

He nods. "I can do that."

"Want to try this?" I pass him the bowl and spoon, and it's so small in his large hand.

He scoops some cereal, and when he holds it to her, her mouth pops open. He gives her the bite, and she swallows quickly, ready to go again.

"Check me out." He laughs, repeating the process.

"You got it!" I grin, going to the cabinet and taking out a jar of organic vegetables. "You love her. That's the most important thing. She feels safe with you."

"She's always safe with me." He says it with so much confidence, and I know it's true.

Walking back, I trade him the empty cereal bowl for the veggies. "So what made you think about Dylan?"

His brow lowers. "I was thinking about how broken she was when she lost her dream. She tried to put on a brave face like it was okay, but we all knew. We heard her cry when she thought nobody was listening." He pauses before looking up at me with so much sincerity in his blue eyes. "I'd never want to be the reason you lost your dream."

Damn you, Hendrix Bradford. How dare you try to sneak in and steal my heart this way?

Swallowing the thickness in my throat, I nod. "I appreciate that."

"I put in a call to the station today." His tone brightens as he resumes feeding Haddy. "I talked to one of the reporters I know, and she said for you to come by and she'd introduce you to the station manager."

"Are you serious?" My eyes widen, and I clasp my hands in front of my face. "LA is like one of the top markets in the country!"

"Don't misunderstand. It's a tiny station. I told her you were only here for a few months, and she said you could be a meteorology intern. It's unpaid, but I can cover your expenses."

"Hendrix!" I shriek, jumping forward to hug him. "That's incredible!"

Haddy blows bubbles on her next bite, and he chuckles. "I think she's done."

Straightening, I take the jar and spoon, rinsing and recycling and putting the utensils in the dishwasher. He takes a damp cloth and wipes her mouth before lifting her out of the chair.

"Ready for your bath?" She *ba-ba-ba*s right back at him, and he turns wide eyes on me. "Am I teaching her how to talk?"

Wrinkling my nose, I don't want to tell him she's been making *ba-ba* and *ga-ga* noises for a few weeks now.

"Maybe?" I shrug.

It's hard to know if she connects *ba-ba* with bath, but I'll let him have it. We walk back to my bathroom, and I stand back, watching as he takes over like a pro.

He starts the water and tests it to be sure it's not too warm. Then he puts her in her little foam chair and even manages to wash and rinse her hair while she happily chews on a yellow duckie and slaps the water.

I walk him through putting her diaper on, and she's bundled and in her PJs when I meet him in the small movie theater with Chinese takeout and a bottle of formula.

Tonight, I'm introducing him to the world of *Forrest Gump*.

"You'll like this one." I pass him his Postmates dinner. "The main character's from south Alabama."

The show starts, and I take the first round, holding Haddy and giving her a bottle while he eats. She's mesmerized watching the feather floating through the sky as gentle music plays. Her eyes blink slower, and I expect it won't be long before she's asleep.

"That's not a bad accent he's doing."

"I listened to this whole interview where Tom Hanks talked about traveling to the area and learning the dialect."

The movie continues, and when he finishes eating, Hendrix reaches over and takes his daughter from my arms. She snuggles into his side like it's our new routine, and she falls asleep quickly.

Hendrix doesn't, which I take as a win, considering how intense he says training camp is. We get to the part where Forrest meets Jenny, and he leans closer, speaking quietly.

"Set this in high school, and that's Garrett and Liv."

Chewing my lip, I nod, smiling. I study his handsome profile, his square jaw and full lips, and I think about my conversation with Ameila. I decide to meet this hurricane head-on, Jim-Cantore style.

Leaning closer, I speak just above a whisper. "My sister said something to me earlier, when we were talking…" He blinks those sexy blue eyes at me, and I swallow air. "We're in this for three months. That's a long time for no… you know."

I shrug, waving my hand side to side.

His brows furrow, and an amused grin curls his lips. "Are you referring to sex, Raven?"

"I'm just saying, we agreed we wouldn't blur the lines, but I don't expect you to go that long without… *doing it*." A pit is in my stomach, but I clear my throat, forcing it out. "If you need to date someone or you know… whatever, I'll understand."

"You will?" It's less a question and more an implied *I don't believe that for one second*.

"I asked you for this enormous favor. I'm well aware how wrong it would be for me to expect you to live like a monk the entire time."

His face turns serious, and he looks down at sleeping Haddy. "If I go out with someone, it'll be all over the gossip sites. Then it could get back to your father, and then he'd be out here ready to kick my ass—and rightfully so. It might even jeopardize our plan."

"I'm sure you could keep it quiet."

"Photographers are everywhere." Shaking his head, he

settles back in his seat. "If we're doing this, I think it's best not to take any chances."

"Can you go that long?" My nose wrinkles, and I don't even consider if I can go that long.

I can. I'm strong.

He shrugs. "I'm not interested in dating anyone. I'll double-down and focus on the game."

"Okay." I don't know why I hold out my hand to shake. "Don't go falling in love with me now, Forrest."

A laugh huffs through his lips, and he shakes my hand. "Don't fall in love with me, Jen-nay."

"I won't." My laugh is completely unconvincing as I sit back in my chair.

Chapter 13

Hendrix

MY EYES OPEN, AND THE LUSCIOUS SMELL OF BLUEBERRIES HAS ME rolling out of the queen-sized bed in Haddy's room.

I was really enjoying the movie last night, but training camp is kicking my ass. As starting tight end, I'm on the field half the game or more, which means I have to be able to go the distance. Which means my training is brutal.

I start the morning with two hours of squats, hanging presses, leg presses, and an assortment of other strength-training exercises, including weight lifting.

From there, I move to footwork drills and running. We spend a few hours working on catching and blocking before breaking for lunch, then I'm back at it with special teams training.

My muscles are sore as I stand, but it'll pass. I'll whip back into shape in no time.

Haddy's crib is empty, and I pull on my T-shirt and joggers before stopping off in the hall bathroom to get rid of my morning wood and drain the vein. From there, I continue to the kitchen to find the source of this mouth-watering aroma.

The closer I get, I hear the inviting sound of cooking mixed with the even more inviting sound of Raven singing. She's got a really great voice, and she's singing some perky tune about the morning and loving Baltimore.

When I reach the kitchen entrance, I stop in my tracks, smiling as I take in the sight. Raven's dark hair is styled in a messy bun on top of her head, and she's wearing a soft-cotton, long-sleeved flowery shirt. She has on matching shorts with a little ruffle around the legs, and she's doing a skippy dance on bare feet with her toenails painted bright red.

Haddy is in her baby chair watching her and chewing on a blue ring that has the head of an elephant on one end. She rocks in her seat to the music, making baby noises as her mother cooks.

It's really cute until Raven dances over to the cabinet, reaching overhead for the plates and those shorts rise higher on her shapely thighs. Then it changes to something else.

My eyes drift to her round ass, and I lick my lips remembering her on her hands and knees looking back at me with hooded lids as I fucked her from behind.

Once again, my dick is hard, and there's no way I can hide it in these thin pants. She spins around, and I quickly step to the side, hiding behind the wall so I can calm down.

"Hendrix, hey—good morning!" She smiles, putting the plate on the counter beside the stove before returning to pick up a medium-sized bowl. "I went to that grocery store site again... *Erehwon*? They had these blueberries, and gah! They're so good!"

Thankfully, she's too preoccupied by her cooking to notice me clearing my throat and running my hand down my cock while I think of cold showers, poopy diapers, cat vomit.

That did it.

"Do they?" I'm somewhat back to normal when I enter the room.

"Yes!" She sets the bowl down and skips over to me, holding a round, deep-purple fruit between two fingers. "They're perfectly firm, and they're like little blueberry explosions in your mouth. Try one."

She holds it up, and our eyes meet. I lean forward, using my lips to pull it from her fingertips into my mouth. As I graze her fingers, her lips part. Her eyes widen, and she exhales a soft *Oh!*

Heat swirls in the air around us, and my semi is back. She quickly blinks down, turning and returning to the stove.

"I, um… ordered some for us, and I'm making blueberry pancakes." I watch her shoulders shimmy as she quickly flips the three round cakes in the pan. "California's mild climate allows the berries to mature longer, which makes the flavor richer."

"You don't say." I walk over to the coffee machine and slip a pod in the slot. "It smells delicious."

"These are for you." She glances at me, giving me a cautious smile. "They say you're supposed to throw away the first pancake, but I never do that."

"Why would you?" I press the button, crossing my arms as I lean against the counter, facing her.

Her eyes drift over my chest and shoulders before she quickly returns her attention to the stove. She did that when I got home yesterday, running her eyes all over my arms and legs before becoming very focused on Haddy.

It makes me wonder how committed she really is to this abstinence rule. I'm sure she remembers how good we are together. It's been almost two years, but I remember every detail, including her on my lap, throwing her head back and riding me like a pony at the fair.

Shit. I've got to stop thinking about these things. Turning away, I adjust my fly as I conjure images of maggots… nose hair… saggy old-man butt…

My jaw is tight, but I've got to kill this erection.

"It's supposed to be the sacrificial pancake." She continues talking, not seeming to notice my struggle. "Like you use it to test the pan or make sure the batter's right. I think it's a waste of a good pancake."

My coffee's ready, and I take the mug out, returning to where she's standing. She quickly scoops three pancakes onto the plate and holds it out to me.

Her pretty brown eyes meet mine, and I study her full lips, her dark hair with the gold highlights around the front. Her soft breasts rise and fall with her breaths, and it all feels...

"I've never used this type of mixture before. It's also organic and back to nature and the best food in the world." She uses a pretend announcer-voice as she walks past me to the coffee maker. "There's butter and honey and syrup on the table, again all-natural, organic superfood."

I look down at the plate and over at my little girl, who's watching me with big eyes as she chews her rubber elephant.

"Good morning, nugget." I lean down to kiss the top of her head, but she's very focused on gnawing that ring.

"I think she's getting a tooth." Raven walks back with a mug of coffee in her hand. "Won't that be the cutest thing? Haddy with a little baby tooth?"

"Yeah," I exhale a laugh, focusing my thoughts on baby teeth and not boning her mother. "Aren't you having any?"

"I ate with Haddy. Those blueberries cook perfectly."

Nodding, I put butter on mine and grab the jar of honey. "Newhope has really good blueberries. There's a farm where you can bring your own bucket and pay one price to pick all you want."

"Really?" Her face brightens with a smile.

"Yeah, I'll take you when we go back."

A hesitant pause falls between us, but she quickly fills it. "I got a message from Star Corrigan at KCLA. She asked if I could come by and meet their station manager today!"

"Hey, that's great!" I take a bite then lean back in my chair with a groan. "Not as great as these pancakes. Dang, Raven, this is delicious."

I cut another big bite with my fork as she talks. "I can't believe you were able to line something up that fast!"

"I told you, I'm a celebrity." I give her a wink, and she does a cute little eye roll. "Seriously—they cover us every week, so I know the reporters. I told you, it's a small station."

"That only leaves one problem." Worried eyes meet mine, and I frown. "What will we do with Haddy? She can't go with me to work."

"She'll go with me." I smile, reaching out to tug on the ring covered in drool.

Raven's brow creases. "She can do that?"

"Sure! We have childcare on-site at the stadium. Everybody uses it, and I'll be able to check on her during the day. It'll be fine."

Her lips press into a worried smile, and she reaches out to slide a finger down Haddy's chubby leg. "She's never stayed with anyone but my sister and me."

"We could fly your sister out here if you want? That would be okay."

"No." She exhales heavily. "Mimi has school, and as much as I think she'd like LA, she's pretty established at Emory. Besides, she needs to live her life and not worry about Haddy all the time."

I polish off the last of my pancakes then take the plate over to the sink. Raven stays at the table threading her finger in Haddy's little fist as she watches her. I can tell she's anxious.

"What can we do to make you feel better?" I walk back to where she stands. "Want to go with me to meet the ladies? From what I understand they're really nice, like sweet old grandmas."

"Do you mind?" She squints up at me.

"Not a bit. Get dressed, and I can introduce you to them before I start my day. If you're happy, Haddy can stay with them, and I'll bring her home with me."

"Okay! Give us twenty minutes." She lifts our daughter out of her chair and hugs her to her chest, looking up at me. "Thanks, Hendrix. For all of this. You've really just been…"

"Stop." I step forward to put my hand on her shoulder. "I

told you how I feel. It's important for you to do the things you've dreamed of doing. It's good for Haddy."

"Yeah, but this is way more than I ever imagined."

"Good." I smile before giving her shoulder a squeeze. "Now hustle up. I've got to get to the stadium before I'm late and Coach makes me do extra drills."

She smiles and trots out of the room with Haddy on her shoulder. I watch her go, letting my eyes trace down her lovely curves. I probably have just enough time to hit the shower and relieve some of this tension before she's ready.

"What a little angel!" Sherri Pace holds out a finger to Haddy, who's sitting on my arm as we do our little meet-and-greet outside the Dutch door of the nursery. "She looks just like you!"

"I had no idea you were a dad, Hendrix." An older woman joins us at the door.

"Ah, yeah..." I squint one eye, doing a little point. "Miss..."

"Martha Torres. Nursery supervisor."

"Nice to meet you." I nod at Raven. "Haddy and her mom are here staying with me for a little while. This is Raven. I brought her to meet you all."

"That's very thoughtful. Did you bring your daughter's medical records? We have an online portal—"

"We can take their word for it today, Martha." Sherri gives her a nudge, then leans closer, lowering her voice. "Martha loves to give the new dads a hard time."

"They probably need it." I wink at her, turning on the charm.

"Oh, boy," Martha shakes her head. "You've got your hands full with this one."

"He's not so bad." Raven's tone is equally teasing. "We've almost graduated to poopy diapers."

"Is that so?" The older woman's eyebrows rise. "Sounds like you can handle him."

Raven's ears turn pink, and I almost chuckle. She can handle me all night long.

Clearing her throat, she looks at our daughter. "Haddy's never stayed with anyone but my sister or me. I'm not sure how she's going to react to being alone with… people she doesn't know."

Sherri gives her a warm smile. "I expect any good parent would want to know who's taking care of their baby."

Haddy clutches my shirtsleeve watching all of us curiously. Axel is under one arm, and she has that elephant ring in her hand. I can't tell if she likes these ladies or not, and I hadn't really considered the possibility she might not like it here.

Now I'm getting worried about leaving her.

"I'll be right in the workout room or on the field if she cries or anything."

It's my turn to get the warm Sherri smile. "We've got a lot of experience with babies." She steps closer to our girl. "Hi, Haddy! I'm Miss Sherri. Would you like to play with me today?"

She holds out her hands, but Haddy doesn't move. It's an awkward moment with Sherri smiling and blinking, palms up and extended to our six-month-old.

Raven steps closer to me, speaking quietly. "Maybe try passing her over."

A knot forms in my stomach, and I look down at my little girl staring at the woman. I'm not sure passing her over is the right thing to do. It feels like I'm forcing her, and I would never do that.

To think I was so confident when we left the house this morning. Now my shoulders are tense, and I'm ready to return to the idea of flying Amelia here. Raven thinks she'll like it. UCLA is a great school, and we could cover all her living expenses for the time they're here.

Martha seems to read the situation at once. "Why don't you walk her in and show her around?"

Her voice is calm and authoritative. She puts her hand on Sherri's arm and opens the door slowly for us to step inside the large playroom.

Five other children are already here. They're all small, and most seem to be around Haddy's age. One is crawling around, and the biggest one is actually walking.

I have no idea whose kids they are. I've never paid any attention to which players had families, and I never cared to find out. All this baby stuff was so far off my radar two weeks ago.

"What do we do?" I look down at the smiling ladies.

Raven is at my side, surveying the room as well. It's bright and happy with lots of toys, blocks and balls all around.

The floor is covered in rainbow-colored foam squares that fit together like puzzle pieces with large letters in the centers. Together they form the alphabet.

One wall has colorful, blobby monsters with numbers on their bellies. On the opposite side of the room, a row of cribs lines the wall. A baby is asleep in one of them.

"Here, have a seat." Sherri motions to a gliding chair near the playing kids, and I walk over to sit in it with Haddy on my leg. "Place her on the floor and see if she'll start to play."

I glance up at Raven, and she nods encouragingly.

I'm not so sure she's ready for that. I'm having flashbacks of my first time taking swim lessons, and even though I grew up playing all along the bay and ocean, I didn't want to jump in the pool.

Garrett finally got sick of watching me pace back and forth and threw me in. He was grounded for that stunt, but I've never been a fan of swimming pools ever since.

"It's okay." Raven's voice is soft. "See what she does."

My jaw clenches, and I look down at Hads. She's still gripping my sleeve in her little fist. She's holding Axel close to her chest, and a very serious expression is on her baby face. This would be a lot easier if she could tell me what she's thinking.

Instead of putting her down, I move to sit on the floor with her. The other children aren't interested in us. One little boy stands beside a round plastic toy that has chutes for colorful balls to roll through.

It makes *boing*-ey type sounds as the balls pass, and he does Haddy's little bouncing trick, bending his knees and squealing. Haddy seems interested, so I move closer to him, putting her on her feet beside it.

Raven picks up one of the balls and drops it into the top of the chute. It spins all around, setting off different noises and lights, and Haddy drops Axel in her attempt to catch it.

"Did you see the ball?" Raven uses her high-pitched baby voice. "Here, you try."

She squats beside Haddy, holding out a small blue ball for her to try. Haddy takes it in her hand, but instead of dropping it in the slot, she puts it in her mouth and starts gnawing on it.

"I think she's cutting a tooth." Raven looks up at Sherri.

The woman smiles, shaking her head. "Don't worry, we wash all the toys every day."

Haddy moves away from her mother, doing her little wobble-crawl maneuver to get inside the ring. She seems okay with this. The other kid is busy doing his thing, not paying attention to our daughter.

"Now might be the time to slip out." Sherri nods at the door, and I glance up at the clock on the wall.

I'm late for practice, but I don't give a shit. I'll do the extra drills to be sure Haddy isn't scared or crying or thinking we ditched her with a bunch of strangers.

Raven puts her hand on my arm. "Let's try."

My jaw tightens, but I stand slowly, going with her to the door but not taking my eyes off our daughter.

Haddy gives up on the blue ball and grabs a red, diamond-shaped block to chew on instead.

"Send somebody to get me if she cries." My chest is tight, and it's a gruff order.

Sherri smiles brightly. "I'm sure she'll be fine, but if she isn't, we know where to find you."

"Here's my number. Text me. Call if I don't respond right away." I make sure she has it programmed into her phone.

Raven gives Martha the big purple bag with all of Haddy's supplies, and we step out into the hall again. Our daughter is still happily putting every toy in her mouth, not seeming to notice we're gone.

Knots twist in my stomach as I watch her.

"She looks okay." Raven's voice is quiet, and I'm surprised at how calm she is.

"You think we should just leave her here?" I sound astonished.

"You said they're like nice old grandmas, and they are." She blinks quickly as if trying to justify her answer. "You'll be on-site the whole time. You gave them your number…"

Frowning, I look back at Haddy once more. My shoulders are still tight, and I exhale a shallow breath.

"I'll check on her in an hour or so." We start to walk in the direction of the weight room.

Raven rubs her hand back and forth over my shoulder blade, I guess trying to ease my tension. "It's good for her to branch out a little, and this isn't too far from us."

I look back in the direction we came. Soft children's music plays through the open top door, and I think about getting one of those baby slings. I could strap her on my back while I practice. It wouldn't work while I was on the field doing drills, but I could have her in one of those baby chairs on the sidelines for that part.

"Hey, man, what the fuck? You're late." Tyler walks out the weight room to where I'm standing with Raven, mentally exploring options for keeping Haddy with me. "Well, hello, there!

I'm Tyler Winslow, starting quarterback for the Tigers. And you are?"

He's turning on all his playboy charm, holding out his hand to Raven, and I snap out of it. "Tyler, this is Raven Gale."

"Hello, Raven." He winks, shaking her hand. "Do you live in LA? Just visiting?"

"Oh, I'm—" Raven starts, but I finish for her.

"She's staying with me." I hit the *me* a little hard, and Tyler's eyebrow arches. "Raven and I have a daughter, Haddy. We just dropped her off at the nursery with Sherri and Martha."

"A *baby*? What the hell?" My friend's chin pulls back. "When did that happen?"

"About six months ago," I start, and this time Raven cuts in.

"I had really bad morning sickness, and then when she was born, it wasn't so easy to get around…"

Her voice trails off, so I pick up the thread. "She's really smart and cute."

"You sure she's related to you?" He quips.

"Har har." I set myself up for that one. "Raven wanted to check the place out."

Tyler's eyes flicker from me to her, and he turns reassuring. "Rusty's kids stay here. They have a two-year-old and a baby. He says the ladies are great."

"They seem very sweet." Raven looks up at me. "I'd better get going if I'm going to make it to the station."

"Take my car." I pass her the fob. "I'll catch a ride home with this guy."

"Sure, no problem." Tyler grins, and I know he's just waiting for her to leave to give me shit.

She puts her hand up, blocking the fob. "The car seat."

"Oh, shit." I smack my forehead. "I forgot about that."

"I can call an Uber or Lyft—or I could come back and get you?"

"Yeah, I'll shoot you a message when we're done."

"Okay, well... You're late." She smiles, taking the fob. "Thanks for helping me out."

My lips twist, and I want to say she doesn't have to thank me for helping with my daughter. I want to say a lot of things to her, none of which I recognize as stuff *the* Hendrix Bradford would say. Who am I these days?

"Good luck today," I reply. "Let me know how it goes."

"Let me know how it goes with Haddy." She turns to leave, then glances back to wave at my friend. "Nice to meet you, Tyler."

He smiles, running his eyes along her face and then lower. "*Very* nice to meet you, Raven. I hope to see more of you."

His flirty tone snaps me out of my mini-identity crisis. If anybody's getting in Raven's pants, it's me.

"That's enough." I punch his shoulder. "Let's get moving before Coach notices we're not there."

Raven continues walking, but Tyler walks backward beside me, licking his lips. "Baby mama, eh? Where you been hiding her?"

"Remember when I had to go to Newhope last week?" He nods. "That's why."

"Now I get why you didn't want to go to Jaguar's." He lifts his chin in approval. "I don't blame you."

"Just keep your mind on your business." I haven't even gotten to the whole marriage part, mostly because I haven't thought it through.

If I tell my teammates, it'll leak to the media, then all my family will know. My throat tightens, considering what will happen if they all know we're married. They'd do everything in their power to keep us together, and that's not the plan.

Coach yells our names, and we jog into the weight room. My friend has no idea what I'm dealing with, and to be honest, I'm not sure I do either.

Chapter 14

Raven

"As you can see we're just getting off the ground." Star Corrigan is a petite blonde dressed in high-waisted navy slacks and a cropped, short-sleeved ivory sweater.

Her hair is styled in a stick-straight bob, and her features are sharp. She's all business, and she looks very much like a fast-talking news reporter. I wish I'd worn something a little more official.

As it is, I'm wearing black jeans and a scoop-neck burgundy sweater. I look like I'm headed to the grocery store instead of to a job interview. Chewing my lip, I'm already planning my next outfit if they actually give me the internship.

"Hendrix has been such a great help," she continues. "So many of the players only talk to the big guys, but he always stops to give us a word or two. He said he has a soft spot for the little guys… something about his brother-in-law?"

"Yes—Logan Murphy." I jump in, glad I have something to contribute. "He bought a radio station in Newhope, and he's working hard to get it established. He wants it to be a premiere sports hub."

"Sports is a tough market to break into." She gives me a wry smile, "But I remember Logan Murphy. He was the star wide receiver for the New Jersey Pirates. He has quite the reputation."

"It's true, then he married Hendrix's little sister Dylan. She's a friend of mine."

"And now you're dating her brother?" Star smiles, but my throat tightens at the question. "Have you two known each other all your lives?"

"Ah, no, actually, we met at Dylan's wedding."

She gives me a playful nudge. "Sounds like I need to get off the apps and get invited to more weddings."

I exhale a laugh, unsure what to say. I don't know how long we can keep our marriage a secret, and if she finds out, I don't have a reason for not telling her. Other than we're planning to end it in three months… which gives me an unexpected pain in my chest.

I have no cause for pain. This was my idea.

She continues talking as we walk through a large room filled with tables and desks. "This is the main newsroom. We only have two full-time reporters, and they work out here."

I follow her down a narrow hall, past an office with large windows. An older man sits inside it behind a desk, talking on his phone. His dark brown hair is styled like a helmet, and with his thick mustache, he's giving total *Anchorman* vibes.

"Ward Cabrera is the owner and station manager." She nods in his direction. "I'll introduce you before you leave."

"Okay." My voice is quiet, and I search for something to say. "Have you always worked in news?"

Shaking her head, she exhales a laugh. "I started out trying to be an actress. With a name like Star…"

Her eyes roll, but I disagree. "I like your name. It's memorable."

"My mom was a big fan of that old vampire movie *The*

Lost Boys." Lifting her hand, she cups it around her mouth and stage-whispers, "I look nothing like Jamie Gertz."

Her confession puts me at ease. "Still, it's a fun movie."

"She named my sister Chloë. She claims it was for the perfume, but I suspect it was really for the Kardashian."

"Isn't she the favorite sister?"

"I don't know." She arches an eyebrow at me. "I like Raven. It's a great weather name. Aren't ravens the smartest birds?"

"My mother said she chose it because my hair was almost black when I was born." I lift a strand. "It lightened up some."

Looking at the shiny brown lock, I wonder if that was the first time I disappointed her.

"It's still a great name for TV." Continuing down the hall, we pass an open area with desks arranged in a circle holding large-screen computers, sports memorabilia, mugs, and a baseball-player bobble head. "The sports crew works here, and the meteorology desk is right this way."

She leads me to a dimly lit room where four huge computer screens are arranged on a large, metal table with keyboards and cheap office chairs around it. Two screens display satellite images of LA and the entire country. The third is traffic reports, and the fourth has lines of code I recognize as weather data from when I was at the station in Louisiana.

A smaller screen off to the side has a calendar with colored blocks arranged throughout the weeks. It looks like a schedule.

"I guess you can tell we're pretty low-budget." For the first time since she greeted me at the front door, her confidence wavers. "So when Hendrix mentioned free help, I jumped on it, and who knows what might happen in December?"

"It'll look great on my résumé, that's for sure." I try to be encouraging.

"We're small, but we want to be a fresh, independent voice." We walk to another glassed-in office containing another older man. "Wilt McCloud is our chief meteorologist."

She seems less enthused about this guy, and I hold off on commenting about his name. "Okay?"

"Ward was thrilled when he managed to talk him out of retirement. Wilt's been covering atmospheric events in LA for decades." Her lips press into a thin line. "He's got quite the reputation around town."

"Good morning, Star." The door opens, and a polished male voice greets us. "What are you doing hanging around my door?"

"Hello, Wilt." Her shoulders stiffen, and she seems to brace herself. "This is Raven Gale, our new intern. She's an aspiring meteorologist, so she'll be working with you for a few months if that's okay."

"Nice to meet you, Raven." His voice is loud and laced with approval. "I'd love to have you. We need more full-figured gals reporting the news."

My brows rise, but Star speaks before I can. "That is completely inappropriate. Raven is an intern, but I expect her to be treated like a colleague."

"How was that inappropriate?" He places a hand on his chest as if he's wounded. "Aren't we concerned with representation now? After all, this is a newsroom."

I give him a tight smile. "Is my appearance news?"

"We'll find out."

"Her appearance is not a topic for discussion." Star's tone is firm.

He holds up both hands like she pulled a gun. "My sincerest apologies, Miss Gale. I intended it as a compliment. You're like those girls on that reality show, which is very popular from what I understand. I hope you'll be great for ratings."

I don't bother to point out the bodies on most reality shows are notoriously manufactured. The sooner we move away from the topic, the better.

"Apology accepted." At least all the years living under my mother's criticism gave me some backbone. "I'm more interested in your meteorological knowledge than marketing."

"All of which I'm glad to share." He lifts his chin, giving me a smile that makes my upper lip curl.

Star takes my arm, pulling me away. "I'll let you get back to whatever you're doing."

"I look forward to having you on my team, Miss Gale."

"Call me Raven." The Miss vs. Mrs issue only adds to my discomfort, and I follow Star down the narrow hall in the direction we came.

As soon as we round the corner, she abruptly pulls me to a stop. "I am *so* sorry, Raven. I am horrified. I am livid. I want to strangle him." She exhales, and her shoulders drop. "I understand if you're ready to leave this place and never look back."

I won't lie, the prospect of working with someone like Wilt McCloud is less than appealing, but Star's clear disappointment makes me hesitate. She seems like a potential friend.

"He's not the first inappropriate male I've encountered in this field, and I'm sure he won't be the last." I exhale my annoyance. "It wasn't even the worst I've heard. In my first job, one of the female anchors suggested I join a gym, since the camera adds fifteen pounds."

As if my mom hadn't told me that one—and my dad thought it was a good idea to remind me.

Star exhales a high-pitched growl. "Can we normalize not commenting on people's bodies? I'm totally talking to Ward about this. If you say thanks but no thanks, I'm telling him why."

Her display of protectiveness actually bolsters the decision I've already made. It's good to know she has my back, and I'm not afraid of some old dick.

I give her a friendly smile. "What makes you like working here?"

"Well…" She straightens. "I love broadcasting, and I like that we're an indie station. Not to mention TV jobs are hard to get in this town."

We're at Ward's office, and he's still on the phone. Star

doesn't even pause, and I guess it's because she thinks I'm passing on the offer.

Stopping at the exit, I think about the jobs I've had where coworkers were only focused on their own careers and didn't give me the time of day. I think I could learn something here.

"I still think it would look great on my résumé." Her eyes widen, and she lifts her clasped hands to her lips. "What he said was not cool, but if I let every unevolved person turn me away from opportunities, I'd never get anywhere."

"Are you saying...?" Her eyes light, and I'm pretty sure this is the right call.

"I'd like the internship if it's still available."

"It is!" She squeals, jumping up and hugging me. "If he does anything to make you uncomfortable, come straight to me, and I'll handle it."

She takes my hand, leading me back to Ward's office. "I'll introduce you to the big boss. Ward's pretty old-school, too, but he tries, which helps."

Nodding, I see her point. "I can work with that."

A sly smile crosses her lips. "If worse comes to worse, we can figure out what night Wilt's working late and let Hendrix know so he can kick his ass."

She's teasing, but my stomach clenches. I don't plan to say one word about this to Hendrix. I have a feeling I know how he'd respond, and I'd prefer Haddy's dad *not* be in trouble with the law.

Chapter 15

Hendrix

> Hey, man, got time to give me some advice?

> Jack: Did you wake up with sticky stuff in your bed again?

I chuckle, remembering my confusion after my first wet dream.

> Nah, I got that part figured out.

Any time I was worried or didn't know what to do or my body changed, my big brother Jack was there to reassure me.

Mama gave Dylan to Zane after she was born, and he took her under his wing. I went to Jack.

He wasn't on my back all the time like Garrett, pantsing me or putting monster masks in the refrigerator. Jack taught me to throw a perfect spiral. He carried me up to my bed when I'd fall asleep on the couch hugging a football.

He was the golden boy, star quarterback. He was seven

years older than me, but he'd still stop and scoop me onto his shoulders after a winning play. He'd give me his jersey and let me tag along with him. He made me feel like one of the guys.

> Poopy diapers—I can't get past the smell. I feed her, bathe her, put her to bed… She even stops crying when I hold her, but I can't do it. I don't want to let Raven down.

Jack: When I was in Houston, a pediatric nurse gave me this.

> He sends me a link, and I read the title. StinkBalm.

Jack: Swipe it on your upper lip, and you won't smell a thing. It looks like chapstick, so no one will ever know. You should be able to get it at any drugstore. In the meantime, try Vaporub.

> Damn, bro. Does Garrett know about this?

Jack: Nope.

> How come?

Jack: He never asked.

I huff a laugh at his reply, feeling like one of the guys again.

> Thanks.

Jack: You okay? It's a big change going from single guy to dad.

It's true. I've never made my feelings a secret, but I couldn't run away from Haddy. It's not who I am. Not to mention all three of my brothers would've kicked my ass if I tried, and don't even get me started on Dylan.

> Haddy's the best. She's cute and smart and curious and funny. I want her to like me, and I want to be part of her life.

Jack: But?

I don't know how to answer him. I still want my legacy. I still love the game. I still want to play until I'm too old to run. What's it going to take to make that stop?

> It's a lot.

> Jack: And Raven?

> It's complicated.

He doesn't reply, but I can hear my big brother's low chuckle from two thousand miles away. If I were in Newhope, he'd see it all over my face. I'm trying to follow her rules, but everything about this situation is messing with my head.

Raven is the smart, beautiful woman of my dreams, and she's here in my house with my perfect baby girl. She's also a fucking goddess with her shiny hair and sexy curves and quick smile and those damn red toenails.

I want to spend every minute with her.

Every minute I'm not on the field, of course.

I love that she has dreams and goals, too. I love that she's not looking for me to make her life complete. She doesn't want to be a WAG and nothing more. It's the main reason I'm doing all I can to help her.

I've heard too many stories about women giving up their dreams for their husbands' jobs or because they had babies. A few times I wondered if my own mom did that, as much as she loved us.

It's not fair, and I would never ask Raven to do that.

At the same time, doing all I can to help her gets us closer to saying goodbye, and I don't want that either.

What would it be like if she decided to stay here full-time with Haddy? What would it be like to wake up every morning with them in my house, singing songs about Baltimore and making blueberry pancakes?

I'm smiling like a dope, and Tyler busts me on it.

"What's the deal with you and Baby Mama? You tapping that or is it a just friends type of sitch?"

His question pisses me off. "Why you asking?"

"Because a woman that fine should not be a free agent."

"She's not a free agent. We're together, so back off."

He holds up both hands, laughter twinkling in his dark eyes. "I feel you. Just asking."

My phone buzzes, and I think it might be my brother. Instead it's a video of Haddy laughing and playing with a squeaky toy followed by a photo of her napping in one of those cribs. The attached text from Sherri says she's having a great day, and my chest relaxes.

I quickly forward the message to Raven.

> Just got this—looks like she's having fun.

Raven: She's so happy! I'm so relieved...

> Tell me about it. What did you think of KCLA?

Raven: Interesting... I took the internship (thumbs up emoji)

> Congrats—can't wait to hear all about it! Ready for pickup?

Raven: OMW

I watch the video of Haddy laughing and squealing at the squeaky toy one more time, and warmth spreads through my stomach. I've only seen her that happy when she found my thinking football and tried to roll over it.

It was a proud moment for me. Then she put her mouth on it and probably got every germ in the world, and Raven fussed at me.

I'll have to ask Sherri the name of that toy.

"So is *interesting* good or bad?" I'm giving Haddy her dinner while Raven unpacks our just-delivered grocery order and tells me about her day.

As soon as we got home, she changed out of her jeans and sweater into another pair of shorts that showed off her legs and hugged her ass.

She matched them with a beige, long-sleeved sweater that's loose around her waist and falls off one shoulder. It's thin, revealing a black jog bra underneath with a zipper down the front. It gives me all kinds of dirty thoughts.

"It's a really small station." She rises onto her bare tiptoes to put a box of crackers away, and I stop, mid-bite to watch her calves flex, that shirt rise higher on her back.

"Yeah…"

Dropping down again, she turns, and I quickly resume feeding our daughter. I pop a spoonful of cereal into Haddy's little bird mouth, and her blue eyes track me like she knows I'm not paying attention to feeding her.

"I mean, you warned me it was small, but I didn't expect it to be *that* small right here in the middle of LA." She walks over to smooth Haddy's hair back and plant a kiss on the top of her baby head.

Haddy fusses, wiping at her with her hand and opening her mouth for more dinner.

Raven's wide eyes meet mine, and she laughs. "Excuse me, Miss!"

"She's tired. We had a busy day, didn't we, Hads?"

Raven's expression warms as she trades me the empty bowl of cereal for a jar of baby carrots.

"I really liked Star, though," she continues. "She seems like a good manager."

"She's cool." I nod, giving Haddy a bite of carrots, which

she proceeds to spray all over me while motorboating her lips. "Gah... would you hand me a towel?"

Raven snickers before handing me a damp cloth. "She said a lot of nice things about you. How you always talk to their reporters on the field when some of the other guys don't."

"She's the manager now? I guess their budget's gotten bigger. It used to be her out on the field with the microphone."

"Mm-hm." Raven stands over us, watching my face like she's looking for something.

"What?" I frown up at her.

"Nothing... I was just curious."

I try giving Haddy another bite and she spits it all over me again. "I think she's done."

Standing, I blot Haddy's mouth with the cloth then examine my T-shirt and arms, covered in tiny orange specks. Raven takes the jar from me, but I catch her wrist.

"Hey." I step a little closer, lowering my tone. "Curious about what?"

Her lips twist, and she blinks down to my large hand. "Just wondering if she was a past one-date girl."

Leaning my face to her ear, I whisper, "You're not jealous, are you, Pink?"

"Pink?" Her eyebrow arches.

"Like the tips of your ears." She tries to pull her hand away, but I hold her. "Are you?"

Her breath quickens, and my dick perks up. "Of course not."

"Good." Releasing her hand, I step back, sliding my eyes over her sexy body. "I think you know she's not my type."

Her tongue wets her bottom lip, and she turns, carrying the jar to the refrigerator. I'm pretty sure I catch the hint of a grin on her lips, which makes me smile. Watching her body moving around this kitchen in that outfit has me pent up.

"I need a shower after my carrot spray."

"Go ahead." She waves. "I'll take care of her."

"I won't be long."

Leaving the kitchen, I look down at the semi in my pants. I'm going to need a lot of focus on football if I'm going to go until December in this house with her constantly driving me crazy.

Stepping into the glass shower stall, I flick on the water before walking over to grab a bottle of bath oil. I don't really use the stuff, but it helps in emergencies.

As the water heats up, I toss my gym clothes into the hamper. Raven's full lips and that zipper on her bra cross my mind, and heat surges in my veins. I step under the spray, and my cock is hard and bobbing.

I put a bit of the oil on my palm and lean forward, my forehead against my fist as the warm water coats my back. My eyes close, and I grip my cock, filtering through my favorite memories from that night almost two years ago.

Raven is on my lap, her long hair sweeping around us in thick, silky waves. Her full lips part, and she moans as I fuck her hard and fast.

"Uh," my lips part as the first surge of orgasm races to my pelvis.

Her hands shoot forward to grab the headboard, and her hips rock back and forth over my hips, pulling me deeper into her hot, slippery depths. Her breasts sway in my face, and my hand pumps faster.

"Fuck…" I'm lost in the memory.

My hips drive forward with another low groan, and I imagine it's her and not my hand stroking my need.

She was mesmerizing all around me. I lifted her breasts, sucking one pointed nipple into my mouth before moving to devour the other. Reaching down, she cupped my face in her hands and kissed me so hungrily.

Our tongues curled. Our lips pulled each other's.

"Raven…" I groan, remembering that moment so distinctly.

Was it then she bewitched me? It was so easy to fall, I didn't even try to fight it.

My chin lifts as the orgasm races up my thighs. It's so good. Being with her was so good. I'm right on the edge when my lids part. My blurred vision clears, and I see a face at the door.

Beautiful amber eyes watch me, and I turn to face her, letting her see what I'm doing. Feral need makes me want her to know why.

"Come in." It's just above a growl, and she doesn't move.

Fever is in my brain, and I don't consider how I look or sound. She did this to me.

"I said come in here." My jaw is clenched.

I move my hand slower over my erection, sliding my thumb over the precum seeping from the tip, doing my best to slow things down.

Her lips move, but I can't hear her over the noise of the shower. It seems like an apology, but her face is flushed. Her eyes are heated, and she's breathing fast. Her sexy tits rise and fall, bound by that fucking bra.

"Unzip your bra and let me see you." Her eyes flare, but I'm on the edge. "You won't let me touch you. At least let me see what I had."

She inhales slowly, but she leans her back against the wall just outside the glass partition. Reading her lips, I watch them form my name.

"Do it." I'm desperate with need.

Dropping her chin, she puts her hand under her thin sweater. I can't breathe. A knot is in my throat as I watch her lower that zipper.

The thick material falls away fast and her full breasts rush out pressing taut nipples against the loose weave.

"Fuck..." My fist tightens around my dick, giving it a pull.

Her dark areolas are visible through the fabric, and my elbow collapses.

My head falls against my forearm as I groan. "You're so fucking beautiful."

Water is in my hair and it flows into my eyes. My hand

pumps my throbbing cock, and I ache with the need to finish this.

My thighs tremble as I watch her hand move inside her shorts. Her eyes are on my dick in my hand, and I move it agonizingly slowly, doing my best to make it last.

But I was on the edge of the cliff when I saw her, and now...

"If I could, I'd put both my hands on those tits and pull them into my mouth." My hand tugs slowly. "I'd kiss them, suck your nipples between my teeth... I'd consume them until you cried out for more."

Her hand moves faster between her legs, and her lips part.

"I'd lay you back on my bed and spread your thighs apart so I could feast on your pretty pussy." The first jets of orgasm escape my cock, and I exhale a groan. "God, it's so good. You're so beautiful. I'd eat your pussy so good. I wouldn't stop until your legs shook, until my face was covered with your come."

Her chest jerks, and she bends forward slightly.

"Do you remember how it feels to have my face between your thighs?" My eyes hold hers, and they squeeze shut as she nods. "Remember how good it felt when I made you come?"

I watch her lips form the words, *Oh, God, yes.*

"Then I'd put you on your stomach, and I'd take that ass." Her lips part, and I hear her moan. "Do you remember how you loved it?"

Yes...

"I remember all of it." My jaw is clenched. "This is what you do to me, Pink. Do you see this?" I'm desperate as I start to come, dropping my head back with a shattered groan. "Fuck... I could have any woman in LA, but all I want is my wife."

Her knees bend, and she shakes as she finishes with me. I milk my cock as the rest of my orgasm spills onto the stone tile of the shower and washes down the drain.

My head is against my forearm, and for several moments I hold, shuddering as the intensity of what just happened recedes.

When I lift my head to look, she's gone.

Chapter 16

Raven

I can't breathe. I went into Hendrix's room looking for... God, I don't even remember what I was looking for. I think I was going to ask if he was still up for a movie tonight.

He'd been back there long enough to be finished showering. I never intended to walk in on him naked. When I heard the spray of the water, I started to go.

I had every intention of leaving and giving him privacy, but then he groaned. He gasped and moaned, and his sexy voice swore in a tone I'd heard before.

It was a tone I remembered so well from a night so long ago, and my body lit up like I'd touched an electric fence. I had to see him. I couldn't stay away.

The door to his bathroom was cracked, and I knew it was wrong. It was an invasion of his privacy. Still, I was hypnotized by the sight of him naked, covered in water.

His perfect ass flexed and his hips rocked. The muscles in his back tensed as the water ran in rivulets down every sculpted line.

I rationalized it, saying I was only appreciating his beauty. I wasn't insanely turned on at the sight of his hand frantically pumping his cock. The muscles in his thighs flexed and tensed. Every muscle in his body was tense. He was the statue of David.

Then he said my name.

Correction, he *groaned* my name.

Shock froze me in place. Was he jerking off in the shower and moaning my name? I had to be dreaming. I'd fallen asleep and was having a dream.

Staring through the door, I waited to see if he'd say it again, only he didn't say it again. His eyes locked on mine, and I was a deer in the headlights. I was caught and there was no escape.

I've never been into domination or taking orders from men, but the ferocity in his voice as he told me what to do, the hunger as he said what he wanted to do to me...

You won't let me touch you. At least let me see what I had.

Simply remembering his words in my head makes my stomach tremble. I can't even think about the fact that I came right there with him.

Now I'm in my bathroom with Haddy in her little chair, doing my best to get control. She's bathed and ready for bed, and she's chewing on that elephant ring like she's so close to getting that tooth free.

I could have any woman in LA, but all I want is my wife.

Another tremble moves across my shoulders, and I go to my toilet, taking a moment to clean my orgasm away. I made the rules. They're very important rules.

"Mamma has lost her mind, Hads."

"Da da," Haddy takes a moment to inform me.

"Yep, he's the one." I stand quickly going to my lingerie chest for a dry pair of underwear. "He looks too good, and he smells divine. And those abs and that..." I think of his thick cock fisted in his large hand, and heat flashes down my neck and chest. "It's a lot."

She blows a raspberry through her lips smiling up at me.

"I know." I pull on a pair of leggings and a thicker sweatshirt this time. "You won't remember any of this, but trust me. It's not easy. And the night we made you…"

"Da da da!" She rocks in her chair, and I lift her out onto my hip.

"I'm not surprised we broke a condom. We broke everything else."

She puts the ring in her mouth again, watching me with big blue eyes just like her father's.

Inhaling a deep breath, I square my shoulders. I can do this. I might have slipped up just now and shown my hand, but we can get this back under control.

I'm a grown woman, a scientist. If I can't handle one hot-as-hell tight end, how do I ever plan to handle a major storm?

Walking from our side of the house to the living room, I fortify my resolve. It was a moment of weakness. That's all.

When I enter the living room, he's standing with his back to me, and my resolve tries to falter when I see that ass.

Haddy's head pops up, and she lets out a high-pitched *Dada*! There's no doubt, she knows what it means now.

Hendrix turns, and our eyes meet briefly before he walks over to lift her out of my arms. "I made her formula."

He's quiet, more in control as well, and I follow his cue. "Do you still want to watch a movie?"

"Sure." He shrugs, kissing the side of our daughter's head, and she leans into him, putting her little arms around his neck.

Blinking, I watch her love him, thinking *if only*…

"*Driving Miss Daisy*." It pops out of my mouth, and his brow quirks. "It's sweet and iconic…" *And safe*. I don't say that part out loud. "Haddy loves it."

"Sounds good."

We go to the movie room, curling up in the chairs. Tonight we're having Nashville hot chicken from a place Hendrix said one of his teammates wouldn't shut up about. I'm taking the first shift with Haddy, but he's not eating.

"You know, I could cook dinner for us sometime." My voice is quiet. "We don't have to order out every night."

His blue eyes lift to mine, and he smiles. "I don't want you to have to come home from work and do more work making us dinner."

"I don't have to do it every night, but it's an option."

I look down at Haddy drinking her bottle and sliding her fingers back and forth on Axel's gills. It means she's content.

"I'm sorry about what happened just now." His voice is quiet, and his eyes are on his dinner. "I was a bit keyed up. I shouldn't have said those things to you. I broke your rules."

My chest is tight, and I swallow the knot in my throat. "I shouldn't have invaded your privacy. I apologize as well."

Blue eyes blink up at me, and my breath stutters. We hold each others' gaze for several heartbeats, and thinking about him naked in the shower, only wanting me, I'm not sure I am sorry.

He looks away, and I can finally breathe again. Lifting the small remote, I press play on the screen, and wistful clarinet music begins.

Haddy's eyes are fixed on the images as she drinks her bottle. We watch Miss Daisy back her giant old car off the side of the driveway and her son hires Morgan Freeman to be her chauffeur.

Hendrix sets his tray to the side then reaches to take our daughter from my arms. "I need to get you a car."

A short laugh rises in my throat. "Am I Miss Daisy? You'll get me a car?"

"Or a car service if you don't want to drive around the city."

"You can do that?" I still can't get over how easily he says these things.

"I make a lot of money, Pink." His eyes level on mine. "*A lot*. And up till now, it's just been me. So yes, I can do that."

My lips twist, and I think about his offer. "I don't mind driving."

"Okay." He shifts, moving Haddy to his side where she likes

to cuddle. "I'll hop online and find you a Rover. I want my girls to have the best."

His girls.

My stomach tingles, and I pull my bottom lip between my teeth, doing my best to keep my eyes from drifting to him as the movie continues.

Haddy's asleep as the credits roll, and I'm surprised to see he's still awake. It's a pretty quiet film, and I know his days are physically taxing.

Standing, I collect our plates, Haddy's bottle.

"I have a maid service that comes once a month," he says, standing as well with our sleeping baby in his arms. "Tomorrow's the day. They're really good, but if you're uncomfortable with them in your room, just close your door."

"I don't mind." My voice is quiet, and my eyes slide over his muscled arms in that tee holding our little girl with so much confidence.

I think about the first time I handed her to him, and he almost turned her upside down.

"Did you like the movie?"

"Yeah, I'm surprised." I look up to see a glint in his eyes. "It was good."

"You're surprised?"

"I mean, come on. It's about an old lady and her chauffeur."

"I wouldn't *steer* you wrong," I tease.

He grins, tilting his head to the side. "I'm glad I didn't live in those days. I'd have gotten into a lot of fights."

"It's hard to imagine."

We walk to the kitchen, and I leave all our things by the sink. Following him to Haddy's room, I do my best not to gaze at his perfect ass flexing in those thin joggers.

Clenching my teeth, I remind myself of his one-date rule. I remember his love of the game, his dream of building a legacy and playing football until he's too old to throw a good pass.

It actually works.

I wait at the door, watching as he bends down to put Haddy in her crib. The nightlight casts a galaxy of stars on her ceiling and the temperature is right. A baby monitor is on the side table, and he picks up one of the small receivers.

Slowly, he walks to where I'm standing at the door, hesitating like he might stay.

"She'll be okay," I whisper. "I'm right across the hall."

His shoulders drop, and he nods. "I know. I just… I don't ever want her to be afraid."

My heart melts a little more as I close the door. "You're a good daddy."

He stands in front of me in all his rock-hard gorgeousness, and that naughty smile is back as he looks down into my eyes.

"What?"

"It didn't work, Pink." A tease is in his tone.

A tingle moves through my stomach. "What didn't work?"

"The movie. It didn't work. I still want you."

"Hendrix…" I try to argue, but I don't have a leg to stand on.

"Don't worry, I know." Leaning forward, he kisses the side of my cheek, surrounding me with the scent of seduction and soap. When he straightens, his eyes linger on my lips, which are heavy. "See you in the morning."

With that, he walks away, and I lean against the door trying to catch my breath.

Chapter 17

Hendrix

I'M REALLY NOT TRYING TO WEAR HER DOWN, I PROMISE, BUT WHEN Raven walks into the kitchen wearing a curve-hugging black skirt that ends at her knees and black heels, I sit back in my chair.

"Dang, my wife is fine." Haddy is in her baby chair waiting for her next bite of cereal, but I need a minute.

Raven's ears turn as pink as the linen top she's wearing, and she goes to the coffee machine. "You shouldn't say that."

"What? That I have a hot wife?" I pop a bite of food in our little girl's waiting mouth. "But it's true."

"Thank you," she answers primly, pressing the button on the coffee maker. "How'd you sleep?"

"Not great." I give Haddy another bite. "I missed having this little nugget right across the room from me."

"You need your sleep." She takes her mug and walks over to where I'm giving Haddy her last bite of cereal. "It's how your body heals."

I imagine Raven threading her fingers in my hair. Maybe

leaning down to give me a kiss. Standing, I walk over to the sink to rinse the bowls and put them in the dishwasher.

When I turn around, I catch her giving me a hot look over the edge of her mug. A grin lifts the corner of my lips, but she quickly turns away, lifting the washcloth to clean Haddy's cheeks.

"Hey…" I walk over to where they are. "Give me that. You'll get cereal all over your skirt."

Stepping back, she puts her hands on her hips, exhaling a little noise. "I have been taking care of her since she was born, you know."

"And now I'm helping you."

I stand, and her full lips tighten. Her eyes flash with heat, and she grabs my arm, pulling me roughly across the room to the walk-in pantry beside the refrigerator.

Her heels click on the stone tile floor, and I chuckle as I let her drag me away.

Inside the closet, she pushes my back against the shelves of crackers and bread and who knows what the hell else I have in here. She's breathing fast, and I guess I'm in trouble for something.

"What?" I laugh, but she reaches up with both hands, grabs the sides of my neck and pulls my mouth down to crash against hers.

A groan rises in my throat, and my arms wrap around her, pulling her to me. She's taller in those heels, and I move her across the narrow space so her back hits the opposite shelves.

She exhales a soft whimper, and my dick is fully hard. Moving her mouth with mine, I part her lips, sweeping my tongue inside to find hers.

She tastes like expensive coffee and she smells like my vanilla body wash. *Interesting.*

Her soft body moves against mine, and fuck, I want to turn her around, rip that skirt over her ass and fuck her brains out.

"Pink…" I kiss her cheek, moving lower to bite the side of her jaw then drag my nose into her hair, inhaling deeply.

She exhales a growl, stepping out of my arms. As she backs

away, my eyes consume her—her chest is heaving and her hair is a sexy mess around her cheeks and shoulders. She's fucking gorgeous.

"What am I doing?" She gasps, placing a hand on her forehead.

"Giving me a raging boner, that's what."

"Stop!" Her eyes blink closed, and she holds up her hand. "We can't do this."

"I beg to differ." I take a step closer. "We're *very* good at this. Remember?"

Shaking her head, she turns. "I have to go to work."

Crossing my arms, I grin, watching her sexy ass move in that tight skirt as she walks away in those heels. "Give me a minute, and I'll be ready."

We still have to ride together until I pick up her car.

"I'll take care of Haddy." She lifts our little girl out of her chair and walks out of the kitchen.

When we get to the stadium, our daughter goes straight into Sherri's arms like they're old friends. Raven passes the diaper bag to her, and Haddy doesn't even look back as we stand at the door, watching her carry our daughter away.

"I guess that's that." Raven takes a step back. "Pick you up at five?"

"Yeah."

Her eyes move to the exit. She hasn't looked at me since she attacked me in the pantry. On the drive here, she played the radio loud enough to prevent us from talking. Now she looks like she's about to run.

"Hey, it's okay, Pink." I step forward, catching her chin. "I don't mind if you attack me in the pantry."

Her slim brows furrow over her pretty amber eyes. "I don't know why I did that."

"I should've warned you. I'm irresistible to women." I give her a wink. "It's my aura."

A laugh bursts through her pursed lips, and she shakes her

head. "Still. I'm not trying to send you mixed signals. I think getting physically involved is a bad idea. For our plan."

"I know." I pat her shoulder. "It'll be our little secret."

"No secrets." She shakes her head. "We're not sleeping together."

"Okay." I nod, doing my best to be supportive.

"I'll see you this afternoon." She turns on that heel and strides to the door.

Stepping back, I watch her go, wondering how long that resolve will hold. After the last twenty-four hours, I'm not so sure.

Back in the weight room, Tyler holds the bar as I do my bench presses. Only 250 pounds are on the bar, but I'll do twenty reps. It's more about strengthening my passing arm than beefing up.

"How long is Raven staying at your house?" he asks.

Exhaling a loud *twenty*, I hold the bar for him to place in the hooks.

"As long as she wants." Sitting forward, I pull the weight glove off my hand, not really wanting to think about an end date for Raven or Haddy being with me.

"You tapping that?" He walks around, and I stand, letting him have the bench.

"No—not that it's any of your business."

"What?" His voice goes high. "Why not? She's a fine-looking woman."

"She's the mother of my child." A warning is in my tone.

"Right, so you already banged her once. What's stopping you from doing it again?"

We trade places, walking around the weight bench, where he sits then lies back.

"We decided it wouldn't be like that." I lift the bar, placing it in his waiting palms and staying close while he does his reps. "She's here so I can get to know my daughter."

"So why aren't you dating anybody?" His brow furrows as he does his last rep.

Because she's my wife... It sure would be easier if people knew that fact.

Or would it?

"I heard Mikayla's single again." He hands me the bar, and I guide it between the hooks.

"No, thank you." I can't even imagine being with another woman—which is new.

"Give me one good reason."

"Because I got off that crazy train." He stands, and we walk to the leg press machine. "Anyway, it feels... disrespectful."

"I give you one week."

"Nope." I sit on the chair while he loads up the weights.

"You can't go that long without sex. It's not healthy."

Exhaling a laugh, I push against the panel beneath my feet, letting the burn in my quads distract my mind. "Maybe my play will get better."

"If you get any better on the field, you'll start breaking your own records."

I finish the heavy reps, letting the last one fall hard. "Thanks, man."

Stepping off the machine, my legs feel like jelly. "Let's take a break. I need to check on Haddy."

He makes some comment about not knowing me anymore, but I wave him away. Tyler and I were always just alike, players, jokers, but good guys at heart.

He knows me pretty well, and he's right. All of this is out of character for me.

"Are they coming to the game Sunday?" he calls after me. "They're running out of your number in the team store."

My mind drifts to that scenario. Raven and Haddy in the box wearing my jersey number, watching me play and the way my chest squeezes, the way I can't stop a smile, just confirms the whole thing.

Chapter 18

Raven

"It never rains in southern California." Wilt announces.

I'm not sure if Star had a chat with him, but he's been on his best behavior since our first encounter. He didn't even make a comment about my outfit today, which I'd prepared myself to deflect.

"People write songs about it," he continues. "It's how I got my tagline."

Everyone deserves a second chance, so I take his bait. "What's your tagline?"

His voice turns into polished TV newsman. "This is Wilt McCloud, and there's not a *cloud* in the sky."

"Oh, no!" I lift my hand to my nose, laughing. "That's terrible!"

"It's memorable and accurate." He points briefly, walking with me to the satellite computer desk. "Most days it's seventy-one and full sun."

He's the rhyme guy.

"So if it never rains, what do we talk about?"

"Traffic. Random meteorological facts. Whatcha got, Gale? Hit me!"

My brows rise, and I blink, thinking fast. "Ahh... The next Halley's comet is July 2061!"

"Is that true?" His lips poke out and he nods. "I didn't know that one."

"I actually looked it up for my sister a couple weeks ago," I confess. "It's pretty easy to find online."

"Still, good work."

I follow him over to the desk. "I gotta say, reporting traffic is kind of a downer for a meteorologist."

"It's still useful, potentially life-saving information. And if you hang around til Christmas, the Santa Anas might shake things up."

I remember the Santa Anas from that Christmas movie *The Holiday*. "What are they like?"

"Depends. They're called 'devil winds.'" His eyes take on a storyteller cast. "They sweep in from the desert, and some years they can be incredibly destructive."

"Ugh." My nose curls. "Sounds like tornadoes. Hurricanes are more my speed."

"Is that so? Hurricanes?"

"Yes. They're also powerful and destructive, but you know they're coming. They give you plenty of time to prepare and get out of the way." His expression remains doubtful, but I continue. "They're what got me interested in the field."

Leaning against the table, he crosses his arms. "You love hurricanes?"

"That's not really the right word." I look down, feeling self-conscious. "Did you know the first major hurricane to make landfall in the US was Hurricane Alma in 1966? It was only a Cat 3, but ninety people were killed." My lips turn down. "Today, that number could've been zero with all we know and our capabilities. I love saving lives."

Wilt studies me, nodding slowly. "You might be all right, Gale."

"Don't grab my ass." I point my finger at him, giving him a threatening glare. "I'd like to learn from you, but I won't put up with any nonsense. I'm a mother."

That makes him laugh, and he sticks out his hand. "Deal. Here, I'll show you how the traffic cams work."

"How's it going back here?" Star breezes into the room. "Getting a feel for things?"

I'm pretty sure she's checking on me, and I appreciate her concern.

"Going good, actually. Wilt was just about to tell me about this traffic situation. I've never been a traffic reporter before."

"You're going to love this." Star steps up beside us. "You'll be an expert at getting anywhere in a city with a notorious traffic problem. It's like a perk."

"Are you saying no salary but great benefits?" I tease.

Her nose wrinkles, and she tilts her head in Wilt's direction. "I hope so?"

My phone lights up, and I glance over to see a photo of Haddy on the screen.

Star notices as well, and gasps. "Is this your little girl? Can I see her?" I tilt the phone so she can see Haddy. "Wow, she looks just like Hendrix... She's so cute!"

That gets Wilt's attention. "Hendrix Bradford?"

"Yeah, he's Raven's... partner?" Star frowns at me. "You never said."

"Something like that," I demure.

"Hendrix Bradford is one of the best tight ends I've seen in a long time. I expect he'll get a championship ring this year."

"Really?" My brows rise. "I knew he was popular..."

"That's putting it mildly," Wilt huffs. "Are you going to the game Sunday?"

My lips part, and I don't know what to say. "I don't know. I didn't get a ticket..."

"I'm sure he'll take care of everything for you." Wilt almost seems annoyed. "Those box seats are ridiculously priced."

"We haven't really talked about it."

"I'll tell our guys to look out for you if you're there." Star breaks in, nodding at my phone. "What's her name?"

"Hayden Lucille Bradford." Saying her full name puts an unexpected twist in my stomach.

It's not the first time I've said her name, but it's the first time I've said it where it feels like she really is his daughter, too. The *Bradford* part has real meaning now.

"Who is she named for?" Star asks, and I smile, thinking of our earlier conversation.

"I just liked the name Hayden. We call her Haddy for short, but Lucille was Hendrix's mother's name."

"That's so sweet," she coos. "You'll have to get her one of those baby jerseys with Hendrix's number on it. Can you imagine how cute that'll be?"

My lips part. I don't even know his jersey number. "Where do I get one of those?"

"Lots of places, but if you need it by Sunday, go to the stadium store. We should call them right now and get them to hold it for you. Number 85 sells out fast." She snatches the receiver off a phone sitting on the desk and presses one button. "I have the stadium on speed dial."

I chew the side of my fingernail as she speaks, wondering what else I don't know about my husband. These are basic facts about his job. His jersey number? Jeez, Raven.

Star puts her hand over the bottom of the phone. "Sizes?"

"Haddy's six months old."

Star waits, and I blink at her. Finally she gives me a nudge. "And you?"

"Me?"

"Don't you want one for the game? All the wives and girlfriends wear them."

My lips twist, and I think about it. If that's true, I can't show up in regular clothes. What would my dad say? We can simply tell all the Bradfords it's a supportive thing.

"How do they fit?"

"Like a football jersey."

"Better get an extra large. I'll manage if it's too big." I hear her saying Hendrix can pick it up, and I catch her arm. "Can they deliver it to the house?"

"I don't see why not." She continues, telling them where to send it, and I smile, thinking it'll be a fun surprise for him on game day.

Assuming we'll be there on game day. I wonder why he hasn't mentioned it.

"Now that that's all settled, we were discussing the traffic report." Wilt's tone is impatient, and I shake my head, blinking fast.

"Sorry, yes. Traffic and weather."

Hendrix's hair is damp when I pick him and Haddy up at the stadium like he showered before meeting us. I guess it's safer that way. No risk of walking in on him again.

The memory of him naked with water running down every flexed muscle in his body flashes in my mind, and my entire body heats right up.

I study him in the rearview mirror as he buckles her into her car seat, then kisses her little nose. She blinks up at him, chattering like he's her favorite thing in the world, and I'm not even jealous.

Apparently everyone in LA shares her opinion—at least everyone who watches football. I'm pretty sure he's told me so more than once.

When he hops in the car, he leans in my direction like he might kiss my cheek, and I freeze.

He stops short, huffing a laugh like he surprised himself as well. "How was KCLA? Still interesting?"

My cheeks flush, and I grip the wheel, driving us to the house. "Much better today. I'm actually learning all kinds of useful things."

I take an unexpected turn, and Hendrix sits forward, looking out the window. "Where are you going?"

"Check out this shortcut." I drive the new route Wilt and I plotted from the stadium to the hills. "Since there's not much happening at the weather desk, I'm also doing the traffic report. This way shaves off two whole minutes!"

"Two minutes, eh?" He leans back, giving me an appreciative grin. "Hey, I meant to tell you, there's a game on Sunday. I know you're not really a football fan, but it's the first game of the season, and…"

"I'd love to go." Glancing over, I give him a little smile. "Haddy needs to see her daddy in action, and I'm a little curious to see you play, too. I've been hearing rumors you're pretty good."

He laughs. "I can't wait to hear the verdict. I'll see if I can get you in the box with Rusty's wife. Pretty sure her name is Heather."

"You don't know your teammate's wife's name?"

He shrugs. "I kind of avoided the married guys, and Rusty's on the D-line."

"Is that one step above Fail? The *D*-Line?"

Hendrix laughs. "He's on the *defensive* line. I'm on offense, so we don't really practice together."

"You'll have to give me a crash course in football before Sunday, or I'm going to be so lost."

"So instead of a movie night, we'll have a football night? I can go for that."

"Maybe we can watch *Friday Night Lights*? It's the movie that led to that TV show, remember?"

"High school ball is nothing like professional ball," he scoffs.

"Isn't that what your brother Jack does now? Dylan said he's the head coach?"

"At our old high school." He looks out the window as if he's annoyed.

I'm not sure what that's about, so I don't push it. "Well, I think it sounds fun. I might not know what's happening on the field, but I'll keep my eyes on Number 85."

His mood shifts at once. "It's really pretty simple. The only complicated part is the penalties and the plays, but you'll pick those up in time."

Time. The thing that's ticking away with each passing week. A knot is in my throat again, but I swallow it away.

Chapter 19

Hendrix

Garrett: Has the baby had her dip-tet?

I've gone a while without answering his texts, and I'm starting to feel bad. Garrett and I've always been close, even if his life's purpose is to give me a hard time.

Okay, I'll bite. WTF?

Logan: He's alive! Dude, I was starting to think you'd blocked us.

Zane: More like they're drilling you to death.

Not me. I was back in shape in two days.

Zane: I do not miss training camp at all.

Garrett: You mean stretching and kicking camp, twinkle toes?

Are you roughing the kicker?

Zane: He's just jealous.

Garrett: Nice try. I can run rings around all of you with Dylan on my back.

Logan: Don't you mean Liv?

Garrett: Liv, Kimmie, anybody.

> What's a dip-tet? Sounds like something for fleas.

Jack: It's the diphtheria-tetanus shot, but I don't think they give it to babies anymore. Did Gigi get a dip-tet?

Garrett: It's a line from Raising Arizona.

> Oh yeah, I forgot that movie!

Swiping on my phone, I send a quick text to Raven.

> We should add Raising Arizona to our watch list.

Pink: The Cohen Brothers are brilliant, but it's kind of loud for bedtime.

> Garrett mentioned the dip-tet—should we be doing that?

Pink: IDK, but we do need to find a pediatrician here.

> I don't want her getting a shot. If she cries...

Pink: Why are you texting me—aren't you in the kitchen?

I'm frowning at my phone, thinking about my baby girl in a sterile doctor's office, when a text notification from Garrett appears on the screen.

Garrett: Gigi is in the 95th percentile for height.

> With a dad like you, I'm not surprised.

> Garrett: What's that supposed to mean?

> You're a big guy, Sasquatch. Even Liv's tall for a girl.

> Garrett: Are you insulting my baby girl?

> Dude! I'm saying she'll probably be tall like her mom.

> Jack: Okay, okay... Looking forward to the game—you all ready?

> I was born ready.

> Garrett: Oh, man...

> Logan: When do you think you'll have time to record again? We miss you on the show.

> Not sure, but I'll let you know. And I wasn't insulting Gigi!

My jaw is tight, and I'm starting to wish I'd maintained my code of silence. Since when did Garrett get so touchy?

Actually, I kind of get it. If somebody even implied something critical about Haddy...

"Why are you frowning?" Raven walks into the kitchen, where I'm standing with my back to the bar. "They have alternate schedules if you're worried about it. She just has to have all her shots by the time she starts kindergarten, but that's four and a half years away."

"No, I'm just..." Shaking my head, I shove my phone into my pocket. "What's that?"

She's holding a box. "Not sure. The UPS guy left it. It's really light."

My name is on the package, so I quickly cut it open and move all the packing peanuts away. It's a large pillow, dark brown on one side, beige on the other, and on the brown side is cross-stitched the words, *Marriage, babies, and* a smiling poop emoji.

"What in the world?" Raven glances up at me confused. "Who sent you that?"

"Garrett."

"You guys are crazy." Shaking her head, she walks over to the cabinet and pulls down a wok. "I think I'll try making stir-fry tonight."

I lift my phone and take a photo of me holding the pillow up by my head, then I send it to the brother's chat.

> Garrett: Yasss... I've been waiting for that to arrive.

> Thanks, bro. Can't wait to sleep on it every night.

> Garrett: How's it going with those poopy diapers?

> Great—no sweat.

> Garrett: Why don't I believe you?

> Because it's a total lie.

I have no idea how it's going with the poopy diapers, because Haddy hasn't had one since I bought the Stinkbalm. I've been wanting to try it out and impress Raven.

Frowning, I look over at her. She's standing beside the counter, reading the directions that came with the wok.

She changed out of her work clothes, and now she's wearing leggings and a long-sleeved tee. Her long hair is pulled back in a scrunchy, and I decide to open a bottle of wine.

"Do you think Haddy's constipated?"

She blinks up at me. "Not at all. She had a big poop this afternoon."

My shoulders drop, and I exhale. "Why didn't you tell me?"

"You wanted to know?" Her brow crinkles. "You said, and I

quote, you do football. Not poop. So I just take care of it." She tosses the manual onto the counter. "I'm used to it."

"Well, I want to help now." I pick up the corkscrew and quickly open the wine, pouring us each a glass.

"You really don't have to. I don't mind skipping the drama."

Handing her a glass, I give it a little tap. "There'll be no drama."

"If you say so… I'll let you know next time." Her eyes narrow, like she doesn't believe me. "Hand me the sesame seed oil. I got julienne veggies at the store, and I'll make rice in the rice cooker."

I prep Haddy's dinner while Raven whips up the stir fry. Before long, the kitchen smells delicious, and my stomach growls.

"I don't think anyone has ever used this wok." She takes out bowls while I set the table.

"I don't think anyone has ever cooked in this kitchen. At least not as long as I've lived here."

"Seriously?" Her voice goes high as she spoons a serving into my bowl. "Enough?"

"If it's as good as it smells, I'll have seconds."

That makes her smile, and she preps her own bowl, following me to the table, where Haddy sits, waiting for the rest of her dinner.

I refill our wine glasses, and we all sit at the table. "To our very first family dinner."

"Aw! I should've made something fancier." Raven looks down at the brown rice with bright red, green, and yellow peppers and small white shrimp.

"We're not too fancy around here." I take a big bite, sitting back as the savory flavors fill my mouth. "Dang, Pink, this is as good as anything you'd get in a restaurant. How'd you do it?"

"Fish sauce." She nods, like it's a secret. "Most amateur cooks don't remember to add it."

"I had fish sauce?" I glance at the pantry, thinking about her dragging me in there for a brief makeout session and kind of wishing she'd do it again.

I only go in there when I need snacks. Or when Haddy needs a snack.

"You have all kinds of stuff in that pantry. It's all very expensive, braggy food, too."

"What's braggy food?"

"It's all labeled like it's the best food ever made on the whole entire planet and if you eat it, you'll turn into some kind of superhuman Marvel character who lives forever."

"Well, hell, why do we order out so much?"

She laughs, shaking her head. "I was just following your lead. I'll cook more."

"Only if you want to." I hop up to grab Haddy's veggies, studying the jar as I walk back to the table. "Who taught you to cook?"

"I taught myself." She sits back, taking a sip of wine. "I'd watch the cooking shows on the Food channel, and I just liked it. It was relaxing to me. It's how I met your sister—she was really into peppers and using them in dishes, and we both took the cooking excursion on that Caribbean cruise."

"That's right. Dylan told me about that." Her expression dims, and I glance back as I give Haddy her bite of creamed spinach. "What's wrong?"

"I just... nothing." She seems embarrassed, and she's not smiling.

An unexpected surge of protectiveness rises in my chest, and I'm ready to find out who to punch. "Tell me what you're thinking."

"It's nothing. Just my mom." A sad little curve lifts the side of her lips. "She always had something to say about my dishes. She liked to tell me what girls eat."

Sitting straighter, I frown. "Do girls eat different foods than boys?"

"Absolutely. For example, a handful of almonds is a better snack than a bag of chips."

"I mean, that's true. Nuts have protein and other stuff..." I catch her annoyed expression. "But they're way better covered in chocolate."

The tension eases slightly, but it's not entirely gone. "She would say I could chew a bite of candy bar, but I had to spit it into the trash instead of swallowing it."

"That's fucked up." I give our daughter another bite of spinach, and she hums as she eats it. "See, even Haddy agrees with me."

"She would've been so proud I lost weight when I was pregnant." Raven stands, carrying her bowl to the sink. "She'd tell me to brush my teeth to make the hunger go away. Once she even popped me with a hairbrush for eating a cupcake."

"Okay, that's just shitty. Who do I punch?"

"I don't know. Maybe I'm exaggerating." She sits at the table again, lifting her glass of wine with a sigh. Then she shakes her head. "No, I'm not. And Lawrence Calder O'Halloran was right there with her. He started the nickname Biscuit—right after I'd made a plate of drop biscuits for him."

"I'd like to meet that guy." *So I can punch him in the face.* "Your dad never defended you?"

"He started calling me Biscuit, too, like it was cute or something." She moves her fingers around the stem of her glass, and I try to imagine how I'd respond to her treating Haddy that way.

"I couldn't do it," I confess. "I'd have to say something if you were treating Haddy that way."

"Because you love her." Her lips tighten. "The messed up part is my Mom was so certain about everything... all the time. Now, with the way people act about bodies and size, I wonder if she might've been right all along. She was an important woman after all."

A note of bitterness is in her tone, and I put down the spoon. I slide to my knees in front of her, reaching for her hands.

"Look at me, Pink." It takes a minute for her pretty amber eyes to drift to mine. "Your mom was wrong. You're beautiful, and I happen to love drop biscuits. I hope you'll make them for me someday."

Her eyes mist, but a tiny smile teases her lips. "Maybe I will."

"You'd better." I chuckle, rising back into my chair. "Do whatever you want in here. Make the place your own."

"Okay." She nods, glancing around the kitchen. "It's a shame to let such a great room go to waste."

"It's all yours."

I don't even feel awkward saying it. It simply feels right.

Chapter 20

Hendrix

GAME DAY IS THE BEST DAY EVER, AND THE FIRST GAME OF THE SEASON is even better.

We're all back, we've been training hard, and today we find out if we'll come together as a team. We'll see where our strengths are and where we need more work.

Raven has her Rover now, and I kind of miss carpooling. But it's fun to have Haddy alone in the car with me. We rock out to The White Stripes and Dwight Yoakum.

She kicks her little feet when I play "Fireball" by Pitbull, and I imagine all of us hanging out on a Thursday night at Cooters & Shooters.

My chest warms when I think of having her and my family all together. We'll be back in Newhope in December for Zane and Rachel's wedding. Dylan straight up told me I was in the wedding party, walking down the aisle with Raven like before.

I wonder if she told Raven that.

Raven instructed me on how to navigate game-day traffic, as if I didn't already know how bad it is. I live close enough that

I don't have to stay in a hotel overnight like some of the guys do. Then she plotted out a route to the stadium that avoids it all. Gotta say, that KCLA gig is paying off.

She has all the directions and everything she needs for parking and getting to the box, and I talked to Rusty. Heather's going to take care of them. The next time I'll see them will be from the field.

I spend the rest of the afternoon hydrating, eating carbs, watching videos and reviewing plays with Tyler. We've been together long enough that we can read each other's minds. I'll keep my eyes on him and get clear, and we move the ball down the field like clockwork.

We meet with Coach, suit up, and it's on. Following the Tigers chant, we jog from the locker room to the stadium entrance. All our PR folks line the path, and I give them a thumbs up to post on social media.

Music plays in the stadium, and some of the guys dance and shout to get hyped. Fans love that shit, and Tyler and I usually do a little hand jive routine.

"Ready to do this?" He grins, bumping my fist with his.

"Born ready," I shout back, doing a point and a hip move.

We're on the sidelines surrounded by the roar of the crowd, the voices on the jumbotron, and "Start Me Up" by the Rolling Stones. They always play that one or "Welcome to the Jungle" by Guns N' Roses.

"Hey, bro!" Rusty walks over to slap me on the back. "You weren't back there crying over Taylor Swift again, were you?"

Shaking my head, I look at my cleats. "I'll never live that down, will I?"

"Nope."

Rusty's about three inches taller and one hundred pounds heavier than me, with fiery red hair. He invited me to join him and a few other players in buying a VIP box for our families. I can afford my own, but I didn't want Raven to be by herself during the game.

"Check it out." He points across the field to the glassed-in case above the forty-yard line.

Looking up, I expect to see Raven and Haddy with a bunch of the other WAGs. What I don't expect is to see them both decked out in royal blue jerseys with the number 85 in bright yellow on both their chests.

"What?" I shout, breaking into a laugh.

I point up at them, not sure if they can see me, but Raven lifts Haddy's little arm and makes her wave. The announcers say something about Hendrix Bradford pointing to a new face in the player's box.

The screen flashes, and I see a full shot of them on the jumbotron. They look really good in blue. Raven's pretty hair is down around her shoulders, and Haddy has two tiny blue puff balls on the top of her head.

I can't help another laugh at how cute she is. I really like seeing them up there watching me—*a lot*. Looking down, it's getting harder to keep in mind this is all a business arrangement, a means to an end, temporary. My jaw clenches.

"We're up." Tyler jogs to me from the field. "Ready to show them how it's done?"

"Let's do it."

O-line gathers around, Tyler takes a second to call the play, and we head onto the field. The Commanders line up in a split-T defense, and my eyes are downfield.

At the snap, I shoot up the center to where it's clear, looking back as Tyler falls to the right. I dig in, getting away from a big lineman, and as soon as I'm open he sends a tight spiral into my waiting arms.

Digging in with my toes, I break to the left and head in the opposite direction, barely missing a cornerback, who goes down at my side. Another guy heads at me, but at the last second, he inexplicably goes down. My legs go up, and I sail over his back like a hurdler.

Two more steps, and it's a first down.

The crowd goes wild, my teammates are around me, and we quickly slap hands before heading back to the line. It's pretty much the same every time. Tyler calls it, and I execute. Play by play, we work the ball down the field until it's fourth and goal.

"You're going down, Bradford." A big lineman snarls across from me. "I've eaten burritos bigger than you."

Pressing my lips together, I snort a laugh. Garrett loves to chatter on the line, so I'm used to talking trash.

"Hope you like greens," I holler back at him. "You're about to eat turf."

The ball snaps, and dammit, that guy shoots right across the line. I take a spin and fake to the right, looking back at Tyler. His eyes are on me, and he fires the ball hard.

It's a good pass, but 53 is hot on my heels. Vince, our wide receiver is across from me, and I flick the ball to him just before I'm down with a loud *Oof!* Looking up from the ground, I see the crowd go wild.

The big guy is off me, reaching down to pull me to my feet, and I see Vince run it in for the touchdown.

"Nice try, bro," I shout before jogging to the sidelines.

Everybody's happy when I get there, slapping shoulder pads and laughing. Vince jogs off the field and we do a fist bump. "Way to be there."

Our kicker heads out, but I look up at the box. Last night I went over the basic plays with Raven. I told her about first downs and field goals, touchdowns and extra points. I explained to her what a tight end does, and how Tyler and I work together.

When I look up, she's looking down at me, and I give her a wave. She's bouncing Haddy, waving her little arm at me, and I smile. They're really cute up there.

"Man, I taste blood." Tyler steps in front of me. "Did I bust my lip?"

"I don't see anything—you're good." I pass him a plastic squeeze bottle. "Rinse and repeat."

Harlow is on the field, kicking all the way to his nose for the extra point. Looking around, this is my tribe. These are my guys. For years we've worked together every week. We're a team.

Glancing up at the box again, I rub a hand over my mouth as I watch Raven and Haddy bouncing and smiling in those bright blue jerseys with my number on them, one little arm waving at me. *A team or a family…*

"Let's go." Tyler slaps my shoulder, and we're back on the field.

With my head down, I put the conflict out of my mind. I focus on the burning in my thighs as I run, on locking eyes with Tyler as he waits for me to be open, on rolling out of the way of 53, who seems determined to break my ribs, and stiff-arming the cornerback.

More plays, more movement. We're in the lead by a wide margin, and I can tell everyone was right. This is the year we'll go all the way.

Tyler snaps the ball on the last play of the game, and I shoot down the field, looking around to discover I'm wide open. Dang, the Commanders' coach is going to hand them all their asses after this one.

I lift my hands, and Tyler grins, quickly sending a pass to me. It's an easy score. I trot right into the end zone, toss the ball to the side, and beat my fist to my chest as the guys surround me, jumping on my back and shoulders.

Our other tight end Rogers butts his helmet against mine. "That's how it's done!"

Blue and yellow confetti falls on us, and everybody rushes onto the field. In the past I'd be jumping up and down with the guys, pulling them in for hugs and dancing to the music.

I'm still smiling, patting my teammates' backs, but like a homing beacon, my eyes rise to the box. It's empty now, and I expect Heather is bringing them down to meet us.

The reporters charge out to get their post-game sound bites. The woman from ABC goes straight to Tyler, and Steven from KCLA holds a mic in my face.

"You gotta tell us what happened out there." He's excited. "How did you get so far ahead of the pack?"

"I just put my head down and ran." My helmet's off, and I wipe the sweat from my brow. "Tyler's got the arm, and he'll find me."

"I've got to ask you the question on everybody's mind…"

I know it's going to be about Raven and Haddy, and a pair of arms encircles my waist, surprising me. I didn't expect Raven to do such an open display of affection out here on the field in front of everybody, but we're all pretty amped.

"Great game, babe!" My insides wither at the sound of her voice. "The boy is back, and you're all in trouble!"

"Mikayla." I clasp her forearm, taking it off my waist and moving to the side, out of her embrace. "What are you doing out here?"

"What?" She laughs, whipping her shiny dark hair behind her shoulder. "I'm always out here for my boo!"

She's dressed in a form-fitting red dress that hugs her hourglass figure. Her lips are velvet red, and she puts her arm around my waist again, hugging her body close under my arm.

"What are you asking, Steven?" She turns to the reporter. "Predictions for the year ahead, as if we need them? Championship ring right here!"

Her voice is loud and laced with laughter, and I feel like I've been caught by an octopus. I can't get out of her tentacles.

"Actually, the question is who was the mystery woman in your box? The one with the baby?"

"Some family member from Newhope?" Mikayla blinks up at me, and my jaw clenches.

"No." My voice is flat, and again, I try to get her off me.

"Let's get out of here." She leans forward, speaking seductively into my ear. "I know what you need after a win like that. I'm wet just thinking about it."

"Bradford!" The ABC reporter is finished with Tyler and comes to me. "Great game, man."

Straining my eyes, I find Heather on the sidelines with Rusty. She's holding his little girl, and he's holding his baby son.

Heather's eyes are on me, and she's frowning like she's annoyed. Raven and Haddy are nowhere to be seen.

The house is quiet when I finally get home. The lights are off, and it looks like they've all gone to bed. My chest falls. They were so cute in the box, and I'd been so anxious to see them since that first moment on the field.

I don't know when Raven left, although I suspect it was as soon as Mikayla showed up climbing all over me. I've been grinding my jaw since it happened, and now it aches.

I'm still hyped up from the game, and I expect it'll take a minute for me to come down. In the past, I'd leave the stadium with the guys and hit the clubs. Maybe I'd bring somebody home, a ball bunny or someone I didn't have to worry about sticking around.

Now the thought turns my stomach.

Going to the kitchen, I figure I'll grab something to eat and then crash out in the movie room watching football all night. I pull up short when I see Raven standing at the counter with a glass of water.

Her back is to me, so I speak softly. "Hey, I thought you'd gone to bed."

She emits a little yelp, turning to face me with a hand on her chest. "I didn't expect you back so soon."

I walk closer to where she's standing, my chest rising. "I wanted to see you guys."

She's dressed in soft white pants and a thin cotton T-shirt. Her hair is down, but her face is freshly washed. She looks ready for bed. She looks really good.

"Haddy was fussy, so I gave her a bottle. I thought we could get back ahead of traffic."

"Did you?"

"No." She's acting cool, not like she's upset or anything. "She fell asleep in her carseat, so I put her to bed when we got here."

"I got here as quick as I could." We're standing, facing each other, and a charge is in the air. "What did you think?"

"You were really good!" Her eyes rise to mine. "I wasn't sure what was happening most of the time, but you're fun to watch. I couldn't take my eyes off you."

I couldn't take my eyes off her.

"I liked having you there. Haddy was cute in my jersey." I quietly add, "So were you."

Her chin drops, and her ears light up. "Star said it's what everyone does."

"I really liked it." I'd really like to reach out and pull her to me, but I wait.

"You must be excited. I know I am." Her brow furrows, and she peeks up at me. "Didn't you want to go out with your friends?"

"No." My throat tightens, but I put it out there. "I wanted to find you."

"But—"

"I'm sorry about Mikayla." Reaching out, I take her hand. "I don't know how she got onto the field."

Raven's shoulder rises, and she slides her hand out of mine. "She's very pretty—a curvy, brunette, celebrity. She's way more your type than I am."

"She's not my type at all." I think of her propriety behavior, running onto the field and grabbing me when we've been over for so long. "She's the one I told you about."

"Your one long-term relationship?" Her nose wrinkles.

"It wasn't a relationship." Frustration burns in my throat.

"She only used me to blow up her socials. She's an influencer. We never talked about anything like movies and shit."

Like we do.

"She seems very comfortable with you."

"I'm not comfortable with her. I told the guys not to let her near me again."

Raven's brow furrows. "Why?"

"Because..." My voice rises. "I would never do you like that, Pink. It's disrespectful."

Her full lips pull downward. "You don't owe me anything, Hendrix. You can see whoever you want."

"She's not who I want to see." *Doesn't she understand?*

Holding out her hand, she's so logical. "Maybe we could use her as our excuse... when it's time."

"No!" Her eyes blink wide, and I exhale slowly. "I'm sorry. I didn't mean to snap at you. I don't want to use her for anything. I don't want her."

I want you...

With a little nod, she turns away. "Still... I think it was a good thing. I was starting to forget why I'm here." She looks over her shoulder at me, attempting to smile, but it doesn't reach her eyes. "I think maybe you were, too."

Shaking my head, I exhale. "I remember."

"We were getting, *shew*, way too close." She waves a hand, pretend-talking to herself. "Like, what are you doing, Raven? This is strictly a means to an end. Get it together."

"Right." My voice is quiet, and I rub my hand over the ache in my stomach. "It's also so I can spend time with Haddy."

"Yes." She straightens, doing a little snap-point like I found the right answer. "We're doing this for Haddy."

Our eyes meet, and the air around us feels heavy. I want to argue. I want to say everything has changed. What's happening here *is* different, and maybe it's worth the risk.

But whose risk is it? Who's ready to give up their dream to make it happen?

So instead, I say goodnight.

It's only been a few weeks, and yes, I remember why she's here. I remember who I am.

I'm a player. I love football. We made a deal, and in the end, we'll shake hands and walk away, just like she said.

Like nothing ever happened.

Chapter 21

Raven

ALL NIGHT, I TOSS AND TURN.

I've been fighting tears since that woman appeared on the field, hugging her body so close to his, smiling up at that reporter and acting like he belonged to her.

Which is wrong and fucked-up, and goes against everything I've told him since the day we moved here.

We'd been having so much fun. Heather was sweet, and Haddy had a blast, squealing and waving. She played with Heather's daughter Shelby, who she seemed to remember from the nursery. Everyone was talking and screaming and laughing.

Hendrix was electric on the field. Watching him break through the line, run the ball again and again, scoring, celebrating with his teammates. Every time he'd look up and wave or point at me, my insides would vibrate with pride.

I did my best to deflect to Haddy, bouncing her on my hip and making her wave. I'd tell her to look at Daddy on the field, but she was more interested in playing with the other children.

Not me. I couldn't take my eyes off his elegant moves, his complete control.

I understand why everyone is in love with him. He's a healthy, red-blooded, hot-as-fuck professional athlete, and watching him play, I was practically drooling for four hours.

Then she appeared, the wake-up call I needed.

Turning hard in my bed, I'm hot and cold, and my head is starting to hurt. Haddy cries from across the hall, and I go to her, doing my best to sing and rub her back and try to get her back to sleep before creeping into my own bed again.

Only, I'm not doing much better. My neck is sweaty, and my stomach cramps. Haddy cries again, and I'm too sad and exhausted. I pick her up and carry her to my bed.

Still, she squirms and struggles. At one point, I look over, and she's on all fours with her little face on her hands, rocking back and forth. It makes me wonder if somehow she's picking up on my emotional turmoil.

Another hour passes. My head hurts worse, and my stomach is empty. I tuck several long pillows around the baby and go to the kitchen to search for a snack.

Picking up my phone, I intend to search for foods to help you sleep. Instead, I see a text from Dylan.

> Dylan: Please say my brother is not seeing Mikayla again. She's the worst!!! And I'd kind of hoped the two of you might... you know... (winking emoji) What's going on? I miss you all!!!

Exhaling a sigh, I take a banana from the basket on the table. I don't really like bananas, but I read somewhere they help you sleep. Bananas and cherries, right?

Going to the refrigerator, I dig around until I find the plastic bin of cherries on the back shelf and take them out as well.

Then I stare at Dylan's text and want to cry. Then I mentally scold myself for getting too attached. I asked Hendrix for a favor, and he very generously agreed.

I promised I wouldn't ask more of him. Then I masturbated in front of him while he was naked in the shower. Then I kissed him in the pantry.

My head pounds, and I feel... really bad.

Opening the plastic container, I take out a cherry and slip it into my mouth. Instead of a splash of sweet-tart flavor, it tastes like dirt. Not like it's rotten, more like it's old. Tilting the package to the side, I see it's not past the due date.

I peel the banana and take a small bite. It doesn't taste right either. Returning to the fridge, I put them all inside. I don't like to waste food, and perhaps I can use it for a smoothie or something tomorrow.

Lifting my phone, I see it's almost 4 a.m., and I stagger to my bedroom.

I crawl into the bed and put my hand on Haddy's back. She's so warm, but she seems to be sleeping at last.

Lying in the dark, I look at Dylan's text on my phone. I think about texting her back. It's almost six in Newhope, and I miss them so much. I miss Mimi and Dylan and all my friends.

Scooting closer, I put my face at the top of Haddy's head and inhale her sweet baby scent, letting her gentle perfume comfort me. I deny the tears heating my eyes. I'm exhausted, that's all.

I'm not lonely. My heart isn't broken. Good lord, where is *that* coming from?

Still I ache, and I'll never fall asleep.

At some point, I must've, because Haddy's crying wakes me. Morning light filters through the blinds, and I'm covered in something wet and stinky.

Stinky is the wrong word. I'm covered in something *foul*.

"Ugh..." I sit up slowly, looking down to see I'm covered in baby vomit. "Oh, Haddy..."

She hiccup-cries, and I lift her into my arms. First stop is the bathroom. I switch on the water in the large, garden tub, then I go across the hall to her room, searching for a clean pacifier.

Her crying is weak and sad, and when I give her the pacifier, she closes her eyes, scrubbing her head against my arm like she's searching for comfort. She's hot, and I'm sure she's running a fever.

"My poor baby." I cuddle her, grabbing a fresh diaper and a clean onesie.

My head hurts worse, and I really need to find baby Tylenol. Placing Haddy on the soft carpet, I go to the bathroom for a towel, but as soon as I enter the room, my throat tightens.

My mouth goes dry, and I race to the toilet, stumbling on the rug as I hit my knees. I slam the lid open and vomit hard into the bowl. I heave and retch, and my elbow bends as tears flood my eyes.

"Oh, no…" I pull the handle to flush it away and crawl to the sink to rinse my mouth.

Haddy's crying in the other room, and I fish around in the drawer for a scrunchie to tie my hair back.

Using the counter to help myself stand, I take a clean washcloth and hold it under the cold water. I only feel a little better when I hear his voice.

"Hey, what's happening?" Hendrix is coming up the hall. "What's wrong with Haddy… Oh, whoa!" He skids to a stop at the bathroom door, bending forward and holding his mouth. "What's that smell?"

"Vomit." My voice is hoarse from my own barfing session.

"You don't look good." He holds up a hand, taking a step back.

"I need Advil. We should have baby Tylenol…" I start to gag, my chin jutting forward, and I spin around to the toilet.

I make it just in time, but nothing comes out as I heave.

My shoulders shudder, and tears stream down my cheeks. Resting my hot head on my arm, I whisper, "Help."

Hendrix places Haddy on the rug and shuts off the water in the nearly full tub. Haddy cries, then she leans forward onto her baby arms and barfs on the rug.

"Oh, shit." Hendrix gulps, his body lurching forward like he's about to vomit. "I don't have the balm…"

"You're kidding me?" I wail, looking up at him.

He pulls his shirt over his nose, holding up a finger. "I'll get help!"

"Hendrix," I cry as he races out of the room.

Haddy is still leaning forward, crying in her stinky barf, and I go to her, picking her up and removing her clothes and diaper.

"My poor baby." I remove my dirty clothes as well, dragging myself to the garden tub and lowering us into the warm water.

I'm weak and shivering, but the water helps. Using my hands, I scoop fresh water over Haddy's chin and face, doing my best to clean her. Then I do the same for myself.

Reaching for a clean washcloth, I hold it under the cold water and give it to her to chew, wondering where the hell Hendrix went.

I'm so tired and my head is pounding. I have no idea how much time passes. The water starts to cool, and we have to get out before we catch a chill. It's just so hard.

Haddy's tub seat is nearby, so I strap her in while I dry myself and wrap my body in the thick bathrobe from my closet. Then I take her out, wrapping her in an equally thick towel.

The fresh diaper I got earlier is around her waist, and I limp into the bedroom only to be hit by the scent of baby vomit.

It smells like rancid milk, and I start to gag again. A knock on the door helps me grasp control.

"Come in?" My voice is weak, and I expect it to be Hendrix.

Instead, a tall woman with kind brown eyes and rose-colored scrubs enters the room. "Are you Raven?" Her brown hair is back in a ponytail, and she crosses the room quickly. "Here, let me help you. Sit."

"Who are you?" I allow her to lead me to the large chair near the window away from the bed and all the smells of sickness.

"Raven, this is Sally McKenzie," Hendrix calls from the crack in the door. "She's one of the team nurses. I called her to come and help us."

"Sally?" I look up at the woman sliding an infrared thermometer across Haddy's head, then mine.

"You both have fever." Her lips tighten, and she shakes her head, going to the door where a canvas messenger bag is sitting. "We'll start with the baby."

My eyes are heavy, and I watch as she gives Haddy a dose of liquid ibuprofen. She then takes out a red bottle and a white bottle.

"Liquid or pill?" She holds them out to me, and I shake my head. "Whichever works fastest."

We're both dosed, and she holds out a hand. "Stay right there."

I couldn't move if I wanted to. Holding Haddy takes all the strength I possess, and I watch as she quickly strips the bed all the way to the mattress.

My eyes are heavy, but she moves fast. In no time, she has the bed remade with all our soiled linens in a pile on the floor. Haddy is asleep in my arms when I look down, and the hammer in my head has at least stopped pounding.

"Can you stand?" Sally's hand is on my back, and her voice is so soothing.

I hold her arm, and she helps me, wrapping her other arm around Haddy. We walk to the freshly made bed, and she guides me to a sitting position.

"Her crib is clean if you'd like me to put her in it?" Shaking my head, I look over my freshly made, king-sized bed.

"I'll just keep her here with me if that's okay?"

"It's perfectly fine. I'll be here." She helps me get settled under the covers with Haddy on my chest sucking her pacifier and clutching the washcloth I gave her. "I'll bring a bottle of pedialyte for her—and for you?"

Nodding, my eyes are heavy, and I'm sure I won't be awake

much longer. She picks up a plastic trash bag of what I assume are all our dirty clothes and linens, then she goes to the door.

Hendrix is in the hall, peering through the crack over her head. "I'm out here if you need anything," he calls. "Just tell Sally, and I'll get it for you."

My bottom lip puckers, but exhaustion is taking over. I don't understand why he's out in the hall, but I'm too exhausted to question it.

Closing my eyes, I succumb to sleep.

Everything that comes next seems to happen in a dream. I hear Haddy being sick, and when I try to sit up, gentle hands guide me down again. We take more Advil or Tylenol—Sally says it's okay to alternate to keep our fever down.

Thankfully, I don't vomit again. I do my best to sleep, and as time passes it gets easier. Haddy's body relaxes, and she seems to sleep as well. The storm finally passes, and we drift into calm waters.

When I open my eyes again, I have no idea what day it is. Haddy is beside me holding a freshly cleaned Axel and chanting *da-da-da*. A large vase of bright pink flowers is on my bedside table, and golden sunshine filters through the blinds.

I slide my hand over Haddy's little body, and she's cool.

"How are you feeling?" Sally's soft voice greets me as she slides the thermometer over both our heads.

"Like I've been hit with a sledgehammer."

"You're dehydrated." The device beeps, and she looks at it. "The good news is your temperature is normal. It seems to be a fast-moving bug. Try to drink some more."

I take the cup from her hand, taking a pull of clear liquid from the straw. "What happened?"

"Oh, you know—24-hour virus. All the kids from the preschool have it or just got over it." She holds up a near-empty bottle. "Haddy's keeping the Pedialyte down. I'm giving her a few more hours, and if she acts hungry, I'll see if she can eat some cereal. You can decide when you're hungry, but for now, hydrate."

With an exhale, I shift in the bed, taking the cup she's holding for me and giving it a little sip. "Who sent these?" I point to the oversized bouquet of flowers.

"Hendrix." She leans closer, raising an eyebrow. "He's been sitting outside your door around the clock. He hasn't left since I got here."

Chewing my lip, I pick up my phone and send him a quick text.

> Sally said you're outside my door.

Hendrix: How are you feeling?

> Exhausted, but no more fever—and hopefully no more vomit.

Hendrix: I'm sorry I couldn't help with that 🫣

> Are you sick?

Hendrix: No—I seem to have dodged that bullet, which is good. I've got to play this weekend. The team needs me.

We need you... I don't text that. I've taken care of Haddy all by myself, and heck, with Sally here, we're being waited on hand and foot.

> What happened to all our soiled clothes and sheets?

Hendrix: I sent them out to be laundered. Don't worry, I warned them it was a biohazard.

> Thanks 😊

Hendrix: I'm sorry I'm not in there helping.

> It's for the team...

> Hendrix: But I promised to take care of you when you're sick.

Frowning, I study my phone trying to remember.

> When?

> Hendrix: Right before we said "I do."

My chest squeezes... and the only reason my heart is melting is because I'm fatigued from the illness. Not because I'm falling in love. I'm not.

> It wasn't a real promise.

> Hendrix: I made a vow. I should be in there holding your hair back when you barf instead of hiring a nurse to do it 😒

> I used a scrunchie... and I don't really want you to see me barf. Sally's helping out a lot—I've never had a private nurse.

> Hendrix: It's not the same. I'm sorry I let you down.

> You didn't.

> Hendrix: I'm right here if you need anything.

> Will you come running in?

> Hendrix: I almost did, twice.

Settling back in the pillows, I study the phone, trying to figure out what to do with these emotions turning in my chest. We're really good together, but our dreams and goals are so far apart. How do we get them closer?

My head hurts, and I exhale a quiet growl.

Sally steps forward and takes my temperature again. "Your temperature is still normal, which is good. Does something hurt?"

My heart? I shift in the bed. "I have a headache."

"Try taking a few more sips. I have liquid acetaminophen if it's too painful."

"I think I'm good for now." I force a little smile and dutifully sip the electrolyte drink she made for me. "Thanks, Sally."

"I'm happy to help." She gives me a wink, calling over her shoulder as she walks to the bathroom. "I'm also being paid time and a half."

"You're worth every cent." I exhale softly.

Haddy kicks her foot, reaching over her head and making baby noises. At least she seems to be all better. Scooting down in the bed beside her, I trace my finger along her chubby arm.

"What is Mama going to do, Hads?" I whisper. "I'm supposed to be securing our future, not falling in love with Dada."

My phone lights up again, and I see a text from Heather on the face. We traded phone numbers at the game.

> Heather: Are you okay??? Hendrix told Rusty you got it, too 🙀

> We're better, but it was a hard couple days.

> Heather: I'm so sorry my rugrats got you and Haddy sick. They were both barfing everywhere. Rusty took Shelby and I tried to nurse Tuck all night. He had it the worst.

> It's not your fault—they put everything in their mouths at this age.

> Heather: Rusty's worried he's going to get it. Coach told him to stay home to be sure, but he's worried about missing the game. He thinks they can't win without him 🙄

> These guys.

I glance at the door, wondering how much Hendrix missed by staying outside our door.

> Heather: Keep me posted. Sending healing vibes 🙏

I heart her message and shift on the pillows. I run the back of my finger over Haddy's little cheek, and her mouth opens to the side like a baby bird. Sally's on it.

"Hunger is a great sign." She walks over and takes her temperature again. "Still no fever. I'll take her and see if she'll eat some cereal. You try and rest a little longer, get that headache under control."

I nod, taking another sip of my drink. "Thank you."

Hendrix might feel bad not being at my side, but I've never had a Sally helping me this way. It's pretty great.

Turning onto my side, I close my eyes hoping I might sleep, and when I open them again, my phone face is covered with texts. It's also eight o'clock.

My head doesn't hurt anymore, but my sleepshirt sticks to my body. My hair is gross, and I really need a shower. Turning slowly, I put my feet on the floor. I'm a little weak, but I'm well.

I quickly wash my body and hair using the body wash I stole from Hendrix's bathroom. I dry myself and braid my damp hair, grab a pair of leggings and a long-sleeved T-shirt, then I stop to read all the texts from the girls.

> Dylan: Way to ghost, Rave!!! What the heck??? 👻

> I'm sorry! I didn't mean to ghost—Haddy and I got sick 🤢 but we're beter now 👍

> Dylan: Oh no!!! And I know my silly brother—he's a sympathetic barfer 🤮 Are you okay???

My lips twist with a smile, and I want to tell her not to worry. She has no idea how okay I am. Instead, another text appears in the chat.

> Allie: Rave!!! How's the city of angels? I'm so jealous. I've never been to LA. Are you staying? What's this about being sick?

The Way We **COLLIDE**

> Dylan: Nooooo!!!!!! Don't even say that! You have to come home 🏠

> Rachel: You're definitely coming back for my wedding! It's Bradford Wedding 2.0, and you're walking down the aisle with Hendrix again. Maybe we'll get more babies!

>> Not from me—it's you and Allie's turn 😉

> Allie: I think seventeen years is too much of a spread.

> Liv: And Dylan! Don't forget Pepper Spice. Logan's been saying he's ready for a little wide receiver.

> Dylan: My babies are not playing football. They can play golf.

> Allie: Good luck convincing your husband 😉

> Dylan: I miss my baby Haddy so much. Send me pictures—no, I want video!

>> I actually have something. Hang on…

I quickly track down the video Sherri sent us from the nursery of Haddy laughing and squealing at that squeaky toy and send it. All four friends reply with *awws* and heart-eyes emojis. I could watch that video all day.

> Dylan: She loves that toy so much! Listen to her laugh!!!

>> Hendrix has been scouring eBay trying to find that old toy. He can't get over how happy it makes her.

> Liv: She is one happy baby—are you okay? You've been sick?

>> *We're better now—no worries! I got a job at one of the TV stations. It's just an

> internship, but I'm learning a lot! I went to my very first football game... again, learning a lot! 🤓

Rachel: Haddy was so cute in her little jersey—you too!

> I was lucky to get them before they all sold out. Your brother is very popular out here.

Dylan: I'm glad to hear you're having fun, but don't get too attached. I want you all back home.

My chest squeezes. My spirits are so lifted by their happy words and upbeat energy. I glance in the direction of the kitchen, wondering how Hendrix would feel about moving to Newhope. I'm pretty sure I already know.

I'd better run—I'll do a better job keeping in touch. Love y'all!!!

Dylan: Miss you, Stormy Spice!

We all sign off with hugs and kisses and our Spice Girl emojis, a pepper for Dylan, a cherry for Liv, books for Allie, grapes for Rachel, a thunder cloud for me. My lips twist, and I wonder if I need a new emoji. I should have a police car for all the traffic I'm reporting.

Wandering into the kitchen, I hear Haddy squealing and saying *Dada*, little traitor. A laugh huffs through my nose, and I can tell I'm better.

"There she is!" Hendrix's voice is bright, and he bounces Haddy on his knee.

"Thank you for the flowers." I pat my hand on his shoulder as I pass.

"The lady at the flower shop said they symbolize 'get well.'"

"I had no idea there was a specific flower for that." I take another electrolyte beverage from the refrigerator. "They're very happy."

"Do you feel like eating? Want to watch a movie?"

My phone lights up, and I look down to see a text from Star.

> Star: Sorry you're sick—stay home until you're sure you're well. We've got you covered.

Turning the phone, I let Hendrix read it.

"It's probably a good idea. Get your strength back."

Pressing my lips together, I nod, quickly sending a reply.

> I should be fine by Thursday. Sure you're okay?

> Star: We're good—seventy degrees and sunny 🌞

I send back a thumbs-up and put my phone on the table, watching as he stands, moving Haddy to his arm. "I put off a check-in with the med staff, and I'll have to train a while tomorrow."

"Are you hurt?" I completely forgot about the game, and he took more than one rough tackle.

"Nah, it's just routine, but I'll try to duck out early. I'll say you're still recovering." He gives me a wink, and all his hovering steals another little piece of my heart.

"I haven't even seen your whole house yet."

"Rest up, and I'll give you the tour."

He carries Haddy from the room, and I sit back watching his tight end go.

Chapter 22

Hendrix

WE'RE ON THE COUCH IN MY HOME THEATER, WATCHING BILLY Crystal and Meg Ryan talking on the telephone while they watch an old black-and-white movie.

"They make it look so easy," I muse. Raven is beside me, and our baby girl is snoozing peacefully on my chest like always. "I've never talked like that on the phone with anybody."

"It was different then." Raven takes a bite of soup. "Now we can text around the clock."

"I guess." I don't know anybody I text that much, besides my brothers.

When I got back from the stadium, I gave her the official tour of my bachelor pad, which is actually a pretty massive place. Raven declared it *ridiculous* for one person.

I showed her the wine cellar, and she grabbed a few bottles to carry upstairs; the game room, complete with a nerf basketball goal, a ping pong table, *and* a foosball table—which led to threats of her kicking my ass at foosball, as if that would ever happen.

I showed her my personal gym, which she waved away, saying she prefers outdoor exercise. If outside wasn't crawling with photographers, I'd take her on a hike.

From there we went to the library where I lost her for about an hour as she perused every single one of my shelves, pulling out books, reading the first few pages, then putting them back.

She declared the place desperately lacking in the romance department, so I told her to stock it.

I showed her my very small art collection. I only have a few pieces, but I really like them. Two by Edward Hopper and a drawing made of colorful shapes by Frank Lloyd Wright that matches the house.

For dinner, we ordered pizza from a local restaurant that also makes the best Italian wedding soup in town, and now we're watching *When Harry Met Sally* at Raven's request. Anything for my girls.

"I think women and men can be friends," she continues. "Guys have put me in the friend zone many times."

I reach for the tray, grabbing a slice of pizza. "I don't believe it."

She gives me a nudge. "We're friends."

My eyes narrow, and I glance over at her and down at our sleeping daughter. "I think we're more than that."

She hesitates, putting her bowl of soup on the tray. "What are we? When I'm asked, what do I say?"

"You're my wife." Satisfaction warms my chest.

I've tried out saying the word to her around the house, and every time it gets easier.

"I know, but do we want to put it out there? You were worried about your family finding out. To be honest, I'm a little worried about that, too."

"They're an intimidating bunch." I put my slice on the tray, my hunger waning.

"They mean well." Raven gives me a weak smile. "They love you a lot."

"I love them." Looking down, I study Haddy's cute little nose, her rosebud lips, her expression so relaxed in my arms.

I keep turning over the idea of our dreams being on opposite sides of the continent, and what it would take to make them stay.

"Let's just see what happens."

"What are you doing?" I stretch out on the hotel bed in the luxury suite in Wisconsin.

By Thursday, we were back to our normal routine—with the addition of Tack Lancaster, the personal bodyguard I hired to stay with the girls.

He came highly recommended by the athletic staff, and his signature is never letting them know he's there, which is what I want.

I don't want them to live in fear, and I don't want this big guy hanging around reminding them to be anxious. Hell, I don't think anything bad would happen, or I'd never let them out of my sight. Tack is merely an insurance policy against overzealous photographers.

I do not call them *journalists*, especially not after what I saw them do to Logan and Dylan and what they tried to do to Garrett and Liv. Nobody's writing shit about my baby or my wife.

"Lying in your bed," she answers.

Hello, dick perking up. My tone lowers to suggestive. "What are you wearing?"

"Black leggings and your cotton jersey." Her tone is decidedly not sexy. "Haddy's been fussy all evening, and I can't calm her down. I don't know what's going on. She's whiney and pushes everything away—she wouldn't eat."

"She's not sick again, is she?" Sitting higher in the bed, I wonder if it's possible to get to LA and back by 2 p.m. kickoff.

I've felt like shit ever since they were sick and I called Sally.

She did a great job, but I sat outside their door, listening the whole time and feeling like an asshole.

Even if Raven backed me up on prioritizing the team, I'm not letting it happen again. I'm Haddy's dad. I should face down illness the same way Rusty did when his kids were sick.

My knotted stomach tells me it's more than that. It's for Raven, too. I want to hold her hair and put a cool cloth on her cheek. I want to wrap my arms around her and hold her until she's well. The team needs me, but I'm starting to need them.

"I think she's missing you." Raven's voice is thoughtful. "I brought her in here to test my theory, because your scent is on all the pillows and sheets."

"And?" I'm over here on a cliff.

"She's curled up at my side, sound asleep."

"Damn," I exhale, relieved. "Send me a picture of my baby girl." Seconds later, my phone buzzes with a photo of the two of them. Raven is looking down at her in profile, and Haddy is curled up beside her with her little arm raised. "She looks content. You look beautiful."

"Thanks." Raven's voice is softer. "We'll sleep here tonight."

"I wish I was there." I think of holding them both in my arms in my bed, sleeping with them safely at my side. "Want to watch a movie?"

"We should watch *Casablanca* since we're on the phone. Like Harry and Sally."

My nose curls. "It's black and white."

"It's an iconic Hollywood romance."

"It's black and white."

"Filming in black and white is a stylistic choice. The shadows and light enhance the mood and create drama."

"Is that why *Casablanca* is black and white?"

"No, I think it was their only option at the time, but give it a chance. It's really, really good, I promise."

Inhaling slowly, I relent. "I won't promise I'll stay awake."

"You might."

We navigate to the same streaming service, and on the count of three we press play. Fanfare and trumpets begin, some guy starts talking as a line traces from Paris to north Africa.

"It's like *Raiders of the Lost Ark*."

"Spielberg was highly influenced by classic Hollywood. *Casablanca* is on the Library of Congress's list of the best movies of all time."

"How do you know all of this?" Skepticism is in my tone.

"I told you, watching movies is my hobby."

We settle into a comfortable silence as the actors all go to this fancy restaurant with live music. A pianist plays jazz, and a small man with an accent is shot dead.

"Wow, they shot him right there in the restaurant." I'm lying in bed with the phone on my shoulder, under the covers. "People could've been killed, and Rick didn't even help him."

"He sticks his neck out for nobody."

"Tough guy."

"Until she walks in…"

I don't say I know how he feels. The beautiful female lead appears, and then it gets really crazy. Drinking, shooting, gambling, sneaking out past curfew… It looks more and more like Raiders, and in the end, we watch the two lovers say goodbye.

"I can't believe he did that. He made her get on the plane."

"It's one of the most iconic movie moments of all time."

"It sucks." I frown, not liking the tightness in my chest.

"I wonder if they ever tried to find each other when the war was over."

"No." My tone is annoyed. "He sent her off with that guy."

"That guy was her husband." I don't know why she sounds amused. "He was a famous war hero. He was fighting the Nazis."

"Whatever."

"You didn't like it?"

"It was fine."

"Okay." She says it in a funny voice, and I can practically feel her grinning at me. "Haddy and I'll be watching you play tomorrow. We'll be in front of the TV in our jerseys cheering for you."

That melts my annoyance. "Send me a picture. I'll wave to you from the field."

"Dylan said Logan used to do a hand gesture for her from the field."

"He did?" I'm frowning again, thinking I can't let that guy show me up. "What did he do?"

"That little thumb and index finger twist that means *I love you*."

"Like the K-pop singers?" I sit back, thinking of how to top that. "I could hold up my ring finger. It doesn't mean I love you, but it means I'm thinking about my wife."

"Okay." Her voice is soft and a little high.

"It's just the first thing I thought of on the spot." I feel bad, like maybe I disappointed her. "I can think about it some more and text you something different tomorrow."

"No, I like it," she answers quickly. "It's good."

I hang on the phone a moment, listening to her breathe, thinking about her and Haddy there in my bed. "I guess I should let you sleep."

"Yeah, you, too." She sounds content, and calm eases my chest. "Sweet dreams."

We hang up, and I stare at the picture of them both in my messages.

Sweet dreams.

According to the sports announcers, after a few early losses, our winning streak has begun. I can't have a phone on the field, but before I leave the locker room, I get a photo of my girls. Both are in blue jerseys, and the little pom poms on Haddy's head are yellow this time.

With a laugh, I send back a selfie of me doing the last-minute hand gesture I made up for us. I'll have to give this one a little more thought. She gives the picture a heart, so I guess she's okay with it.

"Come on, bruh," Tyler slaps my shoulder. "Time to win."

I put the phone away, but their image is in the front of my mind. I think of them being two thousand miles away watching the game, being there when I get home, and I'm happy.

I'm ready to get out there and clean up.

Wisconsin has a good team, and it's clear they've been studying us from the start. They're not about to let us walk away with the game, and they come at us hard.

The trash talk on the line is fierce. Tyler is sacked twice, and Coach is all in the faces of our offensive line. Hell, I've got a linebacker staying on me like white on rice. He brings me down more than once, forcing Tyler to find another receiver.

We're not walking away with any brilliant plays, and I don't expect to be the talk of sports coverage this week. Right at the end, I manage to give my guy the slip and get down the field. Looking back, I lock eyes with Tyler, but he's in trouble.

He barely gets the pass off before he goes down, and it's too high. I'm afraid it's over my head, but I dig in, pushing off with all my strength and reaching hard. All my focus is on the ball, and my fingers curl just scooping it out of the air and into my arms.

The stadium goes wild, but coming down, Sam is right there on me. I break the tackle, jerking out of his grasp. Then I use the strongarm on Will to regain my balance, and I can't believe I see a path to the endzone.

My vision tunnels, and I run with everything I've got, crossing the line as the whistles blow.

The guys surround me, slapping my back and shoulders, and I hold up my hand, pushing my thumb against the third finger of my left hand and laughing my ass off. *That's for you, Pink*.

That was some sweet shit.

We actually lose this one, but we played well. We're pretty

beat up as the reporters run out with their mics, ready to get their sound bites.

Tyler is at my back talking to CBS. I've got one of the ESPN gals on me. She asks about that catch, and I confess, sometimes it all comes together.

But she's not letting me off the hook. "Answer the burning question for us, Hen, who was that mystery lady in your box?"

My throat tightens, and I look down. "She's… She's my…" I feel the weight of six pairs of Bradford eyes on me, and I straighten my shoulders, staring directly into the camera as I say it.

"She's my wife."

Chapter 23

Raven

> Dylan: WIFE?????? RAVE!!!!! What's going on?

> Rachel: Looks like I need to update my wedding program 🐷

> Allie: You little sneak. You ran off and got married on us?

> Liv: Now we really have to talk.

> Dylan: Tell my stinky brother he's in trouble… Rave??? Where are you???

I'm in Hendrix's giant bed again, wrapped up in linen sheets holding Haddy. She had her bottle and her bath, and she's falling asleep with a pacifier, Axel, and her daddy's pillow. I'm chewing the side of my nail trying to decide what happens now.

He did it.

He yanked off the Band-Aid and told the whole world we're married. My mouth dropped open when he said it.

We watched him on the giant television in the living room, and Tack peeked his head in to offer congratulations. It's the only time the giant, six-foot-four, 250-pound, former football lineman-security guard has spoken to me.

I said a quiet thank-you back, and he disappeared again.

On the one hand, having the news out is great for me. It takes the pressure off, no more hiding. It might even speed up the release of my trust fund.

On the other hand…

"One year. Six months! And we can separate after three…" I remember the day I proposed this unorthodox plan so clearly. I remember my promise not to intrude or try to change his plans. I remember promising it would be over so fast, and we'd go back to how we were before.

Now I realize how foolish I was.

My phone buzzes, and I expect it to be Hendrix. I can only imagine his family is blowing up his phone as well.

> Amelia: Cha-ching! You're rich, bitch 💚

I exhale a shaky breath, not really feeling her joy and not really certain why, since that's the whole reason I'm here in the first place.

> Yeah.

> Amelia: When are you coming home? I miss my squishy baby.

I chew my bottom lip as I watch Haddy sleep. Her face is so relaxed and peaceful after being so fussy. Every few seconds she'll give her pacifier a little suck, but otherwise, she's perfectly content snuggling in her daddy's bed.

Going home…

The shades are open, and I look out the wide windows at the golden horizon. I'm rich. I have everything I wanted. I can make my dreams come true now. Why do I feel so sad?

Curling around Haddy, I watch the clear blue sky grow gradually darker. It's another day of sun, not a cloud in sight.

I must've fallen asleep, because when I open my eyes again, it's completely dark. I'm still lying on my side curled around Haddy, but a large, warm body is curled behind mine. It only takes one breath to recognize his rich vanilla scent.

Turning my head, I look over my shoulder at his sleeping face, and warmth rushes from my stomach to my toes. I shift carefully, doing my best not to wake him, but he blinks.

Blue eyes capture mine, and my chest squeezes.

"Hey." My voice is quiet. "What are you doing here?"

Full lips lift with a smile. "I wanted to sleep with my wife."

Another squeeze in my chest. "You said it. On national television."

"My phone's been blowing up ever since," he chuckles. "My brothers either want to kick my ass or dogpile me."

A laugh huffs through my nose. "The girls are going crazy, too."

Sliding his hand over my cheek, he traces the hair off my forehead with his finger before leaning down to kiss me. Our lips part, tongues curling together. I turn fully to face him, and our bodies move together.

Heat radiates through my core. My hands move to his waist, drawing us closer, pressing my soft chest to his firm one. His cock is a hard bulge against my stomach, and he exhales a groan.

Oh, God, what are we doing—and why can't I stop?

Rolling me onto my back, he kisses my cheek before lifting his head and looking over at our sleeping beauty. "She's the cutest little cock blocker."

With a quiet laugh, I turn my head to look at Haddy sleeping on her back with both arms over her head. "She missed you a lot. The entire time you were gone, she fussed."

He smiles, watching her a moment longer before looking down at me. "Are you mad? I might have upended our lives, at least for a little while."

"No." Lifting my hand, I trace my finger along the edge of his square jaw. *How could I be mad at him?*

"Good." He leans down as if to kiss me again, but I straighten, pulling my body from beneath his.

He releases me at once, but my core is slippery and tingling. I'm a live wire of need, and I'm searching for anything to slow this down, to calm this hurricane.

"Fun fact..." I clear my throat. "Aristotle believed wind was caused by the earth exhaling."

Leaning back on his elbow, a frown pierces his brow. "What?"

My nose wrinkles, and I scrub my fingers over my forehead. "We're forgetting why I'm here."

He falls onto his back, speaking as if he's reading a script. "You're here because you needed to get married so you could inherit your trust fund. So you could be financially independent. So you could follow your dreams."

"That's right." I bend my knees, hugging them to my chest to calm my racing heart.

He rises again, hitting me with those gorgeous blue eyes like a lightning strike. "I said yes because I wanted to help you, because I wanted to know Haddy, because..."

A knot is in my throat. "Because?"

"Because you're beautiful and smart, and I'm not sorry we have a daughter." He moves closer, his heat invading my space, and my breath comes faster. "Up to this point, I've let you take the lead, Pink. I've let you set the rules, but I have needs too."

"What do you mean?"

"You needed a husband, but it's not a real marriage if it's never consummated."

"Hendrix—" I don't know what to say.

"I'm not fucking my hand tonight, Pink." His voice drops, and he holds me with his incredible force. "Tonight I want my wife."

My nipples tighten, and my lips part. "What about…" I glance at Haddy, and he's off the bed in one fluid movement.

I watch him moving silently, my body vibrating with need. In a careful sweep, he lifts her from the bed along with his pillow and strides out of the bedroom.

My hands are trembling. My whole body is trembling. One word, and I could stop this. I could hold the line and insist we're making a mistake.

He returns to the room, standing in front of me in boxer briefs and a gray tank top. His broad shoulders rise and fall with his breathing, and he hesitates.

Rising onto my knees, I can barely breathe as I move across the mattress to where he's standing.

His bicep flexes, and he reaches up to slide his thumb across the top of my cheek. "I want to sleep with my wife. Will you let me?"

Reaching up, I put my hand in his. It's small and cool in his firm grip. I can barely breathe as our eyes meet. We've done this before, but this moment feels different, sacred somehow.

"Yes," I answer softly.

I put my hand on his shoulder as he leans down to cover my mouth with his. His strong arm circles my waist, and he pulls me flush against his hard body. His lips open mine, and I exhale a moan.

His tongue invades, caressing mine, and my knees turn to liquid. Reaching down, he lifts me into his arms, and I cup his face in my hand, leaning closer to kiss his neck and inhale his warm scent of wooded vanilla.

Placing me on my feet, he holds my cheeks in his hands and leans down to kiss me again, pulling my lips with his as our movements grow hungry.

"Fuck, I've wanted to do this so long." He groans, moving his face into my hair, to my ear, and shivers race down my arms and legs. "I've dreamed of this body every night. I don't want anyone else."

"Hendrix," I exhale, lifting my arms around his neck.

My nipples pierce the thin fabric of my sleepshirt, and he cups my breast in his hand, rolling the stiff peak between his fingertips. "Take this off."

I quickly lift the shirt over my head, and he does the same, standing in front of me with his lined chest heaving.

His blue eyes darken with desire, and I exhale a whimper. I'm going to regret this so much, and I don't even care. I'll sacrifice my heart for what I know he's going to do to me.

"So beautiful." His hand cups my bare breast, and he sits on the edge of the bed. "Come here."

I turn, and he puts his hands on my waist, sliding my thin cotton pants down my hips, following his movements with his lips.

My head drops back with a moan as hot kisses grow closer to my core. Large hands slide up the back of my thighs, and he grips my waist, turning me as he stands again.

"Lie on the bed, so I can taste you."

"Hendrix…" I start, but he leans down to kiss me, stealing any protest.

I do as he says, and he drops to his knees, wrapping his arms around my thighs and spreading me open before him.

"Fuck, you look so good." He leans down, kissing my inner thigh, dragging his mouth to the center of my pussy and pulling the fabric of my thong with his teeth. "Delicious."

Heat races through my veins, and I feel the wetness slip from my core. With one hand, he reaches around, pulling the front of my undies to the side, and I yelp at the first pass of his tongue over my clit.

He goes to town, licking and sucking like he can't get enough, like he's ravenous for my body, and it isn't long before the orgasm twists tighter and tighter in my lower stomach.

The scruff on his cheeks brushes my inner thighs, and he groans, kissing and pulling until my legs shake.

My orgasm explodes in my torso, jerking my hips and

bending my body. I moan louder, trying to move away, but he holds me, kissing my stomach and biting my ribs as he rises higher between my legs.

"I love the way you come." He's over me, pulling my lips with his mouth. "Let's make a little brother or sister for Haddy."

"Hendrix…" I start to laugh. "I got an IUD after she was born."

"Thank fuck, because I want to fuck my wife bareback." Energy races through my core, and he rises above me, looking into my eyes. "Is that okay?"

Deep, mesmerizing blue steals my breath, and I ache for him to fuck me hard. It's been so long, and as much as he says he's wanted this, I've wanted it too.

"Please…" The word slips from my lips, laced with so much need.

Leaning down, he seals our mouths, and with one firm thrust, we're together. We break apart with a groan, and he fills me, stretching me in the most delicious way.

My knees rise, and I move beneath him, rocking my hips to take him deeper. He groans into my neck, *so good…* it's undeniable, friction, heat, rising tension.

Lifting his head, our noses touch. He kisses me again. A bead of sweat is on his cheek, and I kiss it, salt filling my mouth. His thrusts are relentless, my body feverish.

I pull his hips with my hands, digging my fingers into his firm ass. It flexes beneath my palms, and when he finds that place inside me, I break again, arching off the bed with a cry.

His knee shifts, lifting him higher, fucking me harder, until he holds, shuddering with a groan. Thrusting again with another moan, he fills me.

It's intense and erotic, and I hold him as we melt into each other. We drift down together, his lips caress my cheek, moving to my temple. His hands smooth my hair away from my face, and our eyes meet.

We don't speak. I reach up to place my fingers on his cheeks.

My husband is beautiful. He's passionate and forceful and sensitive and kind… and I'm afraid it's too late.

I'm afraid I've fallen in love with him.

Sunlight wakes me. I'm curled in the middle of Hendrix's large bed, surrounded in linen sheets the color of sand. My body is deliciously sated, and I reach for his pillow, pulling it to my chest and pressing my face into the down. Inhaling deeply, it smells like my new favorite blend.

After our first, desperate consummation, he pulled my back to his chest, wrapping his arms around me as we drifted to sleep. Then sometime in the middle of the night, I noticed a hard rod at my backside and scooted around so I could ride it.

Then early this morning, just as the light set the horizon aglow, I felt him lifting and teasing my breasts and nipples. Reaching behind my neck, I pulled his face down for a kiss, and that started Round 3.

I exhale a sigh into the pillow, grinning at all the happy memories of fucking my gorgeous husband when loud baby squeals echo through the house.

They're followed by Hendrix's teasing voice saying, "Dang, girl, that poop is bigger than some of the guys I tackle."

My eyes cut to the side. *Did he just say…?*

"That poop is as big as *you!*" he continues.

I don't believe my ears.

Throwing back the covers, I look around for my clothes. My underwear is destroyed, and my pajamas are too thin for walking around with Tack here.

Going to his drawers, I pull out a white cotton jersey with a royal blue number 85 on the front. Pulling it over my head, I creep through the house, following their enthusiastic noises through the living room, down the hall, and all the way to Haddy's bedroom.

She lets out an ear-piercing squeal followed by *da-da-da*.

"Yeah, you're proud of it, I can tell." He leans down to kiss her forehead. "I can't wait to embarrass the crap out of you if you try to bring a boy home." Another baby squeal, and he continues, leaning down. "That's right. My Haddy breaks toilets."

He kisses her neck, and she laughs so hard it makes me laugh. "What the hell?"

He straightens quickly, casting me a disapproving glance. "Cover your ears, Haddy. Mama said a bad word."

"Oh, no!" The foul scent of baby poop hits me, and I wave my hand in front of my nose. "Where's your snorkel mask? It's a four-alarm poop!"

"She's also a wimp, Hads." He lifts the poopy diaper, actually attempting to wrap it up and nearly dumping it on the rug.

"Stop—let me do that!" I rush forward, sliding the mess away and quickly wrapping it tightly to hold in the smell. "Phew, that is foul."

"I don't know what you've been feeding her, but that rotten egg was the size of a dump truck." He smiles down at her, and Haddy kicks her legs happily, squealing and doing her best to chatter right back.

"Maybe that's why she was so fussy." Crossing my arms, I watch as he fastens the fresh diaper around her waist.

Then lifts her off the table to his chest. "She was fussy because she missed Dada."

She pats her hands on his shoulders, blowing raspberries and clearly thrilled he's here taking care of her.

I can't argue with him. The swoon bursting in my chest is almost too much. He kisses her little neck again, and I step closer to rub my hand on her back.

She points a drooly finger and says, "Ma-ma!"

My eyes widen, and I lean closer. "What did you say?"

Hendrix turns as well, giving her a little bounce. "What was that?"

"Mmma-*ma*!" She says it again with a little more force.

"Check her out. She did it!" Hendrix gives her another bounce, but I lift her out of his arms, doing a little spin.

"That's right! Mama!" Haddy giggles, and I pull her close, kissing her baby cheek. She pats my face with a sticky palm saying it again like she's practicing.

Hendrix leans against the changing table, crossing his muscled arms over his chest, but even all his gorgeousness can't distract me from this moment.

"Yes, I am! I'm your mama!" I nuzzle my face into her neck so happy.

"Breakfast?" he asks. Our eyes meet, and I nod, thinking about kissing his cheek, too.

"Let me get cleaned up, and I'll meet you in the kitchen."

"I'll take care of her. You make the biscuits."

I head to my bedroom to clean up and slip into a fresh pair of underwear and leggings, and when I get to the kitchen, my sexy husband is standing at the coffee maker bare chested and wearing only those thin joggers.

Haddy is on his hip with her finger in her mouth, like it's the most natural thing in the world to be held by a shirtless Adonis. I guess he is her *Dada*.

Her little eyes widen when she sees me, and she points, letting out another, "Mama!"

My heart squeezes, and I skip over to where she's standing, cupping her hand in mine and kissing it. "That's right! I'm Mama!"

Then I go into the massive pantry to search through the shelves. I find all-purpose flour and a small bottle of oil, carrying them out to the counter, and I grab a carton of milk and dig around under the cabinets for a large bowl.

Hendrix mixes up her cereal while I make a little valley in the flour for rolling out the biscuits, one at a time.

"I can't get over you changing her poopy diaper." I watch him stirring. "How did you do that?"

"I got over myself." He walks back to where Haddy sits in her little chair kicking her feet. "I figured if Garrett can do it, anybody can."

Pressing my lips together, I don't say a word. I'm not buying his story, but I'm not about to stick my nose into that sibling rivalry.

"How'd you sleep?" Hendrix walks to where I'm making biscuits and takes down a jar of puréed fruit, pausing briefly to kiss my lips.

A flash of heat rushes through my stomach, and it takes me a second to recover. I blink at his muscular back, before returning to the pinch of dough in my hands.

"Good…" I chew my bottom lip, giving him a sly peek. "Although, I kept waking up to find a hard, thick object in the bed."

"That's odd." He sits back in his chair, straightening his shoulders in a way that is utterly sinful. "I kept waking up to something incredibly soft and warm… and *wet*."

The heat in my stomach moves lower. I swallow air as I fight the goofy grin trying to break across my face.

"Gotcha." He points Haddy's spoon at me. "Pink ears."

Shaking my head, I roll another biscuit before dropping it on the pan. "I guess we're officially married now."

"Yes, we are." His low voice is firm. "Where's your ring?"

"It's on a necklace in my bedroom." My mind drifts to the simple gold band I'll treasure forever. I can't imagine I'll ever find someone this good to marry again. "Where's yours?"

"In my wallet." He frowns. "Why is it on a necklace?"

"It's a little tight…" I didn't want to say anything, since he was so sweet to even think of it.

"I'll have it resized. Give me another ring to use."

"But it's the one you gave me!" I poke out my lip, and his

blue eyes flicker to my mouth. The heat in them makes me feel all tingly and electric.

In a blink it's gone, and he finishes feeding Haddy, lifting her out of her chair so she can stand on his legs. "The paps are camping out today. We're big news."

Haddy leans forward to put her mouth on his nose, and I swoon watching them together.

"What do we do?"

"Try to go about our normal routine." He shrugs. "We're not hiding it anymore, and Tack is here."

"Okay." I nod, watching my hands.

He plays with the baby, and I continue rolling out the biscuits until the pan is full. We fall into a comfortable silence. He rinses up the dishes and cleans her with a cloth.

I drop the last biscuit on the pan then slide it into the preheated oven. "Fifteen minutes, and those will be ready."

My phone lights up on the counter, and I know I'll have to reply to the girls soon. I don't expect the text that's waiting.

> Hendrix: Your husband needs you in the pantry.

Looking around, I see Haddy is in her Pack 'n Play, squeezing a crinkly book in her hands before ramming it into her mouth. My eyes slide to the pantry, and I walk over to where the door is cracked.

I've just pushed it open slightly when a large hand closes over my wrist and pulls me inside the dim space. My back slams against the shelves, and Hendrix covers my mouth with a demanding kiss.

Heat flashes through my body as his lips part mine, his tongue invades, curling ours together, and I exhale a whimper. Our hands are everywhere. He grasps my waist, and I hold his neck so I don't collapse into a puddle.

"I wanted to do this all morning," he groans, lifting my shirt and cupping my bare breasts in his hands. "Fuck, you're so fine."

"Hendrix…" I whisper, need flashing through my body as

he pulls a hard nipple between his teeth, giving it a suck before turning me to face the shelves. "Oh, God."

"You can call me God, Pink." His face is at my neck, and his morning beard ignites my skin. "Hold on. This is going to be hard and fast."

Another whimper, and my fingers clasp the smooth wooden shelf. He shoves my leggings down, and my heart beats faster. I'm wet and tingling, and I moan when his hand moves between my legs.

He presses something hard and cool against my clit, and I squeal when it begins to vibrate.

"Oh, shit!" I moan as he slides it up and down my pussy.

Wetness spills onto my inner thighs, and I'm about to come.

"Like that?" His voice is rough, but I can't speak.

His rough kisses and demands already had me on the edge, and now my legs start to tremble. Nodding quickly, a low groan comes from my parted lips, and he takes it away.

"Hendrix!" I wail, aching at the loss.

"Wait for me," he laughs, and I feel rustling at my backside as he shoves his pants down. His hard cock is against my ass, and he nudges my legs. "Spread 'em."

My lips part, and I do as he says, my stomach twisting in anticipation. Another loud moan scrapes from my throat as he invades with a hard thrust, sending me onto my toes with the force.

"Fuck..." he groans, wrapping his arm around my chest and pulling me up so he can kiss my neck. "It's too good."

His legs bend, and he thrusts harder, faster. I'm so wet as his hand goes between my legs again. The vibrator ignites, and he slides it up and down my clit prompting another loud moan.

"Yes?" he gasps, but I'm too far gone to reply.

My palms press against the wood. I buck my ass against his thick cock, doing my best to take him all the way before I explode from the orgasm twisting tighter and tighter in my core.

His hot body is behind me, and I'm wrapped in his arms.

His mouth is at my neck, and he pants, moaning as he chases his own release.

We're wild and primal, desperate for what's just within our reach. My knees collapse, and I shudder through the waves of intense pleasure as I come.

Covering his hand, I move the vibrator away from my sensitive clit, and he drops it. He places both hands on my hips, thrusting again and again until he holds.

His body tenses, and he groans repeatedly as his dick pulses again and again, filling me. Strong arms circle my body, and his mouth is on my neck again, kissing and biting, moving to my jaw as I turn my face to meet his.

Our mouths seal, lips parting, and our tongues curl together. I reach back to thread my fingers in the side of his hair, pulling him closer. His hand braces the shelf in front of my chest, and we make out like insatiable teenagers, biting and gasping.

He pulses once more, groaning into my mouth before moving down to kiss my chin. "Fuck, you make me crazy, Pink."

We're both breathing fast, and I press my head against his neck, smiling. "No complaints here." He always takes good care of me.

"I've wanted to do this ever since you pulled me in here and kissed my face off." He takes a step back, pulling out, but he places his hand on my lower back. "Wait."

I look down at my leggings around my ankles, our come on my thighs. He steps into the narrow room again, holding a damp cloth. "This will help."

"Thanks." I use it to clean up when the alarm on the stove buzzes. "The biscuits!"

Pushing the towel into his hand, I reach down and jerk my leggings up before dashing across to take the pan out of the oven. They're golden brown and crisp, and I smile, setting it on top of the range to cool.

"They look delicious." Hendrix walks up behind me,

wrapping me in his arms again and kissing my cheek. "When can we eat them?"

"Make some coffee, and I'll get the butter and honey." I walk over to the kitchen entrance to check on Haddy, who is now standing in her little playpen looking at me. "And the baby."

Two cups of coffee, buttered biscuits with honey, Haddy is on my lap, and my gorgeous husband sits across from me, raving about how good they are, and how he's going to eat the entire pan all by himself, which means I have to make more if I want some.

Smiling, I shake my head. I hold my little girl's hand, and I think about being alone, doing my best to make ends meet, wondering if I could still have my dream and my baby.

I remember thinking of Hendrix and our brief encounter. I remember all the things we said to each other, and I remember making the decision to ask him for help.

I convinced myself coming here, doing this would be like facing down a hurricane. If I sensed things were getting out of control, if it seemed like my feelings were growing too strong for me to handle or that they might spiral into something overwhelming, I'd have plenty of time to move to safety.

I could protect what I didn't want to lose, namely my heart. I'd pick up the pieces when it was over, and I'd be okay.

Now I realize how foolish I was. Hendrix Bradford isn't a hurricane, he's a tornado. He blasted in without warning and took everything. I thought I was safe. I thought I was in control, but he tore through my little trailer park, ripping out trees by the roots and throwing everything into the air.

He didn't just steal my heart, he transformed the landscape. My life will never be the same, and even if I rebuild, I'll always carry his mark.

Chapter 24

Hendrix

Jack: I can understand not wanting to tell all the guys, but you could've at least told me you were married.

Zane: I don't understand not telling the guys. WTF, Jack?

Garrett: Yeah, dummy, why didn't you tell us? We love Raven. You finally got your head out of your ass.

Logan: It's really cool, bro. Congrats.

Garrett: Don't be a brown-noser, Logan.

> We didn't want to tell you in case it didn't work out.

Jack: Why wouldn't it work out?

Zane: Yeah, man, what's the problem?

Garrett: Prioritize her needs. It's not the Hendrix Show anymore. I'm saying this with love—it's how I got Liv back.

> I know.

I do know. My big brother gives me shit all the time, but his words are true. It's also why I haven't let myself slow down long enough to think about it since that night after Wisconsin.

If I had my way, Raven would give up her silly notion of moving back to Atlanta and just stay here with me. Star never misses a chance to tell me how much they adore her at the station. I'm confident they'd give her a full-time job. It wouldn't pay much, but she doesn't need it. She has her money and mine.

So what if the job at KCLA is boring? So what if we have no weather in LA? I've learned to like the eternal sunshine. She might, too, if she tried.

Staring at my phone, the pit in my stomach tells a different story. I know what motivates Raven. She's about making a difference, saving lives, and as the weeks fly past, faster and faster, I can't deny what's coming.

"I can't believe it's already December!" Raven stretches out on the oversized, buttery leather seat of the private jet.

Her face is freshly washed, her lips glossy, and with her hair swept back, she's so pretty. Her amber eyes shine, and she's wearing black yoga pants and a long-sleeved black tee. A glass of champagne is in her hand.

I can tell she's excited to be going home. It's the first time in three months…

Three months that passed like three days.

Every year, when the season takes off, it's the same. Between training all week and games every weekend, I wake up and it's Christmas then the playoffs and counting down to the final big game.

Sports media spent a minute on my personal life after my

big announcement. They posted pictures of Raven and me with Haddy leaving the house. They had pictures of me carrying Haddy into the stadium when I went to practice.

For the most part, the coverage was neutral, not nasty or invasive. The gossip site TMI tried to make a big deal out of me being a father, but they didn't have much dirt to turn.

Somehow our courthouse wedding escaped their notice, likely because the old people running the show don't have smartphones and only basic internet.

Everyone was way more interested in my gameplay.

We've had an incredible season. After a few early stumbles, we haven't lost a single game. Tyler and I are the talk of the league, and commentators are already predicting us to win the Super Bowl.

They're calling me one of the best tight ends in history, and it's the capstone of what I've worked for my entire career.

It's our bye week, the one week every season when we don't have a game, and we're making the most of it, starting with Zane and Rachel's wedding in Newhope.

From there, we'll drive to Atlanta to visit Raven's father and sister—and sign off on her inheritance. After that…

My mind drifts to her nervous proposal, and all the things she said. At the time, she was desperate for me to help her. She was working with the old "no marriage, babies, or poop" Hendrix Bradford, and hoping I wouldn't turn her down flat.

I don't even know that guy anymore.

Raven rests her head on her hand, smiling at our baby girl in her carseat sucking a pacifier and holding Axel. "It seems like yesterday we were getting ready for her first Halloween."

"She was the cutest little football." I reach over and squeeze Haddy's foot.

It was a funny joke about the first time I tried to hold her. What a dumbass I was.

We walked around the neighborhood trick-or-treating, getting a bunch of candy she couldn't eat. Then Thanksgiving came, and we ordered plates and shared puréed turkey with her while we chatted on FaceTime with the family.

At the end of the day, I watched Raven holding her, giving Haddy her bottle, and like a punch in the chest, I realized how fucking thankful I was for them.

"She's nine months old," Raven playfully wails.

"Yeah." I clear my throat, thinking how much they've become a part of my life in such a short time.

"She has four teeth—four!" Raven's pretty brown eyes are wide as she holds up four fingers.

"I know. She bit the crap out of my shoulder the other day."

"It's because you're delicious." She cuts me that sassy look that always brings my dick to the party.

If my wife wants to join the mile-high club, I'd never tell her no. Hell, maybe it would take my mind off all these damn thoughts.

I watch her gaze out the window, a happy smile curling her full lips. For the past week, all she could talk about was seeing her family, my family, our friends, being home…

Going back makes her happy. That's what I want… right? What does Garrett like to say? It's not the Hendrix show anymore.

Placing my hand over hers, I check my watch. "There's a good chance we'll make it in time for Dare Night."

It's the night of Dylan's weekly special, where she tests out a surprise, super-hot-pepper recipe for customers brave enough to try it.

Craig and the rest of the gang turned it into a fire-themed dance party years ago, and it's become the restaurant's most popular night of the week.

"I hope so!" Her eyes dance as she looks up at me. "Last time, I only caught the end, but it seemed like a blast."

"It's pretty crazy." I stand, bracing my forearms against the overhead compartments.

Looking down, I watch her slide a piece of hair off her

cheek, behind her ear. She's still so beautifully mine. I don't want to think about a day when I'll be flying back to LA alone.

In the beginning, I told her I was okay with that. I've lived by myself for five years. Of course, I'd be okay with that.

I'm not okay with it.

These two ladies came into my world and changed everything. From the first night when we waited, holding our breath outside Haddy's bedroom door as she cried. To every single bedtime movie that followed.

Even on away games, we'd go to sleep on the phone.

Then they started sleeping in my bed.

How the fuck do I go back to being in that massive, "ridiculous" mansion all by myself?

My phone buzzes, and I pull it out to see the text.

Jack: ETA?

Looking out the window, we're somewhere over Texas. A screen in the wall shows a map of the United States and our little plane shooting across the bottom.

Looks like we'll be touching down around nine.

Jack: Perfect—see you then.

Taking the seat beside Raven, I hold her hand, studying the gold ring I had resized so she could wear it all the time. "Are you ready for this?"

"For the wedding?" Her brow furrows.

"This might be our last quiet moment for a while."

Her face relaxes with a grin. "Are you saying we'll be torn apart by wild Bradfords?"

I lift her hand to my lips to kiss her knuckles. "More like we'll be smothered by them."

Scooting closer, she puts her head on my shoulder. "Haddy's going to love her family."

Leaning my head against hers, I'm sure she's right about that part. Haddy already loves music and dancing. She'll fit right in, and they'll be ready to make her one of us, just like her mother.

Still holding hands, I think about us being only friends. I think about explaining our breakup to my brothers. I think about the promise I made three months ago.

"Whatever happens, I had a lot of fun."

She blinks up at me, and her lips press into a smile. "Me, too."

Haddy dozes in her seat while Raven reads a book on her Kindle. I have my phone out watching highlight reels from the past season on YouTube.

A light touch on my shoulder draws my attention.

"We're making our final approach." The flight attendant's voice is smooth and low, and we scoot around to prepare for landing.

It's not long before we're on the ground. I help Raven collect Haddy's things. She slept through the flight, which I hope means she'll be ready for the craziness that's to come.

We walk down the short steps to find two familiar teenage boys in jeans and hoodies waiting for us. It's a cool, breezy night on the coast, and Raven pulls the hood over Haddy's head and ears.

"Coach Jack sent us to pick you up." The taller boy I recognize as Austin Sinclair, QB-1 for Jack's high school football team and Dylan's best friend Allie's son. "He said to drive you straight to the restaurant, no detours."

"They've planned a surprise party for you." Edward Wells is Rachel's brother, and he's a hoot.

"Edward!" Austin punches his arm. The younger boy frowns, rubbing the spot with an *Ow!* as Austin scolds him. "You weren't supposed to tell them that."

Raven ducks her head, covering her mouth with her hand, and I step forward, lowering my voice. "It's okay. You never told us."

"But I did tell you." Edward is confused, looking from me to Austin, who lets out a groan. Then he shrugs. "Adults are weird."

Shaking his head, Austin takes Raven's suitcase. "Whatever, just act surprised."

"We'll be the most surprised people you've ever seen," she reassures him.

Following the boys, I help put our luggage in the bed of Garrett's oversized Ford pickup. We fasten Haddy's car seat in the second row behind the passenger's seat, and I take the front with Austin while Raven and Edward sit in the back with the baby.

It's a short drive to the restaurant from the small airport south of town, and when we pull into the parking lot of Cooters & Shooters, it's so obvious they're planning something.

"Did they cancel Dare Night for us?" Raven's voice is worried as she leans forward.

The restaurant is almost completely dark, and the parking lot is empty except for a few cars, Jack's truck, and Logan's SUV.

"No, they just told everyone to park at the house, and they're going to jump out and yell when you walk in the door," Edward explains without a hint of irony.

"Edward, Dang!" Austin stage-yells, and I can't help a chuckle.

"Rachel told me not to walk in with all of you. It's going to be loud with poppers and shouting."

Austin looks at him in the rearview mirror. "That was for your information, not for you to tell the whole truck."

"I thought they should know for the baby. Gigi cries when everybody yells."

"You make a very good point, Edward." Raven pats his arm. "Thank you for warning us. I'll let the guys go in first and cover Haddy's ears."

Edward nods his head. "No problem. I'll see you tomorrow. Welcome home."

He slides out of the truck and walks up the hill to the house. Austin puts the truck in park and piles out like a typical, annoyed teenager.

The three of us follow him down the short walk to the front entrance, and I bump his shoulder. "If it makes you feel any better, they're being pretty dang obvious. There's no way this place is this quiet on a Thursday night."

His lips twist with a smile, and he grabs the handle. "That's true."

He doesn't even get the door open before the lights flash on and everybody yells *Surprise!*

"You're finally here!" Dylan rushes forward to pull me into a hug. "We've been waiting and waiting."

"I can tell." I lean down to give my sister a squeeze.

"My new sister!" She turns to hug Raven. "How did my big brother propose? Show me your ring!"

"Oh…" Raven's smile falters, and her panicked eyes fly to mine.

"It wasn't really like that…" I start, but Dylan's holding her hand.

"No diamond?" She frowns up at me.

"We decided so fast, we just picked these up…" Raven starts.

"It's temporary," I finish.

"Okay, and you'll have anniversaries and holidays and whatever!" Dylan smiles, supportive as always. She waves my misstep away, turning to smooth the hood of Haddy's coat off her head. "Where's my little Haddy-boo? Here she is!"

Haddy isn't crying. In fact, her blue eyes are huge as she looks around the festive room.

All four of my brothers gather around us, along with Liv, Rachel, and Allie. A lighted sign over the bar reads *Welcome Home!*, and the place is packed with family and friends and patrons here for Dare Night.

It looks like we caught them mid-Dare.

Once the initial surprise part is over, "Disco Inferno" kicks off on the PA system, and a few of the female servers hop onto the bar to dance, *Coyote Ugly* style.

"Welcome home, Hen!" Craig says over the mic from where he stands behind a long picnic table.

He's in his blonde Sandra Dee from *Grease* wig, and a waitress I recognize helps him hand out little white cups of this week's spicy pepper dish to the line of brave customers.

"How was your flight?" Jack grips my shoulder, pulling me in for a hug.

"She's so big!" Liv is at my side holding Gigi and hugging Raven and Haddy.

"Well, if it isn't my married, baby-having, poopy-diaper-changing little brother." The loud voice is followed closely by massive arms around my chest, lifting me off the floor.

"Put me down, Sasquatch!" I yell, twisting against Garrett's vise grip.

He puts me on my feet again, and I turn to see him in his own Sandra Dee wig, grinning down at me. "You don't look too worse for wear."

"He looks happy." Zane walks up reaching for my hand before pulling me close and slapping my back. "Being a dad agrees with you."

Nodding sheepishly, my eyes instinctively search for Raven. She's drifted off with the girls, laughing and hugging. They're all talking at the same time, fawning over the babies.

Haddy has her pacifier in her mouth and Axel in her hand as she watches them all in amazement. I don't think she's going to cry.

"He's a Bradford." Garrett laughs, leaving us to join Craig, who's yelling at him from the top of the bar. "He can't help himself."

Somehow he drags his six-foot-four frame on top of the bar in one move as the music changes to "Fireball" by Pitbull. The lights flash around the room, and our welcome home is swept up in the commotion of Thursday nights at my family's restaurant on the bay.

"Want some?" Dylan dances up to me holding a paper cup and a spoon. "It's Red Savina chili with sweet potatoes and corn and a little apple cider vinegar and lemon juice to cut the heat."

"I do!" Raven skips up beside me, taking the small serving. "Red Savinas were the hottest pepper in the world until ghost peppers were discovered."

"No, thank you." Logan holds up both hands, stepping away.

"Same!" Liv calls from where she's bouncing Haddy on her hip. "I prefer my taste buds remain intact."

My pretty wife takes a small bite of the daring dish. As soon as it's in her mouth, her brown eyes widen, and she squeals, waving a hand in front of her face.

"It's delicious!" Her eyes water, and her nose starts to run as she laughs, still waving her hand. "Smoky…"

"Are you getting any of the sweetness?" Dylan is beside her, watching like they're in a laboratory.

Raven shakes her head fast. "It's burning my mouth off!"

"Here!" Allie holds out a small cup of vanilla ice cream.

Raven takes it, ripping off the cardboard top and sticking her tongue straight into the cup.

"Want some, Hen?" Dylan turns to me, holding another small cup.

Both my hands go up like she pulled a gun. "I'm good for now."

Rachel snorts a laugh, taking the serving. "In that case, you'd better get dancing. Your big brother's been waiting for you."

I look up at the bar where Garrett, Craig, and several waitresses in cutoffs and Cooters & Shooters T-shirts shake their hips in time, then I look at my bride holding a party-sized vanilla ice cream cup to her mouth.

Our eyes meet, and she blinks with a smile.

"I think I'd rather dance with my wife." Stepping forward, I hold out a hand. "Are you okay with that?"

She tosses the ice cream into a nearby trash can and puts her hand in mine. "I was born okay with it."

Chapter 25

Raven

HENDRIX WRAPS HIS ARMS AROUND ME, PULLING MY BODY TO HIS, and we groove to the strains of "Stars Like Confetti" by Dustin Lynch.

He sings in my ear about climbing in his jacket, and like my heart, you can have it, and warmth slides through my veins.

Leaning back, I smile up at him. "You have a really nice voice."

Pulling in his chin, he grins down at me. "I'm not sure I'm pageant material."

"Don't worry. I never was either."

His arm tightens around my waist, and he hugs me closer. "Don't sell yourself short, Pink. You could be the queen of my double-wide trailer any day of the week."

My head falls back with a laugh. The crowd around us sings the chorus, and Hendrix moves his hips in a way that fills my mind with dirty thoughts.

I'm right there with him, wrapping my arms around his shoulders and letting him take the lead. "Is this our first dance?"

He looks around as if he's thinking. "We didn't dance at Dylan's reception?"

Slanting my eyes, I smile. "We left early."

"Yeah, we did." His eyebrows waggle. "I wouldn't change a thing."

Dare Night is everything I imagined it would be, from the crazy food to the wild lights and dancing, to the Bradford family all around laughing and teasing. The music alternates between fiery dance tracks and country hits, but it all comes winding down when the clock strikes eleven.

"You're glowing." Hendrix holds my hand as we exit the dance floor again. I've lost track of how many times he's dragged me out to sway in his arms tonight. "You seem really happy."

"It's like the family I never had." I look around the room wistfully. "I'm happy for Haddy."

A gentle pull of my hand has me snug at his side. "I'm pretty sure they think of you as family, too."

Chewing my bottom lip, I think about his words and wish…

"Have we lost our daughter?" I deflect, looking around the room.

Zane and Rachel are behind us, and they've been inseparable all night, holding hands and dancing close like almost-newlyweds.

I spy our little girl at a table with Dylan and Miss Gina, the sweet old blind lady who owns the Italian-style villa on the bluffs where Dylan and Logan were married. She's like the family's honorary grandmother.

"Uncle Henny!" Kimmie Joy shouts, and I've been wondering where that little voice was all night.

Jack's daughter marches up to where we're standing like she's ready to fuss, and Hendrix bends down to sweep her onto his hip. She's in first grade, and she's already a lot like her aunt Dylan.

"Uncle Grizz said you told me a fib. He said my American

Girl doll won't come alive at night when I sleep." Her six-year-old arms cross, and she frowns hard. "He said you were trying to scare me."

My hands cover my mouth to hide my laugh, and Hendrix presses his lips together, I'm sure to do the same.

"It's true." He nods, looking so contrite. "I was teasing you, but I didn't mean to scare you."

Her dark head tilts to the side as she considers his apology. Then all at once, her expression brightens, and she pats his shoulder. "That's okay, Uncle Henny. I tell fibs sometimes too."

"What?" He almost laughs again. "Like when?"

"Like one time I told Daddy a snake was under my bed because I didn't want to sleep all by myself."

"What happened?"

"He said I could sleep in his bed until I fell asleep, but I shouldn't tell stories."

He lifts his chin. "Your dad's right. We should always be honest. I'm sorry I told a fib. If I promise not to do it again, will you?"

Her dark eyes slide to the side again as if she's considering her answer, and he gives her a little shake. "Kimmie!"

"Well…" Her reply bursts into squealing laughter as he starts to tickle her, until she finally relents. "Okay! *Okay!!!*"

Then he puts her on her feet and she scampers away to where Dylan is holding our daughter.

Shaking his head, he looks over at me. "That girl is going to be trouble when she gets bigger."

"I think she's adorable." Stepping closer, I hold his arm, rising onto my toes to kiss his cheek. "And I think Haddy has a great dad."

Blue eyes darken when they meet mine, and lust sizzles in my veins. His low voice tickles my stomach as he asks, "When can we get out of here without hurting people's feelings?"

"That didn't stop us last time." My tone is sassy, and the muscle in his square jaw flexes.

I heat right up when I see him struggling for control. "Everybody wants to see Haddy now."

"You're not trying to get out of here, are you, Hen?" Garrett walks up, slapping him on the back. "Logan wants us down at the station tomorrow to record a show."

A poster of Logan and Zane hangs on the wall near the pool tables. It's an image of them both in headphones with broadcast mics in front of them and the words *Lightning & Thunder* splashed across the bottom.

Dylan walks up to where we're standing, bouncing Haddy on her hip. "She is the sweetest little baby, Rave. Just look at that smile!"

As if on cue, Haddy pulls her pacifier out of her mouth and makes her *Zzz* sound, showing off her four teeth.

"I think it's time we added a little boy to the team." Logan walks up, wrapping his arms around his petite wife, then he nods in my direction. "Hey, Rave, I've got an idea for a meteorologist position if you're interested."

My ears perk up, and I do a little bounce. "I'm interested!"

His eyes drift to Hendrix and back to me again. "We'll talk later. It's a school night. You guys coming to the station tomorrow so we can record the show?"

"We'll be there." Hendrix's low voice is at my side, and his arm is around me, like it's so natural.

"Bachelorette tomorrow night!" Allie skips up to where we're standing, scooping Haddy out of my sister's arms. "I'll bring the purple drink."

"Oh…" I look from Haddy to her. "Who'll watch the babies?"

"Austin already offered to help. He'll have Edward and Kimmie and Benji Maxwell on hand."

"Sounds like a full house," Hendrix laughs. "What are we doing?"

"Crashing, of course." Logan dips his face to nip at Dylan's neck.

"You are not!" she cries, batting his arm. "You boys need to find something to do on your own. Give Zane a lap dance."

"On it," Garrett answers fast. "Craig has our outfits in his car."

"Now I want to crash their party," Allie laughs, looking from Grizz to me.

Hendrix stands straighter, reaching for our daughter. "We'd better get Haddy to bed before she starts fussing."

"Damn, keep it in your pants, horndog," Garrett quips.

"Uncle Henny's not a corn dog!" Kimmie skips into the circle, holding up her hands to jump on Garrett's back.

"Ha!" Hendrix punches his brother's shoulder. "Busted."

"Don't teach my daughter new words." Jack's weary complaint joins the group, and I can't help a laugh.

"You've got your work cut out for you with those two," I say, and he smiles, wrapping his arm around my shoulders.

"You and Rachel are the only ones with my back."

"That's not true!" Allie cries, but she's laughing along with Dylan and Liv.

He just shakes his head, lifting his chin at me. "Good to have you here, Raven. Welcome to the family."

My chest squeezes, and my silly eyes burn. Blinking quickly, I look away, inhaling slowly. I didn't expect that from Big Brother Jack, and it's like I'm really a Bradford now.

I whisper a thanks as I reach for Hendrix's hand. He smiles at me like he's feeling the same way as me—happy, loved, and so conflicted.

With hugs and plans for tomorrow, we tell everyone goodbye. Garrett says we can use his truck while we're in town, since it already has our things and Haddy's car seat in it.

The staff at the hotel greets us like old friends, and Hendrix leads us to his usual, gorgeous suite overlooking the bay. It's just like before, only this time a portable crib is in the corner.

Haddy fell asleep on the ride here, and as I look down at her sleeping peacefully, her daddy steps up behind me, wrapping his arms around my waist.

"What are you thinking?" His voice is quiet.

My reply is equally quiet. "How I'd like to stay in this moment."

We both watch our sleeping daughter in the pale light of the full moon.

"It's a pretty good moment, Pink." Sliding his lips along the side of my neck, I feel him smile against my skin.

I rest my head against his, thinking how right now, even with the silvery moonlight around us, this place is golden.

"Ahhhnd we're back, hoes and hookers, for the notorious, the infamous, the potentially dangerous, third-annual round of Marry, Fuck, Kill!" Rachel cups her hands beside her mouth, making whispery cheer noises.

"We've created a monster." Allie leans into my side as she pours five glasses of her infamous purple drink. "Tell me, Rach, what's the difference between a ho and hooker?"

Rachel waves her away, and I inspect the cup of grape Kool-Aid mixed with what I'm pretty sure is jet fuel. "It's only the second time for me. And the first round was two years ago."

"We have a correction, ho-ho-hoes…" Rachel says in her fake-announcer voice, digging in her bag and taking out pens, slips of paper, and the little hourglass. "It's the second, biennial, notorious, potentially dangerous…"

"Speaking of danger," Dylan sing-songs as she dances out with a tray of gorgeous finger foods. "Who's ready for ghost pepper toast points with goat cheese and honey?"

"Me!" I cry, holding up a hand.

"And the non-spicy option is…?" Liv takes a Solo cup of purple drink, scooting onto the stool beside me.

"Pizza rolls." Dylan plops a basket filled with little rectangles on the table between us.

"Yum, I'll have some of those, too." I lean into Liv's side, and we both laugh.

"They're Garrett's fave," Liv informs me.

"I brought hummus and pita." Allie digs out a plastic bag holding a tub of store-bought hummus and a package of pita. "Don't judge—I was working in the library all day."

"No judgment here." I walk around to help her arrange the items on the table. "You brought the purple drink."

"That part's easy," Allie whispers. "Two parts Kool-Aid, one part Everclear."

"Oh, shit." We snort a laugh, and Dylan holds up her plastic cup for all of us to cheer.

Then we slam it back, and I don't even wince. This drink is dangerous.

"Okay, ladies, get those pens ready." Rachel takes out her phone. "First round is coming in hot!"

"Why am I suddenly nervous?" I giggle, and Dylan grips my hand.

"It's the battle of the Elvises." Rachel's voice turns ominous. "Jacob Elordi, Austin Butler, Bruno Mars... GO!"

"Bruno Mars?" I frown. "When did he..."

"He was an Elvis impersonator as a little kid." Allie explains. "He was so cute. He was this little bitty—"

"The clock's ticking, Bookish Spice," Rachel fusses.

"I'm not entirely sold on that nickname." Allie frowns. "It sounds kind of boring."

"You're the sexy librarian." Dylan waggles her eyebrows as she quickly writes her answers. "Take off your glasses, let down your hair, and... Done!"

"I should start wearing glasses," Allie muses, quickly folding her sheet of paper.

Rachel isn't far behind, and she and Liv put down their pens and finish their cups.

"Dang, y'all are fast!" I'm still staring at my blank sheet.

"Just write anything." Allie gives me a hip-check as she refills everyone's red Solo cups. "There are no wrong answers."

My lips twist, and I quickly scribble down the names as Rachel yells time.

"Me first!" Dylan bounces on her toes.

"Shouldn't it be Rachel first, since she's the bride-to-be?" Liv catches her sister-in-law around the waist.

"Let's read them all together," Rachel suggests, and I wait as they all read them out.

"Fuck Jacob, Marry Bruno, Kill Austin." Dylan cries, which starts the debate.

"I'm having a hard time with the name Austin," Allie complains. "I can't do any of these things without thinking of my son."

"It's a *game*, Allie," Dylan leans into her. "You're not really doing it."

"Okay, I have to know…" Leaning forward, I grab a handful of pizza rolls. Purple drink is sneaky, and I'd better eat something before I'm drunk. "Did you name your son after that old TV show?"

"I was eighteen!" Allie cries, her face turning bright red. "It was my favorite show!"

"Oh, my God, you did?" Liv collapses into laughter against Rachel's back.

"I knew it!" I hold up my glass for a cheer.

"My turn, my turn…" Dylan leans against the bar, grabbing a toast point. "Vin Diesel, Paul Walker, The Rock."

"Ooo, *Fast & Furious* edition." My eyes widen, and I quickly write my answer.

"See, you're getting the hang of it." She elbows me, folding her sheet in half.

The final grains slip through the plastic hourglass, and Rachel calls time.

Holding up my hand, I announce the correct answer. "Fuck The Rock, marry Paul Walker, kill Vin Diesel."

More screams break out, and Allie says I've got it all backwards. Liv is on my side, but Rachel and Dylan both marry The Rock.

"It's a valid choice," I concede. "But I'm a sucker for blue eyes."

"I know you are." Dylan pokes my side, and we fall against each other.

The party continues with the purple drink flowing. We eat all the finger foods and argue over whether to marry or fuck Jensen Ackles or Milo Ventimiglia. We're all united in killing Zac Efron. Poor Zac.

Both Hemsworths go in the fuck category, since there's not a third hot one, and halfway through the night, Dylan, Rachel, and Allie's phones all go off at the same time.

"Are you kidding me?" Liv turns wide eyes on me. "We're *still* not in the family group chat?"

"I have an iPhone!" I hold up my device. "It's easy to add me."

"It's Jack," Allie explains. "He always pulls up the old thread by mistake."

We crowd around Dylan's iPad, watching as Logan drags Zane to a chair in the middle of the dance floor at the bar where they're having the bachelor party.

Zane tries to object, but we hear Logan say if he had to do it, Zane does, too.

Then the lights change to disco, and "Pony" by Ginuwine starts playing. We all scream as Garrett and Craig dance out in their blond wigs. They're both in sequined halter tops, and they move their hips in time like exotic dancers.

Zane drops his head forward like he's about to be killed by firing squad, and his brother gives him a lap dance while Craig runs his fingers through his long, dark hair.

Rachel wipes tears from her eyes as she laughs, but Dylan

and I both scream when Hendrix saunters out. He's not wearing a wig, but his shirt is off and his jeans hug his ass and legs so well, I have to fan myself.

He turns his back to his brother and bends forward, shaking his ass in his face. Naturally, Zane pushes his brother's butt with his foot, but Hendrix is prepared, catching himself in a push-up and doing a smooth, arching lift off the floor like a real exotic dancer.

"That was hot as those toast points," I say, still waving my hand in front of my face.

"My brother's got moves!" Dylan does a little hip shake, and I can't argue.

He turns around, dancing off the stage, and while Garrett and Craig are hilarious, Hendrix is pure sex. Or maybe that's just me speaking as the person sleeping with him.

"Oh, my gosh." Rachel collapses on the chair. "We'd better get some rest if we're going to be at the stables at ten."

"I'll bring hair of the dog!" Allie picks up the empty platters, and I help collect the cups and napkins, tossing them in the trash.

"You're going to die when you see what Clint did with the place," Rachel gushes. "It is absolutely gorgeous. I cried."

"He really is talented," Dylan adds. "He's getting more confident now, too."

The restaurant is cleaned, and we follow a weaving path together up the hill to the Bradford house.

"The ceremony will be in the alley between the stalls. The big doors will be open, and we'll face the green pasture. Everything is decorated with pine boughs and twinkle lights, and my bouquet is camellias and winter jasmine. He got those scented pine cones, so it smells amazing."

"It's almost Christmas," I wistfully note, thinking of the holiday just around the corner.

"I wish y'all would stay with us." Dylan rests her head on my shoulder. "Haddy needs to know her aunt Deedee."

"Hendrix has a game." My voice is quiet, and I think about how I'd like to spend Christmas with him.

It's so close. Even though it's past our three-month limit, I wonder if he'd be okay with that. I think he would.

Dylan and Rachel are settled at the house. Austin picks up Allie and me, driving me to the hotel before taking his mom home.

When I get to our room, Haddy is asleep in her crib, and her daddy is breathing heavily from the bed. I quickly wash my face and slip between the sheets beside him. Thinking about his sexy moves on the dance floor, I press my lips against his warm skin.

Without hesitation, he turns, cupping my cheeks and pulling my mouth to his for a hungry kiss.

We don't speak. We don't question the way my legs part, the way he moves above me, the way our bodies come together like it's the most natural thing in the world.

His hands are on each side of me on the mattress, and as he rocks his hips, sending his cock deeper into my slippery core, I slide my hands up his muscled arms.

I remember the way he moved on the dance floor, rolling like a wave on the ocean, and a moan slips from my parted lips. I grip his shoulders, lifting my back so I can trace my lips along the lines of his chest.

My tongue slides over his salty skin. I press my teeth against his hard muscles, causing him to groan deeply. Arching my back, I meet his movements, taking him even deeper.

He stretches me, caresses me, sends me straight to the edge. It's a primal dance, so basic between a man and a woman, a husband and a wife.

He's mine. I'm his.

We get closer to the end and our movements become feverish. We moan and kiss, chasing our release, and when it happens, I'm more sure than ever this is how it's meant to be.

Chapter 26

Hendrix

THE BARN SPARKLES WITH WHITE LIGHTS, AND WEDDING GUESTS flood the dance floor as the reception continues past twilight.

Leaning against a sturdy wooden beam, I watch our friends dancing to the music. Gloria and Sandra are the owners and partners here at Second Chance Stables. They gave Zane a place to heal when he came back angry and injured. Craig, who I haven't seen enough on this visit, and his wedding-planner-boyfriend Clint groove together.

I don't know a whole lot about weddings, but this one seems custom-designed for Zane and Rachel's quiet, smoldering romance.

Standing beside Jack and Garrett, watching Zane look so intensely into Rachel's green eyes as he recites his vows, watching her hold him so close after their kiss, I'm really kind of gratified my loner older brother has found his person.

I like how Rachel's floor-length dress has a square neck and a lace skirt that hangs in three layers down the front. I think

Raven would look beautiful in something like that. She's so pretty in white.

Rachel's bouquet of white and red flowers is one of the biggest I've ever seen. Raven said they're camellias and white jasmine, and they smell really good. Hell, the whole place smells really good, like Christmas.

A wreath of flowers is woven into her blonde hair, similar to how Raven wore her hair at our wedding, and as pretty as my brother's ceremony is, with the horses hanging their heads over the stalls like they're taking part in it, I think our wedding at the courthouse was just as special.

I know for sure my ladies were just as beautiful. A little smile crosses my lips as I remember Haddy in her cute white dress trying to get that wreath off her head. Raven's eyes were so scared when they met mine, but I had it all under control, rings and everything.

My brothers and I wear traditional black suits, but the bridesmaids wear floor-length, pale green dresses with different styles up top. Raven is the hottest in her off-the-shoulder gown. It's my favorite look on her.

Her dark hair hangs in soft waves, and the way that top moves, I have to distract my thoughts from her luscious breasts.

Last night, I'd meant to stay up and wait for her, but I must've dozed after getting Haddy to sleep. Waking to her warm lips pressing against my skin, I didn't hesitate. I took her.

It was so easy, so fundamental, like breathing or walking or catching a perfectly thrown spiral when I'm wide open in the end zone and ready to score.

Complete satisfaction.

The final bridesmaids photo is taken with all the girls surrounding Rachel under the arch near the open back doors. The pale moon is just visible in the light blue sky. Garrett lifts Gigi out of Liv's arms, and I watch as Dylan runs to Raven to take Haddy.

My sister hasn't stopped holding Haddy since we got here, and I know she's trying to get in all her auntie time before we leave for Atlanta in the morning. Dylan loves her family so hard. I try to play it off, but I always feel guilty when it's time to go.

Watching the whole scene, Raven holding hands with Liv and laughing with my family, the thought of a brief separation and a quickie divorce grinds my jaw. It's all wrong, and it just doesn't make sense.

"Hey, bro, you okay?" Garrett walks up to where I'm standing, holding a beer, and thinking all these thoughts.

Clearing them away, I smile, nodding. "Dylan hasn't put Haddy down since we got here."

My brother laughs, and his little girl wraps her chubby fingers around his bow tie, intent on putting it in her mouth. Gigi has strawberry-blonde hair like Liv's, but she has Garrett's big blue eyes. It's how you know Haddy's her cousin—all the Bradford boys have them.

He laughs, following my line of sight to our sister.

"You know I like messing with you, but seriously. Isn't this the best thing in the world?" He puts his hand on his baby daughter's back. "Did you ever think you could love someone this much? I mean, Liv is the love of my life, but Gigi's something different."

I can't argue with him. "It's pretty life-changing."

"This little lady depends on me." He kisses her head, and she pulls his now-untied tie into her mouth. "I catch myself having pretty ferocious thoughts when I think somebody might try to hurt her or make her feel bad."

"You always stood up for the underdog. Look what you did for Craig."

"That's what I mean. Kids can be really shitty in school." He shakes his head. "I'd better not hear about it."

Chuckling, I nod. "I'm pretty sure Liv knows this about you."

"Speaking of school, you were a jock, but you were really smart. You always made straight *As*." Squinting up at him, I wonder what he's getting at. "Maybe you could work with Jack, be his assistant coach and teach... I don't know... something."

Shaking my head, I look down. "I'm not interested in being a teacher."

"Logan would put you on the air in a heartbeat. You're a natural at sports radio."

My throat tightens, and I look up at him, doing his best to give me options to move home. "I'm not ready to retire, Grizz. I still love the game."

"I know." He nods, exhaling a laugh. "You want to play until you're too old to run. I remember. But maybe one day you'll want to be closer to family. Just letting you know, we have a lot of fun. You wouldn't be sitting around watching the grass grow."

Raven gives Dylan a hug, and her eyes meet mine. She smiles, walking to where I'm standing with my brother, and I nod, blinking up at him.

"Thanks, man. I believe you."

This little town where we lived all our lives surrounded by people who knew and loved us has a lot to offer. If only I knew how to make it enough for me.

"It's nice to meet you at last, Mr. Bradford." Jeffrey Harrison Gale shakes my hand, and a heavy Rolex watch slides down his wrist.

After all the drama of saying goodbye to my family this morning, which included tears and hugs and kisses from Dylan and more hugs and pictures and promises to FaceTime every day and "stop being such a stranger, Hendrix," we made the drive to Raven's father's estate just south of Atlanta.

I gotta say, it's a lot bigger than I expected. Hell, this place makes Miss Gina's mansion on the bluffs look like somebody's fishing camp.

Raven said her family had money, but this is a ten-foot-tall, wrought-iron gates at the end of the driveway, massive fountain in a circle drive, tall columns at the door, and even a marble foyer with a table holding a bowl of roses as big as something you'd see in a hotel lobby mansion.

I've been to grand estates like this for charity events in Hollywood, but I honestly didn't expect this to be Raven's scene. She's so down to earth—and cheap.

I remember the time she was so excited to find a pack of ten tube socks for a dollar at the Safeway. Then she got a twelve-pack of Jolt cola from the dollar store. I didn't even know they made that shit anymore.

She showed them to me like she'd found buried treasure. Treasure nobody wanted, I pointed out.

"It's nice to meet you, sir." I stand straighter, wishing I'd worn my blazer over my short-sleeved navy T-shirt and jeans.

Raven is as casual as I am in an off-the-shoulder burgundy sweater, leggings, and brown Uggs. Haddy is wearing her *On Sunday, we watch football* onesie with pink baby joggers. As usual, she's taking in the whole scene with big eyes, a pacifier, and Axel in her grip.

My muscles are tense, and I'm ready to go protective daddy-bear at the first sign of trouble.

A man about my age stands behind Raven's dad watching us with a scowl. His dark hair is smoothed back from his face, and a gold chain peeks over the collar of his gray sweater. He's wearing a pinky ring.

Not that I'm judging. I'm not much of a jewelry guy, but some of the fellows on the team are into it. What I don't like is the way his brown eyes follow Raven's every move like he has some ownership stake in her.

"Raven." Her dad steps forward, putting both hands on her upper arms and kissing her cheek. "You look good."

"I am, Dad." Her voice is bright and strong. "I'm very good."

I'd like to think I have something to do with that, but I imagine inheriting six million dollars helps.

"May I see your ring?" He takes her hand before she can answer, and his tone rises. "That's *it*? You can get that for fifty dollars at an outlet store."

My chest tightens, and, *Fuck me—again!*

I was so proud of myself for remembering to bring rings to our ceremony. Now I feel like a cheap, unromantic asshole.

"We decided quickly," Raven sputters. "Anyway, it's not about the ring. It's about me doing what I want to do, and Haddy being healthy and happy and getting to know her dad…"

"Doing what you want to do," her dad huffs. "Chasing down hurricanes? Doing your best to stand still in a windstorm as trees fly past your head? That's what you want to do?"

His challenging tone sends a surge of adrenaline through my chest, but Raven lifts her chin, not the least bit shaken by his attitude.

"I haven't exactly been doing those things, but I'm getting there."

"When you could be here, working in a plush office space in Atlanta, making a good salary with your family around you." He exhales a huff. "It doesn't make any sense, Biscuit."

My jaw clenches, but Raven beats me to the punch.

"Please don't call me that." Her voice is sharp, and he throws up a hand like she's being impossible. "I see you have Larry by your side, as always."

"I heard you were coming into town." Lawrence Calder O'Halloran stops lurking and steps forward to join the conversation. "I take it this is *him*."

My eyes clash with his dark ones, and I nod.

"Hendrix Bradford." I extend a hand. I'm not afraid of this guy, and I don't like the way he's looking at my wife. "I'm Raven's husband."

"Lawrence O'Halloran." He places his hand in mine, and I give it a nice firm, *back the fuck up* squeeze.

He winces, and I'm ready to go, when a sweet voice I recognize from their weekly FaceTime calls interrupts the face-off.

"Raven! Haddeeee!" Amelia calls, and Haddy starts to squeal when the younger woman races into the room.

"Mimi!" Raven grabs her sister, and they hug each other so tightly, swaying side to side. "Oh my goodness. I've missed you so much."

Raven laughs, and they both wipe tears from their smiling eyes.

"Give me my baby girl!" Amelia takes our daughter from Raven, squeezing her and swaying side to side.

Haddy squeals and talks baby talk, patting her shoulders like she's reuniting with an old friend. Amelia is a little taller than Raven and skinny, but they have the same amber eyes.

"She has *teeth*!" She blinks at her sister then at me. "And... Hendrix? Is that really you?"

"Nice to meet you in person." I smile, reaching out to shake her hand, but she skips forward and hugs me.

"It's so nice to meet you!" Her hand is on my chest, and at least somebody in this house is friendly and warm. "I've missed my Haddy boo-boo so much. She's just my little squishy baby—yes, she is!"

Mimi wrinkles her nose, shaking her head in Haddy's face, and my daughter lets out the loudest squeal. I chuckle, but her grandfather recoils.

"Honestly, Amelia." He puts a hand on his chest. "Must you make her scream like that?"

"She's just happy, Pappy!"

"Don't call me Pappy."

"You got it, Pops!"

"Amelia." His tone is sharp, but neither of his daughters seem particularly intimidated by the tall, elderly gentleman before me.

I'm not completely sold on the guy, but their attitudes soften me. Still, I remember what Raven said about her mother, how she used to be treated, and how her father never stood up for her. So while he might be okay eventually, I'm ready to have her back when she needs me.

Amelia, on the other hand, leans into Raven. "I'll take her to my room so y'all can do whatever you need to do. Come find me."

Raven slides her hand down Haddy's little arm, passing the purple bag to her sister then turning to face her father again. "How have *you* been, Dad?"

His expression relaxes as Amelia leaves with the baby, and he takes a step toward the large window at the back of the room.

"I've been better," he sniffs. "I know you aren't interested in what we do here, but you could come around a little more. At least you could call once in a while. Pretend to care."

Her gaze slides to mine, and I can tell she's holding back an eye roll. *Pity-party much?* "I do care, Dad. I just don't like being manipulated."

"Who's manipulating you?" His tone is offended. "Is it manipulation for a father to want the best for his daughter? Is it manipulation to want my family close in my old age?"

Her jaw tightens, and I take a step forward, between them. "It's true, my job keeps her away from home." Clearing my throat, I put my hand on Raven's shoulder. "But Raven talks about you and this place all the time. She cares about her family."

It's not a lie. She's told me things about him, things she wished she didn't care about, and it seriously pissed me off. I'm ready to find my baby girl and take them both out of here, but I'm trying to let Raven lead—at least until her business is settled.

The man's brown eyes search my face, and he takes a beat. "I've watched you play, young man. You're very talented."

"Thank you."

"I believe I read you're originally from south Alabama?"

"Yes, sir."

"Perhaps you'll consider moving back to this area in the future."

My brow lowers. "Eventually, I'm sure I'll move back to Newhope, but we're pretty set where we are."

Raven puts her hand on my arm. "Hendrix's career plans aren't up for discussion. We came here to settle my business, so if you would just let me know what I need to do…"

"I don't understand the rush." Her dad glances from her to me.

"Hendrix has a game, and I have work." I don't like her explaining herself to him.

I don't like this *manipulation*, which is exactly the right word regardless of how he tries to spin it. He should understand her needs and cooperate, make it easier not harder.

Instead, he walks over to the table where a few envelopes are lying. "Donald is the trustee. He'll want documentation that you've met the requirements your mother outlined…"

He glances up at Larry, whose expression is tight. Raven doesn't seem to notice, but I don't like these two exchanging glances. I don't like Larry's judgmental sneer.

I'm having a hard time not grabbing that guy by the collar and telling him to get the fuck out. *Why is he even here?*

"I sent the official papers to you and Donald three months ago," Raven notes.

"Yes, but he'll want to verify where you'd like the funds sent and other things, I don't know. He'll tell you."

Raven's lips twist, but she doesn't argue. "I assume he'll be in his office tomorrow?"

"I can have him come to the house if you'd like."

"I can go to him. I'd like to wrap this up as soon as possible."

"Of course," he huffs. "You can never get out of here fast enough, can you?"

Her shoulders drop, and she crosses the space. She puts a hand on her father's chest and gentles her tone. "I love you, Dad. I'm just not interested in being a jeweler."

"Trust me, you've made that abundantly clear."

Her lips press into a frustrated half-smile, and she rises onto her toes to kiss his cheek. "I'm sorry we don't see eye to eye on this, but I hope one day you'll understand."

"We had a plan, Raven Lorrain."

"*You* had a plan, Dad. I was never consulted on it." She returns to where I'm standing. "Let's find Amelia. I want to see my baby."

"I'll be right behind you."

She walks out at a pace that I recognize as anger, and I turn to the two men watching her go. Their eyes meet mine, and I take a step forward.

"I don't know what's going on here, and I appreciate that we've just met. But I'm going to make one thing clear, and I won't say it again." My voice is quiet but firm, and I like that I'm at least an inch taller than both of them. "Raven is my wife, and while she's clearly strong enough to stand up to you, I don't like her being made to. So listen up, I'm not going to stand around while you play with her emotions and *manipulate* her." I hit the word hard. "And if I hear either one of you call her Biscuit again, you're going to wish you hadn't. You got me?"

Her father's dark brown eyes narrow, and he places a hand on his midsection, sliding it down his blazer. My shoulders are bowed, and I'm at the point now where I wish one of them would test me.

After several seconds, he lifts his chin and offers a simple "Understood."

Lawrence Calder O'Halloran scowls, falling back. "I've heard enough."

He turns and leaves quickly through the front door, but I stay a minute, holding her father's gaze and allowing him to assess my level of seriousness.

His lips quirk, and he nods, dropping his eyes and leaving me alone in the room.

Looking around, I wonder how the heck I'm going to find my girls in this four-story museum. A happy baby squeal gives me a hint.

Chapter 27

Raven

"He's always ready to pile on the guilt, isn't he?" Stomping around Amelia's old bedroom, I can't keep the frustrated growl out of my voice. "We had a plan…" I imitate my dad's pompous tone. "What about my plans? I have never, since Day 1, had a say in anything having to do with my life."

"At least you found a way out." Amelia lies on her stomach on the rug, bouncing Axel up to Haddy and booping her on the nose with him.

Haddy squeals and belly-laughs every time she does it, and it's the one thing strong enough to melt the anger in my chest. I've managed to shield my baby girl—and clearly my little sister—from their manipulations.

Hendrix leans against the wall with his muscled arms crossed like some protective god. Amused affection fills his eyes, and I imagine he's glad he dodged a bullet with this family after coming off the love-fest, party-bus of his own.

I walk over to kneel beside my sister on the floor. "Do you want to work in the family business, Mim?"

"I don't mind." She shrugs, pushing into a sitting position facing me. "I'm an accountant, so it'll just be one boring office or another. I'd rather work at a place where I know everybody and I can do what I want than be at a place that doesn't give a crap about me."

Reaching out, I slide a clump of dark curls behind her ear. "I'd argue this place doesn't give a crap about you."

"Aww, you're just grumpy. You know that's not true." She smiles up at me. "Dad loves you. He just wants all his little bitties under one roof."

"Where were those protective urges when Mom was alive?" I grumble, my eyes on Haddy chewing Axel's gill. "He never said a single word to her."

I can't fathom making my sweet daughter feel inferior or less than perfect. I notice Hendrix shift his stance, and I appreciate him holding back in there, letting me take the lead. I know it's not easy for him.

"I almost forgot this!" Amelia bounces to her feet, skipping over to the bed to grab a brand-new, baby blue axolotl with pink gills fanning around its head. "Meet Axelita! Sorry, I never mailed her to you. I got so busy and—"

"You don't have to apologize." I reach out to give her a hug. "You've been busy with school and having a social life, and Axelita is adorable."

"When are you coming back to give Jim Cantore a run for his money?" She wraps her arm around my waist. "I graduate in May. I can help you with Haddy now!"

"We almost moved you to LA to help with her." I give Hendrix a wink, and he smiles, walking over to us.

"You don't say?" Mimi tilts her head to the side. "LA, eh? That's pretty far from my family and friends. Don't you miss us?"

"I miss you a lot, but I'm having fun." Hendrix's eyes are on me, and I know he's listening closely to everything I say. "I'm making friends, mostly at the station, but I've met some of the wives, and they're nice. I'm happy."

"I've got your new alter ego!" Mimi nudges me, and I cringe. Hendrix knows nothing about my alter ego. "Liz Pantore!"

"Like Jim Cantore." His low chuckle joins the conversation. "I get it!"

"It's way better than Tasha Scarce." Amelia's nose wrinkles. "Who's—"

"It's just a game we used to play." I quickly cut off his question.

Her chin drops, and she's doing her best not to laugh. I could pinch her, when she rises to her feet.

"Tell you what. You two go out." She lifts Haddy off the floor, swinging her onto her hip. "I'll snuggle my baby boo-boo, and y'all can have a little date night."

Chewing my bottom lip, I glance up at Hendrix. Our eyes meet, and he's doing such a good job being the protective husband. He's already a great dad. He has no idea my sister knows everything about our arrangement.

"I like that idea." He steps up beside her, putting his hand on her shoulder.

She blinks up at him with a little swoon, and I'm about to pinch her again. I can tell she's up to something, but Hendrix reaches for my hand to help me up.

He's so gorgeous and confident and everything I want in a man, in a partner.

I take his hand, stepping into his side as I look at my sister. "Text me if you need anything."

"I won't need anything. Now scoot!" She flicks her fingers at us. "I'll put her to bed and everything. You officially have the night off."

"Thanks, sis." I step forward to kiss her cheek.

"Don't rule out LA so fast." Hendrix gives her a little point. "You might like it."

"Okay..." She leans her head against Haddy's, and I'm pretty sure I see hearts in her eyes.

Shaking my head, I follow him out of her bedroom. "See you later, alligator."

"After while, crocodile," she calls back.

The Peach Pit is an old townie bar just outside Peachtree City where my dad lives. It's the bar all the local kids frequent. As soon as you turn twenty-one, you head to the Pit for your first legal bender.

I'm sad to say I don't recognize a single face as we walk through the open space with its ancient booths lining the perimeter. Black metal tables surrounded by folding chairs are arranged in the center of the room, and neon beer signs hang on the walls.

A cluster of kids surrounds a pool table in the very back, but tonight, the front of the bar is filled with people. A makeshift stage is cleared in the front, and I see the poster on the wall announcing karaoke night.

"I put your name in." Hendrix walks up and places two beers on the round wooden table between us.

"Oh no!" I put a hand on top of my head. "Don't..."

"Too late." He grins, leaning closer to kiss my temple before speaking in my ear. "You're going to blow them away."

"I don't know about that." I look down at his strong forearms leaning on the counter beside me.

It's time. I know it's time, but I don't know how to start this conversation.

I can't find a gentle segue from all the things we've shared to "it's time to say goodbye." I'm not even sure I even want to.

But I promised...

The music changes to a familiar keyboard and drums intro,

and I glance to the front to see a young man holding the microphone. There's a spoken word part, and my skin prickles as he begins to sing "End of the Road" by Boys II Men.

My chest tightens. A knot is in my throat, and I look up at my husband. It's the stupidest, perfect theme for what I'm about to say, and while I'm afraid, confidence is all over his features.

"It's the first moment we've had alone since our flight here." He reaches across the table for me.

My gaze lowers to his large hand covering my left one. "Sorry, I slept the entire drive here from Atlanta."

I'm not sorry.

He continues, "Feels like we've been holding our breath all weekend, when we have this decision hanging over our heads." Our eyes meet, and his thumb slides across my fingers, turning the gold band on my third one. "What's going on in that pretty head of yours, Pink?"

It's a teasing question, but my throat is so tight.

I struggle to inhale, to swallow the pain as I say the words. "I think, for better or worse, all our family is here. They want us to come home, and I want Haddy to know them. The only thing is…"

A sad smile curls his lips. "The only thing in LA is me."

It's not exactly what I was going to say as I study the gold band shining in the glow of the Yuengling sign. "You're a big thing, a very important thing. But I know, being married and having a family isn't what you want."

His brow furrows, and his thumb stills on my hand. "Is that really what you think?"

"It's what you said," I whisper as the guy sings. *Still, I can't let go…* "It's what we agreed."

Hendrix steps around the table, standing in front of me. He looks down, smiling with so much emotion. Emotion I want to believe is love.

"Then why are there tears in your eyes?" His voice is low.

If I blink, they'll spill onto my cheeks. *It's unnatural...*

"There are?"

"I know you better than that, Pink."

The song fades out, and the DJ's voice is on the microphone calling my name. My chin quivers, and I look over to where he's holding it out to me.

"That was fast." I do my best to dry my eyes.

"I tipped him twenty bucks."

The intro saxophone and drum beat for "Good Morning, Baltimore" begins, and I walk forward, taking the mic and losing myself in the song I know by heart.

It's a song of optimism and defiance, of believing in dreams and not letting anyone hold you down.

I belt it out, losing my sadness in the joyful words, and when I look around, several kids in the crowd are singing along with me. A girl and a few guys stand on the edge of the makeshift stage, doing the dance from the show.

When we get to the chorus, they sing it loud with me, and for a moment, everything fades away like it always did—my mom's cruel words, Larry's echoing backup, my powerlessness, the ache of wanting to leave and feeling trapped.

In that song, I'm strong and fierce, and the crowd is behind me. No one can say we're not good enough.

I sing the final words, and everyone cheers and holds up their hands for high-fives. I'm smiling as I walk off the stage, after handing the mic to the DJ, who gives me a thumbs-up.

My smile melts when I see Larry standing at a table not far from where Hendrix is walking up to greet me.

"I love it." Hendrix gives me a hug. "You're a superstar."

"Thanks." I'm a little breathless, shielded by his strong body, but when he straightens, I can't ignore the man standing beside us. "Larry? What are you doing here?"

"That massive talent." His voice isn't exactly congratulatory. "I remember when your mother chose that song for you."

I do, too. Vividly. She said it was to "match my new look."

"She hoped it would embarrass me." My voice is sharp, and I lift my chin. "Too bad it backfired. It's a great song, and it's perfect for my voice and my range."

"She killed it." Hendrix stands beside me with his arm around my shoulder.

Larry scowls at him. "I know all about you and this fake arrangement. I hired a private detective the minute you sent that marriage certificate. I know it was only for the money. There's no way a guy like you would marry someone like her."

He says *her* in a tone that catches me off guard. Shame burns in my chest, and I'm too thrown to argue.

Good thing I don't have to. Hendrix's arm is off me in a flash, and he steps into Larry's space. "We discussed this, *Lawrence*. Is this really what you want to do right now?"

Unbelievably, Larry doesn't back down.

"You ruined everything," he hisses angrily. "I was supposed to marry you, not him. That was the plan. Half of that trust fund belongs to *me*! It was *our* wedding present from your mother."

"Wait a minute." I grab Hendrix's arm, pulling him to the side, so I can get in Larry's face. "She wanted me to marry *you*? Why? So you could take over demeaning me for the rest of my life?"

"You are mine, Biscuit." It's a whiny shout, and Hendrix grips his upper arm.

"That's it." He practically lifts Larry off his feet, dragging him to the front door of the bar and out into the parking lot.

I jog after them holding my hand out, unsure what's about to happen. Hendrix shoves him in the direction of the parked cars, and Larry stumbles before regaining his balance.

"I told you never to call her Biscuit." Hendrix's voice is angry.

"Fuck you, Mr. Football Star." Larry staggers forward, actually stupid enough to get closer. "Mr. Johnny-come-lately. You think you're special? Anyone can get a girl pregnant. It just makes you careless. Irresponsible. I know your type."

"You don't know shit," Hendrix snaps. "I love her. I want to build a life with her. What do you want?"

"Oh!" My heart jumps in my chest, and I take a step back, my eyes fixed on my husband.

"You call that love?" Larry shouts. "You want her to be average. I want her to be great. Her mother saw it, and I see it. She lacks discipline. She's lazy, and she overeats when she—"

Hendrix grips the front of his jaw and slams him back against our rented Range Rover SUV. "Shut your idiot mouth before I break it. Raven is smart and focused. She's caring and fierce. She's the sexiest woman alive, and I wouldn't live in your world where everyone looks the same and every woman is starving and miserable for one second, let alone a lifetime."

"I want what's best for her," Larry argues.

Hendrix leans into his face. "If you know what's best, you'd better get the fuck out of here before I kick your ass so hard, you spit leather."

The entire karaoke crowd is outside the bar, and I look around at all the phones on us. I count at least ten kids recording videos, and I can't let Hendrix get into trouble for defending me.

Rushing forward, I catch his arm. "We need to go. They're all watching."

"Let them watch." He shoves Larry with both hands, and the loser staggers backwards, falling against another car before landing on his butt in the dirt.

Hendrix takes a step forward, and with a little yelp, Larry turns onto all fours and quickly crawls away like the coward he is.

For a moment, I watch Hendrix's broad shoulders heaving, then when he turns to me, his blue eyes are blazing.

He's vibrating with adrenaline, and when he closes the space between us, my skin prickles with heat. My body is on fire, and I want to climb him like a tree.

"I'm finished talking, Pink. You're coming home with me." His hands are on my arms, and he looks straight into my eyes.

"Garrett said it's not my show, but it is my family. You're my wife. Haddy's my daughter, and we're staying together."

My heart swells bigger with every word he speaks. "For Haddy?"

His chin drops, and he nods. "For Haddy…" His eyes hold mine again. "And for you and me. I love you, Pink."

I hiccup a breath and hot tears hit my cheeks. "But you love football…"

"Fuck, Raven, I love you more than football."

"But the team needs you…"

"And I need you more."

A sob breaks through my throat, and I quickly wipe the tears off my face. My emotions are flying. "Are you sure?"

The fierce expression tensing his brow breaks, and he smiles, putting his hands on my cheeks. "Remember when we watched that movie about how men and women can't be friends?" I nod, and he continues. "It's like that guy said—when you realize what you want for the rest of your life, you want the rest of your life to start right away."

"I'm not sure that's what he said."

"Then I'll say it." He glances at all the people and shakes his head. "I love how you get up early to make drop biscuits for me, even when they remind you of an idiot who teased you and made your life miserable."

"You reclaimed them for us." I sniff, my chest squeezing with every word.

"I love how you make me watch all those crazy old movies I don't care about, then I end up liking them."

"I knew you would, though."

"I love the way you sing 'Good Morning, Baltimore' to our daughter, and how you never throw away the first pancake."

"It's wasteful…"

"I love that you used *Driving Miss Daisy* to try and distract me from how sexy you are and how much I wanted to fuck you."

Stepping forward, I put my forehead against his chest. "You remember everything."

"I'll never forget that I didn't hold you when you were sick."

The regret in his voice tugs my chest. "You never left our door."

"I never should've left *you*." He cups my cheeks, lifting my face and catching my tears with his thumbs. "I know you have dreams, but I have dreams too. It's to wake up every morning with you by my side. It's to go to bed every night with you in my arms. It's to hold your hair when you're sick and fuck your brains out when you're horny."

"Hendrix…" My voice breaks as more tears come. "My heart…"

He leans down to kiss my lips. "You saved me, Pink. I didn't know how lonely I was until you came crashing into my life. You taught me to love. You showed me how to take care of another person. Give me a little time, and I'll help you save the world."

"Oh…" I sniff, holding his shirt.

"What do you say?" His pretty blue eyes are so wide, so vulnerable, as he waits for my reply. "Will you give me time to make your dreams come true?"

"You already have." Reaching up, I hold his neck.

"Let's stay together, Pink." He pulls me into his chest, pressing his lips to my forehead. "Let's keep our family together."

I'm nodding before I can get the words out.

Chapter 28

Hendrix

"YOU DESERVE A BLOW JOB FOR THAT SPEECH." My wife's hand creeps across the console from where she sits in the passenger's side of the Rover I rented for our drive to Atlanta.

Her fingers trace the growing bulge in my jeans, and I shift at the tingling sensation. "This looks like a good place to park."

I pull the vehicle behind a large structure at the back of her family's estate and slam it into park. Quickly shrugging out of the seatbelt, I reach across the space, placing my fingers behind her neck and pulling her full lips closer to mine.

"As much as the thought of that sexy mouth sucking my cock has me hard as a fucking rock, I'd rather eat your pussy until you're calling me God again, then fuck you til you can't walk."

Her amber eyes blink fast at my words, and her breath catches.

"Sound good?" My brow arches, and I lean closer to trace my lips along the line of her jaw into her hair.

"I think I just had an orgasm," she whispers.

A smile curls my lips, and I reach down for the button on the side of her chair, lowering the back so it's almost flat. "Get those leggings off. Now."

She does as I say, and I remove my jeans at the same time. My cock is so hard, I need some relief. Bending down, I hook my arm under her thigh, lifting it open so I can drag my tongue along her clit.

Her hips jump, and she moans as her fingers thread in my hair. She's juicy and sweet, and I give her a few more passes with my tongue, a few more concentrated sucks, to get her right to the edge. Then I shift my body, moving my chair forward, so we can climb into the backseat.

"Come on, babe." I reach for her. "Get back here and ride me."

She sits up and follows me across the console, straddling my lap and lifting her ass so I can line up with her core. Our faces are close, and our mouths seal together.

Tongues curl and taste. We're salt and freshwater, and we smell like flowers and vanilla and sex. I lift my hips, and she drops, taking me all the way into her tight, gripping heat.

My head falls back with a groan, and she leans forward, holding the headrest behind me.

"Fuck, yeah," I hiss, shoving her sweater higher.

Her arms raise quickly so I can lift it over her head, and my hands cup her breasts, wrapped in black lace. She grips the seat again, rocking her hips back and forth over my cock, taking me deeper as I shove her bra higher.

Her breasts spill out, and I pull them into my mouth. Lifting, biting, sucking, her tits are all around me as she rides, chasing her orgasm and blowing my mind.

My cock thickens, and I feel my control slipping. Her lips are at my ear, and I hear her pants and moans as her pussy grips and massages me. I'm lost in sensation, doing my best to wait and go with her, but I'm not sure I can.

"That's right," I gasp, gripping her ass and moving her faster on my waist. "I love the way you ride my cock. You're so fine."

She kisses my ear, my neck, and her low moans grow in urgency as she moves faster.

Spreading her cheeks, I slip my finger into her ass, and she jumps with a little wail. I press, using it to pull her forward, and her pussy clenches.

Another back and forth, and she breaks into spasms. Her thighs shudder, and her body jerks as she comes on my cock. It's so damn sexy.

"Fuck me," I groan, letting go of my orgasm.

I lift my hips thrusting again and again until the mind-altering pleasure explodes through my pelvis. I hold, letting it pulse into her.

She's leaning forward, still gasping and shuddering, and I wrap my arms around her waist.

"You are so fucking gorgeous, Pink."

Her head lifts, and silky dark hair falls around us. Her mouth covers mine, and we chase each other's kisses, tongues sliding out and in, lips moving from cheeks to jaw to lips again.

Another pulse of orgasm moves through my dick, and I groan.

Delicate hands cup my cheeks, and she meets my eyes. "No one's ever said those things about me before."

"Which ones?" I study her pretty amber eyes, so earnest.

"The things you said to Larry."

"That fucking dickhead." My teeth clench, and I wrap her tighter in my embrace. "I meant every word. You're the most beautiful woman in the world."

"I worked hard to grow past their judgment. It took a while, and sometimes I still fall back into old thoughts." Her cheek is next to mine, and I kiss her neck. "It's nice to have someone else on my side."

"I'm always on your side." Reaching up, I smooth her hair back from her face. "If we hadn't had an audience…"

"I love you, Hendrix." She blinks, shy as she says the words that send me over the moon.

"I love you, Raven." My thumb is on her full bottom lip, her chin. "There's not an average bone in your body."

She leans closer, kissing the side of my cheek as she moves her hips. "You're right. It's an exceptional bone."

My stomach tightens, and I bark a laugh. "It's going to be in your ass when I get you home."

A little moan comes from her throat, and she kisses my ear. "That's motivation to get back to LA."

"Let's get to bed. I want to fuck you a few more times then get up early, get our baby, and get out of here."

"Me too," she sighs, leaning her head against mine.

Donald Becker's law office is in the heart of downtown Atlanta, overlooking a landscaped courtyard between three tall buildings.

After Amelia's tearful goodbye at her father's mansion that rivaled anything Dylan might do to make me feel like shit for leaving, we drove here to finalize the paperwork and have Raven's trust transferred into her name.

My chest was tight the entire drive, watching my pretty wife dabbing tears from her eyes and rationalizing going back to LA with me and leaving her family behind.

We had a pretty amazing night, but I don't want her getting cold feet on me now. I've always been pretty confident in my effect on women, but at the moment, I'm glad to have our baby girl on my hip, tilting the scales a bit in my favor.

Donald sits across from us behind his desk, and he's reading off the controlling terms of her mother's trust while sliding the documentation into the folder showing compliance.

"I don't know why I'm nervous." Raven's voice is quiet, and I reach out to hold her hand.

"You got this, babe." I give her a squeeze, and she gives me a brief, sweet smile.

As much as I know about her early life, I can't imagine the emotions she's wrestling with right now. This document was meant to hold her down. She was ready to walk away, but instead, she turned the tables for our daughter.

"It's all pretty standard procedure." Her family's lawyer takes a sheet out of the folder and slides it across the shiny desktop to her. "If all of this is correct, sign the highlighted blank at the bottom, and my secretary will wire the money to your account."

I've arranged for Raven to meet with the guy who does all my financial planning when we get back to LA, but for now, her money will go into a regular bank account.

Her full bottom lip disappears into her mouth, and she studies the sheet. "It's all correct."

A wobble is in her voice, and I can't tell if it's nerves or something else.

I watch as she signs, and Haddy chews the little fan thingie on the side of Axel's head. Or is this Axelita? I can't tell.

"I've got your marriage certificate here, which fulfills your obligation." Donald stands, closing the folder and reaching across the desk. "Congratulations, you're officially a millionaire."

"Minus taxes, of course," Raven deflects, standing and tucking her purse under her arm.

"Actually, there is no inheritance tax in the state of Georgia." He walks around the desk to where we stand, nodding at me. "Or the state of California for that matter. By all accounts, you're a rich woman. You don't need anyone anymore."

Raven's eyes drift to the window, and I wish we were on the jet headed back to my place. I want to argue everybody needs somebody. I want to tell her we need her.

I want her to tell me what she's thinking.

Donald puts his hand on her shoulder. "Your mother was a hard woman. It's how she was raised, and I guess it's what she thought was right."

My wife's chin drops, and she looks over at Haddy and me then back to him. "I don't know what she thought, but it's over now."

The older man's lips tighten with a smile. "You've always been strong, even as a little girl. I've never worried about you."

Raven's smile doesn't reach her eyes, and she hesitates before simply saying, "Thank you."

We're out on the street when she finally breaks. "I was strong, so no one ever fought for me? Is that the message here?" She shakes her head, walking ahead of me on the sidewalk. "Strong people need someone to lean on, too, you know."

My legs are longer than hers, but I still have to do a quick step to catch up with her. "Hey, slow down a minute."

"He never protected me." She stops, looking up at me, and I see the glisten in her eyes. It hits me right in the chest, and I pull her into my arms, wrapping her up tight and holding her close. "He stood by and let her do all these things, and not once…"

Her voice breaks, and I kiss the top of her head.

"I'll always have your back, Pink. Anywhere you go, whatever you face, I'm here. I'm your husband, and I'm fighting on your side… And Haddy's. I protect my family."

One more shudder, and her body melts into mine. Her arms go around my waist, and the tension in my chest eases. She's mine. It's the most precious gift I've ever been given—besides Haddy.

The air around us is cool, but our embrace is strong and warm. It's bonding, and if I had my way, it would go on longer… But our daughter starts to wiggle, making squeals and raspberry noises, and we both laugh.

Raven turns her head, kissing her little face. "That's right, Hads. We're a family." Her chin lifts, and she meets my eyes. "You, your daddy, and me."

"And maybe a little brother or sister." I put my arm around her shoulder as we walk slowly to the rented Rover.

"Let's get this one out of diapers first."

"That wasn't a no…"

Chapter 29

Raven

"I THOUGHT YOU WERE GOING HOME FOR A WEDDING, NOT TO SET the Internet on fire." Star leans beside me, staring at my phone.

"It was... I mean, we were." My voice fades as I swipe through video after video of men and women breathlessly breaking down Hendrix and Larry's encounter in the parking lot.

"It's every woman's dream to have a husband who will fight for her." A woman called @hoosierdaddy spends three whole minutes extolling the virtues of an overprotective spouse and Hendrix's pretty awesome speech about staying together.

"He's a brute just like every other professional athlete, beating up a weaker man for looking at his girl wrong," a user named @captainchalupa argues.

"As if Hendrix wasn't already all over the news," she continues. "Now he's in the running for swooniest husband in the league."

"When they're not calling him a brute." My brow lowers, and I don't like Captain Chalupa.

At least the consensus seems to be he's a good husband, committed to his family and defending his wife from a body-shaming bully—which, as someone who was present for the whole thing, is what actually happened.

Still, those haters have my blood hot, not to mention the haters who say it's all my fault, and I provoked the whole thing.

"This @lizardsarelife person says I was having a secret affair with Larry all along." I tilt my phone in Star's direction. "Like he didn't show up at the bar saying Hendrix stole half his money, which was actually my inheritance."

"Ignore that." She waves a hand over my device. "There's always going to be some dummy ready to blame the woman for everything."

Exhaling a sigh, I'm ready to slide my phone into my pocket and take a break from the chatter when the next video pulls me up short. "Is that...?"

"Ew, Mikayla," Star groans, and we both stare at the screen.

"I can verify she has definitely changed him." The curvy brunette slides her stick-straight hair behind her shoulder, fluttering her caterpillar eyelashes like she's so bored with the world. "The Hendrix Bradford I knew would *never* get into a fight in a parking lot. Not once the entire time we were together did he even worry about another man. He's a lover, not a fighter."

My jaw drops, and I can't stop a laugh. "What is she even talking about?"

"I guess she doesn't realize how bad that makes her sound." Star leans in beside me. "He wouldn't fight for her."

"Lawrence O'Halloran has it right—she's definitely average," the woman continues. "She's a *weather girl* at KCLA? Who even watches KCLA?"

"Easy, bitch," Star laughs, turning wide eyes on me. "Now she's going after us!"

"Weather girls were actually enormous stars in the

mid-1950s." Wilt steps up to join the conversation, completely serious. "There was a time when Ms. Monitor was the most recognizable female voice in the country."

"I've never heard of her," I say.

"It's where the American Meteorological Society seal of approval comes from." He pulls out his wallet and produces a card showing his. "Weather girls weren't really about the weather. They sold sex and vacuum cleaners. The AMS did not approve, but it launched the careers of several stars like Gilda Radner, Diane Sawyer..."

"We should do a special segment about them!" Star clasps her hands, and I see the wheels turning. "You could host it, Raven, talk about how times have changed."

"I'm all for reclaiming another slur in my lifetime." I slide the phone into my pocket for real this time, done with the noise for the day. "I'm just glad it doesn't seem to be hurting Hendrix's standing in the league."

I would be devastated if all of this led to him being suspended from playing in the Super Bowl. He might love me more than football, but he still loves football.

"He didn't hit the guy, which I think shows a lot of restraint." Wilt walks around the traffic computer, crossing his arms. "If it were truly a roid rage, he'd have beat the shit out of that guy. Personally, I don't know what I'd have done if some man said those things about my wife."

"Wilt?" Tilting my head, I slant my eyes at him. "Are you saying Larry was wrong?"

"Of course, he was wrong." Wilt straightens like anyone would agree. "I can attest there is nothing average or lazy about you, Mrs. Bradford. I've worked with you too long."

My chest squeezes, and I step forward to put my hand on his arm. "Thank you, Wilt. That means a lot to me."

Clearing his throat, he turns to the screen. "Now, about these Santa Anas. They're not as strong this year as last, but it's early. Last year, we clocked winds up to sixty miles per hour."

My eyes widen. "That's as strong as a Cat-1 hurricane."

"And with less warning." Wilt casts me a glance. "Perhaps the weather here isn't as boring as you thought?"

"Perhaps."

Before we left for the wedding, he caught me on the phone with Amelia, complaining how my life in LA was a blur of activity everywhere but at work, where it was slow, slow, slow.

I know how to get everywhere in LA at any time of day and during any major event. I know more random meteorological facts than the encyclopedia Britannica...

Until now.

"We'll keep an eye on things. This time of year, we work closely with the fire department to try and help them get where they need to be." His jaw is tight. "We just got this special software that can help us locate within a mile of where an incident occurs."

"Are you telling me traffic saves lives?"

"You'd better believe it." He points a finger. "Now let me show you what's happening out there."

For the rest of the day, we take a break from social media while I learn how to read the warning signs of high winds and learn the Rapid Response system we use to help emergency workers in bumper-to-bumper traffic.

"Tell us your thoughts heading into the playoffs." Logan's smooth broadcaster voice comes from the speakers on Hendrix's desktop when I enter the house.

He's recording his guest appearance on *Lightning & Thunder*, Logan and Zane's sports radio show based in Newhope. It's not strictly radio anymore, though. Now the guys also post a video recording of the interviews on their YouTube channel.

Hendrix has a small camera mounted on the top of his

computer, and on his screen, I see Logan, Jack, Garrett, and Zane all sitting around a long, brown conference table wearing headphones with black mics in front of them.

Hendrix is on a large flatscreen television behind them, and they all face each other as they chat about the week's football news and the last round of games leading up to the final one of the season in New Orleans.

The Tigers are heavily favored to go all the way, but they have a few more games to win first.

"We're going to stay focused and play the way we've played all season." Hendrix has a great voice for radio, and he looks really hot on screen, too. "Tyler and I've worked out the kinks, our D-line is strong, and we're ready to take it all the way."

"How are you feeling about the championship chatter?" Logan is so polished on-air, I sometimes forget he was a wide receiver in New York with Garrett only a few years ago. "Sounds like they're looking at you, kid."

"Pulling some classic Hollywood on me there." Hendrix laughs, and I mentally pat myself on the back for him catching that *Casablanca* reference. "I remember the year when you were in the running for it. You know how it feels."

"It feels like your year," Logan deflects. "I'd be surprised if you didn't win it after the way you've played this season."

They move to dissecting the past week's games and discussing plays and players I don't know. I put Haddy down, and she takes off crawling fast to the football her daddy left lying on the floor.

She dives face-first onto his "thinking football," and I have to scoop her up and out of the room before her squealing breaks up the show.

His next game will be here in town, and if they go all the way... sorry, *when* they go all the way, we'll go with him and stay for a while. New Orleans is only a two-hour drive from Newhope.

"How are you handling the social media firestorm?" Garrett's cocky voice joins the chat.

My ears perk up, and I peek around the corner to see Hendrix's expression doesn't change. "I'm just going to keep my head down, and play—"

"Yeah, yeah, tell us how you really feel." Garrett interrupts him, and they all laugh.

Hendrix laughs, but he only says, "I think it's best not to give it any additional oxygen."

"Well, I'm proud of you, bro." Garrett leans forward in his chair. "Don't listen to the haters. You've got to defend your lady, and tell Raven if that guy ever shows his face in Newhope, I've got a dumpster with his name on it."

Hendrix glances at me, and I mouth, *I love you*. He smiles and shakes his head. His brothers all have their own personalities, and Sheriff Grizz loves "taking out the trash."

I wouldn't mind turning him loose on Lawrence Calder O'Halloran.

My lips twist as I think about how my actual father never stood up for me the way the Bradfords do, and instead of being sad, I'm angry this time.

For so long, I made excuses for him. I was embarrassed, and maybe I secretly, deep down worried that it was because I wasn't worth defending.

Hendrix and his brothers put an end to that. They cross their arms and dare someone to try and hurt me. It's healing and stirs emotions I've never experienced.

I've got some work to do if I'm going to forgive my dad.

The guys finish up recording the show, then they hang out a few minutes longer shooting the breeze. I unload the back of the Rover, and I've just put my latest find on the kitchen table when my phone lights up with a text.

> Liv: Best idea ever—since their birthdays are a week apart and you'll be here anyway, how do you feel about a joint first birthday party for Gigi and Haddy???

My fingers can't move fast enough.

> OMG... I LOVE IT!!!!! LET'S DO IT!!!

> Liv: I was talking to Clint, and he wants to break into the world of high-end birthday parties. He has the whole thing planned out, and let me tell you, he is going ALL OUT...

She sends me pictures of his ideas, and it's straight out of the Kardashians playbook. Or any other rich-person party here in LA, to be honest.

> Liv: The theme is Mermazing, and he has a balloon entry and water slides and super soaker games and fish ponds and crafts and party favors—and he'll do it for free if we post pictures all over social media and give him credit.

> I LOVE it so much, but he can't do all that for free!

> Liv: That's what I said—Garrett insists on paying... Are you in???

> Absolutely! Haddy's going to love it and we'll go halfsies!

> Liv: I'll tell him to do it then—I'm so excited!!!

> I can't wait to see y'all again!

My chest squeezes when I think about all the time we'll spend with the Bradfords this summer.

I'll miss Heather and Star and the group of friends I've made here in LA, but I can't wait to be with our family, especially now that they're really my family, too.

"That's a big smile." Hendrix walks into the kitchen, pausing to kiss the side of my head before scooping Haddy off the floor.

"I was just thinking I'm a real Bradford now." I look up at him.

His expression warms, and he puts his arm around me, pulling me into his chest. "You always were."

My hands are around his waist, and I think about everything that happened starting with Dylan's wedding. From that first night, it felt like I was meant to be there.

"The first time I met Dylan, she felt like a sister to me."

"My sister loves a big family."

Haddy starts to struggle and squeal, and he steps back, putting her on the floor where she takes off in a fast crawl to the living room. We both laugh, and I shake my head.

"When she starts walking, we're never sitting down again."

"What's this?" Hendrix picks up the large package on the kitchen table.

"Oh my gosh, can you believe it?" I hop over to him. "I got eighteen rolls of toilet paper for only two bucks!"

His nose curls. "You realize you're a millionaire now, right? And you're married to me... And Haddy isn't even potty trained yet."

"Waste not, want not!" I hold up a finger, digging in the cabinet for penne pasta.

"I don't think that applies in this situation."

"That's a great deal." I walk over to where he's standing. "When I had Haddy, and I was living by myself, I'd have freaked out to find a deal like this. You've never had to worry about money like I did."

"Actually, I have." He pulls me into his arms again. "When my parents were opening Cooters & Shooters, their business partner ran off with all their loan payments. We were left with nothing but a huge debt."

"What did they do?" A familiar fear squeezes my throat.

"They pinched pennies, Dad took a job painting houses and Mom did odds and ends." He shrugs. "We had to go to the food bank a few times, but the restaurant took off, things got better... and now I can afford the good toilet paper. And so can you."

My nose wrinkles, and I lean closer, whispering, "But it's such a good deal!"

"That's also why I always donate to the food bank and shelters—which is where I'm taking this tomorrow."

"I told Haddy you were secretly sweet." Rising onto my toes, I kiss his lips.

He releases me. "You're not going to turn into a hoarder on me, are you?"

"No," I laugh. "But I am going to cook our dinner, and we can watch *The Holiday* for our bedtime movie."

"It's after Christmas." He walks into the living room to check on our wandering daughter.

"Haddy won't know, and Jack Black's funny." I dig around for ingredients to make tomatoey pasta with beef tips and rosemary. "He talks about *Driving Miss Daisy*."

"You know that makes me horny." Hendrix sticks his head around the corner to waggle his eyebrows at me and make me snort.

We didn't do a big Christmas, since Hendrix had an out-of-town game. Haddy's too young to remember much about the holidays, but we took pictures with Santa and bought her way too many toys.

Hendrix found the squeaky toy that made her laugh so hard in the video Sherri sent us from her very first day in the nursery. He spent hours scouring every vintage toy store and online retailer, but it was worth it just to hear her baby belly-laugh.

We finish the day like always, cuddling together in front of the big screen, only now we raise the armrests, and Haddy and I both curl up at Hendrix's side.

She falls asleep halfway through the film. Hendrix declares it a decent holiday movie, and we put our daughter in her crib before going to his bedroom to celebrate our own holiday in his bed.

Chapter 30

Hendrix

"THAT WAS A PRETTY SPECTACULAR PLAY AGAINST THE ADMIRALS last week." Garrett's voice is amped, and we're on the show again to break down the recent playoff games and what's coming as we count down to the Big Game.

We're barrelling through the playoffs, and the games are coming fast. Raven and Haddy don't travel with me. Babies aren't so great at staying in hotel rooms, but when we're in town, they're in the box, cheering us on.

I look up to see them in my jersey waving their hands or Raven chewing her nails when it's close. She's understanding the game more, and I'm finding it harder to keep my eyes off her and on the field.

"I'd argue if it hadn't been for the handoff you made to Rogers, they might've won it," my brother continues.

"It was close." I exhale a laugh, thinking about the final play of our last game against Baltimore. Their defense wasn't letting me do anything, and in the final minutes, Tyler passed me the ball, which I tossed to our other TE, who ran it in for the score.

"A little too close for my taste," I confess.

"I think if they had a better kicker, you'd have been in trouble." Logan's polished voice joins the chat. "Too bad for the Admirals there's only one Zane Bradford."

"Thanks, bro." Zane's smile is self-effacing. "Jackson's getting there. He'll be one to watch next season, mark my words."

"He's no first-round draft pick," Jack says, and Garrett holds up his hand for the high five.

If I can't play football with my brothers, I do enjoy getting together and talking about it. Maybe Garrett's right, and taking a job like this with Logan would be something that would make me happy.

"What's happening on the college front, Coach?" Logan turns the conversation to Jack, who is an occasional guest, filling us in on which high school seniors to watch.

He mentions boys I don't know, and I watch our daughter across the room, standing beside a plastic ball-toy similar to the one at the nursery. She crawls inside and takes the balls from the base then pulls herself up to drop them in one by one.

It feels like an advanced move to me, but maybe it's typical ten and a half month-old behavior. I should ask Garrett. Maybe send him a video and see if Gigi's doing anything like this.

Knowing Liv, she's probably already reading.

"Austin Sinclair is drawing a lot of attention from the college recruiters," Logan says, and my ears perk up at the mention of Allie's son.

"Yeah, he'll have his pick of schools." Jack leans on his forearms not making eye contact. "He needs to think about where he'll be happiest, and what he wants for his future."

"If anyone can help with those decisions, it's you, bro," Garrett says, slapping our oldest brother on the back. "You held all our hands through those difficult decisions."

"Not yours." Jack laughs, deflecting the compliment. "You knew where you were going from the time you could walk."

"Yeah, and maybe I should've thought a little more about

what I wanted for my future." Garrett looks down, and I know he's thinking about Liv. "It would've saved me a lot of heartache."

"Heartache's part of life," Jack says. "It's how you learn."

A half-smile pulls my lips, and I study my oldest brother. For the first time, I wonder who guided Jack through those difficult decisions.

"It all worked out," Zane says. "Now about this week's championships."

We're back on track, and everyone's making predictions about the last two games. We wrap up the chat. The guys wish me luck, and I head out for a run.

I'm training hard, doing my best to stay offline and keep my focus on winning—when it's not on my ladies, of course.

The championship game is on Sunday, and after our last near-miss against Baltimore, the tension in my chest twists hard. So much has happened this season I never accounted for. So much has changed, but one thing is the same. I still want a legacy. I still believe this is the year for us, and I still want to go all the way.

Sitting in the locker room in Seattle, I smile down at the faces on my phone.

"We'll be here cheering you on the whole time." Raven is in my royal blue jersey with her dark hair pulled into a ponytail.

"Dada!" Haddy stands at the coffee table, also in her Number 85 jersey, bending her knees and bouncing.

Her hair's getting longer, but she still has the two little blue puff balls on the top of her head. She's active and so close to walking.

"I'll miss seeing you guys when I play." The twist in my chest tells me just how much I've gotten used to looking up and seeing them smiling and waving.

"I wish we were there, too." Raven's tone is wistful. "Seattle's so close, maybe we should've just made the flight?"

"It's okay. Either way, I'll be home tonight."

"Then we're headed to New Orleans!"

The excitement in her voice makes me smile. "That's the spirit. All the way."

"You bet we're going all the way! We didn't come this far not to win it!" Her enthusiasm is just what I need to get me hyped. "When I hang up with you, I'll FaceTime with the family. We're all behind you."

"Thanks, babe. I love you, Pink." Her chin dips, and she blinks a few times like I just said it for the first time. "What?"

"That's the first time you've said it in your uniform."

"Is it?"

She nods. "I had to catch my breath. I love you, too."

Nodding, I give her a wink. "Sleep in that jersey tonight, and when I get home, I'll say it so many times, you'll lose count."

Her pretty eyes shine, and she lifts my daughter's little hand to wave to me. I blow them a kiss just as the guys start yelling it's time to get moving.

I end the call and put my phone in my locker, exchanging it for my helmet.

Jogging to the field, Tyler slaps me on the shoulder. "Man, that's some good shit."

"What?" I frown as we head out onto the sidelines.

The noise is deafening between the cheering fans and the blast of the music and the voice of the announcers.

"Having a sexy mama like that and a cute little lady at home cheering for you." He holds out his hand, and we do our fist bump, hand-jive, point routine with our shoulder rotation at the end.

The fans do it with us, and I can't resist a tease. "You see something you want?"

Pulling his helmet over his head, he shrugs. "Maybe I do."

Nodding, I can't argue. It's a pretty sweet gig. I hang back thinking about them as he runs onto the field for the coin toss. My eyes lift out of habit, but we're not on our home turf.

"I remember when you were more focused on the team than the spectators." Rusty stands beside me waiting to get the signal. "It's funny how it changes."

"I never even felt it happening." I look up at him as we hear we won the toss.

He gives me a salute before jogging onto the field. "Best feeling in the world."

For years Seattle has been a sleeper team, but it's been a breakout year for them. They've made it all the way to the championships and they want it bad. Which means they're fighting hard.

Every down is a battle. I've got big guys forming a wall to keep me from getting open. A rookie cornerback is on Rogers, and he's a fast one. Tyler's forced to throw the ball many times, resulting in dumb penalties and turnovers that should've been first downs or scores.

At halftime, Coach hands us our asses for being sloppy. He lets me have it for not breaking out and running down the field. He's right.

We didn't get here because of luck, and we can play better than this. We have played better than this all season.

Tyler grabs my pads and gives me a shake. "Get clear. I need you."

Nodding, I study the guys holding me back. It's two big guys, and they've got my routine memorized.

"It's time to mix it up," I say, and he nods.

"Keep your eyes on me."

Tyler and I've been playing together long enough that we can read each other's minds, but their defensive end has come close to sacking him twice.

I do my best to keep him away while dodging the linebacker

coming at me, but we don't make much progress through the next series of downs.

My jaw is tight, and it's a low-scoring game. We're at six and three after failing to get the extra point in the last half. Seattle's kicker is better than ours, and standing on the sidelines watching our D-line work, my mind flashes to Zane. He never missed a point.

Just then the unthinkable happens. Their running back breaks free and makes a thirty-yard break to score. Then their kicker gets the extra point.

Their fans go crazy, and my chest sinks. We only have a few minutes left on the clock, and if we don't get this, it's all over. My throat is dry, and Tyler gets in my face.

"It doesn't end here!" he yells, going from player to player.

We stand behind him, yelling *yeah*, then we head onto the field. I think of my ladies at home watching us play. I picture Raven chewing on the side of her fingernail, and I'm doing this for her.

Down after down, we slowly make our way closer to the goal. Less than a minute is left, and Tyler runs up, getting in my face.

"See if you can get clear," he says, and I nod.

I only need a few feet, and I can take it over the corner. Lining up, I just touch turf when the snap happens. My guy heads straight at me, but at the last moment, I dig in with my toes, zagging in the opposite direction.

For once, I'm open, and I turn back to see that fucking DE headed straight for Tyler. Our eyes lock, and he manages to get the pass off just before he goes down.

It's not a great throw. It's too high, and it wobbles. The safety is coming at me, but I'm not looking at him. My eyes are on the ball.

I jump, reaching out with both hands as hard as I can while stretching my feet to stay in the zone. We fall together, going all the way down in the end zone, but I'm holding on with everything I've got.

This one's for the win, and every muscle in my body flexes as I hold the ball tight against my chest. We hit the grass with a loud *oof*. Our arms are tangled, but I turn onto my side with only half my body outside the goal line.

It's good, and the stadium explodes. Vince gets to me first, pulling me up, and I stagger to where Tyler is running straight at me.

"We're going all the way!" he yells, jumping and pulling me into a hug.

The fans go wild, and everybody's flooding onto the field. It's chaos, and I wish the girls were here in the box. They'll be with me for the big win. It's time to start packing.

Chapter 31

Raven

I'M HOARSE FROM SCREAMING AND JUMPING AROUND HENDRIX'S bedroom.

Haddy conked out at halftime, and I carried her to her crib, grabbing a monitor and taking it to the other side of the house.

I started the game on FaceTime with the family, but after a while, we switched to texting with the girls' group.

That big guy is not letting Hendrix do anything!!!

> Liv: He's the strong safety—it's his job to cover Hendrix

> He's doing a great job! I'm ready to kick him in the nuts!

> Allie: That would be a personal foul, unsportsmanlike conduct.

> I've chewed the side of my fingernail off watching this game. NOOOO!!!!!! 😭

Dylan: What happened? What happened????

Liv: Seattle scored. This is not looking good. 😱

Rachel: I can't watch. It's like I'm having a panic attack.

Dylan: What is Jack saying? He always knows.

Allie: Nothing. His jaw is tight, and he has that look.

What look? WHAT'S THE LOOK???

Allie: No expression. Kind of like he's trying to mind-meld with your husband.

Dylan: If Henny doesn't win, I'm going to sob my eyes out.

I can't watch—tell me what happens.

Dropping the phone on the bed, I pace the bedroom. If Hendrix doesn't win, I'm going to have to get some quick advice on how to handle it. This game means so much to him.

My stomach is in knots, and I'm queasy. Still, I can't not watch.

Placing both hands over my eyes, I watch as they get closer and closer to the other end of the field. To think, I've only been watching this sport for one season. Last year, I was blissfully ignorant of all this.

Now my heart's beating out of my chest, and I can't take my eyes off Number 85.

Scooping up my phone, I see the girls are still going.

Liv: This is good. Solid plays. Come on, Tigers…

Did that clock speed up?

Allie: It feels that way sometimes, doesn't it?

Liv: Last play… they're doing the goal line formation.

> How do you know all of this?

Allie: You pick it up after years of watching, although NFL play is different from high school and college.

> HE'S OPEN!!!

Liv: Oh, shit, Tyler's about to get pancaked… He got it off!!!

I can't breathe. The ball wobbles wildly through the air. It's too high for Hendrix, but somehow he takes a flying leap. He's moving so fast, it looks like his body actually stretches.

The Seattle guy is on top of him, and together they fall to the ground, the ball caged somewhere between them.

> Did he get it?

Liv: I can't see… HE GOT IT!!!

Allie: TOUCHDOWN!!!

Dylan: THAT'S MY BROTHER!!!

Liv: See you in NOLA!

My phone is buzzing nonstop, but I'm jumping up and down, screaming into a pillow. The cameras are on Hendrix and Tyler and all the guys smiling and dancing and fist-bumping.

The kicker-guy trots out onto the field and easily kicks the ball through the post-thingies, and everybody is on the field. Hugging the pillow, I watch him on the screen smiling so big as the newscaster asks him how he feels about the game.

"I don't like when it's so close, but at this level, every team's a winner." He's so generous. I'm so proud.

The woman asks him about the final catch, and he laughs,

shaking his gorgeous head. "I expect to see that one on the reels. That was a miracle."

She thanks him, and he holds up his hand, extending the ring finger on his left hand and mouthing the words, *I love you.*

I huff into my hand, my eyes filling with tears. "I love you, too," I say to the screen.

I'm shaking from all the adrenaline, and I feel like I could run a marathon… or at least a 5K. Sliding my phone into the pocket of my leggings, I go to the kitchen to pour a glass of wine, preparing to chew my nails until he gets home.

A buzz in my pocket has me pulling out the device, and the text I've been waiting for appears.

> Hendrix: We did it.

> That catch was incredible. I don't have a voice anymore 🎤

> Hendrix: Another squeaker. Coach was on our asses.

> Where are you now?

> Hendrix: Headed to the airport. I'll be there in three hours. Wait up?

> OFC!!!

I check on Haddy once more. She's still sleeping soundly, so I grab the monitor, refresh my glass of wine, and go to the theater room to pull up *La La Land*.

It's long and musical, and it'll distract me until he gets here. Curling up on the couch, I watch the opening scene of cars all stuck on the freeway, and I think about Wilt saying traffic reporting saves lives.

Lying on my side, with my head on the armrest, I wonder if I could merge my desire to save lives and make a difference with what I'm doing here. Being a mom and raising a responsible, productive member of society is an important job—and it doesn't put me at odds with my sexy husband, who I love.

Emma Stone dances on the screen, singing about meeting someone in the crowd who can make all her dreams come true. I watch the actors dive into the pool as she meets Ryan Gosling dressed up like a 1980s pop singer.

She has a dream, and I know how this story ends…

"I see where Haddy gets it from." The low voice wakes me, and when I open my eyes, excitement floods my veins.

"Hendrix!" He's kneeling in front of me, and I sit up, wrapping my arms around his neck and hugging him. "I missed you so much."

Leaning back, he slides his finger along the side of my hair, moving it off my cheek. "That's a greeting worth coming home to any time."

Our mouths meet in a kiss, lips parting, tongues curling. His body is warm, and his mouth tastes like minty water. He smells like heaven.

"Is it late?" I whisper as his lips trace a line along my jaw.

"After midnight."

"Are you tired?"

"I'm getting my second wind." The hunger in his voice sparks my own.

"Are you hurting?"

"I'll have a few bruises tomorrow." His mouth moves lower onto my neck, and my nipples tingle.

The air around us is hot with desire.

Turning my face, I kiss the side of his cheek. "I'm still wearing your jersey."

"Good girl." His low tone tickles my stomach.

I place my hand on his cheek. This man is mine. He owns my heart and my soul, and I love him from the ends of my hair to the tips of my toes.

Leaning forward, I brush my lips across his, speaking against his luscious mouth. "I love you, Hendrix."

"Not as much as I love you, Pink."

A teasing smile curls my lips. "How do you know?"

"The thoughts that keep running through my head." He smiles, sitting back on his heels. "There's no other explanation."

Sliding his hands up my outer thighs, he catches the sides of my leggings, yanking them down and off quickly. Pushing higher, I sweep my hair around my shoulders, rubbing my knees together and giving him my best sex-kitten pouty smile.

Blue eyes narrow as he hisses. "Hell, Pink, the things I want to do to you."

My core clenches, and I bite my lip. "Do them all."

"Lie back." I quickly comply as large hands grip my knees. "Now spread those sexy thighs and show me that pussy."

With a sigh, I happily obey, letting my legs fall open. Dark eyes meet mine, and he dives forward, covering me with his mouth and growling as he slides his tongue over my clit.

"Oh, God," I gasp, stabbing my fingers in his hair.

I'm reclining in the chair with my legs draped over the arms, and his face is at my stomach. Two thick fingers invade my dripping core, curling as my back arches with a wail.

His hand slides higher, under the jersey to my breast, twisting a nipple between his fingertips as I moan.

The caresses of his tongue grow stronger, more persistent, and my mind tunnels. My core clenches, and I gasp, pulling his hair, riding his face. He growls against my sensitive skin, and I jump. The muscles low in my stomach twist tighter and tighter with every pass.

He doesn't stop, and my mouth opens. My back arches, my toes curl, and with a snap, orgasm floods my brain and body. I cry out, shuddering as my body jerks.

Warm lips pull my skin, and he kisses me again before sliding his mouth to my lower stomach. As he unfastens his jeans, he nips my sensitive skin with his teeth, making me squeal. Then with a quick rise, he slides his cock into my still-clenching core.

Strong arms are on both sides of me as his mouth consumes mine. I reach up to grab his neck, sealing my lips to his. Our kisses chase and pull, then he leans back with a smack, holding my thighs and pulling me forward as he thrusts.

I fall back, letting him use me. My hair falls around my shoulders, and I lift the jersey to let my breasts peak out.

He groans, and I feel him thicken as he moves faster. "You're so fucking gorgeous."

His chin drops, and he's fucking me hard, keeping the orgasm swirling beneath my skin. I wrap my legs around him, and we move together, riding the growing waves.

"Yes," he hisses, holding the back of my neck and pulling me closer.

A bead of sweat traces down his cheek, and I kiss it, savoring the taste of his desire.

"I want you in my mouth," I groan, and he moves back as I drop to my knees.

Lifting his cock, I pull it between my lips, swirling my tongue over the tip as he moans. My hands spread over his tight ass, and I feel the muscles flexing. I feel him fighting his orgasm, trying to prolong it.

He can't. I press my face to his stomach, lifting my chin so I don't gag, and he breaks with a shuddering groan. His hand is behind my head, and he holds me, pulsing again and again as I swallow, taking every last drop of his essence.

I'm twisted in his sheets when I wake to the dim light of morning.

After making love in the theater, we moved to the bedroom to clean up, showering together, running our hands all over each other's naked bodies… which led to another round of fucking.

Eventually, we made it to sleep, but everything has changed since our visit home, since we agreed we're in this forever. Every act of love with my husband feels like it bonds us closer.

Knowing his body is mine, my body is his, has brought us to a place I didn't know existed. He's in my mind even when I don't know he is. He's moving with me, and one look fills me with lust and need.

Hot lips trace a line up my back, and I straighten, exhaling a happy sigh.

"How are you feeling?" His warm voice at my ear sends tingles down my back, through my breasts, pointing my nipples.

"Horny," I say with a quiet laugh.

His strong hand slides down my back, squeezing my ass. "Give me this, Pink."

A thrill tickles in my stomach, and I nod. "Okay."

He disappears briefly, and my heart beats faster. Last night he fucked me so hard, I could barely walk. He had to carry me to the bed, and still I wanted more.

Now I'm breathless as he returns to the bedroom holding a small bottle.

"Get on your stomach." It's a low order that makes my stomach jump.

"Is that from Erewhon?" I tease breathlessly, and he grins like a devil.

"It claims to be very pure and organic. Perfect for anal." He kneels on the bed behind me. "And I have this."

I hear the soft buzz of the vibrator, and I'm instantly wet. "Oh, God."

Leaning down, he scrapes his face along my lower back. "I love when you call me that."

My knees rise, and I rest my face on my arms, looking back at the god above me. Warm drizzle falls between the line of my butt, and I watch him fisting his cock, covering it with oil.

"I'm so hard for you, it hurts."

My lips part, and I swallow a whimper.

"Pretty little pucker," he whispers as his fingers coat me with oil.

I'm dying with anticipation and need, and with every pass of his finger over my hole, I tense.

"I love watching your pussy clench like a good, hungry girl." He puts the vibrator in my hand, but I don't need it yet.

If I use it, I'll come before we even begin. This buildup has me on the very edge.

"Ready?" Two thick fingers push gently, spreading, preparing me.

I gasp, nodding. "Yes, please."

The sound of his fist sucking with oil as he prepares his cock almost makes my knees give out. One large hand braces my hip, and my eyes squeeze shut as he presses the large, mushroom tip slowly, slowly, waiting for the muscled ring to relax.

"If you need me to stop, I will."

I nod again as more oil flows around the place his dick is nudging. Fingers caress my lower back and cheeks, and with a gentle pop, he's inside me. My mind bends, and I let out a cry at the feeling of him hard and large, a thick rod in my ass.

"Fuck, that's a tight fit." He groans, holding still. "You okay?"

"I'm okay," I gasp, my pussy clenching wildly. "Oh..."

He moves slowly, stopping and starting as my body relaxes, as heat starts to move through my thighs. My body trembles, and I put the silver bullet on my clit. In an instant, I start to move more, taking him deeper.

I'm lost in sensation, crying out and pressing my ass against his hips. I feel his balls slap the back of my thighs and I hear him grunting. I hear him say *my wife*. I hear him say *such a sweet ass*. I hear him say I'm a *good girl*, and I come apart.

His words morph into sounds I've never heard before, deep and animalistic, as his movements become wilder. He's fucking me harder, and I feel wetness spatter on my inner thighs. *Did I just squirt?*

I'm wailing, coming harder again and again, until I feel him start to withdraw.

"Oh…" I whimper as he pulls out, and the vacancy he leaves behind is real.

More sucking sounds as his fist rapidly jerks his cock, and with another deep groan, hot come coats my lower back, slipping over my warm backside.

I'm lying on the bed utterly boneless, my orgasm still pulsing through my thighs. His strong hand is beside me on the bed, and he kisses my cheek. I turn my face so he can consume my mouth, licking his tongue inside and biting my lips.

"You okay, love?" His low voice is hoarse, and I nod. "Come with me."

My eyes are still closed as he lifts me in his arms, carrying me to the glass shower stall. Warm water flows over us, and he gently cleans me, holding me in his arms and covering my face with kisses as I hold his shoulders.

"My beautiful wife," he whispers, gently massaging my body, kissing my lips, worshipping me. "I love you so much."

My heart melts, and I lift my chin to meet his kisses. "I love you," I whisper, and in that moment we're one.

Chapter 32

Hendrix

TWO WEEKS GO BY IN A FLASH OF TRAINING AND DRILLING.

Our win against Seattle was too close for all of us, and I remember this Wisconsin defense. We're not going to win if we don't prepare, and I'm not looking forward to facing off against Number 53 again.

To be honest, the cocky swagger I've projected through the playoffs took a hit that last game. We're the two best teams in the league. Nobody's walking away with any prizes. They're going to be earned.

It's hard to sit still in the small jet as we fly across the country to where all our friends and family will be waiting to greet us in the Crescent City. I stand, rubbing my stomach as I walk the aisle, and Raven glances up at me from where she's curled up in her black sweats.

"You okay?" Her voice is soft, the one thing that soothes me, and I walk back to lean down and kiss her lips.

"Just getting ready."

"You're ready." Her smile is warm. "You've worked so hard these last two weeks."

It's true. I've gotten up before dawn and come back after dark. I hated being apart from them so much, but once this game is over, we've planned an extended vacation.

Newhope is only a two-hour drive from New Orleans, and I've booked a cute little cottage off the scenic highway on the bay for us to stay in while we visit.

Haddy squeals in her carseat, kicking her little feet and waving Axelita at me. She'll be a year old next month, which is hard to believe, and the ladies have planned a massive, joint first birthday party with Clint's help.

Raven's been buzzy and thrilled and excited the entire time we've been packing. Her internship at KCLA ended, and as predicted, Star offered her a full-time position as a meteorologist and all-around reporter, producer, pretty much whatever she wants.

Star's obsessed with my wife, and Raven told me she has plans for several special assignments, including one on weather girls, who she said played a significant role in the entry of women into broadcasting.

My phone buzzes, and I pull it out to see a photograph of a rust-colored, three-piece suit. "Aw, man," I groan.

"What?" Raven frowns, and I take the seat beside her, turning the screen so she can see it. "What's that?"

"They hired a fashion coordinator for our entrance to the stadium."

"That's fancy!" Raven gives me a half-grin.

"It has something to do with hockey. Apparently those guys go all out for their entrance to the games."

"I've seen the video. It's hot."

My lips twist as I study what they want me to wear. "I'm going to look like Napoleon Dynamite."

Her head pulls back. "You've seen that movie?"

Lowering my phone, I think about it. "For some reason it was on all the time at the house. That and *The Big Lebowski.*"

Her pretty amber eyes curl with her smile. "Because you were in a house full of guys. Did you also watch *Road House?*"

"Garrett did—when Liv wasn't making him watch *Dirty Dancing.*"

"Liv's so great," she chuckles.

"Pretty sure he only did it to get in her pants." Lifting my phone, I show it to her. "Back to this."

"I mean, it's different..." My eyes narrow, and she shrugs. "It's designer—have fun with it."

"I think we have different ideas of fun."

"You know that's not true." Her sassy tone makes my dick jump.

"Dada!" Haddy squeals, pointing at me as if on cue.

"Shew," I shake my head. "She really is the cutest little cock blocker."

"Those better not be her next words."

My thumbs fly across the screen as I reply to the email. "I'm telling them okay. I hope I don't regret it."

"Win the game, and no one will care what you wore." Her nose wrinkles, and I lean down to kiss her soft lips.

The flight attendant comes through and lets us know we're preparing to land. I cover her hand in mine, ready to get the show on the road.

"Their defense is strong." Vince stands beside me, holding an Uncrustable peanut butter and jelly sandwich as I slide the burnt-orange blazer off my shoulders. "But we've got the best offense in the league."

"They beat us last time with that defense." I put the fancy coat in the bag provided.

"Good evening, ladies." Rusty walks in wearing a teal-colored suit and matching tie, then he gives me a nod. "No crying tonight, Bradford."

I exhale a growl, shaking my head. "Nice suit."

"It was my dad's." He goes to his locker to start getting ready for the game. "I'm not cut out for that designer shit."

"These guys went hard the last time we faced them." Rogers is two-fisting Uncrustables, when he and Tyler walk up to us.

"We have to be in each other's heads at all times." He's already suited up. "We've been together long enough. We know what to do."

Adrenaline surges in my veins as I pull on my gear. I left Raven and Haddy at the hotel with the family. Everybody was cheering and supportive, and they'll all be in the box watching.

I got my own box this time, since the whole family plus Thomas drove down to watch the game. They even closed the restaurant, which is a first. Dylan said the customers would understand.

Music plays, and I alternate stretching and warming up my muscles. Right before we leave the locker room, I see a text on my phone from Pink.

It's a photo of her and Haddy in their jerseys waving. Haddy's showing her four front teeth, which is how she smiles now, and I exhale a laugh. She's really cute.

Underneath the photo are the words *We love you*, with a heart emoji. I give the photo a kiss and decide it's my good luck charm.

It's time to go out.

Tyler's hand is on my shoulder as we jog through the entrance onto the sidelines. "You might have a hard time getting clear, but I'll be looking for you first."

I nod, and we stop, doing our usual fist-bump routine. The noise of the fans is louder in this stadium than others, and I hear cheers mixed with boos. Looking around, I see different faces on the jumbotron.

They flash to the players' boxes, and for a split second, I see Raven holding Haddy. They're bouncing to a rhythm, and she's waving Haddy's little arm. It makes me smile, and I wave up at them.

Cheers break out, and I guess they're for us. It's hard to tell in the chaos leading up to the coin toss. Rusty is beside me on the sideline, pacing, and I can tell he's ready to start.

We win it, choosing to defer, and Tyler runs to where I'm standing as our D-line heads onto the field. The guys line up, and at the snap, they're moving forward, putting pressure on the quarterback.

He gets the pass off, and they make it down the field. It's moving fast, and I'm not smiling, watching as they close in on the end zone.

"Fuck, if they score right out the gate…" Tyler doesn't finish, but I know what he's thinking.

They beat us last time. We can't miss a single play this rematch.

Our guys manage to hold them, and we're up, heading onto the field. We line up, and 53 is right across from me, looking straight in my face.

"We meet again, hot shot," he growls.

Pulling my chin back, I can't stop a grin. "Ready to shoot right past you."

The ball snaps, and I rush forward, holding him off Tyler, who's getting pressure from the sides. I manage to evade the safety, but Tyler has to run it. We're close, but no first down. The next down goes pretty much the same way, lots of holding plenty of blocking, little movement.

We're back on the sidelines, and D-line is headed out again.

"These guys are a fucking wall," Tyler grumbles, walking up and down the side. "We've got to mix it up, guys. We can do this. We've done the work."

It's true, and we've been studying the tapes and drilling.

We've practiced new plays they haven't memorized, and when it's time to take the field again, we gain more yardage.

I'm ready for the next snap, taking a quick twist away from 53 in a very dancerly move. Dylan would be proud. Hell, Garrett is probably yelling right now.

Digging in, I run for the opening, looking back to see Tyler's in trouble. Again, he's about to go down, but he fires the pass to me. It's short, and I have to double back, but I manage to scoop it out of the cornerback's hand, preventing an interception.

I get some yardage, but again, no score.

It keeps going, possession after possession. The tension is so taut on the sidelines, my neck hurts, and I look up to see Allie holding Haddy and waving her little hand.

Frowning, I scan all the faces in my box. Allie is standing beside Liv, who's holding Gigi, but Raven's not there.

Maybe she had to go to the bathroom? I don't like it, but I have to get back on the field.

The snap goes, and I start to spin, but 53 is ready this time. He has me around the waist, and I hit the turf.

Chapter 33

Raven

I'VE NEARLY CHEWED A HOLE IN THE SIDE OF MY FINGER. THE WISCONSIN team is killer, and the Tigers don't progress much when they have the ball.

"It's hard when the defense is this good." Jack patiently explains to me what's happening on the field. "We have a strong offensive line, but it's hard to break through that wall."

"Oh!" Half the stadium echoes my groan as Tyler is forced to run out of bounds.

"They've got to do a better job covering him." Garrett's arms are crossed, and I remember his position was offensive lineman.

"That big guy's keeping Hendrix in place." Liv is right beside me, bouncing Gigi on her hip.

We're all wearing our jerseys and the babies are wearing royal blue and yellow pom-pom headbands. They're adorable, but the game is stressing us all out.

I know how much it means to Hendrix to win, and it's the

last and biggest game of the season. My stomach is in knots and my blood pressure is spiking.

My phone goes off, and I jump, looking down to see a text from Star. Frowning, I take a step away to read it.

> Star: Can you talk? I know it's the biggest game of the year, but major 911!!!

Walking up to Allie, I give her a nudge. "Would you mind holding her for just a second?"

"I won't mind at all!" Allie cries, taking Haddy off my hip. "Hello, Haddy-boo! Remember me?"

Haddy pats her shoulder, holding Axel and blowing bubbles.

"That's right!" Allie laughs. "Books."

"I just have to make a call, but I'll be right back."

"Is everything okay?" Allie studies my expression.

"I think so? I got a text from the news manager back in LA. I'm sure it's no big deal."

"We've got you covered, lady." Rachel puts her hand on my shoulder. "Take your time."

I wave to Dylan, who's sitting in the back of the box away from the windows, watching with Thomas on his tiny, portable black-and-white television. I've been told it's his lucky TV, and he watches all the games on it.

Going into the breezeway outside the box, I quickly return Star's call. She answers on the first ring.

"I'm so sorry to bother you!" She's speaking high and fast. "I can't find Wilt, and we just got a report that a private, two-seater plane went down in the hills. EMS needs us to use the mapping software to help find them, but I don't know how."

My heart drops. "Star, oh my God, were they killed?"

"We don't know, but the clock is ticking. Can you talk me through it?"

Blinking fast, I try to visualize the console. The stadium erupts into cheering, and I walk away, doing my best to find a quiet space where I can think.

"I've got her on the line now." Star is on the radio talking to emergency crews, and I chew my lip.

"Pull up the Scout Master software, and you'll need to draw a radius around the area. Are you able to do that?"

I hear clicking on the other end of the phone, and Star speaks softly to herself. "Let me ask if they can give me an idea..."

She moves the phone away from her mouth, and I wait as she returns to the EMS workers. "He said it's somewhere between Bell Canyon and Hidden Hills."

I'm still learning the area, but I've sat beside Wilt several times as he showed me how to pinpoint locations. He said it was for wildfire detection, but I don't see why it won't help us now.

"All planes have a black box. It should transmit a signal." I scrub my fingers across my forehead, trying to think. "It's something megahertz. Wilt has the number written on the desk. Look beside the keyboard."

"Give me a second. I'm not at his desk."

More cheers erupt in the stadium. I'm missing the game, and I know Hendrix will wonder why I'm not there with Haddy cheering him on. I don't want him to worry or be distracted.

"I found it!" Her voice is high. "Hang on!"

She's back on the line with the EMS guys, and I'm chewing the side of my fingernail, blinking at the door to the stadium.

"That's it. It's got to be them!" Star's voice goes high. "We found them. Raven! You helped me find them!"

"That's great, Star. That's great. Can you guide them how to get there? I really need to get back..."

"I'll text you." We disconnect, and I dash across the concessions area, heading to the box entrance.

"Shit!" I forgot my key card, and I have to bang on the door. "Guys—let me in!"

They're all facing the field, and I slam my palm against the glass repeatedly. More cheering breaks out. They're all jumping and hugging each other, and I almost scream, fumbling for my phone so I can text Dylan to let me in.

Her head turns and her eyes widen. I see her yell my name and she runs to the door to let me in the box. "Where have you been? You're missing everything!"

"Life or death situation." I hold up my phone. "What did I miss?"

"Okay, you're going to have to explain that. Tyler dodged a sack and was finally able to get a decent pass off to Hendrix, but that 53 guy pulled him down. Now they're lined up, and Jack says they're going to do a tush push."

"Tush push?" I wrinkle my nose.

"It's exactly what it sounds like."

We run to the window in time to see all ten guys in a tight huddle. The snap goes, and they shove forward as a group, literally pushing Tyler's butt over the line for the touchdown. The guys laugh and slap hands. Dylan and I exchange a glance and blow a laugh through our lips.

"Here you are!" Rachel scurries up to me holding Haddy. "Hendrix keeps looking up here, and I know he's trying to find you. Get out there!"

I rush past her to the window, and sure enough, my husband is standing on the sideline looking up. I wave both hands before blowing kisses, and through the helmet I can see the smile spread across his face.

We're in the last quarter, and the score is so close. One touchdown will cinch it. Reaching for Haddy, I hold her on my hip, bouncing as I watch.

"She's my little security blanket," I say to Dylan.

"Thomas is mine," she replies, and I see Logan standing with the brothers.

They all have their arms crossed, brows lowered, and they're watching intensely.

"Sacked!" Garrett yells, and both Gigi and Haddy jump, twisting around to look at him.

Gigi starts to fuss, and Garrett takes her from her mother. "It's okay, baby. That was a good thing."

Logan gives him a high five, and they're back to watching the field so hard, I imagine them burning a hole in the glass. My phone buzzes, and I pull it out quickly to see Star's text.

> Star: They just found them!!! EMS says we saved twenty minutes of searching. He has a head injury and is bleeding. They said we saved his life! Raven!!!

My eyes heat as I read her words, and I almost forget to watch the game.

> Really???

> Star: It was a student flight. He was only seventeen.

> I'm so glad!!! Tell them I'm so glad.

> Star: Now get back to that game. We need Hendrix to do one of his magic plays and win this thing!!!

It feels like an emotional roller coaster. My mind is a whirl, thinking I helped save someone's life two thousand miles away.

"Are you okay?" Liv is beside me, rubbing her hand up and down my back.

"Traffic reporting does save lives." I sound as stunned as I feel.

"Okay?" Her brow furrows, and she doesn't understand.

It doesn't matter. The guys break into yells, and we hurry to the window again. Garrett tosses Gigi in the air, and she lets out a loud belly laugh.

"What did we miss?" Liv yells.

"Hendrix just caught a forty-yard pass," Logan explains from the other side of the box.

"This is it!" Allie bounces up and down beside me, hands clasped. "They're about to do it! Dylan, get over here!"

She complains, but she runs to stand with the four of us. I'm holding Haddy, and we're all holding hands as the guys line up in what Jack said is goal formation.

Chapter 34

Hendrix

I'M BREATHING HARD, AND 53 IS SNORTING AT ME FROM ACROSS THE line like a raging bull. He's going to plant me like a tree, but first he's got to catch me.

The clock is running down. We're one point behind. The game could go either way, and every play counts. We need to score; they need to stop us.

We're facing each other eye to eye at the 20-yard line. It's first and ten.

The snap happens, and 53 races forward, but I roll. A safety is coming up from the side, and I step out of his way. Roger is covering Tyler along with two other guys, but their defense is coming in like a wall. All I can think is *run*.

I dig in and head for the end zone. Looking over my shoulder, I lock eyes with Tyler, and he nods. He has one second—all the time he needs to plant his feet and fire off a perfect pass.

I'm not entirely open, but without interference, I've got it. Running at top speed, I'm one with the ball. It's soaring to me like a bird preparing to land. I reach out, ready to snatch it, but a cornerback is right there.

It doesn't matter. I've got it. It's smooth as silk, right into my arms, and I fly, sailing through the air, bracing for impact.

Don't think hitting the ground doesn't rattle my brain and hurt like hell. It does, but nothing is sweeter than completing this pass.

The catch is good. I hold it to my chest just long enough for the ref to call the touchdown, then I'm up, tossing him the ball and holding out my hands as my teammates plow into me.

We're laughing and yelling. Some of the guys beat their chests. Rogers bangs his helmet against mine.

Tyler grips the front of my pads and shakes me, yelling. "That's what I'm talking about!"

He pulls me into a hug. He's so fucking happy, and I can't stop laughing.

Our kicker comes out and handily sends it through the uprights, and it's all over. We bagged the big one.

Confetti rains down on the field, and everybody rushes out to join us. I look up at the box where the family *was*. I can't wait for them to get out here.

The stadium is a mass of people yelling and waving their arms over their heads. Some people are twirling yellow flags. Tyler is at my side as the reporters surround us.

"How are you feeling right now, Hen?" The woman from ESPN leans close.

"Pretty darn good." My cheeks ache, I'm grinning so hard.

"That last play—tell us what was going through your head."

"I kept expecting somebody to hit me," I laugh, moving side to side. "I turned around, and nobody was there."

"Congratulations." She smiles, and I turn for the next reporter only to freeze in place.

"You were amazing tonight, boo!" Mikayla stands in front of me in a body-hugging, royal blue dress holding a mic. "Congratulations!"

She steps forward to hug me, but I block her advance. *What the fuck?*

"What are you doing out here?" I can't keep the annoyance out of my tone, even if her mic is still in my face.

"I'm a reporter for WeGot Sports!" Mikayla has the nerve to act excited. "I'm here to congratulate you on your win!"

"No." I shake my head. "You don't congratulate me. You don't touch me. And I'm not your boo."

"Hendrix..." she puts a hand on her chest. "What has that woman done to you?"

"That woman is my wife, and this is me." I take a step closer, causing her to take a step back. "Raven is an incredible human being, who cares about people not follower counts, and I'm sick of you talking out your neck about shit you don't understand."

Her jaw drops, and I feel strong arms around my shoulders, holding me back. "Hey, bro, that was a killer play—get over here!"

The anger burning in my chest mixes with the adrenaline, but Garrett's pulling me away. He's about the only one who could after all the shit she's said online about Raven since my near-fight in the parking lot.

I would never hurt a woman, but I seriously want her out of my celebration.

"You know I love to take out the trash." My brother's mouth is at my ear. "Let it go."

"Hey, baby! That was incredible!" Raven is at my side with Haddy on her hip, and I pull my two girls into my side, wrapping my arms around them.

Turning to a different reporter, who is still holding the mic in my direction and just taking it all in, I give her a wink. "Would you like a real scoop?"

"Definitely!" She blinks, stepping back for me.

I nod at the line coach I asked to help me. He steps forward with a small blue pouch, and I turn to Raven. "Raven Lorrain Bradford, you've made me a better man. I couldn't have done any of this without you."

"Hendrix!" Her hand flies to cover her mouth as Haddy reaches for me.

I take my baby girl, holding her to my chest, but I'm not letting go of her mom. A body pushes up beside me, and I see it's Dylan.

"Give her to me." She takes Haddy, but I catch her arm, making sure they stay close.

"Raven, my beautiful wife…" I take her hand, sliding the diamond ring on her finger. "I should've done this before."

Her lips press together, and she looks at the round diamond surrounded by tiny baguettes. "It's so beautiful…"

"I wanted it to be like a storm cloud, then I wanted it to be like the sun that comes after the rain." I shrug, still holding her hand. "Then I just wanted it to be something that would make you as proud as you've made me. I want the whole world to know it. I love you, Pink."

She blinks, and tears hit her cheeks. I pull her to me, but before I kiss her, I look into the mic. "I'll fight for her any day of the week because she's worth it."

Her hand goes around my neck, and she pulls me down for a kiss. I hold her close, and the reporters drift to Tyler. I look up to see the officials surrounding him. They have the crystal trophy, and they're ready to make the announcement.

"The MVP award goes to Tyler Winslow!" The crowd goes wild, and I couldn't be happier.

Tyler's eyes meet mine, and I give him two thumbs up. I've got a heap of blessings on my head, and I'm glad my friend got one, too.

"I'm going to Disney World," he yells, and we all laugh.

My brothers surround me, slapping my back and congratulating me.

Logan pulls me in for a hug. "He couldn't have done it without you."

I know he speaks from experience, and it means a lot. "Thanks, bro."

"Raven really has changed you." Garrett wraps his arms around me, lifting me off my feet. "You're not such a little punk anymore."

"Put me down, Sasquatch!" We all laugh, making our way off the field, ready to pack up and head home for a few weeks.

It's been an amazing season. More than I ever imagined when I stood on my balcony in September thinking about what I thought I wanted, what I thought would make me happy.

When Jack called me home, I had no idea I was on a collision course with a wife and baby, and I wouldn't change it for the world.

"Your sister has stolen our baby." Raven is under me in our bed, her dark hair stuck to the sweat on her neck, and I haven't stopped kissing her since we crashed through the door of our hotel suite.

"She loves babies." I cover her mouth with mine, my cock still buried deep between her thighs.

After the game, we partied in the VIP box for a few hours. Allie wanted to take us all over New Orleans, which is her hometown, but Jack said it was probably safer to stay where we were.

He was right. The fans were having a party, and it got crazy out there. Also, I was just as happy to come back here and make love to my wife all night.

"Remember that first night we all slept together in the theater room?" She blinks her pretty eyes at me, and I smile, kissing her lids. "We've come so far."

"Yeah, but I knew then we'd stay together forever. Didn't you?"

Her brow furrows. "No—I couldn't see either of us giving up our dreams."

"And now?" I lean onto my arm, tracing her hair off her cheek with my finger, thinking about what she told us in the VIP box.

I'd asked where she went for so long during the game, and Dylan asked what she meant about traffic saving lives.

She told us how Star called her needing help. Then she got a little emotional telling us how they were able to find the small plane using some kind of software.

My question was why they needed KCLA to do it when I needed her. She didn't know, other than Star is friends with everybody in Los Angeles, including emergency workers. I guess that's why she runs the station.

"When I got into meteorology, it was to help save lives. I guess now that I've done it, I can keep doing it."

Rolling onto my back, I pull her to my chest, tracing my finger down the smooth line of her back. "I'm thinking I'll be too old to outrun those blockers around the same time we're ready for a new little tight end."

That makes her laugh, and she pinches my side. "Is that so?"

"Then we can move back to Newhope, and you can start chasing storms."

"I can't be Liz Pantore pregnant." She turns her face to kiss my skin, and I'm ready to go for another practice round.

"It's only nine months." Turning, I pin her beneath me once more, loving the big smile piercing her cheeks. "I'll be clear and ready for you to pass him to me."

"You can't hold a baby like a football."

"I've never dropped a football in my life."

Lifting her chin, she kisses my lips. "Let's put a pin in that."

"Done." Sliding down, I cup her breast in my hand. "We can still practice. I'll be the hurricane…"

"You're a tornado," she laughs as I pull a nipple between my teeth.

"I won't hurt you, girl. Climb on and let me put an exceptional bone in your body."

Our mouths are smiling as our lips come together. "I'd expect nothing less."

Epilogue

Raven

"Happy birthday to you!" I bounce Haddy on my hip with every word, and she gazes around her birthday party in awe.

We're all in awe. Clint turned Miss Gina's patio and gardens into a balloon-filled oceanic wonderland built around his "Mermazing" theme. The entire place looks like we've gone under the sea, Disney-style.

The sidewalk entrance that leads up the hill to Miss Gina's gardens is lined with balloons of all shapes and sizes in a beige color, as if you're traveling from the sand into the waves.

Opening the wrought-iron gates, guests enter a tunnel of balloons with jellyfish streamers and small tables holding goblets of fizzy pink punch for the kids and glasses of champagne for the adults.

At both ends of the tent, massive arches of sea green, periwinkle blue, purple, and pink balloons of all shapes and sizes open to a patioscape of trees with gobs of clear-balloon tops.

We stand at the back presentation table surrounded by

undersea creatures made of balloons, and arches over the pool hold large, clear spheres.

"This is the second time I really wish I could see my patio," Miss Gina says, laughing as Rachel leads her closer to where we stand with the babies beside their cakes.

"I can hardly believe my eyes," Rachel replies. "How in the world did they do it?"

"They've been out here all week," Miss G says.

Both the birthday girls are dressed in mermaid-inspired outfits with a pink onesie for Gigi and purple one for Haddy. They wear matching tutus in the theme colors.

Liv stands on the other end of the table holding a squirming Gigi, and we barely get to blow out the candles before both girls are on their feet, toddling around the party.

Their daddies aren't far behind them, making sure they don't fall into the pool or knock over a table of cupcakes and treats of all shapes and sizes.

Both girls started walking on the same day, and Garrett and Hendrix have been arguing about who took the first step ever since.

We were at the park blowing bubbles and watching the guys throw the football when it happened.

"It was Gigi, because she loves dogs," Garrett says. "She finally came out of Liv because that lady at the park had a dog."

Liv's eyes meet mine, and I almost choke on my champagne. "It's not a competition, babe.

"They're walking now, and we're never sitting down again," I tease.

"I'm winning this, Cherry." He cuts playful eyes at her.

Hendrix shakes his head. "It was Haddy, because she loves football. She was trying to come out onto the field with us."

"Who wants a mermaid cupcake?" I hold up a lavender-topped cake with a perfectly designed, strawberry-blonde mermaid on top. "This one looks like Liv!"

"I think Kimmie is having the most fun of everyone." Allie

stands beside me holding her glass of champagne and watching Jack's daughter run from the bounce house to the balloon maze then sliding into the ball pit.

She's wearing a dress with a lavender top and pale green tulle skirt, and Clint follows her all over the party telling her to pose here and stop there and taking pictures of everything.

"I think my favorite part is how he did their names." I point to the massive balloon arrangements spelling out both girls' names on each side of the patio.

"That topiary starfish with the seahorse is incredible." Dylan nods at the five-foot structure made of roses, daisies, and hydrangea flowers.

"I've never seen anything like this." The stuffy male voice makes my chest freeze, and I turn just in time to hear my sister's voice.

"This is the coolest party I've ever seen!" Amelia runs through the toddler-sized tables to give me a hug. "It's straight out of the Kardashians!"

"I didn't know you were bringing Dad." I walk back the way she came to where my father stands, seeming bewildered by all the stations of food and candy and balloons.

"Raven, this is quite a party." He leans down to give me a kiss, but the skin on the back of my neck tenses.

"You don't have to pass judgment." My tone is cool. "You can simply enjoy it."

His brow lowers. "I have no intention of passing judgment."

Taking my sister's hand, I lead her away from him to where the Bradford ladies are standing. "Dylan, Allie, Rachel, Liv, this is my little sister Amelia."

"I know Amelia!" Dylan skips forward to give my sister a hug. "It's been four years, but you haven't changed a bit!"

"Do I still look seventeen?" Mimi cries, putting her hands over her face. "That explains a lot."

"You look very youthful." Dylan takes her hand, leading

her to the drinks table. "But I know you're twenty-one. Have some champagne."

"Look at my little Haddy-boo walking!" Mimi drops to her knees, and Haddy squeals, smiling as she wobbles quickly to my sister.

Amelia scoops her up as Hendrix leans down to give her a hug. "Hey, girl. You're looking good."

"I'd say the same to you!" She gives him a wink, and my eyebrows shoot up.

"Mr. Gale." Hendrix reaches out to shake his hand. "Good to see you again, sir."

"Congratulations to you on winning the Big Game. That was a very impressive catch." Hendrix nods, and my dad turns to me. "What was that about you saving a life during it?"

Someone tipped off the big LA newspaper about Star and me helping with the plane crash, and they put it on the front page. From there, the gossip site TMI found it, and after that, we went viral again. Only this time, audiences were unified in their response.

The LA Times headline read "Bradford Saves Superbowl, Wife Saves Councilwoman's Son," but the TMI site went all out with "SUPERBOWL WIFE SAVES A LIFE!!!" I didn't even know the boy we rescued was the son of a city council woman until TMI told me.

Along with the viral posting of the rescue, everyone was discussing how Hendrix shut Mikayla down after the game. It only took a few days and the loss of several thousand followers for her to remove her videos insulting me after the parking lot incident.

"The consensus is I'm not so average anymore," I joke.

"Raven's a hero." Liv pulls up the TMI story on her phone. "I still don't understand why they use so many exclamation points."

My father sniffs at the screen. "It does seem to be shouting at us."

"I'd say that's something to shout about." Hendrix puts his

arm around my waist and gives me a squeeze. The warmth of him at my back eases my tension.

"The station manager where I work needed my help using this new software. She couldn't find our chief meteorologist to help her."

"Did the weather have something to do with the crash?" My father is confused.

"The weather doesn't actually change all that much in LA, so we also cover traffic and do special reports, things like that," I explain.

"Well, that's very good. I'm proud of you."

He gives me a warm smile, and an unexpected knot clogs my throat. What in the world? I am not about to cry over this.

"Thank you," I manage. "If you'll excuse me a minute."

Turning away, I start for the guest cottage when he calls after me. "Raven, I'd like to speak with you. Alone."

I stop walking, and my eyes fly to Hendrix, who's watching the entire situation like a hawk. My eyes sweep over the party, searching for an excuse.

All the guests have returned to eating cake. Liv has Gigi in the bounce house, holding her fingers as she bends her knees and tries to jump. Mimi and Dylan are fighting over who gets to hold a squirmy Haddy.

Craig is suggesting he and Garrett don wigs and mermaid costumes and turn this into a dance party. Kimmie slides into the ball pit, and Clint is taking pictures nonstop.

Everything's under control except my emotions.

Hendrix walks up beside me, taking my hand. "Want me to stick around?"

Pressing my lips together, I'm inclined to say yes. Instead, I give his hand a squeeze. "Keep an eye on things. I'll be right back."

I lead my father down the flagstone path to where a wooden platform faces the bay. A large bougainvillea-lined arch stands over a wrought-iron bench.

"This is a lovely spot." Dad looks out at the water. "Seems like a nice group of people here."

"The Bradfords are wonderful. They build each other up, and they take care of their family."

His eyes slide to mine, and he clears his throat. "I wasn't happy with the way your last visit went. Then Amelia showed me a video of Lawrence saying terrible things to you outside the Peach Pit. I didn't like what I heard."

"Did you know Mom set up the trust the way she did with him in mind?" My tone is pointed.

"I know your mother thought you and Lawrence made a good match."

"Because he demeaned and insulted me my entire life the same way she always did?"

"Because she loved you very much. She came from nothing, and she never wanted you to know that kind of life."

"She was cruel, and you never said a word." My throat aches, and a wobble is in my voice. "You could've protected me, and you didn't."

"I didn't think you needed protection." His voice changes. "You were always quick to speak your mind."

"I was a child." My eyes are wide as I look up at him. "I was hurting. You have no idea what it's like…" Shaking my head, I turn away, doing my best to calm my breathing. "I spent so many years getting over what happened in that house. I'm not about to pretend you were there for me when you weren't."

My chest hurts, and I start to leave. His voice stops me.

"You're right." It's a somber tone. "When I heard the things Lawrence said to you, I was furious. I spoke to Thurman about it, and he has spoken to his son. I expect you will receive a formal apology from him—whether you choose to accept it or not is up to you."

I don't speak. Doing the right thing doesn't require a response.

"As for your mother…" He pauses, then continues at a

slower pace. "I didn't defend you when you were young. I'm sorry."

A fountain trickles somewhere nearby. I watch a line of pelicans glide smoothly over the water in a *V* formation.

Lifting my chin, I look up at him. "Why didn't you? Did you think she was right?"

"Occasionally, you needed correction, but I thought you were a very beautiful, very smart, and very talented young woman."

"So why didn't you help me?" It's a cracked whisper.

He puts a hand on his chest, looking down at his expensive shoes. "I didn't know anything about children. Your mother seemed very sure of herself... and she was your mother."

"That didn't make it right."

"No, it didn't." His voice is quiet. "Perhaps one day, you'll find it in your heart to forgive me."

The knot is still in my throat, but I force a nod. "I don't want to be angry with you, but... I think I need a little time."

"I understand." He takes a step down from the platform. "I'll be heading back to my hotel, then I'm leaving in the morning. I placed a gift for Hayden on the table."

"Thank you."

Pausing one more time, he looks back at me. "I like your husband very much. He's a good man."

"Yes, he is."

"He won't make the same mistakes I did."

With that, he continues swiftly down the flagstone path in the direction of the exit.

"No, he won't," I say under my breath.

The briny breeze touches my cheek. I remember an old saying about salt water and healing... *sweat, tears, and the sea.* Forgiveness is a gift you give yourself... So many mantras. I know them all.

Inhaling a cleansing breath, I know what to do. Healing

will come, and I'm starting at a far better place this time. I have a sweet baby girl and a very good man—and a party to attend.

When I get to the patio, Kimmie is holding a stuffed pink turtle for Gina and a purple one for Haddy.

"They're your new cooters," she announces, and I duck with a snort.

I happen to know a *cooter* is a *turtle*, but it's still hilarious to hear a six-year-old say it so casually. Haddy pushes Axel at her and squeals.

"Axel can be friends with your cooter," Kimmie says, trying to tuck the turtle under her baby cousin's arm. "Tell her, Eddie!"

Edward's brow furrows, and he looks around the decorated patio. "It's probably not a good idea to have so many balloons in a yard full of newborn kittens." Edward's logical tone reminds me of Mr. Spock from the old *Star Trek* movies.

He's got the dispassionate delivery on lock.

"Hey, man, want to head back to the restaurant?" Austin calls as he jogs up to them. "Sadie's bringing Oliver, and we're going to play some pool."

"Aussie!" Kimmie stands, going over to take his hand. "Come with me. Daddy said I could get in the pool if you or Edward would swim with me."

"I'm not swimming, KJ, and Edward's coming with me. Get Miss Dylan to swim with you."

"Aunt Deedee has to peel peppers for tomorrow's Dare Night, and she doesn't have time to wash her hair." Kimmie all but stomps her foot, but Austin isn't swayed. "Then get Uncle Grizz to swim with you. He'll do it."

"Aussie, I want you," she whines, holding his hand in both of hers and shaking it. "I can't watch the babies and swim!"

"Look! A kitten is trying to attack that balloon arch!" He points, and Kimmie gasps.

"Where?" She turns and starts running in the direction of the party, her little shoes slapping on the flagstones.

Austin punches Edward on the shoulder. "Come on, let's go."

"If a kitten is attacking that balloon arch, it could get a real fright. Some of those balloons are huge…"

He grabs Edward's arm and drags him toward the exit. "I made it up, now come on."

"Bye, guys!" I laugh, waving as I go to retrieve my abandoned toddler, who is now shaking Axel in one hand and the stuffed turtle in the other.

"Oh… Hi, Miss Raven." Austin is at least embarrassed. "Great party!"

"It does give the impression of being under the sea." Edward looks around. "It's an interesting concept."

"Thanks, guys." I smile warmly. "And thanks for coming. I know baby birthday parties aren't the most fun at your age."

"I didn't find any kittens!" Kimmie shouts as she runs back to where I'm standing.

Austin pulls Edward's arm again, and the boys take off jogging away.

"Auntie Rave, where's Austin and Eddie?" Her hands are on her hips, and her brown curls are a frizzy mass around her shoulders.

"They had to go." Reaching down, I catch her hand. "Help me take the birthday girls back to the party, okay?"

"I've been helping them walk." She nods, trying to hold Gigi's arm. Gigi makes an angry squeal, waving her arm up and down and out of Kimmie's grasp. "They're a little wobbly."

"They haven't been at it very long," I explain.

"That's okay! I'll help them get better. Miss Allie says I'm good at helping, and Haddy needs to know her cousin Kimmie."

"Yes, she does!" We take their hands and make our way back to the party, toddler speed.

My dad's words are on my mind and emotions twist in my chest.

His apology was one I didn't even know I needed, and while

I do need time and probably some counseling, I accept it. I want to forgive him, and that's a big part of healing.

"I had a brilliant idea, Rave." Dylan skips up to us. "While you're here, we can do all the Thursday Dare dishes together! Want to?"

"Absolutely, I do!"

Hendrix walks up, scooping his daughter off her feet and kissing my cheek. "Everything okay?"

Nodding, I press my lips into a smile, looking up at the two of them. Haddy is already squealing and struggling to get down again.

"He apologized. He even complimented you."

"Hey—that's…" He bends down to put Haddy on her feet again, then he straightens, holding my gaze. "Good?"

"It's really good."

Later that evening at Cooters & Shooters, we're sitting around a big table with Grizz and Liv, Logan and Dylan, Rachel and Zane, and Jack.

Amelia is on the side porch playing pool with Austin, Edward, and the teenage gang. Gigi and Haddy are asleep on their respective daddies. Kimmie is conked out on a bench, using a stuffed cooter for a pillow, and Dylan is showing me her idea for dare recipes on the iPad Pro she uses in the kitchen.

"You fell asleep watching movies?" Garrett frowns. "That sounds like a tough habit to break down the line."

"I always fell asleep watching football." Hendrix leans back, patting Haddy's little back.

"You could transition to books," Zane suggests, and I imagine his low voice reading a bedtime story.

"That would put me to sleep," I say.

"Worked for me!" Dylan chirps up.

"Wait, tell me more—" Rachel scoots forward, smiling brightly. "You watched old movies together? That's so cute... Which ones?"

"Let's see..." I think, counting off on my fingers. "*Forrest Gump, When Harry Met Sally, Steel Magnolias...*"

"Hated it." Hendrix interrupts, and all the girls gasp. "She died!"

"Okay, that part was sad," I agree. "*Rocky...*"

"Now *that* was some good shhhh..." Four pairs of eyes cut to him, and he grins. "Stuff."

"*La La Land...*"

"Worst ending ever."

"*Driving Miss Daisy...*"

"Cock blocker."

"Hendrix!" Dylan cries. "Miss Daisy is not a..." Her eyes meet mine, and she seems to understand immediately.

We fall back laughing, and Logan clears his throat. "Back to what we were saying... Whether you keep going or not, you've got your legacy."

"Yes, I do. It's right here." Hendrix nods, patting his little girl as his pretty blue eyes meet mine. "But maybe I'll keep playing a little longer?"

I reach out to squeeze his hand. "We can do that."

Liv walks over with her phone. "Clint has started posting pictures—check them out!"

We spend a minute laughing and cooing over the candid images. He has a shot of Haddy with her face in a slice of cake and one of Gigi lying on the back of a blow-up octopus.

I follow the social media account on my phone. "I wonder if he can send us the originals so we can make prints."

"We have to frame the Dylan twins' first birthday party," Allie laughs, joining us.

A longneck is in her hand, and Jack isn't too far behind, walking over with his hands on his hips. I'm pretty sure I'm the only one who notices his eyes drift down to her ass. *Interesting.*

She takes out her phone, and I'm about to tell her Clint's business handle when the color drains from her cheeks. She blinks quickly, and it's like she sees a ghost.

"Allie?" Dylan stands quickly, going to her. "What's wrong?"

Allie's always so feisty and fun. I've never seen her like this. She hugs her waist, seeming to shrink.

"It happened," she whispers. "I set up an alert on my phone…"

Jack is at her side at once. "What happened?"

He reads us the brief that Rip Sinclair was released on probation.

"He said as soon as he got out, he'd…" Allie clears her throat, her eyes flying to the pool area. "Don't tell Austin."

"Don't you worry, girl." Garrett steps up to her side. "I happen to know the sheriff."

"And a good lawyer." Liv is right there with him.

I give Hendrix a worried look. "Who is he?"

Allie sniffs, wiping her hands over her face like she's regaining her footing after an unexpected gut punch.

"My ex," she says. "He said when he got out he'd be back for us. Looks like he's out."

Dylan catches her around the waist. "We got you, Al."

Jack and Zane exchange a look, and while I've only been in this family a few months, I can tell. It's about to get real interesting around here.

Thank you for reading *The Way We Collide*!
Be sure to download your **FREE Bonus Scene** HERE:

Up next is *The Way We Win*!
Jack & Allie's small-town, high school football coach
+ school librarian, single dad + single mom (*of his star player*), oldest Bradford Boy + best friend's brother,
romance is going to keep you on your toes, swooning,
laughing, and biting your nails.

Available in ebook, paperback, and on Audio!
Keep turning for a short preview…

Learn about all of my books on TiaLouise.com/Books,
including a downloadable Reading Guide.

The Way We Win

Jack Bradford is always in control. He's lost too much not to be. Forced to step up and take responsibility for his siblings at a young age, he knows better to rush into anything. The one time he did, he was left with a baby girl and a disillusioned heart. Until Allie Sinclair moves to town.

Allie's a single mom with her own share of past regrets when it comes to love. Watching Coach Jack guide her teenage son like a surrogate dad melts her heart. Then, as they start getting closer, as her sexy suspicions about the man hiding behind the controlled exterior prove true, one look is enough to steam up her glasses—and melt her undies.

Winning Jack Bradford is a dream come true. Until her ex-con-ex-husband shows up looking for his family...

(*The Way We Win* is a small-town, single dad, single mom, football romance with a HOT high school football coach, a sexy librarian, Friday night lights, ALL the Bradford fun, SPICE, and a touch of suspense. No cheating, no cliffhanger, and no third-act breakup. Are you ready for Jack & Allie?)

Prologue

Jack

GRAY SKIES SPREAD OVER THE BAY ALL THE WAY PAST DAUPHIN ISLAND as we look southwest. Thomas stands in front of us holding a large blue packet. It's made of heavy, biodegradable paper, and a white sea turtle sits on top.

It's dad.

The thought hits me like a fist in the chest, but I swallow that sob. With a blink, I look down and hold it together. My four siblings stand in a line beside me. We're all in suits and ties except for Dylan. She's wearing a navy dress that hangs to her calves and blows in the wind.

Her dark hair is pulled away from her face in one of those skinny bows, and she rests her head on Miss Gina's shoulder as she openly weeps.

Miss Gina slides her hand up and down my little sister's arm, and I realize it's the first time I've seen that old lady cry. Her blind eyes are typically glittering with joy when we're around, but today they shine with empathetic tears as she holds my sister.

Zane is beside me, his dark hair moving in the nonstop breeze. He's not smiling, but he's not crying. His eyes follow Thomas as he walks slowly to the water's edge. Zane doesn't talk about how he feels, preferring to drift down to the stables south of town and care for the horses.

He doesn't have to tell me. I know.

Garrett stands a head taller at Zane's side. His expression is stoic, but his girlfriend Liv stands beside him touching her eyes with a tissue every few minutes. The wind pushes her long, strawberry-blond hair behind her shoulders, and her dark red dress clings to her legs.

She'll take care of him.

My youngest brother Hendrix is doing his best to stand up straight and not cry. He almost breaks me when he drops his almost fourteen-year-old chin and shoves a fist across his cheek.

We didn't talk as I helped him tie his necktie this morning, helped him straighten his collar in his blazer. We just lost Mom, and now this.

Everybody wants to say our dad died of a broken heart, that he couldn't keep going after losing the love of his life, but I'm not so sure.

Dad would've stuck around for us. He wouldn't have wanted to leave the five of us orphans. The truth is, after Mom's sudden diagnosis and rapid decline, we all saw the extent of our dad's illness as well.

She covered for him, but the effects of his long career as a legendary quarterback during a time in the industry when safety wasn't a priority and players pushed through things like concussions and traumatic brain injuries had taken a toll.

Maybe losing Mom was simply the last hit he couldn't take.

All I know for sure is here we are on this gray day, following his last wishes to put him to rest in his beloved ocean down the hill from our sprawling family home.

Thomas found the container with the turtles on top, and I couldn't have picked a better vessel to send our dad on his journey.

Thomas knew Dad better than any of us. The two of them were teammates for the Texas Mustangs their entire careers. They were the dream team until dad retired. Then when Thomas decided to stop playing, Dad brought him here to our little south-Alabama community to be the head chef at Cooters & Shooters, our family restaurant on the coast.

He's been with us since Dylan was a baby, and now, with

me not quite twenty-one, he's stepped up to get us over these last few months until I'm legal.

Miss Gina greased a few palms as well to keep the state from taking Hendrix and Dylan away—or sending them to live with relatives. Nobody wanted to be the jerk who broke up the family of Art Bradford, local legend and small-town hero.

Thing is, I just got my offer from the Texas Mustangs to be their new starting quarterback. I'm graduating a year early, and the offer is burning a hole in my pocket.

Dad would be so proud, but I'm not sure what happens now.

"We'll never forget Art's sense of humor," Thomas's deep voice draws our attention.

He's also wearing a dark suit, and his large, brown hands hold the small package with so much care. *Best running back in the game*, Dad would say. *I'd trust Tommy with my life.*

It was only right for him to handle his death.

"He loved you kids more than anything." Thomas slides his light brown eyes down the line of my siblings. "Jack, he knew you could step into his shoes, or he would've held on longer. You got this."

My jaw tightens, and I swallow the thickness in my throat, giving him a brief nod. Stepping into his shoes is exactly what I'm doing, in more ways than one.

"Zane, you're going to help your brother Jack take the lead, and Garrett, you keep protecting the little ones."

The muscle in Garrett's square jaw moves, and he's got his game face on as he nods briefly.

"Your dad loved the game, and he'll always be remembered for his accomplishments. But his proudest accomplishment was you five. He'll be watching you from above, standing at your mama's side. Don't let him down."

Hendrix inhales sharply, and Dylan and Liv simultaneously reach for his hands.

"His spirit lives on in you." Thomas looks into my eyes, and nods. "We'll always remember the good times, and we'll think of him now, reunited with the ones who went before."

He's at the water's edge, and he bends a knee to place the blue packet on the waves. "Ashes to ashes, and dust to dust. We release you to the beautiful waters you loved."

Standing on the edge of the bay, my eyes lock on that white sea turtle as it drifts farther out to the center of the water, where it will swirl in the tide and continue to eternity.

I realize every muscle in my body is tight when Dylan's small arms go around my waist. Releasing the death-grip of my arms crossed over my chest, I wrap them around her small frame.

Another pair of arms wraps around my side, and I realize Hendrix has come to me as well. Garrett follows, putting a hand on my shoulder, and Zane turns his head to give me a sad smile.

He's close, at least, attending a small private college not far from Newhope. Garrett has one more year of school before he'll head to Tuscaloosa. Holding my family, I inhale a shaky, fortifying breath.

Thomas returns to where we're standing, takes one look at our huddle, and gives me a satisfied smile.

I'm the oldest. I'm the leader. When we were kids, and we'd have chores or we'd play scrimmage in the park, Dad would say I was team captain.

I wonder if he knew then what he was preparing me to be. Either way, I know who I am. I know what's expected of me, and I'll get us through this.

The Way We Win is available in print, ebook, and on audio.

Books by
TIA LOUISE

ROMANCE IN KINDLE UNLIMITED

THE BRADFORD BOYS
The Way We Touch, 2024★
The Way We Play, 2024★
The Way We Score, 2025★
The Way We Collide, 2025★
The Way We Win, 2025★
(★Available on Audiobook.)

THE BE STILL SERIES
A Little Taste, 2023★
A Little Twist, 2023★
A Little Luck, 2023★
A Little Naughty, 2024★
(★Available on Audiobook.)

THE HAMILTOWN HEAT SERIES
Fearless, 2022★
Filthy, 2022★
For Your Eyes Only, 2022
Forbidden, 2023★
(★Available on Audiobook.)

THE TAKING CHANCES SERIES
This Much is True★
Twist of Fate★
Trouble★
(★Available on Audiobook.)

FIGHT FOR LOVE SERIES
Wait for Me★
Boss of Me★
Here with Me★
Reckless Kiss★
(★Available on Audiobook.)

BELIEVE IN LOVE SERIES
Make You Mine
Make Me Yours★
Stay★
(★Available on Audiobook.)

SOUTHERN HEAT SERIES
When We Touch
When We Kiss

THE ONE TO HOLD SERIES
One to Hold (#1 - Derek & Melissa)★
One to Keep (#2 - Patrick & Elaine)★
One to Protect (#3 - Derek & Melissa)★
One to Love (#4 - Kenny & Slayde)
One to Leave (#5 - Stuart & Mariska)
One to Save (#6 - Derek & Melissa)★
One to Chase (#7 - Marcus & Amy)★
One to Take (#8 - Stuart & Mariska)
(★Available on Audiobook.)

THE DIRTY PLAYERS SERIES
PRINCE (#1)★
PLAYER (#2)★
DEALER (#3)
THIEF (#4)
(★Available on Audiobook.)

THE BRIGHT LIGHTS SERIES
Under the Lights (#1)
Under the Stars (#2)
Hit Girl (#3)

COLLABORATIONS
The Last Guy★
The Right Stud
Tangled Up
Save Me
(★Available on Audiobook.)

PARANORMAL ROMANCES
One Immortal (vampires)
One Insatiable (shifters)

GET THREE FREE STORIES!
Sign up for my New Release newsletter and never miss a sale or new release by me!
Sign up now!

Acknowledgments

I have so many people to thank this go-round. Hendrix is the Bradford's "never say quit" football brother, and I knew he was going to have a hard time letting go of "the Hendrix Show," as Garrett likes to call it... Raven and Haddy are two of my favorite characters, and I loved seeing this little family come together.

Always, always HUGE thanks to my husband "Mr. TL" for everything, including an up-front save. You're so smart...

My amazing PA Kat is my right hand, and we both screamed (*with joy!*) when we saw the illustrated cover from my "dream team," Laura Moore (illustrator) and Kari March (designer).

Jen DeJong is always my rock, cheering me on as I write, and Leticia Teixeira, and a BIG welcome and HUGE thanks to Patti Rapozo for giving me additional eyes as well as the being the NFL expert for this SEC girlie!

Huge thanks to my *incredible* betas, Maria Black, Corinne Akers, Amy Reierson, Courtney Anderson, Jennifer Christy, Heather Heaton, Michelle Mastandrea, and new helpers Jennifer Wolfe (more football help!) and Diane Holtrey. So much **LOVE** for you ladies.

Thanks to Jaime Ryter for your eagle-eyed edits and to the super talented Lori Jackson and Wander Aguiar for the heart-stopping model cover.

As always, the amazing Stacey Blake made my paperbacks gorgeous.

Thanks to my dear Starfish, to my Mermaids, and to my Veeps for keeping me sane and organized and helping me spread the word and all the incredible BookTokers, Bookstagrammers, and book lovers, who I've come to think of as friends.

Last but not least, to my readers everywhere—***thank you*** for allowing me do what I do. Love, small towns, and spice,

❤*Tia*

About the Author

Tia Louise is the *USA Today* and #4 Amazon bestselling author of (*primarily*) small-town, single-parent, second-chance, and military romances set at or near the beach.

From Readers' Choice awards, to *USA Today* "Happily Ever After" nods, to winning Favorite Erotica Author and the "Lady Boner Award" (*lol!*), nothing makes her happier than communicating with fellow Mermaids (*fans*) and creating romances that are smart, sassy, and *very sexy*.

A former journalist and displaced beach bum, Louise lives in the Midwest with her trophy husband, two young-adult geniuses, and one clumsy "grand-cat."

Sign up for her newsletter and never miss a new release or sale—and get a free story collection!

Signed Copies of all books online at:
https://geni.us/SignedPBs

Connect with Tia:
TiaLouise.com
Instagram—@AuthorTLouise
TikTok—@TheTiaLouise

Printed in Great Britain
by Amazon